THE HUNT FOR THE HOLLOWER

THE HUNT FOR THE HOLLOWER

BY CALLIE C. MILLER

ALADDIN
NEW YORK LONDON TORONTO SYDNEY NEW DELHI

❦

ALADDIN
An imprint of Simon & Schuster Children's Publishing Division
1230 Avenue of the Americas, New York, New York 10020
First Aladdin hardcover edition June 2023
Text copyright © 2023 by Callie C. Miller
Illustrations copyright © 2023 by Kristy De Guzman

For information about special discounts for bulk purchases, please contact
Simon & Schuster Special Sales at 1-866-506-1949 or business@simonandschuster.com.
The Simon & Schuster Speakers Bureau can bring authors to your live event. For more
information or to book an event contact the Simon & Schuster Speakers Bureau
at 1-866-248-3049 or visit our website at www.simonspeakers.com.
Designed by Heather Palisi
The text of this book was set in Horley Old Style.
Manufactured in the United States of America 0523 FFG
2 4 6 8 10 9 7 5 3 1
Library of Congress Cataloging-in-Publication Data
Names: Miller, Callie C., author.
Title: The hunt for the hollower / by Callie C. Miller.
Description: First Aladdin hardcover edition. | New York : Aladdin, 2023. |
Audience: Ages 8–12. | Summary: Everyone in his family assumes Percy is the
Septimum Genus their ancestor Merlyn prophesized, but when he attempts a
forbidden spell with his twin, Merlynda, and vanishes through a portal, it is
Merlynda who sets off to rescue her brother and discovers her true powers.
Identifiers: LCCN 2022053726 (print) | LCCN 2022053727 (ebook) |
ISBN 9781665918107 (hardcover) | ISBN 9781665918114 (ebook)
Subjects: CYAC: Twins—Fiction. | Siblings—Fiction. | Magic—Fiction. | Fantasy. |
LCGFT: Fantasy fiction. | Novels.
Classification: LCC PZ7.1.M564 Hu 2023 (print) | LCC PZ7.1.M564 (ebook) |
DDC [Fic]—dc23
LC record available at https://lccn.loc.gov/2022053726
LC ebook record available at https://lccn.loc.gov/2022053727

For Grandmommie, who always cheered me on

"THE HOLLOWER"

Being an excerpt from Lady Phelia's
*Nursery Rhymes to Caution and
Correct Ill-Behaved Children*

The Hollower's on the hunt, my child
The Hollower's on the hunt
Your magic he'll steal
With cunning and zeal
The Hollower's on the hunt

The Hollower's on the prowl, my dear
The Hollower's on the prowl
Your spirit he'll sap
With evil entrap
The Hollower's on the prowl

A Word from Our Narrator

Once upon a time, in a faraway land, there was a wizard named Merlyn. This name might sound familiar, but this Merlyn is not your Merlyn, just as this world is not your world. This story takes place in a magical land, full of fairies, and underwater cities, and a lamentable absence of funnel cake.

Though this story takes place in this magical land, it doesn't belong to it. Stories, you see, aren't confined to a single space or time, as most things are.

Now then.

This story isn't about Merlyn, but it begins with him.

Merlyn, the trusted royal advisor. Merlyn, the greatest wizard in history. Merlyn, who popped out of a magical portal after defeating the villainous sorceress Morgan le Fey and was met by a throng of anxious citizens desperate to know if evil had been vanquished.

"Of course she's been vanquished," Merlyn snapped, his staff still smoking from the battle. Once this was tidied up, he'd have to report to the queen, who'd been cursed into a sheep by Morgan.

"Three cheers for the most powerful wizard of all time!"

"Ha!" Merlyn scoffed. He waved his hand over the smoking end of his staff, and it burst into flames. He shook it irritably to put it out. "Wait until you see my great-great-great-great-great-grandchild!"

In the back of the crowd, a boy with a falcon perched on his shoulder scowled.

The portal Merlyn had appeared from was already gone. The wizard stood alone—except for the crowd—in the midst of a circle of enormous stone pillars, each of them easily five times the height of a grown man.

"Why?" a centaur shouted.

"What will they do?" an old man called out.

Merlyn slammed his staff into the ground. A jet of water shot up from it, finally extinguishing the smoldering bits with a hiss. "You'll have to wait and find out! It's dangerous to know the future."

Merlyn's owl familiar swooped down and perched on his staff. "Don't be rude," the owl scolded.

No one likes being left in the dark, especially a crowd of people who had nearly been destroyed by the embodiment of evil, but Merlyn had an advantage when it came to knowing things. He had the gift of foresight. He was able to look ahead and see things that hadn't happened yet, but probably would. The future wasn't always clear, but it was exceptionally less foggy when he checked in on it than when you or I try.

In any case, it was too late. Word had already swept through the crowd that Merlyn's seventh descendant would do great things. Wonderful things. Miraculous things.

This story is about Merlyn's seventh descendants. Let's meet them, shall we?

They're about to dabble in mischief that's going to take a turn for the worse.

*In which magic goes awry and
a scheme is hatched*

Merlynda of Merlyn Manor hadn't meant to turn every inkwell in the stationery shop into miniature never-ending geysers. She also hadn't meant to give the townspeople another magical mishap to gossip about, but she knew that's exactly what would happen. And she absolutely, positively had *not* meant to practice her magic before she returned home, and not just because that's what her mother had suggested this morning on their way into town. Today's magical bungle had just sort of happened, which unfortunately was a common occurrence for Merlynda.

Inks of every color sprang across the shop, spraying

parchment, waxes, and fancy quill pens. Panicked patrons knocked into Merlynda as they rushed out. Mr. Wintley, the faun who owned the shop, gaped at his ruined goods. Lavender-scented specialty ink burst across his cream-colored shirt and red-brown fur, filling the air with its fragrance.

Merlynda twisted as a jet of blue ink shot toward her, taking the blast on her back but protecting the envelope she clutched. She tucked the envelope into her purple robes, then turned back to Mr. Wintley. "I'm sorry! I'm sorry! I'll fix it!" She closed her eyes to sense the magic and—

"No! You've done enough!" Mr. Wintley wailed, then tried to compose himself. He gripped his horns. "I mean, er, perhaps your mother, or maybe your brother, could . . . ?"

As if on cue, the bell above the shop door rang and Percy, Merlynda's twin brother, stepped in. They shared their mother's deep blue eyes and chestnut hair, but Percy always managed to strike a more collected figure. Probably because he'd never once accidentally magicked a hive of bees into the library, or teleported his lentils into the milk jug, or set off an entire shop's ink supply into never-ending geysers. He wasn't constantly worrying about what his magic might do next. If Percy ever wanted to do any of those things, he did it on purpose, and perfectly.

"Merlynda, haven't you finished . . . ?" He trailed off as a green ink jar's cork flew at him, catching him full in the face. He froze for a moment, taking in the bursting inkpots throughout the small shop, and then started laughing.

Mr. Wintley tugged on his horns harder, hopping from one hoofed foot to the other. "Master Percy, I hardly think this is cause for amusement!"

"It's all right, Mr. Wintley." Percy dodged a spray of ink, unconcerned about his splattered robes. "I'll have everything back before you can say, 'Merlyn's goat.'"

Percy focused on the ink. Magic was accessed through four primary elements: Earth, Water, Air, and Fire. Through these, wizards and other magical beings connected with the Aether—the *real* magic. Percy's affinity was for Air, but it didn't really matter. He was almost as adept with all of the elements.

Merlynda, on the other hand, bungled all of the elements equally.

She watched as Percy found the Water within the ink and used his magic to push past the *Water* and into the *Aether*. It was always at this point in the magical process that things went awry for Merlynda, usually in some form of explosion. She could never quite manage to touch the Aether.

And then, each time, the magic laughed at her. She could feel it now, laughing at the ink raining down all around them.

The magic never laughed at Percy. It apparently did whatever he bid. Percy didn't study half as much as Merlynda (or at all, really), but magic had always come easily to him. The twins were only eleven, but Percy was already one of the most talented wizards to ever live, and he knew it. Which is why instead of calling their mother like they were supposed to whenever

Merlynda bungled something, Percy cleaned up her mess. The inkwells stopped overflowing, and the stray drops and geysers throughout the shop reversed, swimming back to their pots and jars. Droplets peeled away from the parchment, quills, and even Mr. Wintley's shirt, fluttering back to their containers.

Merlynda breathed a sigh of relief. She never meant to do any harm, but her magic always seemed to have a mind of its own.

Mr. Wintley was awestruck. "Master Percy! That was marvelous! Wondrous! Masterful! Why, if you aren't the Septimum Genus, I'll—" He stopped and turned red, as if suddenly remembering Merlynda was there. He needn't have worried. Merlynda was used to such things and wasn't bothered.

The twins' birth had caused tremendous confusion eleven years ago. No one understood how to interpret Merlyn's prophecy about the Septimum Genus—his seventh descendant who was meant to do spectacular things—when there were *two*. Was the Septimum Genus the oldest (Merlynda, by a whole seven minutes)? Or the one who showed the most magical talent (clearly Percy)?

Some people tried to blame their mother, claiming that because she'd married a nonmagical human instead of a wizard, she'd ruined Merlyn's prophecy. Mother fired back that either Merlyn's foresight was right, or it wasn't, but it wouldn't be *her* fault if his words didn't come to pass. She'd marry whomever she pleased and have as many children as she liked, thank you very much.

There was also a good deal of speculation about *what* great things the Septimum Genus would do. For generations, the townspeople had come to Merlyn Manor seeking potions for illnesses or help removing a stray hex that blew in, but after the twins were born, things got out of hand. When they were very young, they'd be approached by townspeople who wanted their gardens to produce year-round without being tended, or travelers who wanted magical powers (magic was common enough in the world, but magical *beings* were a good deal rarer). Once, a young archer dressed in Lincoln green had asked them for a charm that would guarantee he'd marry his true love. He promised to have his friend write a ballad about the twins in return, so the whole land of Faelor would know of their talents.

Mother had shooed the archer away from the manor, with just a touch of Earth magic to speed him along. She also might have shouted after him that clearly too much of the world already knew of the twins' talents, what with how often strangers barged into their affairs, and that she wouldn't have any of it any longer. The archer left in a hurry, and word of Mother's new boundary swept through everyone who knew of the Septimum Genus (which was the majority of the known world, to be sure). They didn't get many strangers after that.

Now that they were a bit older and their talents had had the opportunity to mature, everyone in Avonshire secretly (or not so secretly) believed that Percy was the Septimum Genus. This was just fine with Merlynda, who believed that herself. Besides, who wanted strangers constantly asking you for favors, or expecting you to always perform miracles? Who wanted the world breathing down your neck, to see what "great things" you would do?

This was why comments like Mr. Wintley's didn't trouble her. That, and Merlynda had less lofty goals at the moment. All she wanted was to control her magic, or at least feel comfortable with her powers. Other than that, as long as Percy was around for getting into and out of mischief with her, and as long as her best friend, Neci, was by her side, she couldn't imagine needing anything else.

Merlynda looked at Mr. Wintley, sheepish. "I really am sorry about all of the ink, Mr. Wintley. Is the back room all right?"

Mr. Wintley didn't quite flinch at Merlynda addressing him. "I'm sure it's fine, Miss Merlynda, perfectly fine." The front of the shop was devoted to stationery, but Mr. Wintley also dealt in a number of oddities and knickknacks that travelers brought in. He liked knowing things, and knew at least a little about almost everything. "Master Percy set everything straight now, didn't he? Still got your envelope?"

Merlynda pulled the envelope from her robes. Not a drop of ink had touched it. Neci's birthday present was inside, and if Merlynda ruined *that*, she didn't know how she'd get another one.

"Excellent," Mr. Wintley said, gazing around his shop in a daze. "Wonderful. Well, then, you two better run along." He forced a laugh. "Give your parents my regards."

Merlynda and Percy knew a dismissal when they heard one and took their leave.

"That was brilliant," Percy said, replaying the ink geysers in his mind as they walked down the main street of Avonshire. "It was like an ink rainbow exploded in the shop. Are you all right?"

"No!" Merlynda said. She, too, was replaying the incident in her mind, but it made her shudder. "What if you hadn't been able to fix it? I would've ruined everything in his store!"

"Sure, but I *was* there. How did it happen, anyway?"

Merlynda sighed. "I was signing my name to show that I'd picked up my envelope, and the ink blotted. So I tried to fix it."

Percy tried hard not to laugh. He loved his sister and really wasn't poking fun at her, but he also didn't understand how one of Merlyn's descendants could be so dismal at magic.

"It isn't funny!" Merlynda shoved Percy playfully, and he tried to stifle his snickering.

"An inkblot," he said with a mostly straight face, "that turned into a rainbow of infinite ink . . ."

Merlynda finally cracked a smile. "Maybe it's a little funny. But only because you were able to fix it."

Percy collected himself and waved at a group of towns-people across the street. A gnome pretended not to see and hurried his children on, but several waved back and whispered to one another excitedly. Percy pulled at the Water and Air around him, creating a fluffy cloud that he reshaped with his magic: a flower, a troll, one of the gawking townspeople, and so on. Mother would scold him if she saw (*Magic isn't a plaything,* she always said), but he couldn't help showing off. He *loved* showing off.

Merlynda rolled her eyes. Percy would be insufferable if it weren't for the fact that he always, always had her back. He never lorded his skills over her, and he never even made fun of her for her magical mishaps. He might laugh a bit while cleaning things up, but it was never mean-spirited.

Their family had lived just outside of Avonshire for generations—it was where Merlyn had eventually settled down after defeating Morgan le Fey—so seeing them in town was hardly novel, even if they were the only magical beings around for miles. Since Merlyn's day, the small village had grown into a bustling town. The streets were always busy, particularly in the main square, and as far as Merlynda could tell, they lacked for nothing. She loved it here. It was perfect.

Well, almost perfect. If she could make clouds dance like Percy could, or brew the odd potion like Mother sometimes did, perhaps the townspeople wouldn't look at her with quite so much fear.

For now, she pretended not to notice whenever someone shot her a frightened glance, or even worse, a look of pity. "The magic laughed at me again," she said quietly. "After the ink started springing up everywhere."

Percy let his cloud dissipate and gave his sister his full attention. The magic had never laughed at him, and it sounded terrible. He knew how desperately his twin wanted to understand her magic. "Is it still laughing?" he asked.

Merlynda paused for a moment, listening. "No. But why does it *do* that?" She let the frustration creep into her voice. "It's like it's mocking me anytime I try to use my magic."

"We'll figure it out, Merlynda," he told her, and he meant every scrap of determination he put into his voice. "Together. You're going to be an amazing wizardess."

Merlynda gave him a small smile. Percy might (probably) be the Septimum Genus, and he was certainly a show-off, but at the end of the day, he was always her brother. "Thanks, Percy."

Percy's eyes lit up, an idea forming. "Didn't you say you found an Elemental Focus in the library the other day?"

"Yeeeees . . . ," Merlynda said, guessing at what Percy was thinking.

Her brother did a little leap of excitement. "Let's summon an Elemental Stone! They're really powerful, right? I bet you could use one to control your magic."

Merlynda narrowed her eyes. "And if we're successful, you'd be the youngest wizard to ever summon one."

Percy flashed her a brilliant grin. "Well, sure. Win-win."

Merlynda hesitated, but Percy leaned in.

"C'mon, I'll be there. We're Merlyn's descendants. What can go wrong?"

A lot, they both knew. But Merlynda grinned back and nodded. "I'm in."

+ + +

Across the town square, Neci the Ardent, Merlynda's afore-mentioned best friend, was drooling over the daggers on display at Avonshire's blacksmith. Avonshire didn't have an armory, but the minotaur blacksmith always had a few daggers available for purchase. Neci was expressly forbidden from gawking at them for as long as she had this morning. Not by the minotaur, who found Neci's enthrallment amusing, but by her parents.

Neci was the youngest in a long line of root vegetable merchants. For generations her ancestors had farmed, harvested, and sold beets, parsnips, and carrots of many colors to the good people who ventured to their shop in Avonshire. And venture they did, for Neci's family was famous around the known world for their delectable product. Her mother was especially proud of their wholesome, all-natural growing techniques. NO MAGIC POWDERS, POTIONS, OR SPELLS, the elaborate sign above their shop boasted, along with their company slogan: NATURALLY EXQUISITE CULINARY INGREDIENTS.

Over time this slogan had been shortened to its acronym: NECI (pronounced *NEE-see*). When Neci was born, her parents were so tickled about their business, and how their only child would surely follow in their footsteps, that they named her after their success.

Root vegetable farming was an old and proud tradition, but Neci wanted nothing to do with it. She could never tell her parents this, but the thing she wanted most in the entire world, the longing that filled her dreams to the brim, was to be a knight. Hence, visiting the blacksmith every few days to stare longingly at the weapons. A dagger was hardly the impressive steel carried by noble and courageous knights, but it was a good step closer than nothing.

Neci tore herself away from the blacksmith's. It wouldn't do any good if her mother caught her gawking. She also preferred that her next errand be kept from her parents' knowledge, as she had learned long ago to keep her knightly ambitions a secret, so she set off toward the stationery shop at a brisk clip. She was well stocked up on parchment and quills, but Mr. Wintley was the only merchant in town who sometimes received specialty shipments and curiosities from the city. Including, occasionally, new trading parchments for Neci's favorite game: Ye Knoble Knights Defend the Civilized World.

She had collected nearly every trading parchment available—even the super-rare, nearly-impossible-to-find ones. They were meticulously organized and tucked away in a box hidden beneath her mattress. Her favorites were carefully pressed between the pages of a book, and every day she'd open it to admire them. First was King Arthur, Merlyn's favorite goat. She mostly liked the painting on that one. Next came Tilly the Quick, a brave gnome who was smaller than almost everyone else, just like Neci. And finally Dame Joi, the strongest human knight to ever live. She had dark hair and skin like

Neci, and wielded a beautiful sword but used it only to defend the weak. If Dame Joi and Tilly could become noble knights, then Neci could too.

Every day she tried to be a little more like them. Just last year she'd saved up and sent away for the Ye Knoble Knights Decoder Ring with Customizable Crest. Neci had chosen the gryphon crest because, with the body of a lion and the head of an eagle, they were stalwart protectors. She wore it on a string around her neck, but when no one was looking, she'd slip it onto her finger, proud of what it stood for. Neci kept her most prized possessions hidden because it would break her parents' hearts if they knew that she, their only daughter and assumed beneficiary of their legacy, had no interest at all in root vegetables. She didn't even like eating them very much.

Neci held herself tall as she jogged, keeping her satchel from jostling too much and focusing on projecting a *knightly aura*. That's what one of the stats on her trading parchments called it. She ignored the fact that she was short for her almost-but-not-quite ten years of age. Her speed and swiftness and the short, tight black curls framing her face surely more than made up for any perceived notions of being vertically challenged. She was a force to be reckoned with.

She slowed as a couple of townspeople dashed toward her, splattered with—Neci's pulse quickened—was that blood? Would she at long last get to perform the knightly duty of helping someone in need, and of valiantly defeating an enemy who had harmed an innocent?

"Hail and well met!" she called, even though she already knew it was the florist and his daughter. She said, "Hail and well met!" because that's what the knights in *The Compendium of Knights and Their Noble Deeds* (her favorite book) always said.

The florist and his daughter paused, the panic fading from their faces as they glanced behind them. Neci could see they weren't hurt, even if they were covered in red splatters. She leapt into action. "Hello, citizens! From what do you flee? What fell beast plagues you?"

The daughter, Esme, scowled down at her ruined dress. She was a few years older than Neci. "Hello, *Neci-Queasy*. The fell beast that plagues us is your little witch friend."

Neci felt her cheeks go hot at the insult. Not the jab at her name, which was annoying but uninventive. It was the attack on her friend that riled her. "You mean the great *wizardess* Merlynda? You don't mean *she* attacked you?" Merlynda would never! Well, not on purpose. To her knowledge, anytime the wizardess's magic had gone awry, it had never hurt anyone. Neci thought the magical explosions made things exciting.

The florist surveyed his robes. "That child is a menace," he grumbled. "She should have been named for Morgan le Fey, not the great Merlyn."

A WORD ABOUT
MORGAN LE FEY

As has been mentioned, Morgan le Fey was a dastardly villainess, and had Merlyn not defeated her when he did, the world as it was might have been destroyed. More likely, the world as it was would probably still exist, but be ruled by the evil, finely manicured hand of Morgan le Fey. Really, the outcome of either scenario is the same: misery.

For the florist to compare Merlynda to Morgan le Fey was at best an ignorant oversight of history. At worst, it was a horrible, biting insult.

Neci bristled. She was no stranger to the mutterings throughout town, of course. Her parents, mistrustful of magic, did a
good bit of the muttering themselves. Even so, Neci felt it her
knightly duty to try to help everyone. "Are you injured?" she
asked, already knowing the answer.

"No," the florist answered.

"Was it an intentional act of aggression?"

"I don't believe so. . . ."

Neci crossed her arms. "And was Percy nearby?"

Now the florist and his daughter shuffled, avoiding Neci's
gaze. "He . . . might have been right outside. It all happened
so fast. . . ."

Neci rolled her eyes. "So instead of letting Percy help by
removing the—what is this stuff?"

"Um . . . ink," Esme said.

"Ink," Neci repeated, keeping a straight face. "Instead
of allowing Percy to remove this *harmless ink*, you're rushing
around town spreading lies about a kid."

"Well, I wouldn't say . . . That's not what . . . When you
say it like that . . ." The florist trailed off under Neci's stare.

"Shameful," Neci said. "I hope you've learned your les-
son." Which was another thing the knights in her *Compendium*
often said.

They bobbed their heads in agreement, and Neci took off

again toward Mr. Wintley's shop, grinning. A knight's work was never done.

Percy had just suggested that he and Merlynda should find some sweets before meeting up with their parents when Neci caught up with the twins. "I saw the florist and his daughter on my way back from the blacksmith's," she said breathlessly. "Are you all right? Was this a proper explosion?"

"Ink fountains," Merlynda moaned. "All colors. Dozens of them."

"Hundreds," Percy chimed in. "But we got it sorted."

"*You* got it sorted," Merlynda corrected. "Anything knightly at the blacksmith's?" she asked Neci. The twins both knew of her secret ambition. Merlynda wanted Neci to be a knight as badly as she wanted to control her own magic. Percy thought Neci's dream was silly, but he didn't see any point in telling her that. It wasn't *his* dream.

Neci knew Percy thought this, but she didn't care. Merlynda believed in her, and that was all that mattered. The girls often dreamed about how one day when Merlynda was a wizardess fully in control of her magic, and Neci was a duly appointed knight, they would make a team even greater than Merlyn and Dame Joi.

Merlyn, the most powerful wizard of all time.

Dame Joi, the greatest knight in all of history.

Sure, they had some growing to do. But they were both

working hard, and when that day finally came, it would be glorious!

"The blacksmith made a new dagger," Neci said. "She's brilliant. It's *gorgeous*." The twins knew that Neci didn't mean gorgeous as in "beautiful." She meant gorgeous as in "an artful and efficient weapon."

Merlynda blanched. "Wait a minute. You saw the florist and his daughter running toward the blacksmith's? Covered in ink?"

Neci nodded. "Yeah, but I don't think they were interested in the dagger."

Merlynda locked eyes with Percy, alarmed. "But that's where—"

"Merlynda! Percy!" Mother called out.

Mother and Father hurried down the street, followed by a trail of floating bags. Some of the townspeople pointed and marveled, others crossed to the other side before warily continuing on their way, but most of them carried on as if nothing unusual were happening. Mother scooped the twins up in a single fierce hug, then let go and smiled at Neci. "Hello, Neci dear. I was just coming to collect the twins and hear about their, ah, *errands*."

Like any good knight, Neci knew when to make a hasty but calculated retreat. She offered a sweeping bow. "Good morning! It was a pleasure to see you. Good day!" She gave Merlynda a sympathetic look, then ran off toward the stationery shop.

Merlynda and Percy waved after Neci, then turned to their parents. Mother was almost their mirror image, with her pale skin, blue eyes, and long chestnut hair wrapped across her head in an elegant crown braid. The brooch she always wore sparkled in the sun, and her hedgehog familiar, Hortensia, perched on her shoulder. Father's light hair and dark eyes made him stand out from his family, but not nearly so much as the fact that he couldn't cast even the most basic charm or enchantment. He'd married into the line of Merlyn but wasn't a wizard himself.

Merlynda forced a grin. "Find everything you'll need for your trip?" she asked brightly. After five generations of the Merlyn family engaging in polite communication, the Forfles had at last invited one of them—Mother—to the Forfle homeland to study and give lectures on magic. Given how shy and slow to trust Forfles were, it was no understatement to say that this was the opportunity of a lifetime. Aside from courtesy, an invitation was required because their homeland was in a different magical dimension and couldn't be found on any map. Father was going as well, and they wouldn't be back for ages. Uncle William, Father's brother, was coming to look after the twins.

"We did!" Father grabbed at a new pair of boots that kept bumping into his shoulder, then shoved them into a canvas sack. The sack proceeded to bump into him. "Um, dear?"

Mother glanced at her husband. She waved her hand, and all of their purchases snapped into a neat, floating line. She turned back to the twins. "Now, about this morning. Merlynda—"

"It wasn't her fault!" Percy interjected.

Mother raised an eyebrow.

"No one was hurt," Merlynda said quickly. "And Percy put all the ink and parchment and everything back exactly as it was." She winced.

"I'm sure he did," Mother said, "since what you're *supposed* to do in these situations is come find me immediately, but you two love avoiding what you're *supposed* to do."

Mother's expression softened. "I'm glad no one was hurt. But, Merlynda, dear, I wonder if you might . . . take a break? From practicing. Just until we're back."

Merlynda gaped. "But you'll be gone for months!" she exclaimed. "Maybe longer, you said it yourself! I'm not supposed to practice my magic for that *entire* time?"

"You can still read and study!" Mother forced a cheerful tone. The twins could both see that she was trying to make things out to be better than they were.

"But I'll be here," Percy said. "I can—"

"Get into quite enough mischief on your own, yes." Father looked at his daughter. "Merlynda, I know you're working hard, but Uncle William isn't used to magic. And sometimes, yours gets a little . . ." He paused, searching for the right word.

"Explosive," Merlynda sighed.

"Exciting," Percy said at the same time.

"Extraneous," Hortensia offered.

"Exactly," Father agreed.

Mother smiled gently at Merlynda. "We just want everyone to be safe. Including you."

And for everyone to be safe from *me,* Merlynda thought. But as much as she hated to admit it, they had a point.

"Don't forget the, ah, *explorations,*" Hortensia said with a glower at Percy.

"Yes, I was just getting to that." Mother gave her son a stern look. "No grand experiments. Do you understand me?"

"Yes, Mother." He tried his best to sound convincing and managed to not look at Merlynda. The hedgehog glared suspiciously.

Mother tucked a stray strand of hair behind Merlynda's ear. "All right, darling? Only reading and studying. Just until we're back."

Merlynda fought the devastation crashing in. No magic for months? She'd already read every book and scroll in the manor's library, and even memorized a few of them. If she couldn't actually practice what she read about, how was she ever going to learn to control her magic?

Merlynda mustered every bit of honesty she could. "All right, Mother."

Mother shifted her gaze to Percy. "And you, Percy. No using your foresight. I don't need to remind you that it is far too easy to put stock in shaky visions."

Percy nodded obediently. He'd inherited Merlyn's gift of foresight, which was never something to trust entirely but had occasionally been useful when the twins were dabbling in a spell they probably shouldn't—such as, say, attempting to summon an extremely rare magical item like an Elemental Stone. He'd have to try to get a look at whether or not they'd succeed.

"Excellent." Father rubbed his hands together. "Well done. Now, I believe we have a special farewell dinner planned, and this custard isn't going to make itself!"

"Quite right." Mother smiled fondly at her husband, then back at the twins. "We'll have a rousing feast this evening, and after Uncle William is settled tomorrow morning, we'll be off."

Mother summoned the packages to follow them home. Father walked beside her, holding her hand and whistling. The twins hung slightly back so they wouldn't get knocked in the head by a stray book or sack. The distance allowed Merlynda to seethe in peace. She knew Mother wanted to keep them safe, but forbidding Merlynda from practicing the one thing she desperately wanted to be good at felt like a betrayal.

Once Mother and Father were safely preoccupied with chatting about their final preparations, Merlynda leaned over to Percy. "When Mother and Father are gone, we're definitely summoning an Elemental Stone, right?"

Percy grinned. "I was hoping you'd say that."

In which a number of
alarming portals appear

The next morning Uncle William arrived just in time for breakfast. He looked very much like the twins' father but was a tad stouter. Uncle William lived in town and was a portrait artist by trade. Since there were only so many people in Avonshire who both wanted and could afford portraits, he often traveled for his work. He'd told the family he was looking forward to his stay at the manor as it would allow him time to practice other highly marketable skills, like writing poetry.

After breakfast once the carriage was packed and ready, Mother pulled the twins into a fierce hug. "Behave yourselves while we're gone, darlings."

"And mind your uncle," Father chimed in. "Or at least let him think you're minding him."

Mother shoved Father playfully while Uncle William let out a mournful sigh. "An artist's woes are never ended. Like the ocean's waves, they always lap at the shore." He paused, thoughtful. "Say, I should write that one down!"

Mother handed Merlynda a small looking glass, closing her daughter's fingers around it. It fit easily into Merlynda's palm. "This will work across the magical dimensions, so you can contact us anytime. We'll call as soon as we're settled with the Forfles.

"And if anything goes wrong, I expect you to call us *immediately*." Mother looked meaningfully at each of the twins. Hortensia added her own intense glare. "Understand?"

"Yes, Mother," they both said, doing their best to look the picture of innocence.

There was a final round of hugs, and Mother gave Merlynda an extra squeeze. "You are powerful, my darling," Mother said tenderly as she held her daughter. "When you're ready, you're going to dazzle the world."

And on that confusing note, Mother and Father left on their journey.

The twins got along with Uncle William well enough, but while their father was unmagical, he at least had an excellent sense of humor. The same couldn't be said for Uncle William, and the twins had a strong suspicion that this was partially why Mother had suggested Merlynda refrain from practicing her magic.

The first few days passed without incident, but that was partly because Uncle William had decided the library was the best spot for him to practice his poetry writing. He could be found there at all hours of the day or night, scratching away with his quill. Unfortunately for the twins, the Elemental Focus central to their latest scheme was also in the library, and taking a magical object from a magical library would arouse even their uncle's nonmagical suspicions.

By the time Mother and Father had been gone for a week or so, the twins were deeply bored and still hadn't managed to sneak out the Elemental Focus. So, bright and early before breakfast, they decided that Uncle William ought to meet Harriet.

"Maybe this isn't such a good idea," Merlynda said to Percy while they watched Harriet snuffle around the dining table.

Percy frowned, looking at his pony. "She's perfectly safe."

Harriet's scorpion tail whipped out as she turned, smashing a gravy bowl. It had been a family heirloom. "She's safe for *you*, maybe."

Harriet was a brown-and-white pony who had wandered onto the manor grounds when the twins were very young. Her tail had been injured, all tangled with brambles and knots, so Percy had set about fixing it. Only, he didn't quite get it right. The scorpion tail, stinger and all, was born.

Harriet liked her new accessory, so Mother left it alone,

and Harriet had lived at the manor ever since. She loved Percy. She tolerated Merlynda. She was a living terror to everyone else.

The twins forgot about that last part until Uncle William walked in for his morning tea and locked eyes with the beast. Seeing a pony in the dining room is one thing, but when Harriet's stinger arced over her back, Uncle William nearly fainted dead away. Instead, his eyes focused on the twins.

"Run, children!" he screamed in a pitch higher than the twins thought possible. "I'll protect you!" He demonstrated by grabbing the teapot and hurling it with all his strength, spilling most of the contents all over himself in the process.

Harriet batted the teapot away with her tail and glowered at Uncle William. He gulped.

The twins rushed between them. "It's okay, Uncle William!" Merlynda tried to calm him. "We thought you might like to meet Harriet."

Percy plastered a big grin on his face. He stroked the pony's head and her tail drooped back as she relaxed. "Harriet, this is Uncle William. He's staying with us for a while, so be nice."

Harriet's eyes narrowed.

Uncle William's hand shook as he pointed at Harriet. "You mean . . . You mean . . . you did this?"

"I gave her this tail," Percy said proudly. "She'd been injured."

Merlynda nudged Percy. "I think he meant that we brought her inside," she whispered.

The twins watched in fascination as Uncle William's face turned a number of colors they hadn't realized were possible. He managed to sputter out, "Take this . . . outside . . . monster . . . out!"

"Harriet's not a monster!" Percy insisted.

"OUT!" Uncle William said. "OUT! OUT!"

Percy scowled but walked behind Harriet and opened the double doors that led directly onto the manor grounds. The pony shot Uncle William one more smoldering look, then trotted away.

Uncle William collapsed into the nearest dining chair, face covered in sweat. "My nerves," he kept muttering over and over. "Horrid, horrid beast . . ."

"*You* attacked *her* with the teapot," Percy snapped. "So I'd say you're the beast."

And that is how the twins were banished from the manor until dinner. They left the same way as Harriet, with Uncle William slamming the doors behind them before collapsing once again into his chair.

Percy sulked as the twins walked across the grounds. "He didn't need to throw anything at her. Do you think he'll tell Mother?"

Merlynda glanced back at the dining room. She felt a little bad for Uncle William. "Maybe it would serve us right, but I've got the looking glass with me." She patted her robe where it was stored. "So he at least won't be telling her any-time soon."

Percy kicked a stray stone. "I can't believe we're *banished* for the day. How are we supposed to sneak breakfast if he's blocking the kitchen?"

Merlynda brightened. "We won't sneak breakfast. As long as he's in the dining room, he's *not* in the library."

Percy lit up, all surliness gone. He practically rubbed his hands together in excitement. "Let's summon an Elemental Stone!"

Merlynda's favorite room in all of Merlyn Manor was the library. It was stuffed with books about magical theory, mystical tokens of intrigue, and rare potions recipes that had been folded beneath the cushions for safekeeping. Every time Merlynda entered, she felt like she was in the presence of her namesake, the great enchanter himself.

She had never entered through the window before, so when Percy gave her a final shove and she landed flat on her stomach, that reverent feeling passed almost immediately.

"Oof! Percy!"

"Sorry," he called from outside the window. "Are you okay? D'you see it?"

"I'm fine," Merlynda whispered, standing. "Give me a minute."

Merlyn had built the library to store his books and vials and dangerous magical trinkets all in one place. Then he died, and his sons decided the library needed to be bigger, and *their* daughters thought it needed to be homier, and *their* children thought it needed more alligators (don't ask), and so on. The result was that it now felt less like a room and more like a maze (without the alligators, thank goodness).

What Merlynda loved most about the library was the *potential* it held. All the knowledge and stories gave her hope that one day she might live up to her great-great-many-times-great-grandfather's legacy—or at least be able to cast a simple Finding Charm, or send the broom scuttling around the room.

She crept along the rows of curio cabinets, searching for her prize.

Outside the library window, Percy watched Harriet gallop by and seethed at how Uncle William had thrown the teapot at her. She was a perfectly harmless pony-scorpion. He craned his neck up at the window. Being as adept at magic as he was, he didn't feel the need to bother with books, so he rarely bothered with the library, which was why Merlynda had gone inside and not him.

He *had* tried to contribute to their escapade by using his foresight, despite Mother's warning. It hadn't mattered. That part of the future was dark and blurry, but not knowing how things might turn out made it more exciting.

Merlynda's head popped out of the window. "Got it!" Grinning, she tossed him a flat leather pouch.

"Excellent." Percy helped her down, and they dashed eagerly to the orchard.

The twins stopped in the middle of the trees, well hidden from Uncle William. Percy opened the leather pouch. A rough wooden circlet with glass in the middle, about the size of his palm, slid gently into his hand.

"Look at this." Percy put the lens to his face like it was a giant monocle. "It's only a bunch of twigs."

"Careful! Can't you feel how powerful it is?" Merlynda could sense the tiny vibrations swirling from it.

Percy shrugged, but he stopped fooling around and handed it over. "Right. I'll stand over there and start the spell."

Merlynda nodded eagerly. "And when you're good and ready, I'll add my magic through the Focus." They'd been over this (and really, she'd been the one instructing *him* about how it ought to go, as she was the one who had read about it). She knew they were more likely to fail than succeed—even when the spell was performed correctly, there was no guarantee a Stone would appear. Either way, they hoped to be one step closer to figuring out her magic.

Percy gave her a crooked smile, then moved a few feet away. If anyone could pull this off, wouldn't it be an heir of Merlyn? He'd go down in history as the youngest wizard to ever summon an Elemental Stone. He paused a moment to shake his future fame from his head and concentrate, then reached for the Air. Once he had a tight focus on the magic, he stretched his arm out and traced as wide of a circle between him and Merlynda as he could, his pointed finger leaving a dim glow behind it as it moved.

Elemental Stones were made of highly compressed magical energy and took incredible power and control to create.

Even a grown, fully trained wizard would find this a difficult task—but most wizards weren't from the line of Merlyn.

When the circle's edge glowed so brightly it looked almost solid, Percy shouted, "Now, Merlynda!" Sweat dripped down his face.

Merlynda cradled the Elemental Focus in her cupped hands, then gently blew on it. It lifted gracefully away and floated between her and the circle Percy had made. She steeled herself, hesitating. What if this time she did something more dangerous than creating geysers from inkwells?

"Merlynda!" Percy called again, panting. The circle flickered.

Merlynda took a deep breath and reached out to the Air all around her—that part was simple enough. She funneled it toward the Elemental Focus, and the magic shot through it to Percy's circle, strengthening it. Encouraged, she reached out gently with her magic, trying to move past the *Air* and to the *Aether*—

With a *fwoosh-crack!* the Elemental Focus shattered into a thousand tiny fragments, and with a much larger *bang!* the ground beneath it exploded.

Merlynda yelped and flung her arms up. A light shimmered in front of her, and the splinters and debris clattered against it. As quickly as it formed, the barrier dissolved.

She stared at her hands, dumbfounded. She'd never made a light shield before.

The Air circle had disappeared as soon as the Focus broke, so Percy had not been so lucky. His chestnut hair and deep blue robes were covered in dirt and twigs. He shook his head to get the dust out and coughed. "That was your best explosion yet! How did you make that shield?"

Merlynda didn't know how she'd done it, but she could still feel the magic. It was laughing. At her. Like always.

She didn't get to tell Percy this because at that moment, a great wind roared above the tiny crater left by the exploded Focus. It rushed through the trees and rattled their branches, blasting more earth at the twins. In the space between them, a black void tore through the air. Vicious storm clouds raced around the edges as it widened, chasing sparks and flashes of lightning. Tree branches and leaves broke off and swirled, sucked up into the angry clouds.

It would have been pretty if it hadn't been so terrifying.

The twins scrambled away, circling around to stand next to each other. It was already as big as they were. Inside they could see tiny pricks of light, like stars against the night sky.

"Stop it, Merlynda!" Percy cried. He tried to blast it with magic, but his efforts were sucked up with everything else.

"I can't!" The panic rose in her voice. Had she done this? None of the books about Elemental Stones had ever mentioned this! It looked like a portal, but she'd never actually seen one. She could feel the magic radiating out of the void—*from the* void, *beyond* the void—

The portal belched, then shrank down to a pinpoint and vanished. Earth and brush crashed to the ground, and the orchard was still once more.

Percy cautiously approached where the portal had been. Was this how Elemental Stones formed?

"Percy," Merlynda breathed, understanding. "I think— where is it?"

"Where's what?"

"That was a portal—from the Aether! That's how familiars come—yours must be here!"

"My *what?*"

"I beg your pardon," a small voice said from Merlynda's shoulder, "but I believe you're referring to me."

A Word about Familiars

When Percy said, "My what?" he wasn't asking, "What, sister dearest, is a familiar?" He was saying, "We are clearly not old enough to have familiars, so why are we even talking about this?"

All wizards and wizardesses have familiars, as most magical persons do—witches, necromancers, even the occasional hag or warlock. Once an individual's magic comes of age, their familiar is summoned by the Aether and sent through a portal from the In-Between. Portals are not typically as dramatic as the one Merlynda experienced (hence her initial confusion), but this is the only method *of transportation possible from the In-Between to the rest of the world.*

The age at which magic matures varies depending on the individual, but familiars can be expected to arrive anywhere between the ages of fifteen to nineteen, unless you are exceptionally talented, or exceptionally daft. Rafferty the Portly, for example, didn't receive his familiar until he was seventy-eight, and even then it was an underwhelming guppy. Conversely, Lady Iola of the Moor received her familiar on the exact day she turned thirteen, in the form of a snowy white wolf.

Merlynda and Percy's mother had been fourteen and a half when her hedgehog arrived, which was something to be proud of.

Merlyn, the great-great-many-times-great-grandfather of the twins, had only been twelve when his owl showed up. Twelve.

The twins were a whole year younger than Merlyn, the greatest wizard of all time, but for some reason the Aether thought one of them—just one—was ready for a familiar.

Merlynda whipped her head toward the voice. A thick red worm—or was it a small snake?—perched on her shoulder.

She shrieked and stumbled back, accidentally grabbing at all of the elements at once. Trees swayed toward them and roots cracked as they broke through the ground. Dust and dirt swirled in a mighty tornado.

Percy bellowed a command, and the chaos calmed. He turned to Merlynda, stunned. "What was that about?"

Merlynda whirled, taking in the debris scattered across

the orchard, breathing hard. "There was—something—on my shoulder."

Percy took this in. "On your shoulder."

"It was a—a worm, maybe?"

Percy relaxed. If it was a worm, it had probably gotten tossed on Merlynda when the Elemental Focus blew up and threw dirt everywhere.

"I'm not a worm!" The small voice was defiant but muffled.

Percy whipped around. "Who said that?"

Merlynda knew where the voice was coming from. She could feel it. But she was having a hard time believing it. She was, after all, only eleven, and not a particularly talented wizardess.

Merlynda had fantasized about her familiar's arrival the way children dream and fidget about their next birthday—what form it would take, what name she'd invent for it, and how well they'd get along (it's bad business when wizardesses and their familiars don't get along). Mostly, she'd wondered if it would finally help her control her magic. The magic that laughed.

Percy had fantasized about his familiar too. Namely, he'd imagined the twins would get them at the same time, or (though he'd never say this aloud) that his would come first. So he was more than a little confused when Merlynda tentatively approached a pile of soft debris and crouched down to speak with it.

"Hello?" she asked. But inside she was thinking, *Please let me have seen wrong—please don't be a worm.*

The familiar poked its head out, shook itself to clear

the twigs away, then wobbled across the uneven ground to Merlynda. He—somehow she knew it was a he—did look an awful lot like a worm. Except for his head, which was more like a snake's, and his two little legs, which made him look like something else altogether.

The familiar curled himself around Merlynda's wrist like a bracelet. Walking wasn't needed in the In-Between, but he thought his first steps had been very impressive.

Percy came nearer. If this was Merlynda's familiar, then perhaps his was also nearby. "*Is* it a worm?" he asked.

"I'm not! I am not!" the not-a-worm cried.

Despite her own doubts, Merlynda felt she ought to defend him. "Of course he's not a worm," she said more firmly than she felt. "He's . . . a bit undergrown, that's all. For . . . an arm-less salamander?"

The familiar sulked. "I'm not that, either."

Merlynda held up her wrist so they could get a better look, and the familiar obliged them by uncurling and standing in her hand to show off. He was a deep, rich wine color, and only as thick as her finger. A golden ridge ran down the middle of his back, from his head to his tail. A few inches before his tail were two small clawed feet, and two tiny nubs stuck out from his back.

Merlynda inspected him. "Not to be rude, but . . . what are you doing here?"

The familiar cocked his head at her. "The Aether sent me."

"Yes, of course," Merlynda said. "I mean, *who* are you here for?"

"Oh, that. The Septimum Genus."

The anxiety roiling inside of her vanished. She pointed at Percy. "He's right here."

Percy looked down at the defiant not-a-worm. "Um, hello."

The familiar stared at him, then swiveled back to Merlynda. "That's not my wizardess."

"But . . . he's the Septimum Genus?"

The familiar closed his eyes and curled himself back around Merlynda's wrist. It was exceptionally comfortable. "I'm here for Merlynda of Merlyn Manor, Seventh Descendant of Merlyn the Great, Septimum Genus."

The twins stood in stunned silence.

"Don't you mean *Percival* of Merlyn Manor?" Merlynda squeaked.

"Nope," the familiar answered. "The Aether's very decisive about these things."

Septimum Genus. The words slammed into Merlynda, sending a whirlwind of panic through her. *She* couldn't be the Septimum Genus! She couldn't even magically reheat her tea without blowing up the kitchen. Unless Merlyn considered hiding in the library a miraculous, wonderful thing, everyone who'd been awaiting the fulfillment of his prophecy was in for a big disappointment.

"It's wrong this time!" Merlynda burst out, the panic getting the better of her. "I'm no Septimum Genus!" She looked desperately to her brother. "Tell him! Tell him the Aether was wrong!"

"The Aether has never been wrong before, according to Mother." Percy tried to smile, but he felt like he'd had the wind knocked out of him. Hadn't everyone—including Percy—assumed *he* was the one Merlyn had meant in his prophecy?

He bent down to study the familiar and reached out a finger to poke it. "Did you bring a friend with you?" He tried not to sound too hopeful.

The familiar dodged his finger. "I beg your pardon! And no! Only I was sent!"

Merlynda shielded the familiar instinctively. She already felt a deep attachment to it, though her head swirled. The Septimum Genus? A familiar? She took a few deep breaths, and the panic faded. She still had Percy. They would figure this out, together.

Percy stood up and shrugged. "I suppose it's a relief. My foresight already showed me my familiar will be more impressive than a worm when it comes." This was not strictly true, as all he'd been able to see was that his familiar would indeed one day come, but it helped conceal his disappointment.

Merlynda's familiar reared up like a snake about to strike. "I am a great dragon! Probably! I've only been in corporeal form for a few minutes, so I'm not sure yet." He took a deep breath and glared fiercely.

The twins watched with interest, and Merlynda felt a teeny glimmer of hope. Perhaps her familiar was more than he seemed.

The not-a-worm held his breath a moment longer, then let it all out in a *whoosh!*

A tiny whoosh. And then a sneeze.

"Excuse me," he said, then twisted his head around to get a good look at himself. "Ah, I see." He untwisted to face the twins again. "What did you expect? I'm clearly a very fierce wyvern. It's rare for wyverns to breathe fire before their wings grow in. Everyone knows that."

Percy stared, but it wasn't because of the familiar's pluck. It was because a familiar had come at all, and what's more, it was Merlynda's. Not his. Confusion swirled through him, threatening to blow him over. A hint of something darker chased it, trying to take root and grow. He loved Merlynda, but he couldn't deny his bafflement and, he hated to admit, his envy.

How was this possible? She couldn't even manage basic spells! And wasn't he the one who always fixed things when she bungled her magic? *He* was the most powerful wizard born in generations.

The envy growled inside him, trying to find purchase, but it was rocked by another shaky thought.

If he wasn't the Septimum Genus, then who was he?

"Percy?"

The shake in Merlynda's voice brought him back to the moment. She was terrified. He shoved the confusion and envy into a corner. They resisted, snarling inside him, but his sister needed him. He could sort his feelings out later.

"Let's have a go with him." Percy tried to sound enthusiastic, but even to him it sounded forced. "Familiars help with magic, right? Maybe now you'll be able to control yours!"

Merlynda lifted her familiar up to eye level. "What do you say?"

The not-a-worm craned his head this way and that to admire himself. He didn't know how he'd ever mistaken himself for a dragon. Wyverns were far superior, in his opinion. "After breakfast, perhaps?"

"Just one spell?"

The familiar hunched slightly. "Fine. But remember, I'm new at this."

"Try the fountain one," Percy encouraged, ignoring the dark, snarling things inside him. "That should be easy."

Summoning water from nowhere was *supposed* to be simple, but Merlynda had flooded Father's study the last time she tried. And that wasn't counting the recent ink fiasco, which had been an accident. She looked to her familiar, who was curled back around her wrist.

"Ready?"

"I suppose," he sighed.

Percy stood next to her while Merlynda focused on the middle of the small crater. That would be a good entry point. She could sense her familiar's magic and tried to combine hers with it to move through the elements to the Aether—

Another portal ripped through the air before the twins. Unlike the first one, it was jagged and misshapen and lead to— *nothing*. The nothingness greedily sucked them toward it like a ferocious gust of wind.

Merlynda yelped as her hair and robes were whipped this way and that. She reached behind her as she slipped, grasping a low tree branch. Her familiar clung to her wrist, eyes squeezed shut.

"Merlynda!"

She twisted so she could see the portal. Percy was scrabbling at the ground as he was dragged relentlessly toward the void. His eyes were wide with panic. He tried to magic ropes, to shoot himself forward, but everything was sucked into the emptiness behind him.

He grabbed on to a root sticking out of the ground, feet whipping behind him toward this new, darker portal. Merlynda reached for him, straining, screaming—of all the times to be awful at magic, he wasn't *that* far—but the portal gave a final, enormous heave, and the root Percy clung to broke.

He cried out as he flew back, and the moment he disappeared inside, the portal vanished.

Everything stilled. Merlynda sat up and stared, breathing hard. "Percy!" she screamed. She ran to the empty space where the portal had been. "Percy!"

What had she done?

How?

Right in front of her, a third portal split the air, much smaller than the others. Merlynda caught a glimpse of Percy's terrified face.

"Percy!" Merlynda shrieked. She dove at the portal. Before she could reach her brother, it winked out like the others, leaving only a crumpled piece of parchment that fell to the ground. Her fingers grasped air.

"Percy!" Merlynda screamed again. None of this made sense. Three portals had ripped open before her in the span of minutes, each of them different.

Trembling, Merlynda reached for the parchment Percy had shoved through the portal. On it was a rough illustration of several stone pillars standing next to one another in a crude circle. Other stones were scattered on the ground, and occasionally two pillars had a third stacked across them, as if creating a doorway. Suns arced up over the pillars from the left, and moons from the right, until they met in the middle. At the bottom of the parchment in swirled, looping letters were two words:

The Hollower.

*In which a determined wizardess, a
would-be knight, and a very fierce
wyvern set off upon a quest*

Up in Avonshire, Neci the Ardent was having an exciting morning of her own. She had just put the baker's son in a headlock.

"Your word!" she demanded to his strawberry hair.

She'd spoken out to protect a younger kid from Rupert's bullying, as was a knight's duty, and demanded Rupert promise to change his ways. Instead, he'd thrown a right hook, forcing Neci to defend herself.

They were surrounded by a crowd of jeering kids, mostly older boys. Rupert was the biggest and meanest of them all, but not very nimble.

Neci's smaller size worked to her advantage for once.

"Never!" Rupert grunted, kicking at her. He missed, so he threw himself down, dragging Neci along. She bashed into the ground, the wind knocked out of her.

Rupert stood up, but Neci leapt onto his back, clinging around his neck. Her feet dangled above the ground. "I— said—give—your—word!" she gasped.

Rupert scrabbled at her arms, but Neci held on tight.

"All right," Rupert wheezed. "All right! I give my word!"

Neci let her arms go slack and dropped to her feet, smug.

Rupert turned around and shoved her hard to the ground. Roaring laughter filled Neci's ears. "Cheater!" she shouted. "Brigand!"

"Neci! Get up this instant!"

Rupert scattered with the other children, leaving Neci sprawled in the dirt to face her mother. She pulled herself to her feet, seething. How *dare* he pull such a dishonorable move! It wasn't knightly at all!

But then, Rupert didn't care about being a knight. He'd happily follow in his family's footsteps, baking loaves and sweet buns for the rest of his days.

Lady Ardent was aghast, and Neci cringed. She knew her mother believed that this was no way for the daughter of a respectable merchantwoman to behave. What would her employees or the townspeople think? *"Fighting,* Neci? In the middle of town?" Lady Ardent's skin was the same dark brown as Neci's, and her curly hair was pulled into a perfect bun, but her brown eyes were wide with horror. Probably from whatever new stories the town gossips would be whispering about her only child.

"Sorry," Neci mumbled. She didn't explain that it was *defending*, not fighting. Her mother, always dressed in finery as if the ladies' social club were coming for tea, didn't understand.

Neci found her mother's desire and ability to neatly traverse the social circles of Avonshire just as baffling as Lady Ardent found Neci's utter lack of interest in them. She'd once caught Neci swinging a carrot as if it were a sword and had scolded her for damaging a perfect root vegetable specimen. Neci craved adventure and valiant duels and had cut her hair short herself so that she'd never be distracted by it in battle, just like Dame Joi (she wisely didn't explain this reasoning to her parents). Since even a dagger was out of the question, Neci had crafted her own sling and mastered flinging stones (and the occasional parsnip) at crows and the town boys and other menaces. She wanted a faithful and noble steed named Bone Crusher, or Jawbreaker, or perhaps Morris. She couldn't decide.

Lady Ardent closed her eyes and put her hand to her forehead, defeated. "I think you ought to spend more time with Aunt Prin."

"What?" Neci exclaimed. "No!"

"Needlework and cooking are excellent pursuits for a young girl!"

"Mother—" Neci pleaded. "Please—"

"I'll talk with your father," Lady Ardent sighed. "But not until tomorrow. Happy birthday, Neci."

Neci smiled weakly. At least this bought her some time. It *was* her birthday, and you only turn ten once, so she considered it a big deal.

Morning tea was all set in the great hall when they returned home (with the loaf Neci had been sent to buy in the first place). Lord Ardent sat grinning at the table. Neci's father usually grinned, but this morning there was an extra brilliance to it, and a twinkle in his eye. Neci's customary birthday coin was by her place at the table, but her father also held a short, narrow present wrapped in cloth and tied with a pretty red string. Neci's breath caught—was it possible? It was the exact right size for a dagger. Had they seen her drooling over the one at the blacksmith's?

Her father kissed her forehead, not bothered by the smudged dirt. "Happy birthday, sweet onion."

Hands trembling, unable to breathe, Neci took the present and tugged on the string, and the present tumbled into her hand.

It was not a dagger. It was a brand-new trowel, polished to the point of reflection, engraved with her initials and an inscription:

> *N. t. A.*
>
> *Destiny calls!*

Neci let the words play in her mind. *Destiny calls.* The

disappointment crushed her, worse than Rupert's foul-play shove had.

"Thank you," she mustered. "It's . . . very shiny."

Her parents beamed.

"Why don't you try it out?" her father urged.

"Yes." Neci stood. "Yes, I'll do that."

She picked up her present and walked outside into the gardens. Once she'd found a hidden area, she stabbed the trowel savagely into the ground, over and over and over, until there wasn't a spot of shine left anywhere and the engraving was covered in dirt and damp soil. She dropped the trowel into the fresh hole, covered it up with the loose dirt, and sat and cried.

Crying is no shameful thing. You may not feel entirely well after crying, but you will likely feel better. This was Neci's experience (though stabbing the ground and digging a grave for her trowel helped too). It wasn't the trowel itself that upset her. It was the fact that her parents thought she *wanted* a trowel.

She'd almost finished when bells rang along the road that led to the town center. Perhaps this birthday wouldn't be so terrible in the end.

Neci rushed back inside to grab her satchel, slid her birthday coin into it, and shouted something to her parents about showing off her present in town before sprinting up the road. A two-horse cart trundled along the lane, stuffed with packages. The driver stopped when he saw Neci dashing toward him.

"Do you have a package for Neci the Ardent?" she blurted.

The driver nodded. "Sign here." He held out a ledger, and after she signed, he handed her a small square parcel and drove away.

Neci tore the paper from her package. It was a book, bound in beautiful green leather and embossed with a crest bearing a sword and shield. Glistening silver letters read *The Official Quest Requirements for Knighthood.*

Neci tried not to squeal with excitement—squealing was hardly knightly.

Instead, she rushed off down the road that led to Merlyn Manor.

Merlynda's hand shook as she stared at the words on the parchment.

The Hollower.

It couldn't be. The Hollower was only a myth, told to children to make them behave and eat their root vegetables . . . wasn't it?

Her familiar stared at the words too. "What's a Hollower?" If this was something he ought to be prepared for, he wanted to make sure he could hide.

"A—a story," Merlynda managed.

"I hope it's a good one." The wyvern snuggled up against her wrist. "I could use a good nap-time story."

"Wake up," Merlynda snapped. She sat down hard and cradled her head so the world would stop spinning.

Her familiar had come—she was the Septimum Genus—

Percy had vanished through a portal—then sent her a message through *another* portal—

She and her familiar must have accidentally created the portal that had sucked Percy in. That alone made breathing difficult, but then—if the Hollower was real and Percy had somehow crossed him . . . but how had he gotten her a message so quickly?

Merlynda needed to tell Mother right now. She'd know what to do. Merlynda thrust her shaking hand into her robes, searching for the magic looking glass. She clasped its cold, smooth surface. Her familiar watched, curious but unhelpful.

Merlynda's mouth had gone dry. She licked her lips, then held the mirror up, trembling. It only took a tiny magical spark to activate the mirror. She'd managed that a dozen times before. She tugged ever so slightly at the Air.

Nothing happened. Her familiar cocked his head.

Merlynda took a deep breath. Maybe she should try Earth instead. She reached out and brushed the magic, urging it into the mirror. Still nothing happened, so she focused harder, desperately grabbing at the Earth *and* the Air and shoving them toward the mirror—

Crack! The mirror split into several fragments, falling from her shaking hand.

Merlynda let out a cry of anguish and grabbed her head again.

She stood and began pacing back and forth, thinking through her options. Percy had vanished. She had no way to contact Mother. As far as she knew, there was no one in Avonshire who could get a message to her parents in the Forfle dimension, and there was no one magical around who could help. Uncle William would be less than useless. But she couldn't sit around waiting. The Hollower had Percy *now*, her parents weren't due back for months, and she was the only one who knew what had happened—

The tears came then, stinging her eyes. Had she sent Percy directly to the Hollower? She wiped the tears away angrily as they dripped onto the parchment, the clue Percy had managed to send her.

"What's a Hollower?" her familiar asked again.

Merlynda took a steadying breath. "The stories say the Hollower can appear at any time, in any place. And then he— Merlyn's goat, he's called the *Hollower*. He empties you, steals your life, your magic!" Was he Hollowing Percy already? How did the Hollower even Hollow people?

The familiar scoffed. "That's silly. Magic can't be stolen."

"Then what just happened to Percy!" Merlynda shouted.

The wyvern turned away haughtily. "It looked like *he* was stolen, not his magic."

Merlynda took another deep breath. "I'm sorry," she said. "I'm sorry, but this—this is all a lot."

"Don't blame me," the familiar snipped. "Familiars are plucked from the In-Between and sent by the Aether whenever *your* magic decides it's time. You've no one to blame but yourself."

"I didn't ask for you to come!"

"And I didn't have a choice! Your magic comes of age, and then we're formed based on your potential."

"I only have the potential of a salamander?" Merlynda cried. If that was all, Percy was doomed.

The familiar puffed up. "Take it back! I told you! I am a very fierce wyvern!"

They glowered at each other.

Merlynda stood down first. She didn't have time to bicker, and if she was going to save Percy, she needed to get along with her familiar.

"I didn't mean to offend you," she finally said, wiping her eyes and trying to think. "I only meant . . . I'm awfully young. Maybe you came too early?"

"Nope. The Aether sends familiars exactly when they're meant to arrive."

Merlynda doubted this very much, as the Aether had never been particularly keen on helping her before. She considered the proud, tiny wyvern. "Why don't we start over? Maybe— maybe I should come up with a name for you?"

The familiar twisted his head to catch more of the sunlight. His wizardess might be a nuisance, but he rather enjoyed sunshine. "I like Ignus. Strong, bold—I think it suits me."

Merlynda narrowed her eyes. "I've never heard of a familiar naming itself."

"So? I've never heard of a wizardess who can't do magic."

Merlynda moved her wrist into her shadow.

"How rude!"

They both glared. "Fine. Listen, Iggy—"

"Only my friends can call me that," the familiar sniffed. "My name is Ignus." He turned his head away.

Merlynda bit down a frustrated reply. If this really was her familiar, and she really was the Septimum Genus, then they were stuck with each other. She'd need Iggy's help to save Percy.

"All right, Ignus. I'm sorry I snapped at you."

"And?"

"And threw you into a bush."

"And?"

Merlynda managed not to grit her teeth. "And that I called you a salamander."

He twisted his head to stare at her.

"I'm sorry that I called you a salamander *twice*. You look like a very nice wyvern."

Iggy bared his teeth. "And fierce."

"And fierce," Merlynda agreed. She held out her pinkie finger. "We're in this together. Friends?"

The tiny wyvern eyed her finger, then unwound the tip of his tail from her wrist and shook it. "Friends. *Now* you may call me Iggy."

"Good." Merlynda felt a little better. She folded the piece of parchment and tucked it into her robes, alongside Neci's birthday present. "Let's find my brother."

"Merlynda!" a voice called, startling Iggy and sending him into hiding in Merlynda's sleeve. Neci sprinted toward them through the orchard, clutching her book. "Hey—" She stopped short when she saw the wreckage. "Are you okay?"

Merlynda tried to answer but burst into tears again.

Neci checked Merlynda over for injuries. There didn't seem to be any, but by the size of the crater in the middle of the orchard and the debris strewn around, *something* had happened.

Neci helped Merlynda sit and put her arm around her. The wizardess leaned into her friend, and they sat in silence as Merlynda wept.

As the crying slowed, Neci was still puzzling the pieces together. When Merlynda's magic went awry, things were usually straightened out by . . . "Merlynda, where's Percy?"

Merlynda sucked in a great, shaky breath and haltingly explained to Neci what had happened.

Neci listened, feeling pride at her friend's magic coming of age, then gutted by Percy's vanishing. When Merlynda finished, Neci was speechless. On the one hand, she was extremely proud of her best friend (the Septimum Genus! And getting her familiar at only eleven!), but on the other hand—

"The *Hollower?*" Neci wasn't magical herself, but even *her* parents had tried to frighten her into good manners with stories about the Hollower coming for naughty children. If the Hollower was real, Percy was in extreme danger.

Merlynda offered the now-tearstained parchment. Neci examined the drawing. "This isn't Percy's writing? What's this picture?"

Merlynda shook her head. "I don't recognize the writing, or whatever that ring of stones is. But . . ." She examined the image again. Even if her magic was rubbish, she was an excellent student. She'd never seen an arrangement of stone pillars like that, not even in all of the manor's books. But the way the sun and the moon met above them . . .

"It's the Shadow Sun," Merlynda said. "See? It's an astronomy chart. Maybe Percy was trying to tell me that he'll be at these standing stones when the Shadow Sun happens. But that's not for almost another seven months."

Neci took the parchment, squinting at it. "How does he know where he'll be seven months from now?"

Merlynda threw her arms up. "I don't know! None of this makes any sense! But unless he somehow opens another portal, which is *not* a common magical ability, by the way, finding these stones is all I've got."

Neci nodded, thoughtful. "He wouldn't have sent this to you if it wasn't important. So maybe Percy will be safe until the Shadow Sun! Seven months is a long time."

A tiny hope-spark shimmered in Merlynda's chest, and she began to calm. Seven months *was* a long time.

Would her parents be back by then? She couldn't risk waiting for them.

"Neci," Merlynda said, taking the parchment back. "I'm going after Percy. Right now."

Neci's eyes gleamed. "You're on a quest!"

"A quest." Merlynda tested the word. For all her reading,

she didn't know the first thing about questing. "To rescue Percy. To stop the Hollower."

Iggy had poked his head out of Merlynda's sleeve to wriggle his neck into the sun, but at this he started. "You want to find the person stealing life and magic? On *purpose?*" Just when he thought his wizardess might be all right!

"We've got to, Iggy." The image of Percy's terrified face through the final portal flashed again before her. She had no idea how he'd managed to get her the parchment, but he clearly meant for her to follow it. "He needs us. He'd do the same for me." She stood up.

"You can't just go charging off after your brother when he's been magically swept away," Neci blurted. "You need a plan! Supplies!"

"You're right." Merlynda sat down again. "And I'm sorry. It's your birthday, and that's supposed to be a happy thing."

"Nonsense." Neci looked at Iggy, fascinated. "My parents got me a trowel. Is this your familiar? Hello, Iggy!"

"Only my friends call me Iggy."

Merlynda moved so Iggy caught more of the sunlight filtering through the orchard leaves. "She's a friend."

"I'll be the judge of that."

"Are you a baby dragon?" Neci asked.

"I am a *very fierce wyvern.*"

"He's sensitive about that," Merlynda whispered. "I think people were expecting the Septimum Genus to have something a tad . . . bigger."

"What, like a cat?"

"Cats are *boring*," Iggy said.

"And for witches," Merlynda added. "Besides, I'm allergic. It's one of my many magical failings."

Neci reached out a tentative finger to stroke Iggy's back. He let her. "I think he's brilliant."

Iggy turned to Merlynda. "I like her."

"Of course you do. What's that?" she asked Neci.

Neci grinned and held up her brand-new copy of *The Official Quest Requirements for Knighthood*. "Just the thing to help find Percy. It came this morning. Listen to this." And she read:

> *Dear Candidate,*
>
> *Congratulations on taking your first step toward becoming a dignified man in service to the realm of Faelor! Your journey begins here.*
>
> *In order to qualify for knighthood status, candidates must acquire a minimum of one hundred and twenty-seven (127) points. Points are awarded for completed quests, which vary in value. More difficult quests (e.g., beheading Medusa) will have a higher point value, while easier quests (e.g., helping a fairy who is disguised as a beggar) will have a lower point value.*
>
> *Within these pages are a variety of questing opportunities, along with their associated point*

values. When you feel you have acquired the
correct amount of points to be considered for
knighthood, apply in person to be examined.
Good luck and happy questing!

"What's that about being a dignified man?" Merlynda asked. "Why did it say that?"

Neci hugged the book to her chest. Everything she wanted was in these pages. "I don't care. I'm going to earn my points and become a knight." She could see herself standing tall, a sworn protector of the realm of Faelor, just like Dame Joi.

Merlynda thought only kings and queens could knight someone, but she didn't say anything and looked at Iggy instead. "We need to leave soon."

He stared right back. Of course they needed to leave soon. There were no snacks here.

"But first." Merlynda dug into her robes and pulled out the wax-sealed envelope she'd picked up from Mr. Wintley's shop the day she'd accidentally turned all the inkwells into geysers. "I'm not sure this will earn you any points, but happy birthday."

Neci took the envelope and broke the seal, then slid out the small parchment square and stared. She felt like the wind had been knocked out of her in a jousting match, but in a good way. "This isn't available until next month!"

Merlynda grinned, despite everything. Her father had a friend in the city who had been able to get the gift early. "I may not be very good with magic, but I can still do a trick or two."

Neci stared in awe at the newest addition to her collection. It was a crisp, brand-new, limited-edition trading parchment for the Ye Knoble Knights Defend the Civilized World game. The elegant image featured Dame Joi and Merlyn.

Iggy unwrapped himself enough to get a good look at the card. "You've got his nose," he told Merlynda.

"Thank you," Neci breathed. Not only was this the rarest card *ever made*—it was also the strongest. Most cards featured just one knight, villain, or enchanter, but sometimes cards were created with more.

Two were stronger than one, after all.

Neci removed her decoder ring from the string around her neck and slipped it onto her finger. *Destiny calls*, her birthday trowel had said. Neci doubted this was what her parents had had in mind, but destiny was calling, all right. And she would answer.

"I'm coming," she promised Merlynda. "I'm coming to help you on your quest."

Merlynda leaned back, startled. "But I don't even know where to start!"

"That's why you need me!" Neci exclaimed. "I know all about questing! Knights are always prepared, so I've got everything we need." She dumped her satchel over, and her supplies tumbled free.

Merlynda and Iggy stared at the pile. There was *The Compendium of Knights and Their Noble Deeds*, Neci's sling, a compass, far more stones than ought to have fit into one bag, a few sticks that were suspiciously dagger-sized, a candle, a few odds and ends, and a huge bundle of bandages.

"Have you got any breakfast?" Iggy asked hopefully.

"Hmm." Neci tapped her arm, thinking. "I suppose food would be useful."

"We might be able to sneak into the manor for some food," Merlynda suggested.

"An excellent plan," Iggy agreed.

Neci grinned. "This is going to work, Merlynda. I'll earn my points to become a knight, you'll find Percy, and we'll defeat the Hollower together." A thrill ran through her. What a proclamation! What a glorious adventure! What an excellent solution to avoid embroidery lessons with Aunt Prin!

Merlynda felt another hope-spark. She may have lost Percy, but with Neci by her side, they just might find him.

A quick peep at the manor showed Uncle William still sitting at the dining room table, babbling to himself and staring at nothing, as far as Merlynda could tell. She felt a twinge of guilt about the further distress he'd feel when he realized his charges were missing. She and Neci had agreed not to tell anyone what they were up to. Now that the looking glass was broken, there was no way to contact Merlynda's parents across magical dimensions. The other grown-ups would wait however many months for Merlynda's parents to get back from the Forfle realm, and by then it might be too late for Percy.

Since Uncle William was blocking their access to the manor's kitchen and pantry, the trio headed back into town.

"Are you sure there isn't anything in the manor's library that could help us?" Neci asked.

Merlynda shook her head. "None of the books mention anything like these standing stones. And the only mention of the Hollower is in nursery rhymes, but everyone knows those."

"Yeah," Neci agreed. "'The Hollower's on the hunt, my child,' and all that."

Iggy poked his head out from Merlynda's sleeve. "Are you quite sure we should be hunting a hunter? Wouldn't it be better to, say, learn to make dainty pastries?"

Merlynda could feel how frightened her familiar was, even if he'd never admit it. "I'm scared too, Iggy," she told him. "But Percy needs us."

"I don't see how chasing after a magic-stealer is going to help. And I'm not scared," Iggy sniffed. "I'm a very fierce wyvern."

Merlynda sighed. She and her familiar had a ways to go before they bonded.

Once they reached Avonshire, they headed back to Mr. Wintley's shop. If anyone in town knew anything about the standing stones, it would be him.

Mr. Wintley turned to greet them when they walked in, a wide grin on his face. "Good morning! How may I—"

He froze when he saw Merlynda. She tugged her sleeve over Iggy, who was trying to get a good look at the shop. Explaining how her familiar had arrived and how her brother—the twin everyone *thought* was the Septimum Genus—had vanished was an awkward conversation she'd prefer to avoid. She didn't need everyone in Avonshire gossiping about Merlyn's prophecy when she herself still didn't quite believe she was the Septimum Genus.

"Miss Merlynda!" Mr. Wintley squeaked. "Miss Neci! What terrible timing, I'm just closing the shop for lunch."

Neci looked around, confused. "But it's still morning."

Mr. Wintley ushered them back out the door. "Early riser and all that! Too bad! Do have a lovely day."

"Wait, please." Merlynda ground her heels into the floor, anchoring herself before she was pushed out the door. "I just wanted to ask you a question. I promise I won't make the ink explode again!"

Mr. Wintley stopped shooing them toward the door. Whether because he realized Merlynda had no intention of leaving until this was settled, or he feared another outburst, Merlynda didn't care. He gave her a pained look and forced a smile. "Yes?"

Merlynda pulled the parchment out, careful to cover the words written on it when she showed him. Thankfully, Iggy seemed content to keep hidden around this new stranger. "Have you ever seen these before?"

Mr. Wintley let out an irritated huff. "I apologize, Miss Merlynda, but I really don't have time for silly games."

Neci crossed her arms. "It's not a silly game."

"Please," Merlynda said earnestly. "If anyone in town will know what this is, you will."

Mr. Wintley glanced from the irritated would-be knight to the desperate wizardess. He may have been humoring them, or he may have been genuinely curious in his quest for knowledge, but he adjusted his spectacles and took a proper look at the image.

"Hmm . . . this astronomy chart indicates the Shadow Sun, but we've some time until that occurs. . . . What are all these pillars? Some sort of doorway?"

Merlynda's heart sank, but she tried not to show it. "We were hoping you could tell us. I've never seen it before, not even in our library at the manor."

"I wonder . . . I can't be certain it's what you're looking for, but I've heard a rumor or two about such a place. It's quite a long journey from here."

"How long?" Neci asked.

"Weeks. Perhaps months. Far, far on the other side of Howlwyn Forest, well outside of Faelor in the lesser-traveled parts of the world." Mr. Wintley tried to take the parchment for a better look. "Where did you get this? It's a curious texture."

Merlynda tucked the parchment back into her robes. "Oh, you know, here and there. We must be going now. Enjoy your lunch!"

The girls hurried toward the market to avoid any more awkward questions. Merlynda fought the despair that kept trying to settle in her stomach. She supposed it had been too much to hope that Mr. Wintley would know anything more about the standing stones.

Neci nudged her. "We'll find the stones," she said. "And we'll find Percy. Most knights don't know where they're going when they start their quests—they only know what they're looking for."

Merlynda wiped her wet eyes with her sleeve. "And they always find it?"

"Any knight worth their title."

"I beg your pardon." Iggy poked his head out from beneath Merlynda's now-damp sleeve. "I haven't been in the world long enough to need a bath."

"Oh, I'm sorry, Iggy," Merlynda said, and meant it. "Only, if you can stay hidden until we're out of town, that might be best. Would you like to move to my other wrist? It's dry."

Iggy took a moment to consider. His wizardess might have been careless, but she was thoughtful. Also, there were an awful lot of strangers in this world. He nuzzled back down, content. "I like this one. But I'd like it even better with breakfast?" He peeked at Merlynda hopefully.

Merlynda's own stomach growled. "How do knights find food on their quests?"

"They're sent off with bundles of food to nourish them along their journey, or they hunt wild game."

"We haven't got anyone to send us off, and I don't know how to hunt."

"No," Neci grinned. "But we do have this!" She held up her birthday coin.

Iggy eyed it. "There's quite enough for me, but what will you two eat?"

Merlynda laughed, not unkindly. "You don't eat it—you use it to buy things. Like food."

Neci suddenly shoved Merlynda into a small alley.

"Neci, what—"

"Shh!" Neci hissed. "I just saw my mother up ahead. She must be looking for me." A thrill ran through her. She had her own idea of destiny, and it didn't involve carrots.

Should she feel guilty? Was it unknightly to pursue your dreams, even if it made others worry? She'd consult *The Compendium of Knights and Their Noble Deeds* later.

Merlynda peeked around the corner. Sure enough, Lady Ardent was at the market, speaking to each of the vendors before moving on. "We should probably avoid the main market. Can you get anything to eat from one of your parents' shops?"

"Too risky," Neci said quickly. It was true, but she also didn't want to lug root vegetables around on their whole adventure.

"Let's go around, then," Merlynda suggested. "We can pop over to one of the market stalls on the other side of town, then head to the forest."

The girls took side streets and alleys until they found themselves on the other side of Avonshire. Merlynda hadn't come to this side of town often, but Neci seemed confident enough.

"That one," the would-be knight whispered, nodding toward a round elf selling a variety of cheeses. He was short for an elf, but still taller than the girls. Neci strolled up boldly, and Merlynda tried to mimic her friend.

"Good day, noble cheesemonger." Neci bent low in a sweeping bow to complete the greeting. "Might we purchase some of your fine wares?"

The cheesemonger arched one of his thick eyebrows at them. The tips of his pointed ears curled out slightly from his head. "Money?" he grunted.

Neci held up her birthday coin, beaming. The cheesemonger stared at it for a moment, then slid a tiny wheel of cheese, barely larger than the coin, onto the counter.

The girls stared at it. Iggy followed his nose and tried to poke his head out, but Merlynda darted her hand behind her back to hide him.

"Now, now, my good man," Neci said. "Surely this fine coin will fetch a bit more?"

The cheesemonger swiped the pitiful cheese back beneath the counter and grunted in the direction of another market stall.

Neci and Merlynda stood there for a moment longer, but it was clear the conversation was over. They stepped over to the next stall, and Merlynda tried this time. "Hello," she said to the human girl behind the counter. She was a few years older than Merlynda, with light brown skin and braided hair.

The girl kept staring at the book she was reading. "Yes?"

"We'd like to buy something to eat."

The vendor gestured to the various sweets around her without looking up. "Then pick something."

Merlynda showed her the coin. "What can we get for this?"

The girl shoved a large pouch at them. "Take this and get on. I'm just getting to the good part."

The pouch was stuffed full of candied nuts. They left the coin (which the vendor barely acknowledged) and, feeling quite pleased, made off with their purchase.

Armed with provisions and a scrap of information, the trio headed out of town and toward Howlwyn Forest. Neither of the girls had left Avonshire before. It felt like quite the undertaking, but purpose and determination drove them on. Percy needed them.

"Here you go, Iggy." Merlynda held a candied nut on her palm.

At last! Iggy slither-walked up to it and began munching. Being in this world without arms to hold on to food would be difficult, but he would make do. Iggy considered himself exceptionally resourceful for someone who'd only been born an hour ago.

Merlynda swallowed her own sticky nut. "We've got our food and an idea of where we're going. How else do quests start?"

Neci flipped open her all-time favorite book, *The Compendium of Knights and Their Noble Deeds*, to an image of a knight riding a horse. "Normally, knights begin by galloping away on their valiant and loyal steeds. But we haven't got any of those, so we should skip to what we're questing for."

"We could ask Percy if—oh. Right." Merlynda swallowed against the pang in her chest at the thought of Percy, pushing it down. She'd been about to suggest Harriet, but of course only Percy could make Harriet do anything, and Percy wasn't there.

She'd never been separated from Percy before. They didn't do everything together, but they'd never been *apart* like this. The pang spread into a deep ache as Merlynda tried to grapple with what life without her twin might look like, even if only for the next seven months. She didn't like it one bit.

Merlynda wiped her eyes and focused on the illustration in Neci's book. It didn't look anything like how their quest was starting. "We're questing for Percy. Does your book have anything in it about knights finding the circle of standing stones?"

"Nope." Neci flipped through the pages, showing more paintings of knights and their heroic deeds. "They defeat the monster, find the holy object, save the wrongfully imprisoned captive—that sort of thing. Nothing about stone circles." Or birthday trowels, Neci noted with a vicious satisfaction that was likely unworthy of a noble knight.

Merlynda tried to stay positive. They knew they needed to cross the forest, so perhaps in the meantime she should focus on what it meant to be the Septimum Genus. "Maybe your new book has some suggestions for wizardesses of allegedly great power?"

"And their familiars," Iggy added.

Neci put away her *Compendium* and pulled out *The Official Quest Requirements for Knighthood* (which was now her second-favorite book). She flipped through the pages as they walked.

"How does this sound? 'Scale the Forbidden Cliffs and post your favor upon the highest rock—five points.' Maybe you can magic yourself up instead of climb?"

Merlynda peered at the page. "We'd need to find the Forbidden Cliffs first."

"Good point. What about this? 'Hatch a crimson egg and engage in the noble art of falconry—two points. Postscript: points awarded only if hatchling successfully completes the trials.' You could probably use Fire magic to hatch it."

"Can we cook the egg instead?" Iggy asked. "I've heard wonderful things about omelets."

Neci flipped through a few more pages. "Perhaps there's something about facing an evil magic user. That would come in handy if we're going up against the Hollower, wouldn't it?"

"It would. And we really should practice before then," Merlynda said. If she and Iggy stumbled across the Hollower now, they'd be obliterated, for sure.

Iggy sat up so that he'd seem serious. "I propose we start by searching for funnel cake. With a hint of sugar. You'll get extra knight points for hunting down fresh strawberries to sprinkle on top."

"We'll add that to the list of ideas," Merlynda said.

The trio continued down the path, stopping every so often so that Iggy could smell an interesting shrub, or see what it felt like to slither on meadow grass, and once to scare a rabbit. Merlynda scolded him for that one.

Iggy looked at her innocently. "I was only saying hello."

They finished the candied nuts and smacked their lips, wishing for water to wash the stickiness away. Finally, when the sun began to settle into late afternoon, they at last approached the Howlwyn.

The questers hesitated, mere steps away. Merlynda and Neci had both explored the countryside around Avonshire before, but entering the forest was different.

Moving forward wouldn't just be leaving. It would be committing. The shadowy Howlwyn stretched as far as they could see in every direction—except for home.

"Trees are taller than I expected," Iggy said in a hushed voice.

Neci bounced on the balls of her feet. She couldn't help it. This was a big moment. It was the *true* beginning of their quest, where they left the known behind and embraced adventure.

She wondered again if she ought to feel guilty. Her parents would worry, but it had always felt as if they were more concerned about her carrying on the family legacy and less concerned about her. Besides, knightly endeavors aside, her best friend needed her. "Ready?"

Merlynda nodded. She didn't feel guilty at all. With the exception of realizing that Uncle William would forbid her from doing anything useful, she'd barely given him a thought. Uncle William wasn't in the Hollower's clutches—Percy was, and she intended to find him.

She stood a little taller. Merlynda had left home in a hurry but had every intention of entering the Howlwyn with gusto. Of entering as the Septimum Genus.

They grasped each other's hands, and together they stepped into the forest.

Nothing happened.

Merlynda tested the forest floor. "That wasn't so bad."

"No," Neci huffed. "It wasn't." The sky hadn't even darkened to warn them of impending doom. If anything, the birds sounded cheerful.

The trio traipsed along, scrambling over rocks and rotting logs, taking in the scents of fresh moss and moist dirt and sweet flowers. They found a bubbling stream and stopped to gulp down water and gather wild berries.

"We must forage whenever we can," Iggy said around a mouthful of berries. Juice ran down his entire body. "You never know when your next meal will be on a quest."

Merlynda plucked a ripe berry and set it in her handkerchief. "Yes, but we also don't know how long our quest will take." Which meant they didn't know how long Percy would be the Hollower's captive before they found him, which Merlynda tried not to think about. The images of him disappearing into the portal and his fear-stricken face were burned into her memory. "The point is to gather them for later."

"I knew that." Iggy slipped into the water to rinse himself off and chase minnows. He was pretty sure he was a wyvern at this point, but there was no reason he couldn't pretend to be a sea serpent.

Merlynda wanted to keep charging through the Howlwyn, but the trio needed a rest. The girls sat and watched Iggy play in the very unadventurous stream trickling through the peaceful forest. It was the first real moment of calm Merlynda had felt since that morning. She took in a deep, sweet breath and—

"Achoo!"

The berries in Merlynda's handkerchief went flying. They plunked into the river and sank like stones. Because they *were* stones.

Neci stared at the berry rocks. "That's clever."

Merlynda wiped her nose. "Did I turn all of them?"

"Only the ones you were holding."

"Achoo!"

The flowers next to Merlynda burst into tiny rain clouds.

She pinched her nose good and tight. "I'm not even trying, and I'm bungling my magic!"

Neci stood. "Maybe we should go."

Merlynda had already scooped Iggy out of the water and was on her way.

She waited several minutes before unpinching her nose and taking a few tentative breaths.

Neci squinted at her. "Okay?"

"I think so."

Iggy adjusted himself on her wrist. "I wish you hadn't hexed the berries."

Merlynda glowered at him. "You're supposed to *help* me with my magic."

The wyvern curled his head beneath his tail. "I only arrived this morning. You can't expect me to know everything."

He was right. They were in this together, bungling and all.

"Shh!" Neci stopped, listening hard.

Merlynda listened too. "It sounds like—"

"Adventure!" Neci dashed—quietly—toward the noise. It wasn't hard to track. There was pounding and shouting and singing, and before long she smelled campfire smoke.

Merlynda (and Iggy) scrambled after Neci, stumbling through the dimming light along the shore of the river. Neci signaled for them to stop.

Her eyes danced. She held her breath, then crept forward.

Downriver, dozens of men and women—humans, ogres, gnomes, and more—moved frantically, pulling ropes and gathering logs and skewering pigs and fish to set over blazing fires. Everyone worked in time according to the beat of a drum. Torches lined the riverbank, illuminating a dozen anchored longships.

Merlynda gaped. "They're—"

"Nordvings!"

Neci couldn't help herself. Before Merlynda could say something sensible like *Nordvings murder for fun!* Neci had disappeared for a closer look.

*In which our questers make
several new acquaintances*

The Nordvings were so distracted by their work that Neci could have shouted her arrival and still have been missed. She didn't, because Nordvings tend to have malevolent intentions when away from home, what with plundering villages and murdering innocent bystanders and causing all sorts of other trouble during their exploration of the larger world.

Neci was thrilled.

Merlynda caught up to her, and for several minutes they watched the Nordvings set up camp. "What are they doing this far inland?"

"Settling in, looks like." Iggy sniffed. "Is that roasted mutton I smell?"

"How would you know what roasted mutton smells like?"

"I have an advanced nose."

Neci got her sling out and loaded a smooth stone—just in case. "Maybe they're preparing for a raid," she whispered, "and we'll heroically save the poor victims from their brutality!" She might be able to steal a sword! A knight wasn't much of a knight without a sword.

A horn blasted, and the Nordvings stopped, whipping around to face the sole tent on the riverbank.

"All pay respect to his Honorable Overlord Fenrir!" a voice boomed.

There was a dramatic silence, and then a huge man with a thick braided auburn beard, broad shoulders, and a battle-axe stepped out. The Nordvings erupted into cheers.

"Fenrir the Mighty!"

"Freiydin bless him!"

"Hail, Fenrir!"

Fenrir hefted his mighty axe over his head, and silence fell once more.

Then, with a ferocious war cry, he smashed everything in sight.

"YOOOOOAAAARRRGGGHHH!!!" He smashed his tent in.

"GRAAAHHHHHHHH!!!" He smashed the nearest soup pot.

"HROOOOOOOOGGGHHHHH!!!" He smashed a weapons rack.

Again and again he swung his axe, and his people cheered wildly. Nordving warriors rushed him in groups, and others egged them on. He beat them back, wailing his terrible cry all the while.

Finally, when there were more Nordvings scattered on the ground than not, Fenrir stopped. He wasn't even breathing hard. He slung his axe across his shoulders, trudged to a campfire that had survived his smashing, and sat down. Then he put his face in his hands and sobbed.

The Nordvings exchanged looks. They sighed, heaved themselves up, and set about putting the camp back together.

This was the closest thing to a real battle Neci had ever seen. "Let's get a closer look!"

"Oh no," Merlynda said. "I've read all about Nordvings. They don't like it when strangers sneak into their camp."

Before Neci could argue about the merits of practicing stealth, the same booming voice that had announced Fenrir's arrival bellowed, "The Cherished and Most Esteemed Fenrir would like some entertainment to accompany his meal. Bring forth the prisoner!"

"Aye, the captive!"

"Splendid idea, Your Viciousness!"

"Hail, distraction!"

A human boy who couldn't have been much older than Merlynda shuffled toward Fenrir, escorted by two guards.

His feet were shackled together, but he sat down next to the Nordving lord and brushed his mop of coal-colored hair away from his tawny face to tune his lute. A set of panpipes swung at his hips.

"What would his Noble Nefariousness care to hear this evening?" the boy asked in a clear voice that rang through the camp.

Fenrir motioned to a tall ogre standing next to him and whispered into his ear. The ogre, who happened to be the herald with the booming voice, straightened and said, "His Magnificent Greatness Fenrir would like something sorrowful to match his heavy heart!"

"Aye, sorrow!"

"To stop even Freiydin's thunder!"

"Hail, misery!"

"Sorrowful." The prisoner wasn't surprised. He played a few chords experimentally. "Of course. Your Graciously Powerful and Muscular Sir," he added at a sharp look from the herald. "Have you heard 'When Mordred Went to Market and Found All the Pastries Eaten'?"

The boy played, coming alive as he let the melancholy music overtake him, plucking the strings with ease and singing along in a lovely, lilting way. Fenrir blubbered into his great hands.

Neci nudged Merlynda.

"No," Merlynda whispered firmly.

Neci nudged her again.

"There are too many—"

But all Neci could see forming before her were the words "Save an imprisoned boy from vagrant Nordvings: twelve points." She flung herself out of the trees.

"Fenrir!" Neci shouted, holding her loaded sling. "I demand that you release this helpless—this lost—this musician boy!"

The Nordvings gasped and the music stopped. No one referred to their great overlord without an appropriate honorific (or three).

Neci strode from the forest with strength and purpose. She burned with the fires of authority and justice.

But all the Nordvings saw was a smaller-than-average, ten-year-old girl with a rock demanding absurdities from their leader. They laughed.

Neci stood her ground, but now the fire rushed into her cheeks, and she felt them burn, like they had when the baker's son shoved her. Merlynda came up and stood beside her, despite the likelihood of certain death. Iggy, for his part, kept well hidden.

Fenrir raised his huge hand, and the camp hushed. He motioned to his herald and whispered something.

"His Illustrious and Wonderfully Awesome Fenrir would like to know, who are you, little girl, to demand such things?"

Neci flushed at being called "little girl." "Neci the Ardent, knight in training. This is Merlynda of Merlyn Manor, wizardess of the highest order."

The musician boy cocked his head to the side, and his mop of hair fell away from his light brown eyes. "You're a witch?"

Merlynda scowled. "I'm a wizardess. Witches are evil and have dirty fingernails."

The herald squinted at them through the firelight. "His Affable Eminence Fenrir wonders why he shouldn't order you sunk in the river?"

Neci stepped forward. "Because Merlynda isn't just any wizardess. She's the Septimum Genus." She crossed her arms and smirked.

Merlynda gaped at Neci. What was she doing?

Fenrir looked at his herald, who shrugged. The other Nordvings scratched their heads.

"You're kidding." Neci couldn't believe there was a single person in the known world who hadn't heard of Merlyn's prophecy. "She's the most powerful wizardess of all time!"

Merlynda tried to look like a fierce and powerful Septimum Genus, which would have been easier if she'd felt like one. She wished Percy were there, and the thought brought a tightness to her chest, as though someone were driving a stake into it. *He'd* be able to convince the Nordvings, or at least magic them all out of this mess somehow.

"We know nothing of this Merlyn or serpent Gemini," the ogre said curtly. "What sign have you that this witch is what you say?"

"*Wizardess,*" Merlynda corrected him.

Fenrir raised an eyebrow at her. Merlynda's palms were

sweaty, and nerves nibbled at her insides. Everyone gazed at her expectantly, and she tried not to blush.

She didn't know what to do. So far all she'd managed to do as Septimum Genus was lose her brother and sneeze some berries into stones. Spell after spell flashed through her mind, but what would be enough to impress the Nordvings? And how would she manage anyway, what with all her magical bungling?

Her hands shook, and she tried to push back at the nerves. They were doomed.

"Well?" the herald insisted. "What sign?"

"Aye, what sign?"

"To dazzle even blessed Freiydin!"

"Hail, hexes!"

Merlynda was about to tell Neci they should make a run for it when a small voice said, "Me."

Every Nordving (and also the boy musician) stared at the wizardess. She raised her arm up straight above her.

And in the firelight, a red-and-gold head popped out of her sleeve.

"Me," Iggy repeated, as loud as he could. "I'm her sign!"

"A talking snake!"

"'Tis the evil bringer of Ragnarok!"

"Hail, worm!"

"I'm no snake!" Iggy shouted (he ignored the worm comment entirely). "I am a mighty sea serpent, conquered by Merlynda and shrunk to this embarrassing stature!"

There was an intake of breath. Merlynda slowly turned so

that each of the Nordvings could have a good look.

Iggy kept with the act. "If you don't free the prisoner," he warned, "then she will unleash me, and I will gobble you all up! And then I'll gobble your ships! And then all your bacon!"

The camp stared in silence, then Fenrir let out a guffaw that moved into a full bellow. The Nordvings looked uncertainly at their leader.

The herald bent down for instructions but was waved away. Fenrir stood and everyone hushed.

"I haven't laughed in weeks," he told the questers in a voice that seemed far too rich and warm for a vicious, bloodthirsty Nordving warlord.

The other Nordvings let out cries of joy and sighs of relief. Their great leader was speaking again!

"Therefore," Fenrir continued, "I will not drown you in the river. Yet."

Merlynda lowered her arm but made sure Iggy was still visible. Perhaps they'd manage to avoid this drowning business completely. "It's been that long since you laughed?" she squeaked out.

Neci couldn't believe it. "Don't you have anyone to laugh with?"

"I haven't laughed"—Fenrir sighed a great, sad sigh—"because I have lost that which is dearest to me."

"Rare herbs?" Neci asked. "Jewels? An ancient and mystical sword?"

Fenrir waved his hand, as if ancient mystical swords

bored him. He took a great, shuddering breath, then blew spectacularly into a handkerchief the herald handed him. "What I have lost," Fenrir said heavily, "is my beloved . . . my beloved . . . Vilhelmina!" He bawled, and for a moment Merlynda thought he might start smashing things again (Neci hoped he would).

"Oh, Vilhelmina!"

"Fiercest Vilhelmina!"

"Hail, Vilhelmina!"

Neci leaned over to Merlynda. "What's a Vilhelmina?" But Merlynda didn't know.

Fenrir took the handkerchief back from the herald to wipe his eyes. "She is ferocious yet gentle. So clever, and oh, how she shines! There is none as noble and as beautiful as she!" He broke into sobs again.

Rescue endangered Nordving princess from dire fate: thirty-two points. Neci wasn't positive that she'd read that in *The Official Quest Requirements for Knighthood*, but there had to be something like it. It was the perfect tale of tragedy that needed a knight to step in and save the day.

"Don't worry, Lord Fenrir." Neci used her best knightly-assurance voice. "We'll find your wife."

Fenrir paused his weeping. "I haven't lost a wife." He tossed the handkerchief aside and grabbed the herald's shirt to blow his nose. "I've lost my cat."

Merlynda kept a straight face. "Your cat."

The Nordvings sobbed along with Fenrir. Neci and

Merlynda stood awkwardly, waiting for the warlord to compose himself.

"My greatest trackers have lost her trail. Her favorite food roasting over the open flame fails to lure her home. I fear . . . I fear . . ." Fenrir couldn't bring himself to say what he feared, but the girls understood. "What can you offer, Neci the Ardent, that my people can't?"

Neci grinned. "The heir of Merlyn."

The heir of Merlyn did not feel the same level of confidence.

Fenrir inspected his battle-axe. "I'm afraid we have no faith in your 'heir of Merlyn,' but we *do* always have a use for cabin boys. Or in this case, cabin girls."

"What?" Neci exclaimed. "We said we'll help find your cat!"

"And," Fenrir continued, "I'll be taking that fine ring you're wearing."

Neci clutched her Ye Knoble Knights Decoder Ring with Customizable Crest. "Never!"

Fenrir turned to a Nordving scout. "You say their town is just beyond the forest?"

"What's that about our town?" Merlynda eyed the other Nordvings who had encircled her and Neci. Dust swirled up around her feet, rising with her panic. She could sense the Earth beneath her, around her—but she wasn't reaching for anything, wasn't trying to use her magic.

"We are Nordvings." Fenrir polished the head of his axe. It glinted in the firelight. "And I've got a reputation to uphold."

"Aye, what a reputation!"

"Freiydin's blessing on him!"

"Hail, spoils!"

Neci crossed her arms. "The joke's on you, Lord Fenrir. All you'll find in our town are root vegetables."

Fenrir's great eyebrows came together in a glower. "I like root vegetables."

The dust swirled and picked up bits of grass and twigs around the girls' feet, and Neci stepped back in surprise. Iggy slither-walked up to Merlynda's shoulder and whispered into her ear. The wizardess squeezed her eyes shut, trying to focus.

"Chain them up!" Fenrir called.

The Nordvings surged forward, all axes and shields and nets. Neci whirled her loaded sling around to warn off anyone who got too close.

The ground vibrated and shook. Merlynda tried to gently pull the Earth the way Mother had taught her, or to slip back away from it, or forward into the Aether—anything that would stop what was coming.

But Merlynda couldn't stop it, couldn't settle the power inside her, and even as she flung out her arms to try to direct the magic, the ground erupted into a wave of dirt and grass and soil. It blasted up and out and then rained down from the sky, smothering campfires, spoiling food, blanketing everything in a layer of earth—except for her, Iggy, and Neci.

Merlynda opened her eyes. She and Neci were on a tiny patch of dirt, surrounded by a shimmering light shield. A deep ring cut into the ground around them where the earth had broken. The camp was dark and shushed now, lit only by the moon and starlight. The shield dissipated, and the Nordvings stared at Merlynda with new wariness, hesitating.

Merlynda grabbed Neci's arm. "Run."

They leapt over the broken earth and fled, dashing through the forest, scrambling over tree roots and stones, stumbling on the uneven ground, and helping one another along. The Nordvings weren't following them, but that didn't mean they wouldn't. They'd been frightened by Merlynda's power. *She'd* been frightened.

"Did I hurt anyone?" she panted.

"No. I think the worst anyone got was a mouthful of dirt."

That was a relief. Nordving or not, Merlynda would have felt awful if she'd caused any real harm.

They at last scrambled inside a hollow tree trunk to hide, scratched and bruised and out of breath. Neci couldn't believe their luck. They'd nearly been kidnapped! By Nordvings! This definitely made up for the trowel.

Merlynda could feel the magic laughing at her, at how she couldn't control her power. *Quiet, you,* she thought at the laughing magic, but if anything, that only amused it more.

It was so dark inside the tree, they couldn't see each other. Neci rustled around in her satchel until she found her candle and matches. She lit the candle, then set it carefully down on the ground in the middle of the tree, as if it were a tiny camp-fire beating back the darkness.

"Was I all right?" Iggy asked anxiously.

Merlynda set Iggy down near the candle. She'd still only flubbed her magic ever since he'd arrived, but Merlynda wasn't sure that was Iggy's fault. She was beginning to suspect she and her magic were permanently broken. "You were brilliant," she told him.

Neci flopped onto the ground to check her inventory, but Merlynda couldn't quite settle down. "Neci," she whispered. "We've got to save Avonshire from the Nordvings." Not only were they the reason their town was in danger, but they were also the only ones who knew and might be able to stop it. Even so, Merlynda worried about how long it would take. Every minute that passed was a minute Percy was in the clutches of the Hollower.

That sharp pang tightened her chest again, but she pushed it away and shook her head to clear it. Ensuring the total destruction of her home had to make her the worst quester in the history of quests, not to mention a total failure of a Septimum Genus.

Neci pulled out *The Official Quest Requirements for Knighthood.* "I bet Fenrir will reconsider if we find Vilhelmina. He might even free that lute boy." She skimmed through the pages in the dim light. Saving a cat on its own had to be worth a point or two, but combined with saving an imprisoned minstrel *and* rescuing their town? She'd have her knight points in no time!

Iggy yawned. The candle was the perfect amount of

toasty. "I hope this cat doesn't like wyverns for a snack, or I might have to show her a thing or two."

Merlynda wanted to pace, but their tree was too small, so she slid down the trunk and sat on the ground. "Why did you tell Fenrir I'd find his stupid cat?"

Neci flipped through her book. She'd found *Rescue an ill duchess from the poison which ails her* and *Deliver a young wanderer from an untimely death* but hadn't yet found the line about saving lost pets.

"Neci!" Merlynda cried. "Why did you do it?"

Neci finally looked up. "You're allergic to cats and only cats. You sneezed by the berries. Vilhelmina has to be there."

Merlynda slumped against the trunk and put her head in her hands. "You risked Avonshire because I *sneezed*?"

"Well, not just that." Neci put her book away and lay down. A good night's rest was essential when questing. "You're the Septimum Genus. If anyone can find a Nordving lord's missing cat, it's you."

Merlynda stared at her friend in bewilderment. If only that confidence could be turned into magic.

The questers rose with the dawn. It was strange to Merlynda that one moment they had been walking by the river, and the next they were off on an adventure fleeing from Nordvings. There wasn't much space between the two.

"I know we have to save Avonshire from the Nordvings, but this feels like a distraction. Our quest is to find Percy." She tried to shake away the nightmares where Percy vanished and then a giant portal sucked up their town. It hadn't been a very restful night.

Neci pulled a compass out of her satchel, on the alert for Nordving sentries. "This is more like a side quest."

Iggy stifled a yawn. "What's a side quest?"

"Side quests help you with your main quest." Neci checked the sun. They were headed the right way. "If we find Vilhelmina, maybe we can ask the Nordvings if they know about that picture on your piece of parchment. They've traveled all over, I'll bet."

It would be an incredible help if the Nordvings knew exactly where to find the stone pillars. They'd find Percy and be done with their quest in no time. Merlynda walked a little faster, optimistic.

"And," Neci continued, "you two can practice your magic! That's bound to be useful."

"Or disastrous." Merlynda looked down at Iggy, who was curled lazily around her wrist. "Okay, Iggy. Familiars are supposed to help their wizardesses. How do I control my magic?"

Iggy tucked his head underneath his tail. "I don't know. I've only been in the world for a day."

"What were you doing last night?" Neci asked the wyvern. "When the ground exploded?"

Iggy burrowed his head deeper underneath his body, but there was only so much wrist he could hide on.

"Go on." Merlynda poked him. "Tell her."

When he didn't move, she lightly pinched the tip of his tail.

"I beg your pardon!" Iggy shot straight up, then finally met their gazes. "Fine. I tried to calm her down."

Neci nodded. "Sounds like a good start."

"See?" Iggy said defensively. "It was a good start."

"You tried to calm me down *how*?"

Iggy sulked. "I can't be expected to be the perfect familiar on my first day."

Merlynda sighed. "He was listing all the foods he'd like to taste."

"We don't eat in the In-Between! It's a new experience."

Life sounded much simpler in the In-Between—which, Merlynda remembered, was supposed to be the most magical place in existence. Maybe it held the answers she needed. "What's the magic like there?"

Iggy scratched his nose with his tail. "It's full of the Aether."

"*Obviously,*" Merlynda said. "But what are the elements like?"

"They're all muddled together. You can't tell where one ends and the next begins."

That wasn't very helpful. The only way she could see that the different elements were connected was that no matter which one she used, the magic laughed at her.

Neci adjusted her satchel. "How does your magic feel now that Iggy's here?"

"I don't know," Merlynda huffed, growing agitated. "I don't know how we made those portals appear, and I don't know why Percy was sucked into one. It doesn't make any sense! It's never made any—*achoo!*"

A nearby shrub turned into a flock of dancing napkins.

Neci grinned. "We're close."

Merlynda tried to be excited, but it was difficult when at any moment you might accidentally hex your best friend into an ice sculpture. When she sneezed, it felt like all the magic welled up inside her and then burst out before she could tell it what to do.

"Vilhelmina!" Neci called. "Here, kitty!"

"Vilhel—Vilhel—*achoo!*"

A net of fish flopped around next to them.

"I can't send them back—I can't!" Merlynda moaned.

"We could cook them all," Iggy offered. "It's lunchtime, isn't it?"

Neci leapt over a root. "There isn't *anything* you can think of that triggers your magic?"

Iggy perked up. "I've thought about curry, strawberry shortcake, and cheese, if anyone is interested."

Merlynda stared at the ground, putting her dark thoughts from last night into words. "Maybe my magic is broken," she whispered. "Maybe *I'm* broken." She glanced up at her best friend. "Neci, I'm scared I won't find Percy."

"You can't be broken," Neci insisted. "The Aether decided you were ready. It sent you Iggy!"

Iggy nibbled Merlynda's hand affectionately. "I think I like being a wyvern. We've got a lot of potential, you know."

"And," Neci said with conviction, "we're going to find Percy. We're going to finish this quest."

Merlynda looked from her new familiar to her friend. Perhaps they could do this after all. "I—*achoo!*"

A tree split in two with a loud *crack!*

"Can you please help me?" Merlynda asked Iggy. She didn't bother keeping the pleading out of her voice. She knew he could sense it.

He also sensed something else. "Fairies."

Merlynda rolled her eyes. This wasn't helpful.

"No." Iggy turned sharply toward the sky. "Fairies."

Neci scanned the air. "Where?"

"Everywhere." Iggy slither-walked up to Merlynda's shoulder. "Watching us."

Merlynda squinted. "I don't see anything."

"I am from the In-Between," Iggy sniffed. "They are too. Everything is, but I've been there more recently. So I can see them."

Neci moved closer and readied her sling. "Are they armed?"

Merlynda didn't let herself think for too long. She summoned up a quick breeze—only reaching for the Air, and nothing beyond it—and sent it billowing out around them. The branches swayed, and loose leaves floated to the ground. Success! She allowed herself a tiny smile of satisfaction.

"Oy, beg yer pardon!" a deep voice growled. "Ain't no need for bullyin'!"

"Stop sneaking around, then!" Neci shouted back.

"Who's sneakin'?" another voice called. "You're in our forest, ain't yeh?"

"Yeah!" a third agreed.

"No one owns the forest," Merlynda said. A shower of twigs rained down on her head in response. All around them, deep voices chattered and rustled. "We're looking for a cat," she called out.

The chattering hushed.

"Hello?" Merlynda called. "Have you seen a cat?"

"She speaks of the beast," a voice finally said.

Neci laughed. "Beast? A little cat? Ow!" Something twisted her ear.

"Show some respect, hey?" a voice growled. "They don't show respect!"

"Get 'em, lads!" a voice roared. "They speak of the beast!"

In which a questionable deal is struck

The trees rang with fairy war cries, which is a terrifying thing to experience if you've never had the opportunity. Branches, twigs, and leaves showered Neci and Merlynda from all directions. If the girls had been fairy-sized, this would have been troublesome, but since they were human-girl-sized (except Neci, who was still slightly smaller), it was only irritating.

"Stop it!" Neci said. "We're trying to help!"

"Achoo!"

A nearby tree burst into a cloud of butterflies.

"Where are they?" Merlynda whispered to Iggy. This

needed to end before she accidentally magicked something horrible.

"All over! But the one right above your head is making rude gestures."

Merlynda clapped her hands over her head and heard a satisfying squeak. The fairy struggled and cursed, but she held on tight.

"Enough!" she shouted. "I am Merlynda of Merlyn Manor! Who's in charge here?"

The barrage of forest items stopped. There was a brief rustle through the trees, and then sparkly dust *poof*ed all around them and the fairies appeared. They wore fine fairy clothes and sour expressions and were every color of the rainbow and then some.

"That's more like it," Neci mumbled. Her ear smarted, and a piece of bark had stung her eye. She'd need to invest in a shield at the first opportunity.

Merlynda's fairy was chubby (as fairies go) and had a sharp goatee and a deep, chiseled frown that soured his daffodil-colored complexion. She opened her hands, and he blew a raspberry at her before darting away.

Merlynda sneezed again, and a pungent green slime coated each of the fairies (we don't need to repeat what they had to say about it).

"You heard the wizardess," Neci called out, readying her sling now that she had targets. "Who's in charge?"

The fairy Merlynda had caught blew on a trumpet, then

tucked it under his arm. "Presentin' the Right Honorable Lumont of the Oak Tree, Prime Minister of the Woodland Fairies, Duke of the Dancing Acorns, et cetera, et cetera."

An exceptionally proper, slime-free fairy wearing a many-feathered hat and a monocle flitted forward. He made the slime disappear with a wave of his delicate sky-blue hand, then darted up to Merlynda and flicked her nose.

She felt a tingling, then nothing at all. Iggy growled, and Lumont flew back several feet.

"What did you do?" Merlynda asked warily.

"Cured you. You'll find that you are no longer allergic."

Merlynda wiggled her nose back and forth. "Thank you? But you ought to ask for permission first."

"It wasn't a gesture of kindness. It was a necessary action to protect my people."

Neci glowered. "*They* snuck up on *us*."

"I didn't see either of *you* covered in slime."

"Neither were you." Iggy cocked his head to the side. "Why weren't *you* covered in slime?"

"I arrived right after the assault," Lumont sniffed. "A number of serious attacks have befallen my people. I've been investigating them throughout the Howlwyn."

"I'm sorry to hear that," Merlynda said, "but is the beast your fairies mentioned a cat named Vilhelmina?"

The prime minister glared at her. "The beast was contained due to her possible association with the aforementioned attacks. She did not have the proper documentation to travel unaccompanied through fairyland, and she certainly did not have the proper documentation to engage in acts of attempted murder, as such documentation does not exist."

"I'm not so sure I want to meet this Vilhelmina," Iggy whispered.

Neci lowered her sling, but only slightly. "What attempted murder?" she asked.

Lumont brushed a drooping hat feather out of his eyes. "We have multiple eyewitness accounts of the beast attempting to stalk, maim, and ingest various fairies. This is a gross violation of interspecies law."

"She's a *cat*," Merlynda said.

"That's no excuse."

"But that's what cats *do*."

Lumont buzzed in the air. "This is no cat! It's a weapon of mass destruction and must not be tolerated!"

"You said the eyewitnesses saw Vilhelmina *attempt* to do those things," Merlynda said.

"Yeah," Neci agreed. "And that she's contained. So whatever you were investigating happened *after* she was captured."

Lumont had gotten control of himself and adjusted his monocle. "Someone must be held responsible."

"Give her to us, then," Neci snapped. "We already proved she was locked up before your investigations."

Lumont fluttered back and forth, thinking. "Would the Septimum Genus be willing to trade for the beast? One favor, to be determined at some point in the future."

Merlynda blinked. "How did you know I was the Septimum Genus? I only found out yesterday."

"We have our ways."

Neci narrowed her eyes, suspicious. "What ways?"

Lumont waved his hand, as if being one of the few people to know Merlyn's prophecy had been fulfilled was of no consequence. "You were rather loud about it at the Nordving camp, for starters."

"Oh," Merlynda said.

"Regardless," Lumont continued, "our sources were already well aware. The fairykind have long known of Merlyn's prophecy. Some of us were even there when he gave it."

"Really?" Merlynda tried to sound casual. "Do any of those fairies happen to know what Merlyn meant?"

"No one ever knew what that old wizard meant," Lumont said. "But he was often right." He eyed Merlynda slyly through his monocle. "Do we have a deal? One favor, in exchange for the beast?"

Merlynda glanced at Neci, who shrugged.

"Be careful," Iggy whispered. "Even in the In-Between we know all about fairies."

He didn't need to say it. *Everyone* knew about fairies. They were often tricky things.

But returning Vilhelmina to Fenrir was probably the only hope the girls had of saving their town, and maybe getting another clue about the circle of stones.

"I won't hurt anyone." Merlynda thought through everything she'd read about fairies. "And I won't break any laws. It can't be anything wicked or wrong."

The prime minister bowed. "Of course not. In return for the beast you call Vilhelmina, you will, at a time yet to be appointed, fulfill the obligation of performing one favor on behalf of the Woodland Fairies, to be requested by myself."

"I agree." Merlynda had the distinct feeling that she would regret owing this fairy a favor, but she didn't see any way around it.

The feeling only increased when Lumont smiled. He threw his head back and called, "Release the beast!"

A Word about Vilhelmina

Vilhelmina was not a cat. At least, not in the sense that you might be thinking.

It's true that she had whiskers, a tail, and a penchant for chasing smaller animals. At first glance you might assume that she was a lion—until you got a good look at her blue fur and gray stripes. Then you might guess that she was some sort of tiger. And then you'd realize that she was neither a lion nor a tiger, but she was a bit of both.

Vilhelmina was a great sapphire liger with a terrible streak of vanity. Lord Fenrir had discovered her on one of his many voyages and was immediately smitten. Vilhelmina had not been fond of traveling with the Rusvokian circus and was only too happy to leave with Fenrir.

Living on the water wasn't her favorite thing, but it was much better than being locked up in a cage. The food was better, she could roam where she wished, and even if Fenrir had just returned from a vicious battle, he always scratched her gently in her favorite spot, behind her left ear. He also made sure her luxurious blue fur and sizable claws were kept well groomed.

The other circus animals would say that she'd gone soft, but what did she care? She wasn't locked up in a cage.

At least, she hadn't been, until the fairies captured her. She had been stalking and trying to eat them, because even if she wasn't a cat, she was still a liger. Besides, they'd ruffled her fur on purpose.

She'd been locked up, high in the trees, waiting for the fairies to decide what to do with her. With luck, she'd get a few good swipes in. She'd been practicing whipping out her claws, like this—

Snnkt!

Retract.

Snnkt!

Retract.

Snnkt!

—when the cage disappeared and Vilhelmina plummeted to the ground, claws very much at the ready.

Merlynda could recite magical theory forward, backward, and sideways, and had pored over every magical text in her home with gusto. She'd memorized long passages about the proper way to introduce oneself to centaurs, how to navigate through a bewitched hedge maze, and even the proper time to pluck mintwort based on the phases of the moons.

Given the range of Merlynda's studies, she was fairly confident that the enormous blue streak falling from the sky was not a cat.

Lumont shot his hand out right before Vilhelmina hit the ground. She swirled around in midair, snarling and scratching.

"Sign here, heir of Merlyn." A tiny scroll appeared in the prime minister's hand, which he unfurled with a flourish.

Merlynda accepted the quill that Lumont plucked from his hat and began to read the contract. She knew all contracts should be read before they are signed, especially fairy contracts.

Neci couldn't tear her eyes from Vilhelmina. Even if the liger had been sitting on the ground, she would have been three or four times as tall as the knight-to-be. "She's *beautiful*."

Vilhelmina finally stopped growling at the fairies and gave Neci a scornful look. She began to groom her front paw as if she didn't care at all that she was hovering two feet above the ground and couldn't do a thing about it.

Merlynda scribbled her name on the contract. The ink hadn't even dried when Lumont snatched it back and grinned. "Splendid. The beast is not to travel alone through fairy territories, attack fairy citizens, et cetera, et cetera."

"Of course." Merlynda wondered how they would prevent Vilhelmina from doing whatever she wanted.

"Septimum Genus." Lumont bowed again, sweeping his hat in a grand gesture. "It's been a pleasure." He gave some sort of signal, and the fairies vanished in clouds of sparkly dust.

"Are they actually gone?" Merlynda asked Iggy.

"Yes."

Neci moved closer to Vilhelmina, who continued to pretend to ignore everyone while she groomed herself. "Hello, Vilhelmina. I'm Neci."

Vilhelmina acknowledged Neci with a long-suffering look, then moved on to cleaning her next paw.

Iggy cocked his head. "She doesn't look so ferocious when she's washing herself."

Vilhelmina grinned wickedly to show off her many, many sharp teeth.

"Perhaps I'm mistaken," Iggy amended.

Neci took another step. "I bet you were only teasing those fairies, weren't you, girl? They probably started it."

Vilhelmina flicked her tail. This smaller one wasn't so bad, but she wouldn't give in that easily. These two little humans *had* just made some sort of bargain for her. The beautiful Vilhelmina! Bartered for as if she were nothing more than a bolt of cloth, or loaf of bread!

"Would you like to go back to Lord Fenrir now?"

Vilhelmina looked disdainfully at Neci. *Of course* she would. But there was the tiny problem of her paws floating two feet above the ground.

Merlynda stepped forward. "Hi. I'm Merlynda." She

didn't want to get any closer to those claws than she had to, but it seemed that Lumont had indeed cured her cat allergy.

Vilhelmina yawned, bored. So this was who that loquacious fairy with the absurd bird hat kept going on about. She smelled like the oldest magic. It wasn't a bad smell, just exceptionally obvious to one as clever as Vilhelmina.

Iggy angled his head to get a better look at the vainglorious liger. "You missed a spot."

Vilhelmina ignored him.

"Can you magic her down?" Neci asked.

Merlynda looked down at Iggy, curled around his favorite spot on her wrist. He'd tensed at the suggestion, just as she had. "I'm not sure we should try," she finally answered. "Iggy and I don't exactly have the best track record."

Now Vilhelmina did pay attention, and she didn't like this train of thought one bit.

"You can do it, Merlynda," Neci encouraged her. "I know you and Iggy can."

Bolstered by her friend's faith, Merlynda walked around the liger, getting a sense for the enchantment that kept her afloat—or perhaps it was a hex. Fairy magic was tricky. She concentrated on the fairy spell, tried to grasp the wispy edges of the magic, and gently pushed.

Vilhelmina slammed into the ground, then bounced back up, up, up, clawing and yowling.

"Sorry!" Merlynda said. "I'm sorry!"

Vilhelmina fell back toward the earth and stopped—still hovering.

Iggy examined her fur. "Now you've got to start all over," he told her. "You've got twigs everywhere."

The liger snarled at him.

"That's no way to treat someone trying to help," Neci scolded the liger. "Do you want to go back to the fairies?"

Vilhelmina turned her back to them.

"I thought not. Go on and sulk."

In the end the girls had to push Vilhelmina through the air. This wasn't enjoyable for anyone except Iggy, who called out helpful remarks like "Watch out for that pointy boulder!" and "Vilhelmina, there's grass stuck behind your ear."

The little humans hadn't noticed the falcon that was following them, so Vilhelmina saw no reason to point it out.

After many tumbles, bumps, and a near miss with the river, the girls, the wyvern, and the liger rolled up to the Nordving camp. It was lunchtime, and the Nordvings were all sobbing into their bowls of root vegetable stew while the boy minstrel, still shackled, played a melancholy tune on his panpipes. Weapons and armor were scattered around, ready to be donned at a moment's notice to march toward Avonshire.

Vilhelmina yowled a greeting. The minstrel stopped playing out of shock, and everyone turned to look.

The liger was so excited, she sent herself sprawling through the air. Neci and Merlynda chased after her (it would be just their luck for Vilhelmina to get washed away in the river), but

Fenrir met her halfway and they joyfully crashed into each other.

Enormous, messy tears flowed down Fenrir's face, but they were happy tears. Vilhelmina even wept a little herself, but she pretended it was the campfire smoke getting in her eyes.

Fenrir gawked at the questers, almost dazed. "You found my precious Vilhelmina?"

Neci had her sling ready, just in case. The other Nordvings eyed Merlynda. Iggy bared his teeth at them.

"Yep. We rescued her from some fairies." Merlynda flicked her hand so that a few rocks leapt away from her, startling the Nordvings. "So we're hoping you'll reconsider your whole 'destroying our town' plan."

Fenrir laughed his great booming laugh. "Of course, of course." He scratched Vilhelmina in her favorite spot, behind her left ear. It was more difficult than usual, as she was still floating. "How can I repay you for the return of my beloved Vilhelmina?"

Neci grinned. "The release of your musician."

"And some information," Merlynda added.

Iggy propped himself up on Merlynda's wrist. "And maybe funnel cake?"

Fenrir's brow furrowed, and Merlynda tensed, afraid she might make the ground explode again. But then he leaned back and laughed. "Neci the Ardent and Merlynda of Merlyn Manor, you do fine work." He motioned to two of the Nordvings, and they unshackled the minstrel's feet. "The boy can come and go as he pleases now. They'll say I'm going soft, but anyone who rescues Vilhelmina is a friend of Fenrir's."

Neci beamed. Her first mission was a success! She'd have her knight points in no time.

Fenrir looked quizzical for a moment. "I'm afraid we don't have any of this funnel cake, though."

Iggy let out a long-suffering sigh.

Merlynda watched the minstrel test out walking in freedom. "How long has he been shackled like that?"

The Nordving lord waved his hand. "It's mostly to keep up appearances. He'd never get out of camp unnoticed."

"I have the same problem," Iggy said. "I'm quite noticeable."

Fenrir laughed his rich laugh, then addressed his Nordvings. "Tonight, we feast!" he shouted. "In honor of Vilhelmina and those who brought her home!"

"Aye, and what a feast!"

"Blessed by Freiydin!"

"Hail, celebration!"

The camp burst into activity. Someone was sent to fetch the net of fish Merlynda had sneezed into the forest, cooking fires were stoked, and the Nordvings rushed to see that the questers were comfortable. They were excellent hosts.

"Master Batu," Fenrir said with a bow of his head when the minstrel returned from his pacing. "I hope you'll play for this evening's celebration. As a guest."

Batu plucked his lute and shrugged. His black hair

seemed to perpetually fall across his eyes. "If there's a meal in it."

"Of course, my boy, of course. Though I think you owe some gratitude to your rescuers." Fenrir gestured to the girls. "May I introduce Batu of the Lake."

Batu turned stiffly to Neci and Merlynda. Of the many times he'd imagined leaving the Nordvings, being rescued hadn't been one of the scenarios. He'd intended to escape on his own. "Thanks, I guess." He stalked off to tune his lute.

"He *guesses?*" Neci exclaimed, incredulous, and Merlynda had to agree. They'd rescued him!

"He's always been a surly one," Fenrir said. "Some people won't be grateful, no matter the circumstances they've left or entered."

"Nor some cats." Neci eyed Vilhelmina. The liger yawned once more but reached out her tail and patted the would-be knight.

The feast was magnificent. There was dancing and laughter and—to Iggy's delight—dessert. Merlynda and Neci were the guests of honor, along with Vilhelmina, who had received proper grooming attention right away and no longer had stray burs or tufts of grass stuck in her fur.

Batu played the entire time, plucking lively and funny and joyful jigs. He barely paused to eat now that he was free to choose whatever melodies he wished, instead of those melancholy ballads Fenrir had always wanted.

"Are you going to do much pillaging while you're inland?"

Neci asked Fenrir. Now that they were on friendly terms, the fearsome warlord was much less intimidating, and even kind.

"We'll head back to sea now," he answered. "We only came this far looking for Vilhelmina."

The aerial liger nuzzled the Nordving, then *snnkt*ed out her claw to spear a piece of meat.

"I haven't decided if we'll plunder Francia or Danmorc next," Fenrir continued. "But what of you? It's unusual for two so young to be off on their own."

Merlynda and Neci told him all about being the Septimum Genus, and a knight, and their quest to save Percy from the Hollower.

Iggy swallowed his mouthful of shortbread. It wasn't funnel cake, but it would do. "I think it's a terrible idea."

Merlynda pulled the crumpled parchment Percy had sent her from her robes. "Have you ever seen these stones before?"

Fenrir took the parchment and let out a low whistle. "I'm afraid I don't know about this circle of stones, but I do know about this Hollower. My people call him the Soul Snatcher. Legend has it, he defeated Dahlia the Defiant, the noblest, strongest magical warrior my people have ever seen, in a flash of purple light. When the Hollower finished, Dahlia was a husk of who she once was."

Fenrir leaned back and gave them a level look.

"They say the Hollower can appear wherever he wants, and there's nothing you can do to stop him. If there's any truth to the tales, he's been stealing magic for centuries."

Neci set her cup down. "We'll need to be ready, then. He's bound to be powerful."

"And hungry for magic!" Iggy whimpered. "What's he need it all for, anyway?"

"Hush," Merlynda said soothingly, with far more calm than she felt. "If anyone can stop the Hollower, it's the Septimum Genus and her familiar." She needed to believe this herself, so she put as much conviction into her words as she could.

Iggy laid his head on the table miserably. Merlynda was right. "Fine. What's your plan?"

Merlynda took a sip of the sweet juice the Nordvings had served her. "I haven't gotten that far." Without the standing stones' location, the only thing she knew for certain was that each passing day brought them closer to the Shadow Sun.

"Quests take time," Fenrir said. "We leave tomorrow. Join us! You can take your leave anywhere you like. Perhaps you'll learn more about this circle of stones in one of the harbor towns up the coast. You get folks who've seen all sorts of things in seaside ports."

Merlynda saw the wisdom in this. Neci was nodding before Fenrir had finished the invitation. "Thank you, Lord Fenrir."

"My friends just call me Fenrir."

Iggy looked up, his face covered in shortbread crumbs. "Mine call me Iggy. You're my third friend since arriving." And then he whispered, "I'm not actually a sea serpent."

"I know," Fenrir whispered back. "But you are a very fierce wyvern." And he winked.

Batu played and the Nordvings danced and the questers kept being offered food until they could hardly move. After several renditions of what Fenrir claimed was Vilhelmina's favorite song, the Nordving lord declared it was bedtime.

"All rise for His Joyful and Delighted Overlord Fenrir!" the herald shouted.

"Aye, and isn't he pleased!"

"As tickled as Freiydin with his hammer!"

"Hail, rapture!"

The Nordving lord waved good night and ambled to his tent. Vilhelmina gave a mighty stretch, then was guided after him by two of the Nordvings as she hadn't quite figured out how to move by herself yet.

Grinning, Batu let the last notes fade into the night. His gaze fell on Neci and Merlynda, who were watching him. He'd been so ungracious to them earlier. Should he try to make it up to them? He hesitated. Apologizing got his ears boxed back home. Besides, he would've *eventually* escaped on his own. Probably. So he gave them the smirk he'd learned so well even before being captured by the Nordvings and fled to his tent.

Neci and Merlynda rolled their eyes. They rose and headed for their own tent, but the herald stopped them. With a slight bow the ogre handed a thin bundle to Neci. "A gift," he said.

Curious, she unwrapped the cloth, then stared. "Wow," she breathed.

It was a dagger. The hilt was elegant and carved with trees, and it fit snugly inside a leather sheath that made Neci think of moss and fresh soil. She tugged on the hilt, and her breath caught. The blade was no ordinary steel but was the deepest, purest black.

"Alchemically refined," the herald said, "but not magically altered. For what is metal other than refined Earth?"

Neci cradled the dagger. "But why?"

"Consider it a late birthday present. Earth is strong and loyal, Neci the Ardent, as are you. You may be born to merchantwomen and farmers, but you have the heart of a knight."

"How did you know"—Neci looked up, but the herald was already gone—"that it was my birthday?" she asked the empty air.

Merlynda stared after him. "What do you think of that?" she asked Iggy.

"I'm not sure." Iggy squinted at where the herald had stood. "But that was no ordinary herald."

*In which our questers
take a swim*

The Nordvings set off the next morning, new friends in tow. The questers rode on Fenrir's flagship, which had a beautiful dragon head carved into the prow. Iggy liked to slither-walk up to sit on it (*To keep her company,* he told Merlynda). As the sun set, they worked with the Nordvings to set up camp for the night on the river's bank.

"Merlynda, watch this!" Neci called. She gripped her dagger by the tip of the blade, took aim at a big tree knot, raised her arm back, then threw it.

It *thock*ed against a tree—not the one she'd been aiming

at—and went sprawling into the forest. A falcon squawked and bolted from its branch.

"It was a good throw," Merlynda offered.

"No, look!" Neci twisted so that Merlynda could see the dagger's sheath strapped to her hip—*with the dagger inside.*

"Merlyn's goat!" Merlynda bent down to look at it. It was definitely the same dagger, black blade and all.

"Neat, right?" Neci beamed. "I named it Faithful. The herald said it was made from Earth, and Earth is exceptionally loyal. It's my token!"

"What's a token?"

Only one person had a voice that clear. They turned slowly.

"What are you doing here?" Neci tried to sound cordial, but she was still irked at how ungrateful Batu had been after being rescued.

"Fenrir likes my playing." He plucked a few strings. "I left home to travel. By boat is as good a way as any when it's free."

"Now that *you're* free," Merlynda pointed out.

Batu's hand slipped, striking a jumble of dissonant notes. He took a breath. This wasn't going how he'd hoped, but he hadn't been taught how to make amends, only how to charge ahead. He turned to Neci to try something else. "I saw you practicing with your dagger. You're throwing it like you're trying to punch someone, but you've got to finesse it a bit."

Neci's dark eyes flashed. "You couldn't even free yourself,

and you expect me to think you're some sort of weapons expert?"

Batu glared, then swung his lute onto his back, picked up a hand axe, and threw it in one smooth motion. It sliced through the air and buried itself deep into the tree knot Neci had tried to hit earlier.

"You throw like a girl," he snapped at Neci, then spun on his heel and walked away, panpipes swinging from his hip.

"How else would I throw?" Neci yelled after him. She turned to Merlynda. "Why did we bother rescuing him? And where did a wandering musician learn to throw an axe like *that*?" She didn't mean to sound jealous, but what a throw!

Iggy stared after the minstrel. "I don't like him. He has to call me Ignus."

"He never spoke about it much, but I don't expect Batu had many a role model in his life, before we, ah, *found* him." Fenrir had come up behind them with Vilhelmina, who was still airborne. "But if you don't mind my saying so, your technique *could* use some work."

"But look!" Neci said. "It comes back!" She launched Faithful again to demonstrate.

Fenrir let out a low whistle, and Neci handed it to him. "It's my token," she repeated proudly.

The Nordving lord studied the dagger. "What's a token?"

Neci sighed. "Am I the only one on this quest who's actually read about quests?"

Iggy and Merlynda shrugged.

"Tokens," Neci explained, "are items given to knights—and I suppose other people, sometimes—on their quests. They might help them later, or be reminders of something they've learned."

"Shouldn't I have a token?" Merlynda asked. "Since it's my quest."

Neci nodded. "You're bound to get one."

"And me?" Iggy perked up. "Perhaps something laced with delicate spices?"

"We'll keep an eye out," Neci told him.

Fenrir handed the dagger back. "That is a fine piece of workmanship."

"Isn't it? Your herald gave it to me."

Merlynda looked around. "Where is he, anyway?"

Fenrir scratched his beard. "Before we left this morning, he told me he'd like to retire in the forest. He said the Howlwyn was as good as any."

"What's his name?" Neci asked.

The Nordving lord shrugged. "We always called him Harold."

It turned out that the Nordvings were in no rush to find the open ocean, so Fenrir arranged for Neci to train with his finest shield-maiden, a tall, muscular elf named Brynhild. Neci liked her immediately and accepted the bruises and scrapes that came from her lessons with no small measure of pride (and ignored Batu's remarks about how she could do better).

Now that things had settled, Merlynda jotted down a

note to her parents. She'd been too flustered after the looking glass had broken to even think about it, but in theory magical messages could cross dimensions into the Forfle realm. You didn't magic messages to a person so much as to a location. Merlynda was still sure that rushing off after Percy had been the right thing, but Mother would know just what to do.

She gave up after the third attempt flared into a wasp's nest (Iggy was none too thrilled about the sudden dive into the river, but Merlynda reassured him it was better than a face full of stingers). The wizardess was overtaken by a desperate homesickness. Did her parents even know she and Percy were gone yet? Did they know she was the Septimum Genus?

The Nordvings' leisurely pace was agonizing. As far as Merlynda knew, Percy was being Hollowed *that very moment*. She kept playing that terrifying day in the orchard over and over in her head. What if they had let Iggy eat breakfast instead of insisting they try a spell? What if she had gotten to Percy in time, or somehow reached him through that final, smaller portal?

Portals didn't just happen, either. The portal Iggy came through was explained easily enough by the Aether, but the next two? Guilt seared through Merlynda, hot and empty. She could think of no other explanation for the portal that had taken Percy, except that somehow she and her magic were responsible.

Aside from the guilt, there was the incredible ache of *missing*. She'd never gone more than a few hours without seeing her twin. It had already been days. It would likely be months. Would he be okay when they finally found him? Would he still be the Percy she knew, who spun up absurd schemes and always, always supported her?

Merlynda wanted to rush directly to the nearest town and search for information about the image on Percy's parchment, but she held tight to the hope that they had until the Shadow Sun. She also saw wisdom in Neci using the time to train, and reminded herself that their quest had only just begun. If she wanted any real chance of rescuing her brother, she needed to master her magic.

She and Iggy used the evenings to experiment—carefully. They could sense each other's feelings (and sometimes exact thoughts), and if Iggy wasn't wrapped around Merlynda's wrist or on her shoulder, they still always knew where the other was. Merlynda wasn't convinced they were improving, but practicing helped distract her from worrying about Percy. Once they found the circle of stones—because she kept telling herself they *would* find them—she'd need to be as powerful as she could be. She'd need to be the Septimum Genus, whatever that meant.

"Let's work with Fire," Iggy said. They sat on the riverbank, hopefully far enough away from camp so that magical mishaps wouldn't cause damage. "Fire is useful for cooking."

"Air is safer." Merlynda didn't want to hurt Iggy's feelings, but ever since he'd arrived, her magic had been even more volatile. "And it's Percy's element." She managed to keep the shake of *missing* out of her voice. "Maybe it's mine, too."

She pushed down the cold lump that formed in her throat at the thought of her brother and adjusted the pile of twigs that sat in front of them. Merlynda had tried this exercise a hundred times before, but perhaps with Iggy things would be different. She tucked a stray lock of chestnut hair back behind her ear, took a deep breath, and concentrated.

Merlynda reached through the Air around her, sensing how it filled everywhere, how it was in the grass, the bugs, inside of her and Iggy. She felt for the twigs, found them, and reached into the Air to try to move them. They trembled and shook, and then one gently lifted from the ground.

It was working! She could feel Iggy's magic in tandem with hers. Merlynda pushed with the Air, gently, gently—she could feel the Aether beyond but couldn't quite reach it, like there was a wall in the way. She pushed—

The twigs *cracked* and burst into fireworks, zooming around the camp and up into the sky. Merlynda instinctively blasted them toward the water with a vicious gust of wind so that they wouldn't burn the camp or the ships. Also, it felt good to blast something.

A single twig—one that hadn't moved at all—remained on the ground. And of course, the magic laughed at her.

Frustrated, Merlynda picked the twig up and hurled it into the river. It floated on the water's surface in the most unsatisfying way, which only made her madder. "I don't understand!

Percy can enchant the pots and pans to make dinner, but I can't even move a stick!"

"Making dinner is an admirable ability," Iggy said. "Perhaps we can work on that next."

"Nice trick." Batu flopped down beside her and blew a scale across his panpipes. "How does it work?"

Iggy clambered up to Merlynda's shoulder to put a little more distance between himself and Batu. Batu was *not* allowed to call him Iggy.

Merlynda stroked Iggy along his spine. "How does what work?"

"Your magic."

"I don't know."

"You don't have to be stuck up about it." Batu regretted the words as soon as they'd left his mouth, but it was too late.

The wind gushed around them, rippling through the grass and trees and whistling across Batu's pipes. He held them closer, wary. "Stop kidding around. I was there when you blew up the camp, no need to prove anything."

Merlynda took a deep breath and tried to calm down. "I'm not. I really don't know how it works. How did you learn to play the lute? Or your pipes?"

Batu shrugged. "My mother showed me the basics—scales and things—then I went off on my own."

"Did you want to learn?"

"Of course." Batu stared across the river, remembering those happier times. "More than anything."

The wind settled down, and Merlynda exhaled. "More than anything, I want to learn how to play my instrument— my magic. Imagine that you've got all that passion for music, and you know you'd be good at it, if only you could understand the basics. But for some reason, you *can't* understand them, no matter how many lessons you take or books you study, or how loud everything inside you screams that you want to learn." She jutted her chin out, defiant. "How would that feel?"

Batu looked down at his panpipes. "Awful," he whispered.

"That's what this feels like." Merlynda stood. "So unless you happen to know a wizard or benevolent necromancer willing to take on the subject of Merlyn's prophecy as their student, don't you dare tell me I'm stuck up, Batu of the Lake." She stormed off with Iggy.

Batu watched them go, then flopped onto his back, hands over his face in frustration. He'd finally decided he ought to at least try to make friends since they were traveling together— when was the last time he'd been around anyone his age?—but instead he'd managed to insult both Neci and Merlynda, and it didn't seem like Merlynda's pet thing was very fond of him either.

He sat back up and blew a few mournful notes across his panpipes. Maybe being alone was better after all.

✦ ✦ ✦

At long last the Nordving fleet reached the open ocean. Neci had almost mastered the techniques Brynhild had taught her (and had ignored Batu's further attempts to "help"), Merlynda and Iggy had bonded (even if their magic hadn't improved), and Fenrir had settled on plundering Ispania.

"I hear wonderful things about it," he said. "Excellent pillaging grounds."

"Aye, treasure and glory!"

"To fill Freiydin's coffers!"

"Hail, riches!"

Fenrir invited Merlynda and Neci to join the Nordvings, but they politely declined.

"What about you, Master Batu?" Fenrir asked. "Care to serenade us further across the open ocean?"

Batu swung his lute over his back. "I'm off to be a roaming minstrel, but I'll be sure to compose a ballad about Fenrir the Mighty."

They said their goodbyes (Vilhelmina only flicked her tail), and then wizardess, knight, minstrel, and very fierce wyvern all piled into a small boat and were off. They planned to follow Fenrir's advice and sail along the current to the nearest port town. Merlynda and Neci hoped to find leads about the stones on Percy's parchment, and Batu could go on his merry way singing to anyone who would listen.

Merlynda's pale skin was now a light tan from the days spent in the sun, and she'd taken to wearing her chestnut hair in a long braid. Only a few weeks had passed, she told herself. They had loads of time before the Shadow Sun. Time to find the stones, time to become the Septimum Genus and save Percy. She ignored the little voice inside her that said this effort wouldn't be any different, that she would bungle things like always.

Neci guided the tiller of their ship the way Brynhild had taught her, and Merlynda managed to summon a few small breezes to spur them along. She didn't dare try to push past the Air and into the Aether, but at least she could do this much. Batu watched, idly playing melodies and giving a fuming Neci pointers. The sun beating down made them all testy.

"I heard you magicked your brother away," Batu said to Merlynda. "And now you're looking for him."

Merlynda flinched, his words as sharp as if he'd slapped her. Neci gritted her teeth. "Leave her alone."

Merlynda didn't respond, but she summoned a spray of water with her next breeze and splashed it on Batu. He hugged his lute. "Hey!"

"Oops," she said darkly.

Iggy rose up to stare at Batu. "We, sir, are on a noble quest to *rescue* Percy. What reason have *you* got for being on your own?"

"Reasons that are mine," the minstrel snapped. How did he always manage to say the wrong thing? He just wanted to get to port so he could carry on with being alone. No more annoying questers. No one to be upset with him, or to argue with. Just him and his music. He started to say more, then stopped and cocked his head. "Do you hear that?"

In the distance, they heard a song. It was in a flowing, musical language, laced with magic.

Come, weary traveler
Come to our arms
Come, weary traveler
Find your rest
Come, tired adventurer
Come stay with us
Come, tired adventurer
Find your peace

Batu's face softened. The music seeped into his bones, into his soul. "It's lovely," he murmured.

Neci scowled. "Rubbish."

"It *is* pretty." Iggy cocked his head to hear better. "But there's something else."

"It's coming from over there." Batu jostled the boat as he moved for a better look. "Ahead, and farther out."

The singing grew louder as the current brought them closer. In the distance, a cluster of rocks jutted out of the water like gravestones. Three beautiful women sat on them, swaying with their song. Their hair was long and tousled, their smiles bright and inviting. They held their arms out to the young travelers.

Come, tired questers
Come be at ease
Come, tired questers
Let us heal pain
Come, wounded wanderers
Come find comfort here
Come, wounded wanderers
Your journey is complete

"Get closer," Batu commanded.

"No." Neci tightened her grip on the tiller. "They're out of the current. And their song doesn't sound friendly."

Batu lunged for the tiller.

"What's wrong with you?" Neci shouted, fighting for control. Merlynda tried to grab him, but he flung her away.

"He's bewitched," Iggy hissed to Merlynda. "Those are sirens!"

Chilled, Merlynda looked sharply back at the women sitting on the rocks. Sirens were crafty and malicious creatures of the sea who delighted in sending sailors to an eternity beneath the water.

These particular sirens had been tasked with *not* killing the travelers, but old habits die hard. It had been ages since they'd used their voices to weave spells, and they were now embracing the opportunity to entice all who were unlucky enough to hear their song.

All *men* who heard their song, anyway. Fortunately, Merlynda and Neci were not men, and while Iggy found the song alluring, he was very recently from the In-Between and therefore made of stronger stuff.

"Cover your ears, Batu!" Merlynda jumped onto his back to pull him away from his struggle with Neci, but he shook her off. Their small longship rocked back and forth.

Merlynda struggled to her feet, slipping in the water that sloshed in the boat. Iggy wrapped himself around her head so that he didn't fall away, clutching her hair with his feet.

"Stop, Batu!" Merlynda shouted. "They're bewitching you!"

A screech broke the sirens' song.

Merlynda looked up to see a falcon diving for her, talons first. She yelped and threw herself onto the floor of the boat, violently rocking it. Iggy scrambled around and around her head, frantic.

The falcon screeched again and turned for another pass.

"Look out!" Merlynda shouted. "Stop fighting!"

"Let go!" Batu roared at Neci.

"No!" Neci snarled. Batu had his hands on the tiller now, and they struggled for control.

Neci was determined, but Brynhild hadn't taught her how to fend off an enemy while sailing a boat, and Batu was older and bigger. He shoved her hard, and Neci tumbled overboard and splashed into the sea.

"Neci!" Merlynda cried. She grabbed Batu's lute and

swung it at him with all her strength, hoping to shock him out of the enchantment. It shattered into splinters across his back, but he didn't even notice.

Merlynda left him to the sirens and reached into the magic of the Water, desperate to find Neci. There was so, so much of it to sort through. "Hurry, hurry!" Iggy urged.

She saw a tangle of arms and legs bob up and down, and Merlynda gently, gently urged the water to lift and carry Neci back to their boat, but the falcon darted down once more with a terrible cry. Iggy called out, and they both tumbled over the side and into the ocean.

Merlynda burst through the surface in time to see their longship crash into the rocks. The sirens' laughing smiles turned vicious as they slunk back into the water.

Merlynda reached for Iggy, who coiled himself like a vise around her wrist. As the water pressed in around her, forcing her under, she noticed two things.

Iggy was glowing.

And the magic still laughed at her.

As Neci tumbled into the icy water, she considered the possibility that this might be the end of her quest. She would never be a knight and she would never ride a noble steed and she would never return in glory to her parents and explain why she left on her birthday without even leaving a note, all because some stupid musician boy couldn't resist pretty singing.

If he really was a musician, which Neci seriously doubted. Where would a lute player learn as much about proper fighting technique as Batu knew?

Neci kicked and struggled toward what she hoped was the surface. She'd swum in Avonshire's lake more times than she could count, but that was nothing like the ferocious waters that seemed bent on pulling her down, down, down.

Something wrapped around her waist. She panicked, but she didn't have much air left and her fingers were numb and she couldn't seem to find her dagger, and even though she didn't quite give in, she knew she was done for.

Until she felt herself pushed through something squishy and, with a great squelching sound, found herself surrounded by air instead of water.

She fell on a spongy floor, coughing out water and sucking in deep breaths of beautiful, salty-smelling air. She wanted to lie there forever and just breathe, but she struggled to her knees and grabbed her dagger. Her satchel had been lost to the depths, but at least she had Faithful. The squishy thing she'd tumbled through was some sort of membrane. It seemed to be keeping the rest of the ocean at bay, but Neci took a step or two away from it just in case.

The membrane made another loud sucking noise, and Merlynda tumbled through with Iggy. Batu squelched in right behind them and crashed to the floor. Neci flung herself at Merlynda and hugged her, then scurried back as the wizardess went through her own round of coughing and gasping.

"Iggy," Merlynda finally managed, "you were glowing!"

The wyvern was quite pleased with himself. "I was, wasn't I?" He glowed again, just to show that he could. He squinted at Merlynda. "Shouldn't you be all wet?"

Merlynda and Neci both glanced down. Despite nearly drowning moments before, they looked like they'd never touched the water. Even their hair was dry.

Batu shook his head, bewildered. Now that he was away from the sirens' song, his head was clear. He glanced at the girls, then turned away, ashamed. What had come over him?

A willowy woman with blue skin and watery hair rushed over to them. Her robes were made of seaweed and scales, and shimmered and swayed as she moved. Her eyes were even bluer than Merlynda's. "I will explain everything in a moment, but I must ask you to step deeper into the cavern." She gently but firmly ushered them along.

Neci kept Faithful out, but the travelers took several steps across the spongy ground as they were bid (Batu sulked behind his mop of dark hair, but he didn't argue). They were in an enormous cavern that looked out through the membrane and into the ocean. Not *over* the ocean, but *into* it. Floating balls of water filled with glowing eels and fish and other ocean creatures hovered overhead, providing light. One water lamp bumped into the membrane, and the creatures inside were released back into the ocean.

"Do you know where we are?" Neci whispered to Merlynda.

"No," Merlynda whispered back, "but I think that woman is an Oceanid." She'd never seen an Oceanid, but some of Merlyn Manor's books and journals on Water magic had described them.

More willowy, blue-skinned women hurried past, and a moment later an enormous bubble, easily large enough to fit Merlynda, Iggy, Neci, and Batu with room to spare, burst through the membrane. Two Oceanids emerged with great urgency, a floating stretcher following behind.

"Lady Phelia," one of them said to the woman who had first greeted the travelers. "We've barely escaped, but Lena—" Her voice broke as her eyes flashed to the stretcher.

"Hush." Lady Phelia's voice was warm. "You did all you could."

"As did he," the second woman said bitterly. Her bright blue eyes flashed, and she handed Lady Phelia what appeared to be a withered flower. "He disappeared into a portal before we could get close, just as the legends say. The entire field, gone."

Lady Phelia stared at it, silent for a moment. "It is as we feared, then."

The others nodded, grim.

"Take Lena to the infirmary," Lady Phelia said with a heavy sigh. "I must attend to our guests. They have arrived just in time."

As the stretcher floated past the travelers, Merlynda glimpsed the woman lying on it. She, too, was an Oceanid, but her skin was an ashen gray, and her hair was dry and brittle. Her head turned, and she stared at Merlynda, but her eyes weren't vibrant, as the other Oceanids' were. They were dull, empty—not dead, but also not quite alive.

"Merlynda," Iggy whispered. He pressed himself against her.

She felt it too. Or rather, it was what they *couldn't* feel. They could sense the magic in each other, and they could feel the magic all around them, for they were clearly in an extremely magical place. They saw the Oceanid lying there, but where there should have been a shimmer of Oceanid magic—there was nothing.

"It's gone," Merlynda whispered, horrified. "Her magic . . ."

"Indeed it is, Septimum Genus." Lady Phelia approached as the stretcher moved out of sight, hurried along by the Oceanids.

Merlynda didn't question how Lady Phelia knew who she was. There was likely very little that the Oceanids didn't know, particularly about magic.

"I'm afraid that little can be done." Lady Phelia held out the withered flower, and Merlynda cupped it in her hands.

It was a windflower—or at least, it had been. There was no trace of Air magic left. Iggy uncurled from Merlynda's wrist to get a better look. "It's not quite dead." He sniffed it. "But it's also not alive."

Merlynda looked up at Lady Phelia. "Windflowers only grow by the Lake of Cantor."

"And now they grow no more."

"The entire field?" Merlynda whispered.

"The entire field. Gone." Lady Phelia plucked the empty flower back with her delicate hands. "What you've just witnessed—the windflowers, Lena, and countless other reports over the centuries—is the terrible work of the Hollower."

*In which the mark of an old
family foe resurfaces*

The Hollower.

He was real. The message on the parchment, from Percy—*he was real.* Merlynda had known ever since getting the clue, but part of her had wanted to believe that the Hollower was only a myth, a story, an elaborate prank that Percy had played on her. But now there was no denying it.

Was Percy lifeless like that, empty, drained of all his magic? Or is that what would happen to him if Merlynda didn't find him in time? Her legs went weak at the thought, and she stumbled backward. Neci reached out a hand to steady her, and Merlynda took a deep breath, trying to calm down, to quell the rising panic that threatened to swallow her.

The Hollower.

Lady Phelia looked up from the hollowed windflower, her eyes hard. "We have much to discuss, Septimum Genus. Allow me to properly introduce myself. I am Lady Phelia of Oceanus. You and your companions are our honored guests." She bowed low.

Merlynda was so horrified about the sick Oceanid, and that Percy might share the same fate, that it took her a moment to return the bow. She froze halfway through. "Lady Phelia of Oceanus? You wrote *An Expanded View on Water* and *Water: The Truest Magic*! I've practically memorized them! I'm—" Merlynda flushed at her babbling. "Thank you for saving us," she mumbled. "We ran into some siren troubles." She glowered at Batu, who was staring out into the ocean.

"Ah, yes." Lady Phelia almost sighed. "I'm afraid the sirens were . . . *overzealous* in their task to bring you here. They are in our rehabilitation program."

"Wait," Merlynda said. "*You're* the reasons the sirens came after us?"

"Yes. As I said, you are our honored guests."

Merlynda wouldn't call crashing their boat an honor, but she didn't say so.

Outside the membrane, the three sirens swam past. They twirled and blew kisses at Batu. He turned away, cheeks burning. "I don't suppose you could send a regular sort of messenger next time?" he asked. "And, er, why exactly have you sent for us?" He wasn't keen on becoming a prisoner again, if that's what was happening. He was also still embarrassed about crashing their boat, even if Lady Phelia had just admitted to sending the sirens.

Lady Phelia narrowed her eyes ever so slightly at the sirens. "We shall adjust the sirens' rehabilitation program to address their behavior. And all your questions will be answered shortly."

Neci gestured at the barrier keeping the ocean *out* and the air *in*. "Is that, um, safe?"

"Indeed." Lady Phelia gave Neci a small smile. "I assure you, you are well protected here. Come. Arrangements have been made."

Lady Phelia led the travelers across the cavern and through a large coral door. Above it, a sign hung with an inscription:

ALL WHO ENTER HERE LEAVE CHANGED.

Neci shot Merlynda a questioning look. "Do you think it's safe?"

Change wasn't safe, usually. It meant new things, and maybe good things, but probably difficult things too.

Merlynda gazed back at the open ocean beyond the cavern, to the vast darkness that stretched beyond. "I don't think we have much choice."

A Word about Oceanus
(and Lady Phelia in particular)

O ceanus, while being quite alive, is not quite its own being, but almost. Melded together by the Oceanids from the life of the ocean and the creatures that live therein, it travels the depths, shape-shifting and morphing as needed to navigate through underwater ridges or schools of fish. At times it sweeps along with the currents, and at others it propels itself with steady determination wherever the Oceanids bid it.

The Oceanids themselves are an ancient people and have lived in Oceanus since time out of mind. As so often happens with those who are left to their own devices, the

Oceanids—and Lady Phelia in particular—had become very set in their ways. Convinced of their own correctness, they generously offered their rehabilitation services to those they felt needed reform, like the sirens—whether or not the individuals in question felt the same way.

What the Oceanids did not understand—and Lady Phelia in particular—is that good intentions do not always produce good actions.

The travelers were presented with an extravagant seafood dinner followed by rich tea and tiny cakes. Batu pushed his food around, sulking. Merlynda didn't eat much either, haunted by the empty eyes of the magic-less Oceanid, sick with dread that the same fate would befall Percy.

Neci kicked her under the table, and Merlynda realized Lady Phelia had addressed her. "Sorry?"

Lady Phelia took a delicate sip of tea. "We must discuss what has happened. I've heard whispers of the Hollower throughout my lifetime, but never has he been this bold."

Bold indeed, Merlynda thought bitterly, to kidnap the Septimum Genus's brother. Or maybe the Hollower knew she wasn't a very good Septimum Genus, so he wasn't worried.

Merlynda had had a little while now to get used to the idea of being the Septimum Genus, but she still didn't feel anything like the fulfillment of Merlyn's prophecy. It was quite a lot to ask of someone, to suddenly change everything they thought they knew about the world.

If anything, Merlynda felt even more useless. All those people, waiting for centuries, for her to do something amazing and extraordinary? They were going to be let down. *She* was going to let them down, but she'd never even wanted to be the one they were waiting for! It was supposed to be Percy, the talented twin. Not Merlynda, who couldn't even magically remove an inkblot.

Neci could see that Merlynda needed a moment, so she launched into the story of Iggy arriving, and the portals that appeared, and how Percy vanished but then reappeared to send Merlynda a message. Merlynda was grateful that Neci took over, but hearing it told out loud was almost a worse way to relive it.

Batu listened to the tale in silence. He knew the gist of it already, but seeing Merlynda's eyes well up made him want to kick himself for being so flippant about it on the boat. He knew the pain of loved ones being ripped away, of your life changing in an instant.

As Neci wrapped up, Merlynda offered her mostly full plate to Iggy, who had finished his. "So you . . . You've seen what the Hollower does before?" she asked their host.

"Not firsthand," Lady Phelia said gravely. "But the accounts I'd heard were enough for me to do all I could to warn others."

"'The Hollower's on the hunt,'" Merlynda said. "You wrote that."

Lady Phelia nodded in acknowledgment. "It was meant to

be a warning, for even the youngest to be aware of the danger, but now most use the rhyme as a way to frighten small children into behaving. The Hollower does not drain life, as some of the stories say, but he does indeed drain magic. Magic-filled creatures have always been his targets."

"But why?" Merlynda asked. "What does he want with it? Why did he take Percy?"

The Oceanid bowed her head. "I'm afraid that even we have been unable to ascertain his purpose."

"Percy gave us a clue." Merlynda reached into her robes to show the parchment to Lady Phelia, but the familiar crumpled page wasn't there.

Panic seized her. She searched her pockets, her sleeves, even her shoes. She always kept it on her, always had it close—

"Merlynda," Neci said soothingly. She'd never seen the wizardess like this. "Merlynda, it must have gotten washed away when we fell in the water."

"No—Percy—" It was the one clue he'd made sure she had, and she'd lost it!

Iggy slither-walked up to her and nuzzled his face against her cheek as the tears slipped out. She hugged him tight.

"Septimum Genus," Lady Phelia said after a few moments. "I know this is difficult, but we must press on. If there's any hope of finding Percival, we must find the Hollower."

"How?" Merlynda bit out. "I can't even keep a piece of parchment safe! How am I supposed to defeat a villain who's been stealing magic for centuries?" The table vibrated, and Merlynda tried to calm her boiling frustration. Blowing things up wouldn't save Percy.

"We will do our best to recover your belongings. But in order to defeat the Hollower, in order to restore Lena and any other victims, we need the Septimum Genus. We need *you*, Merlynda."

Merlynda wiped her face with her sleeve. "I can barely do basic spells without something going wrong." Without the magic laughing, she thought. "What about a snow cactus, or Elemental Stones?"

"Those items are powerful, but they are exceedingly rare, as you well know. Assuming the Hollower continues in this way, we'd need far more Elemental Stones than we'd ever be able to conjure. And I'm afraid it gets worse."

Merlynda wasn't sure how that could be possible, but Lady Phelia moved to a cabinet made of bright coral and removed a shell as big as a dinner plate. She raised it up, and a stream of water flowed down from one of the lamps to fill it.

"This is a scrying shell," Lady Phelia explained. "It can show us almost anything we wish to see." She moved her hand over the shell, then tipped it on its side. Instead of spilling all over the table, the water swirled up into the air above them. She spoke a gentle command, and the water shifted and whirled until it formed an excellent approximation of a liger, stripes and all.

"Vilhelmina!" Iggy waddled over to get a better look. His

belly bulged from all the tasty seafood, so slithering was difficult. "Are you in Ispania yet?"

But the water-Vilhelmina only licked her paw and yawned.

"She can't hear you," Lady Phelia said kindly. "The water shows you what is, and only what is. I have tried to scry the Hollower to see his activities. He is clever and evades me, but there is something you must see."

She murmured another command. The water flattened into a disk, then swirled faster and faster. Droplets flew off like sparks, and the edges billowed out like clouds chasing after one another.

A water-falcon burst out of the disk and fluttered across the table. It screeched, then dove toward Iggy.

Merlynda let out a sharp cry, and the falcon burst into droplets, misting everything. Plates and saucers cracked, and the membrane on the window rippled. Batu and Neci inched their chairs farther away from it.

Iggy poked his head out from where he'd hidden in Merlynda's collar. "You said they couldn't see us," he whispered.

"They should not be able to, Ignus." Lady Phelia looked slightly out of breath. For a moment she stared at Merlynda the way the Nordvings had when she'd made the earth explode—but then her face was back to kindness and calm, and the wizardess wasn't certain she'd seen anything at all. "It seems the Hollower doesn't approve of my attempts to spy on him."

"That was the falcon that attacked us!" Neci exclaimed.

"I knew it felt funny." Iggy looked at Merlynda. "You knew it too."

Merlynda didn't, because she'd been preoccupied trying to stop Batu from sinking their boat, but the minstrel had been unusually quiet, and she didn't want to spoil his silence by bringing it up. "It looked like it was using a portal."

"It would appear the Hollower can create them at his whim." Lady Phelia stroked a strand of her long hair thoughtfully. "Familiars are sent from the In-Between via portals when the Aether deems it so. This falcon is twisted, tainted, and the Aether does not send tainted familiars. It is somehow from the In-Between, but not from the Aether."

Merlynda thought back to that fateful morning. The portal Iggy arrived in hadn't been calm, but it was precise. The second portal, the one that formed when she and Iggy tried to use their magic for the first time, had been skewed and violent. "Lady Phelia, how are portals created?"

"Ah, now that is a question that magical theorists have spent centuries debating."

"Great-Grandfather Merlyn used portals to the In-Between to travel through time, and across the world, and to check on his foresight." Merlynda sat back in her chair. "But no one else has ever been able to do that."

The Oceanid inclined her head in agreement. "Until now, it would seem. It's a dangerous skill, which is why Merlyn did not pass on his knowledge. Our Hollower could not do this on his own. He has acquired an object of great power, and greater evil."

Neci leaned forward. "Is this the regular sort of great evil, or something fantastically evil?"

"It poses one of the gravest threats in history."

"Excellent." Neci sat back. She still had no doubt they'd defeat the Hollower. In her stories, good always triumphed. Her knighthood was in the bag.

The Oceanid turned back to Merlynda. "The Hollower has acquired the amulet of Morgan le Fey."

Morgan le Fey. The enchantress who had nearly done Merlyn in. Merlyn, the most powerful wizard in history. Merlyn, who trapped Morgan beyond the In-Between after a brilliant battle. Merlynda had read all about the vicious fight, the sorceress responsible for it, and, of course, the wicked amulet that channeled her magic.

She shivered. The Hollower, who drained the magic away from living beings, had Morgan's power. "But—how?"

Lady Phelia stared out at the ocean. "I do not know the answer to that question. I glimpsed it while attempting to scry the Hollower's whereabouts. He blocked me from further investigation, and I sent for you immediately."

Her ocean-blue eyes bored into Merlynda. "All who are of magic are in danger. Merlyn was a frequent visitor to our city, and we are well acquainted with the prophecy about his seventh descendant." Lady Phelia paused. "Your family resemblance is uncanny. You even have his nose."

Merlynda only nodded and waited for Lady Phelia to continue.

"It can't be a coincidence that such a great evil has come to power at the same point in history that the heir to Merlyn's prophecy is revealed. It is time for the Septimum Genus to fulfill her birthright."

Merlynda felt very small. Technically, this quest was supposed to fulfill her birthright, but so far all she'd managed to do was cause an earthquake and ruffle the fur of a liger. "Can your scrying shell find Percy?"

Lady Phelia waved her hand, and another stream of water trickled down from a lamp. When the shell was full, she offered it to Merlynda. The wizardess hesitated. It was such a pretty shell, she'd hate to break it.

"It's quite simple," Lady Phelia encouraged her. "Think of what you want to see, and command the water to show you."

Merlynda gingerly took the scrying shell. "Um. Show me Percy." The water shimmered inside. She thought of her twin, of his cocky smile and mischievous grin.

The water swirled up into the air above them as it had for Lady Phelia—and that was it. She couldn't even get a scrying shell to do as it was told.

Batu glanced up, then went back to staring at his plate. He didn't know a thing about magic, and he knew Merlynda didn't care what he thought, but he'd hoped for her sake that she would be able to glimpse her brother.

Neci looked at the shell, hard. "Tell it to show you Fenrir."

Merlynda didn't see the point, but she did as Neci asked. A perfect image of Fenrir swirled into shape, eating a bowl of root vegetable soup.

Excited, Merlynda told the water to show her Percy again, but it went back into its blank swirl.

"What does that mean?" she asked Lady Phelia, panicked. "Is he gone? Is he okay? Is he—is he—" She couldn't bring herself to say "hollowed" or "dead."

Lady Phelia magicked the water back into the lamp. The glowing fish guided their water to the window, then slipped through the membrane and into the ocean. The room darkened.

"It is most likely that he is still in the company of the Hollower," Lady Phelia mused, "and that his whereabouts are shielded from prying eyes such as ours."

"But he's all right?" Merlynda's chest felt like Vilhelmina was crouching on it.

"I'm afraid I cannot answer that, but if the Hollower has him, it's for a reason. I suspect your thoughts about the Shadow Sun are correct."

Hope sparked inside Merlynda. "You do?"

"Yes. I believe we have until then to find the Hollower and save Percival."

Merlynda bolted out of her chair. "We've got to go! We've got to find him—"

Lady Phelia held up a calming hand, gesturing for Merlynda to sit back down. "A few moments of planning

are worth a year of swimming in the dark. If I might make a suggestion—stay here in Oceanus. Allow me to work with you and Ignus, to prepare you for what is coming. Together we can stop the Hollower."

Merlynda and Iggy looked at each other. They each felt the hope-spark this time. Could Lady Phelia really help them? She *was* one of the foremost researchers and scholars on Water magic.

"Oceanus has the largest library in existence," Lady Phelia added. "If the image on Percival's message is to be found anywhere, it is likely here."

Merlynda set Iggy on the table. "What do you think, Iggy?"

Iggy still wasn't keen on rushing *toward* the person draining magic, being a magical creature himself. But as much as he didn't want to meet the Hollower, he also didn't want anyone *else* to meet the Hollower. "We can't do much worse on our own, can we?"

"Good enough. Neci?"

"I'm with you." The knight in training had come along to help find Percy, and if this was the way to do it, she was in.

They turned to Batu, who avoided eye contact but shrugged.

"We'll stay, then," Merlynda said to Lady Phelia. "Thank you. Could you . . . Could you also send a message to my parents? I tried before, but . . ."

Lady Phelia bowed. "Of course. You honor me, Septimum Genus. We begin tomorrow."

+ + +

Merlynda, Neci, and Batu were each given their own room, with tubs full of warm water and all the soap, sponges, combs, oils, and fluffy towels they could want. The Nordvings' idea of bathing was to swim in the river and then dry off in the sun, which was better than nothing but still left something to be desired. Merlynda's chestnut hair, now freed from its Nordving braid, was extra soft and shiny after her Oceanus bath, and Neci used the combs and oils to restore her own curls to their typical Dame Joi likeness.

They slept so soundly, they woke up feeling as if they'd never need rest again, and showed up to breakfast refreshed and ready for the day. Batu grunted a hello but sat at the far end of the table and kept to himself.

When they were finished eating, Lady Phelia entered, followed by two Oceanids. "Are you ready to begin, Septimum Genus?"

Neci leapt to her feet. "Of course we're ready!"

Lady Phelia smiled, but it wasn't warm or kind. "I'm afraid Merlynda will need to focus. No distractions. But you will not be at a loss for entertainment."

What sort of knight left their best friend for entertainment? Neci was about to say just that, but Merlynda stood up and smiled. "It's all right, Neci. You've seen me blow things up loads of times." The wizardess actually felt hopeful about learning from Lady Phelia. Nervous, but hopeful.

Neci looked from the Oceanids to her friend. The whole point of Neci joining this quest was so she could help Merlynda!

But the wizardess seemed at ease, so Neci said, "You'll do great."

Lady Phelia gestured to one of the Oceanids. "I think you'll find your time here is not wasted, Neci the Ardent. Arjia is Oceanus' leading master of Oceasha, our highest form of hand-to-hand combat. She has agreed to train you, if you'd like."

Neci had no idea what Oceasha was, but if combat skills were involved, it hardly mattered. She bowed to Arjia. "Yes! I mean, I'm ready! I mean, thank you!"

"And for Batu of the Lake"—Lady Phelia gestured to the third Oceanid—"Xanthe has offered—"

But before she could say what Xanthe would teach, Batu shoved his chair back from the table and stalked past them. He really just wanted to be left alone. "I don't need your lessons."

Neci scowled. "Don't mind him. He's always like that."

Lady Phelia took Merlynda and Iggy to a sparse training room. Dim algae sprawled along the walls in pretty veins, offering calm light. There were no windows, and Merlynda wondered if this was a safety precaution after the way she'd made the dining room tremble. In the center was a large shell filled with water.

Iggy squeezed Merlynda's wrist tighter. He was nervous too. "Is this another scrying shell?" Merlynda asked.

"No." Lady Phelia's robes shimmered as she walked to it. She placed her hands on the rim. "This is simply a shell, its creature long passed back to the Water and Aether that created it." She raised her hands, and the water rose with them, flowing in on itself until it formed a sea turtle, a fish, a larger fish chasing them. Then they swirled back into droplets and splashed into the bowl.

"Now you try," Lady Phelia said.

Merlynda stared at the water and the shell. "Maybe we should start with something less breakable."

"It's perfectly safe." Lady Phelia encouraged her.

Merlynda lifted her wrist so Iggy could crawl onto her shoulder. "Here goes."

She closed her eyes and felt for Iggy's magic, then focused on the water, and past it to the Water—the magical tension flitting across the surface and singing through every droplet. It wasn't only in the liquid, but also in the shell, and the pedestal it stood upon, and in every trace of Oceanus.

Merlynda's eyes flew open. "Did you feel that?" she whispered to Iggy.

"Yes," he whispered back. Progress!

Lady Phelia smiled. "Oceanus is deeply entwined with the Aether. Water is the most fluid of the elements, and it permeates every fiber of our society—as does the Aether."

Merlynda concentrated. She grasped the Water with her magic, then tried to nudge beyond it into the waiting Aether—

Crack!

The shell shattered and crashed, splintering into razor fragments with such force, all Merlynda could do was duck.

She threw up her arm to shield Iggy, and a light flared in front of her. The shell fragments hit her light shield and clattered to the ground. Water spilled everywhere.

"I'm sorry!" Merlynda stepped back to keep her feet dry, embarrassed. "Are you all right, Lady Phelia?"

The Oceanid had stopped the shell fragments in midair. She let them clatter to the ground, perplexed.

"I promise I didn't do it on purpose," Merlynda said. She hoped Lady Phelia wouldn't decide this was too much trouble and cancel their lessons.

Lady Phelia looked at Merlynda differently now—like she was calculating something. "That protection you created. How did you do that?"

"I don't know," Merlynda said. "It happens when I blow things up."

"Did it start when Ignus arrived?"

Merlynda thought back. "Yes. It happened once right before he came from the In-Between, and again when the Nordvings threatened our village. But this time was stronger." *Everything* was stronger with Iggy.

"You're welcome," Iggy said.

Lady Phelia waved her hands, and the water on the floor picked itself up and streamed into a decorative pot. "Your ability to create these barriers began in conjunction with your magic coming of age. I have good news, Merlynda. You have been connecting with the Aether this entire time."

Merlynda rubbed her ear in case some water had found its

way in after all. She couldn't have heard properly. "I've what?"

"Connected with the Aether. I'm not sure how, but you have. That shield was made of more than a basic element. It was made of Aether."

The Aether! Merlynda and Iggy didn't need to look at each other. They could feel each other's surprise, but also delight. The Aether!

Lady Phelia moved the pot into the center of the room. "Let's try again."

On their way to Oceasha training, Arjia gave Neci a tour of Oceanus, which was bigger than she'd ever imagined a place could be, especially a place that was underwater.

She couldn't get over that. They were in an *underwater city*. More water barriers like the one the questers had arrived through covered Oceanus, looking into the ocean like windows. Blue-skinned women tumbled through them as easily as stepping out of a doorway onto a road. There were concert halls and taverns and shops and bakeries. No one asked for coins or goods, just handed over whatever was requested.

For lunch they sat on a coral bench in one of the parks, munching on sweet pies that Arjia had gotten them. If the water lamps had been a tad brighter, Neci might have believed they were outside in the fresh air. She savored each delicious bite of her pie. There were no onions or carrots or turnips in sight. It was bliss.

"Will we start training soon?" Neci asked, licking syrup

from her fingers. She could see other Oceanids practicing farther away in the park. They sparred and tumbled, fluid like water.

"You're sure you wouldn't prefer to visit our museums and tranquil gardens?"

"Merlyn's goat, *no*."

Arjia smiled, and Neci realized she'd been joking. "We will start with the foundations now, if you're ready."

Neci leapt to her feet. "I'm ready, Master Arjia!"

The foundations of Oceasha, Neci soon learned, involved a lot of sitting quietly, which was basically her worst nightmare (other than the one where she had to go live with Aunt Prin and do nothing but cook and curtsy). She fidgeted and twitched and marveled at how Arjia sat like a stone. Neci wanted to make sure the Oceanid was still breathing, but she'd been instructed not to move from her spot.

So she sat and she sat and she wondered when she'd be done sitting and could start jabbing and rushing things like water. But Arjia didn't move, so Neci stayed put.

A knight's path was never easy.

Five broken pots, three shattered bowls, and one cracked turtle shell later, Lady Phelia decided to call it a day. Merlynda had made no progress whatsoever, other than accidentally creating Aether shields. When she tried to make them on purpose, she couldn't.

She and Iggy were exhausted. Magic wasn't supposed to be draining once you'd gotten used to it, but they'd tried and tried to move past the Water and into the Aether, and each time it felt like slogging through deeper and murkier mud.

And then the magic would laugh.

Still, they were in higher spirits than when they'd left home. "Wait until we tell Neci I've been using the Aether this whole time!" Merlynda told Iggy as they walked to the dining room.

"Wait until we tell her how many things we broke!" he answered.

"Septimum Genus, you must not be distracted if you are to succeed."

Merlynda frowned at Lady Phelia. "Neci's not a distraction. She's my best friend."

The Oceanid inclined her head. "As you say. We will continue training tomorrow. Rest well, Merlynda. It will take all your focus if you are to face the Hollower."

Iggy bared his tiny teeth. "It's the Hollower who ought to be ready to face us!"

Batu and Neci were already at the table, sitting as far apart as possible. Merlynda and Iggy sat down next to the new Oceasha trainee.

"We broke things," Iggy said.

"I had a sweet pie," Neci answered. She unwrapped a napkin and offered them each one. Even though they were still on a quest, and faced a terrible foe, and Merlynda was desperate to find Percy—even though they were somewhere in the depths of the ocean, and Batu bolted his food down and then left in a hurry—things weren't as dark as they could've been because Merlynda and Iggy and Neci had one another.

In which Merlynda discovers
a betrayal

After several days in the underwater city, Batu decided that he may as well leave his room for something other than food. He'd spent his waking moments mourning the loss of his lute and panpipes—especially the lute. He wished Merlynda hadn't smashed it. He knew he deserved it, but oh, how he missed his music.

Batu avoided the girls. If he was going to be a solo wandering minstrel, he may as well start practicing now. Besides, his previous efforts at making friends had failed, and he was sure he'd make things worse by trying again (even though at least a tiny part of him wanted to). And this Hollower business sounded serious. He didn't want to get in the way of their training. But listening to Neci chatter during meals made him realize how big Oceanus was, so he figured that if Neci and Merlynda could find things that interested them, perhaps he could too. Or maybe one of those bubble things they'd seen when they first arrived could take him back to land, and he could get started with his wandering.

He let his hand trail along the damp hallway wall as he walked. Veins of pale moss stretched and spiraled along it, offering light that splashed across his tawny skin. Despite being underwater, the city never felt cold or clammy or drippy. It was warm and inviting and wholly foreign to Batu.

He wandered down hallways, through chambers, and around parks, past groups of blue-skinned Oceanids going about their business. Batu walked until he was lost, and then he walked more. He hadn't been able to go where he pleased since the Nordvings had captured him. He could only do it now because the girls had rescued him.

Plinking and plucking sounded in a nearby chamber—music! He didn't need to tell his feet where to go.

A single Oceanid sat at a harp. Xanthe, Batu realized, the Oceanid who was originally supposed to teach him . . . something. He'd stormed off before learning what. She appeared younger than many of the others, except her eyes looked ancient, or like they knew of ancient things.

Xanthe caught Batu listening and smiled at him. She played a deceptively simple melody on a whalebone harp, moving in rhythm with the music as if she were floating on the waves. When she finished, he realized he'd been holding his breath, afraid to miss a single note. "That was beautiful," he breathed.

"Thank you. Do you play?"

Somehow Batu thought she already knew the answer. "Lute, mostly. And a few other things."

Xanthe offered him the stool, and Batu swept down so quickly, it was hard to tell whether he'd sat on it or collapsed. He'd never seen anything as lovely as the harp, with its beautiful carvings that spoke of water and freedom, with all those strings waiting for him.

He poised his hands the way he'd seen Xanthe position hers, hesitant.

"Would you like me to show you?" Xanthe asked.

Batu examined the strings. Was he a musician, or wasn't he?

He plucked a few strings, testing to find strings Xanthe had used. As he gained confidence, he layered in notes and chords until he was playing something that was close to her melody, but not quite.

When he'd finished, Batu stood and smirked. He was starting to feel like his old self again (he didn't understand that this was not a good thing). "Not too bad for a first try, is it?"

Xanthe stared at him, appraising. She swept onto the stool, pulled the harp toward her, and closed her eyes.

A storm of sound thundered inside the chamber, tearing across the strings and piercing Batu's heart with its pain, its joy, its laughter, its sorrow. Whatever confidence Batu felt evaporated. Compared to this, his copycat melody was insignificant. Less than insignificant. His technical expertise and skills were nothing.

He was enraptured. The music flooded his ears, his heart, his soul, and he realized he'd never truly played music before. Not like this. Not with such honesty.

"My music has moved many, Batu of the Lake, but I believe your story is greater than that. Why do your tears flow?"

He wiped at his face. Where to start? Before running away, his uncle never allowed him to cry even when he had good reason to. Then he'd always had to act tough around the Nordvings, which had grown into shoving down his hurt as a matter of practice. But now it felt like everything at last could be free.

"I've been horrible," he finally managed. "Neci and Merlynda rescued me when they didn't have to—without even knowing me!" This was a shallow description, but Batu wasn't sure what would happen if he went deeper. "I couldn't escape on my own. It made me feel small somehow. But that's stupid—of course I'm glad to be rescued. And then I tried to talk to them, but it always came out wrong, and . . . and then I crashed our ship. Because I liked the sirens' song."

Xanthe understood. "The sirens have lured many good men to their deaths."

"But I'm not a good man. I'm selfish." He wiped another angry tear, but he was only angry at himself. "What an excellent way to say thank you, by being a jerk and nearly killing us."

The sound storm continued to wash over him. Batu couldn't get it out of his heart. "Would you teach me?" he asked, earnest. "Music. *Real* music. I know theory and technique, but what you played . . ."

Xanthe stood and gestured to the stool. Batu sat.

Day after day Neci and Arjia went back to the park to sit and meditate and try to be still like water. Neci was a little better at sitting quietly now. Not much, but she didn't fidget as often.

She also couldn't take it anymore.

"Arjia," she said, "I know water is calm, but—it can also be torrential and devastating."

Arjia raised an eyebrow for Neci to continue.

"Could we maybe try a bit of the devastating part?" Neci pleaded.

The Oceanid considered. "All right. Stand."

Neci jumped to her feet. Finally!

"We'll begin with Wave Form. Do as I do." Arjia closed her eyes and slowly moved her hands back and forth in front of her body. "Feel the mighty rhythm of the ocean, in all her depth and power. She doesn't hurry. She arrives exactly when she means to."

Neci suppressed a groan.

She wandered into dinner still frustrated. She'd waved her arms back and forth all afternoon but didn't feel the ocean any more than when she'd been back home weeding the carrot patch in the garden.

Neci found Merlynda half asleep in her soup. Iggy wasn't much better.

"Want to go back to my room after this and check on our quest progress?" Neci asked her. "Arjia said they found my satchel."

Merlynda jerked awake. Soup dribbled down her chin, and she wiped it off. "I can't. Lady Phelia wants to have an extra session today."

The door opened, and Lady Phelia glided in. "Are you ready, Merlynda? Ignus?"

Iggy let out a massive yawn, then curled up with his head tucked beneath his tail. Merlynda poked him. "Come on." She turned to the Oceanid. "Have you found anything about the circle of stones on the parchment Percy sent me? Or heard from my parents?" They still had *some* time, but considerably less than when they'd arrived in Oceanus.

"We continue to search, Septimum Genus. And I'm afraid there's still been no word. Come, let us continue your lessons." Lady Phelia gave Neci a cold smile before following them out.

Neci frowned after her. She'd barely seen Merlynda since training had started, and the wizardess was always exhausted. Even so, she seemed to be having a more exciting time than Neci, which the knight in training tried very hard not to envy.

Batu walked in and shuffled over to his customary seat as far away as possible. He glanced at her, then busied himself with his soup.

Neci grabbed a hunk of bread and stormed out.

True to their word, the Oceanids had found their shipwreck and sent Neci's belongings to her room. They were set up on a little table—her satchel, her books, even her sling. The Oceanids had magicked the water out somehow, and she'd been reassured that her satchel was now waterproof. Everything was a shade or two darker than it was supposed to be, but the deep green leather on her copy of *The Official Quest Requirements for Knighthood* was still beautiful, even if some of the silver lettering had flaked off. She opened it. The pages were only a little wrinkled.

Something fluttered out from the book, and she bent to pick it up.

It was her birthday present from Merlynda, the ultra-rare trading parchment that hadn't been released yet. Or maybe it had now. Time felt slippery ever since arriving in Oceanus. How long had it been? How long did they have until the Shadow Sun? Without sunrises and sunsets, it was hard to tell.

Neci propped the parchment up on the table and studied it. It was all in one piece, but the paint was smudged, and you couldn't make out any of the stats. Dame Joi's and Merlyn's faces were warped. Merlyn was leaning off to the side, as if he had somewhere better to be. Dame Joi reached for him, like she was afraid of being left behind.

She picked up the parchment, then made a fist and crushed it. She felt like Dame Joi.

✦　✦　✦

The next morning Merlynda asked to have the day off. She was exhausted and wanted to catch up with Neci. There also wasn't anything else she could possibly break in all of Oceanus, which worried her because that meant she'd break Oceanus.

The only good thing that had come from Lady Phelia's teachings, as far as Merlynda could tell, was that now she and Iggy were definitely bonded. It was difficult for Merlynda to imagine ever *not* having Iggy around. And somehow, even if they had a hard time believing in themselves, they managed to believe in each other.

Lady Phelia wasn't pleased with the request. "Has the Septimum Genus forgotten the incredible threat the Hollower poses?"

Iggy gave Lady Phelia a slight scowl. She sure was pushy.

Merlynda didn't appreciate the Oceanid's response either. "It's all I think about," she said. That, and the immense ache she felt from somehow creating the portal Percy vanished through, sending him straight into the cold embrace of the Hollower.

"You must not become distracted, Merlynda."

"I'm not. But we're not getting any better, and I'm exhausted. Just one day, to rest."

Lady Phelia's deep ocean eyes turned cold, but she dipped her willowy head in concession. "If the Septimum Genus wills it. We will continue tomorrow."

Merlynda rushed back to the dining room. Batu wasn't

anywhere in sight, but Neci was finishing up breakfast. "Want to go exploring?"

Neci hesitated a moment. She missed spending time with Merlynda, but Oceasha training was supposed to get exciting today. Besides, why should Neci give up her studies for Merlynda when the wizardess never had for her?

To avoid making eye contact she checked that Faithful was strapped to her waist, but of course it was. "I can't. Arjia is finally going to show me some weapons basics."

"Oh." Merlynda said in a small voice. "Iggy and I have the day off."

"Sorry."

The girls stood for a moment.

"See you at dinner?" Merlynda asked hopefully.

Neci shrugged.

"Okay." Merlynda sat down to her porridge with Iggy. The day was going to feel extra empty without Neci. "Okay."

"You are a quick learner, Batu of the Lake." Xanthe stood up from where she'd been listening to him play and moved to a coral cabinet.

"You are an excellent teacher, Lady Xanthe." Batu set the harp down to rest and bowed his head. "Thank you. Not just for the music, for—" He hesitated, not sure how to express what he was feeling. "For change," he said simply.

"What changed?" The Oceanid removed a small chest from the cabinet and sat next to him.

Batu rested his head against the harp to think. "Me. I hated that Neci and Merlynda rescued me from the Nordvings when I couldn't do it myself. I still thought I was better than them. But I'm not. Just different."

"And are they better than you, or just different?"

He met her gaze. "Both, I think."

Xanthe turned the chest around so that it faced him. "No two people are exactly alike, and each is gifted in their own way. Our differences make us stronger. Do you believe this?"

"Yes." How could he not?

"Then accept this gift. I believe your friend would call it a 'token.'"

She opened the chest, and his breath caught. Inside was an ocarina, painted in swirls and spirals that whooshed across it and moved as much as the ocean. Twelve delicate holes dotted the surface to allow air to pass through. Twelve meant it would be difficult to learn, even more difficult to master, but it also meant the possibilities were greater. It was filled with what could be.

"Oh. Oh, I can't." He wanted it, desperately, but he wasn't worthy.

Xanthe picked it up. "This ocarina is made from Atlantean coral, a plant so strong, only magic-infused tools can craft and shape it. Coral is a living thing, Batu. It grows and breathes and is filled with the Aether. It will not fail you in this lifetime, nor in many lifetimes to come."

She placed it in his hands. He sat, almost trembling, but already his mind was racing to translate what he knew of his panpipes to how the air would play and dance across each of the openings.

"Thank you," he whispered. He didn't know what else to say.

So he played.

Because Merlynda felt sad about Neci, and discouraged that her questing could mostly be chalked up under "failure," she went back to something she was good at. She went to the library.

The Oceanus library was at the top of the city, with the ocean stretched overhead like the darkest of skies. Countless water lamps floated in the room, illuminating the books and winding pathways and artifacts on display. It was a treasure trove of history, magical and otherwise, of things barely explored or mostly unknown by land dwellers.

Iggy sniffed the air. "It smells old in here."

Merlynda wandered through the shelves and displays with archaic findings and inscriptions. It wasn't cozy the way the library in Merlyn Manor was, but it was still comfortable. Bookish people tend to find bookish places comforting, no matter where they are.

Iggy craned his neck around. There were an awful lot of books. And that wasn't counting the manuscripts. And that wasn't counting the scrolls. And *that*—

"I know," Merlynda said. But researching was the best plan she had.

She ignored the thought in the back of her mind that this was hopeless. Percy's parchment hadn't been recovered along with Neci's things, but Merlynda had described it in great detail to their hosts. Weeks ago Lady Phelia had assigned her Oceanids to research the circle of stones from Percy's parchment, but they'd had no news.

Merlynda's brow furrowed while she thought. Had it already been weeks since they'd gotten to Oceanus? Whenever she thought about how long they'd been in the city, the days turned fuzzy, so she couldn't get an accurate count. There'd also been no messages from her parents, even though she'd asked Lady Phelia to send a few more.

They wound through the shelves and stacks, looking for anything that might help them. There was *The Compendium of Poisonous Herbs and Their Uses*, a book called *Alchemists and the Errors of Arrogance*, and a particularly large tome entitled *A Truncated History of Life Underwater*. There were displays of coral and shipwrecks and an entire wall full of bones from animals Merlynda couldn't identify.

"Let's look on the other side," Iggy whispered. One of the displays had a skeleton laid out that seemed a little too much like a wyvern.

Merlynda hurried past the bones, turned a corner, and bumped into a desk. A stack of parchments wobbled, then spilled all over.

"What have you done?" a scratchy voice accused. It crashed through the silence of the library like an earthquake.

"I'm sorry!" Merlynda bent down and scrambled to gather the parchments. "I didn't see—"

She glanced up and froze. A face full of sharp teeth was inches away.

The teeth lined a narrow, scaly beaklike jaw attached to a snakish head, with yellow eyes on either side. The head was *big*— big enough to chomp Merlynda in half with one bite. It was part of a long body that disappeared behind the desk. Several brown tentacles snaked out from behind the desk and used their suction cups to gather the parchments Merlynda had scattered.

"Are you helping or not?" The thing moved irritably out from behind the desk and twisted his head to get a better look at her. The head and snakelike body were *attached* to the tentacles, which acted like legs and arms all in one.

"Staring is rude," he snapped.

"I'm sorry," Merlynda said.

The octopus-eel cocked his head to examine them up and down. "You're that Septimum Genus girl. And her familiar."

"Merlynda. And this is Iggy."

Iggy almost mentioned that only his friends were allowed to call him that, but he got another good look at the mouth full of teeth and decided that the octopus-eel should be a friend.

"And you are?" Merlynda prompted.

"The Curator," he snapped, then let out a *humph* and moved back behind the desk.

"The Curator?" Merlynda nudged when he showed no further interest in talking.

"It's part of my rehabilitation," the Curator snapped.

"Would you be able to help us?" Merlynda asked. "We're looking for information on portals, or the Hollower, or stone pillars—"

The eel head flung back and let out an awful screeching sound, then returned to itemizing the scrolls on his desk.

"Sir?" Merlynda squeaked.

The Curator's head turned, one eye looking at them, the other at his work. "I'm busy. I've summoned an aide to help you."

A large droplet of water landed on his head. He looked up and snarled. "Siren!" He shook a furled tentacle at the ceiling. "Lady Phelia will hear of this!"

He was answered with laughter as a siren swam across the ocean above them.

"Lady Phelia sent some Oceanids to research the same things," Merlynda offered. "Maybe they're already set aside somewhere?"

"She's done no such thing."

Merlynda and Iggy both started. "But she said—"

"Come," the Curator snarled, "if it will rid me of you!"

The Curator moved between the shelves, grabbing scrolls and parchments and texts and piling them onto tentacles, sometimes shoving things at Merlynda, who hurried after him with Iggy. She wanted to ask what he'd meant about Lady Phelia but didn't dare upset him further.

"Nothing is permitted to leave the library," the Curator instructed as they walked. "If anything is damaged, I will be *most* displeased." He snaked his head around to stare at them while his tentacles worked. "Do you understand?"

"Yes, sir," Merlynda answered from behind the stack of books she now carried. "This is a very impressive library. You must be proud."

"Proud?" The Curator let out a bitter laugh. "When my rehabilitation program is complete, I will be on my way."

"When will that be?" Iggy asked politely.

"Whenever Lady Phelia deems I am rehabilitated." He placed the books and scrolls into neat stacks on a table, then rolled away on his tentacles.

Iggy walked across the table and stared up, up, up at the formidable stack in front of him. He pulled a scroll out of a nearby pile instead and blew the dust from it.

Merlynda took in the dozens of books, parchments, and scrolls. She wished Neci were there.

Neci wanted to spend the day with Merlynda, but also she didn't. Rather than think about this contradiction, she threw herself into her lessons.

Skilled practitioners of Oceasha looked like they were dancers instead of fighters. Neci didn't look like either. Instead of stepping lightly, she stomped. Her transitions were jerky and harsh. And when she and Arjia sparred, Neci didn't know how to treat it like anything other than a Nordving wrestling brawl.

Neci stabbed Faithful into the seagrass ground after

stumbling over her own feet for the umpteenth time. "Have you got anything to punch or kick?" she growled.

Arjia sat next to Neci in a meditative pose. "You must flow like the current."

Neci pounded the ground. "How am I supposed to flow like currents of water when I'm loyal and grounded like earth?"

Arjia studied her. "You are anchored in Earth, which is strong and loyal. But Earth also has rock and stone, and is difficult to change. Tell me. What has made you so hardened?"

Neci twisted bits of seagrass between her fingers. She knew the answer, but it wasn't very knightly. "I haven't been much of a best friend," she said in a small voice. "Merlynda has this amazing power. Glorious things are expected of her!"

"But?"

"But she never *wanted* any of that. She just wanted to get a spell right once in a while."

"And you would feel differently in her shoes?"

"I'd love her shoes!" Neci cried. "A mysterious quest? Destined for greatness? Knights live for mysterious quests and destined greatness!"

She got quiet again and looked down. "So I guess I feel a little ugly inside. Because she's only ever believed that I could be a knight, and I feel like I've betrayed her."

Arjia gently lifted Neci's chin. "Why do you believe this is only Merlynda's quest and destiny?"

Neci stared back. "Because nothing exciting happens to me. Merlynda's family history is full of epic legends.

Mine is full of people who are good at selling carrots."

"Humble beginnings do not preclude you from great things. No one is truly no one."

Earth might have hardened stone, but it also had soft clay. Neci could already feel the anger shifting. After all, she'd decided to answer destiny's call by coming on this quest, and to make her own future by pursuing her knighthood.

She climbed to her feet. "Can we try again?"

Merlynda risked bothering the Curator for some parchment and a quill, then took note of anything that might help them. The quill was helpfully enchanted to write on its own. This made the process much faster, though she did scold Iggy for writing down a recipe for sea-turtle stew.

Her eyes were bleary, and the words were starting to swirl together when she turned a page in an ancient volume titled *Merlyn's Mighty Accomplishments* and started awake.

"Iggy," she whispered. "Iggy, *look.*"

The wyvern yawned but slithered over, then jerked awake. "You found it!"

It was the page—the *exact* page—that Percy had sent her. There was the circle of stone pillars, with the moons and suns arcing above it, meeting as a Shadow Sun in the middle.

"How did Percy get it?" Merlynda marveled. "We don't have this book at home."

She looked at the quill, poised and ready for further instructions. Merlynda hesitated—defacing books was a great crime, as far as she was concerned—but she had to know. She slid the book under the quill.

"The Hollower," Merlynda instructed, holding her breath.

The quill darted across the page, forming the same swirly writing that had been on Percy's parchment:

The Hollower.

"Merlynda," Iggy whispered. "It's the same! How is it the same? How could you lose a piece of parchment that's right here in this book?"

"No clue!" Excited, Merlynda read:

> *During his final battle with Morgan le Fey,*
> *Merlyn lured the sorceress to the Omnivia, a*
> *place uniquely linked with the In-Between. His*
> *risky but brilliant plan required him to create*
> *a portal not to the In-Between, but to a place*
> *beyond the In-Between, so that the evil sorceress*
> *would be banished forever. (See Appendix R.52*
> *for a full list of Merlyn's known portals.) While*
> *Merlyn jealously guarded his technique for*
> *creating portals, some believe the Omnivia—*

"There you are."

"Lady Phelia!" Merlynda exclaimed. "We found it! We found the Omnivia!"

Merlynda expected Lady Phelia to be pleased, but a frown flitted across her face. "How wonderful," she intoned.

"Now we know where to find Percy!" Merlynda picked up Iggy and hugged him.

Lady Phelia didn't seem pleased at all. "You must stop allowing other pursuits to distract you," she said. "Your goal is to defeat the Hollower. To fulfill the prophecy of the Septimum Genus."

Merlynda paused and looked at the Oceanid. "My goal is to save Percy. I only care about being the Septimum Genus if it's going to help rescue him. Defeating the Hollower just happens to be part of that."

"You must focus!" Lady Phelia hissed. "Your chief weakness is that you allow your affection for others to draw you away from your purpose. Neci has come a long way today in her recovery, working with Arjia. It is time for you to do the same."

Lady Phelia's choice of words made Merlynda stiffen. "Recovery," she repeated. "Do you mean *rehabilitation*?"

Lady Phelia smiled, but it wasn't a gentle smile. "Yes, we would consider this a part of her rehabilitation."

Merlynda stood, Iggy perched on her shoulder. "Neci doesn't need rehabilitation. And neither do I."

"Every creature who comes to Oceanus needs rehabilitation. Neci needed healing from her envy, Batu from his arrogance—and you and Ignus, from your distractions and doubts. You are failing, Septimum Genus, and failure has dire consequences for our very existence."

Merlynda felt Iggy tighten his claws. "We didn't choose to come to Oceanus," she said carefully. "You sent the sirens for us."

Realization hit Merlynda. *All who enter here leave changed,* the sign leading into Oceanus had said. "You always intended to keep us here," she accused. "To 'rehabilitate' us, whatever you think that means."

"Not everyone recognizes their need for healing." Lady Phelia stroked the spine of a book with her willowy blue finger. "But in the end, we ensure others receive the fullness of our generosity."

The Curator's word came back to Merlynda, from when she'd told him that Lady Phelia was supposed to be researching the Omnivia. *She's done no such thing,* he'd said.

"You knew." Merlynda tried to keep her voice from shaking. "All along, you already knew about the Omnivia. That Percy's message led there."

Lady Phelia inclined her head in admission. "As I have said, Septimum Genus, you must focus. If Percy's message is to be trusted, we know where to find the Hollower, and when." Her voice went cold. "Tomorrow we resume your training to defeat him. *Without* distractions."

The table trembled, but Merlynda pushed back, trying to calm down. She bowed. "Of course, Lady Phelia."

Once the Oceanid was out of sight, the shaking stopped. Merlynda breathed.

"We're leaving, right?" Iggy whispered.

"Yep. Tonight."

"What's the plan?"

"I haven't gotten that far."

In which Merlynda uses a
great deal of magic

 eci waited for Merlynda at dinner so she could apologize for being an unknightly friend. It was tough work being thrown around and stumbling over your feet all day, however, so when Merlynda didn't show up, she ate and went back to her room. She'd see Merlynda at breakfast.

Only it definitely was not breakfast time when she found herself being shaken awake and dragged out of bed.

"What?" Neci asked from where she'd tumbled to the floor. "What's happening?"

Merlynda was shoving things into Neci's satchel. "We're leaving. Now."

Neci caught the clothes Merlynda threw at her. "Why weren't you at dinner?"

"I was in the library."

Merlynda looked up when Neci didn't respond. She was pretending to sleep, ignoring her.

Iggy nudged Merlynda's hand. He'd found the crumpled trading parchment, waterlogged and warped.

Merlynda picked it up and sat by Neci. "I'm sorry I've been so focused on training that I haven't made time for you. We're on this quest together. Lady Phelia thinks wanting to save Percy is a distraction. She also said *you're* a distraction, and that tomorrow we're going to continue training *without* distractions."

Neci opened one eye.

"Everyone here except for the Oceanids is in some sort of rehabilitation program," Merlynda continued.

"Even us?"

"Especially us. And as I'm failing mine, Lady Phelia hinted she's got something big planned." Merlynda examined the trading parchment. Everything was connected to the Aether, so it was too, right? She focused on the trading parchment, but she also focused past it, to where the Aether was, to where the magic laughed. She tried to make her magic laugh with it.

She heard a *snap* and looked down, fearing the worst.

The parchment was whole and brand-new again. She grinned, handing it to Neci.

Neci stared at the painted faces of Dame Joi and Merlyn. It was perfect.

She climbed out of bed and dressed in a hurry. How dare the Oceanids carry on such a deception! A secret escape in the middle of the night with her best friend sounded like the perfect revenge.

The trio stopped in with Batu before leaving. "Lady Phelia is doing *what*?" he asked.

"Rehabilitating us," Merlynda repeated. "Are you coming or not?"

Of course Batu was coming. Getting away from the Oceanids sounded like a capital plan, and he was thrilled they'd decided to invite him along. "Yes. Erm—thanks. And I'm sorry about—before. With the sirens. And everything else."

They stood awkwardly.

"Well, let's get on, then," Neci said. "Grab what you need."

"This is it." Batu looped his ocarina's cord around his neck.

"What's that?" Neci tried not to sound too interested, but she'd never seen anything like it before.

Batu looked down at where the ocarina rested against his chest. "An ocarina. Xanthe gave it to me. She said it's my token."

They peeked outside of Batu's door, then stole down the hall. Merlynda trailed behind, and Iggy nipped her ear.

"What?" she snapped.

"Envy doesn't suit you."

Merlynda huffed. "Neci got a dagger, and now Batu has an ocarina. It's *my* quest. I'm the one with a vanished brother. Shouldn't *I* have a token?"

Iggy looked down at himself, then back at her. "Maybe I'm your token?"

Her irritation melted away. "You're much better than a token."

Neci led the way. They snuck along as quickly as they could, ducking into empty rooms and nooks when an Oceanid or water lamp floated by. Before the lamps had seemed beautiful, but now it felt like they were watching everything. And, the questers realized, maybe they were.

They moved faster.

At last they reached the cavern they'd arrived in. Bubble carriage after bubble carriage sat on the spongy ground, like the one that had brought Lena in when they'd first arrived.

"This is the plan?" Batu whispered.

"Do you have a better idea?" Neci challenged.

He didn't.

"Which one should we pick?" Merlynda whispered.

"That one's closest to the membrane," Batu said, gesturing. "Might be easiest."

"But it's the farthest from *us*," Neci pointed out.

They scowled at each other, then turned to Merlynda.

"Um. Let's go for the far one," Merlynda decided. "We'll be able to leave the fastest."

Batu turned to Neci. "What's the plan?"

She started. Not only did Batu not crow that they were going to the bubble *he'd* picked out, but he'd asked her for instructions.

"Looks empty," Neci said. "Let's make a run for it."

Merlynda could feel the Aether throughout Oceanus—she'd been able to ever since that first training session with Lady Phelia, so at least *some* good had come from their time here—and she felt when the pulse of the city quickened.

"Now," Merlynda whispered. "They're coming!"

The children bolted across the cavern, Iggy clinging to Merlynda for dear life. If only his wings were grown!

"Merlynda!"

The shout thundered across the cavern, bouncing off the spongy ground and the rocks and the membrane. They kept running, but the ground rippled and shook. Sections broke away from one another, creating canyons.

Neci leapt over a trench. "Almost there!"

And then the floor shot up in front of her and she slammed into it, and Batu into her, and before they could find their footing, the spongy ground had grown up around their feet and snaked up to trap their arms against their bodies.

Merlynda felt the ground's attack before it struck. Her scribbled notes from the library scattered from her robes as she leapt up and missed the first arm that shot toward her. It didn't matter. Another section jolted from below like a geyser, wrapping around and around her body, pinning Iggy against her shoulder.

Lady Phelia, Arjia, and several other Oceanids filled the cavern.

"Does the Septimum Genus tire of our hospitality?" Lady Phelia asked. "Or is she running from her own destiny?"

"I'm running *to* it!" Merlynda *shook*—with anger, with fear, with magic.

"Arjia, how could you?" Neci shouted. She struggled and thrashed but couldn't budge.

Arjia bowed her head. "I hope you still feel as if you've gained something from your time here, Neci the Ardent."

"Looks like I'll have longer to work on it," Neci spat. If only she could reach her dagger!

"No, Neci the Ardent," Lady Phelia said. "You prevent the Septimum Genus from achieving her true potential. You lure her away from her destiny. But since Merlynda has no interest in avoiding distractions, I've no choice but to eliminate them for her." She cocked her head to the side. Neci and Batu felt spongy arms slither up and circle around their necks.

"No, please!" Merlynda begged.

Lady Phelia's face was set. "Rest assured, Septimum Genus, this is for the good of all. Even now, we race toward the Shadow Sun. You lack discipline but have such potential, such power! Raw emotion triggers this power. Let their deaths be the fuel you need to embrace destiny and defeat the Hollower."

Neci and Batu gasped as the sponge arms tightened.

"Stop this!" Merlynda howled. The ground vibrated, and Merlynda tried to concentrate. She breathed, and the magic welled up inside her, like so many times before. She felt the place where it laughed.

Lady Phelia took a few steps closer, observing the children. "You must focus on the purity of the Aether. These two are not worthy of your attentions."

Iggy let out a vicious hiss, and Merlynda's eyes blazed as she stared into Lady Phelia's ocean-deep eyes. It felt as though Fire itself swirled inside her, ready to pour out. Cracks formed in the sponge beneath her. "We are all of the Aether, Lady Phelia. We are *all* worthy."

Merlynda stopped trying to control the magic. She pushed with all her might past the Water and into the Aether and was met with the same barrier as usual—only this time she was counting on it.

She reached for Iggy's magic at the same time he reached for hers, and when their magics met, everything burst.

Oceanids ducked and cried out as chunks of sponge and coral blasted toward them. Merlynda fell to the ground and stumbled to her feet, catching Iggy and cradling him against her chest. Neci and Batu broke out of their prisons, stomping on twitching sponge arms.

They ran, Neci and Batu charging ahead, Merlynda firing blast after blast to keep the Oceanids at bay. It wasn't refined, there was no technique or elegance, and there was no control. But it was effective.

They leapt into the bubble, popping inside the same way they'd entered through the membrane. Batu scrambled around. It was empty inside, no lever or wheel in sight. "How do you make it go?" The Oceanids had recovered and were already halfway across the cavern—and they knew how to control their magic *and* fight.

"Arjia told me it's intuitive," Neci said.

"What's that mean?"

"Think about where you want to go!"

Iggy peered outside the bubble. Oceanids looked vicious when they were angry. "I would like to leave."

"Me too!" the others chorused.

The bubble drifted up and out, stopping just outside the membrane.

Merlynda glanced back at the cavern anxiously. "Why did we stop?"

"We have to all want the same thing," Neci explained. "It'll get confused if we all give it different directions."

Oceanids leapt through the membrane and swam for them.

"Away!" Neci shouted. "We all want away!"

The bubble shot through the water, faster than even the Oceanids could swim, until the lights of the moving city had disappeared in the darkness of the deeps.

It was a relief to be away from the known danger, but that left another problem. They were alone, in the middle of the ocean, with cold and darkness pressing in from all sides. Iggy solved the last problem by glowing, and everyone shielded their eyes from the sudden reddish-gold light. Pleased with himself, he climbed higher up Merlynda's arm so the light spread better.

"That's clever, Ignus," Batu said after a moment.

Iggy cocked his head in Batu's direction. "Really?"

The minstrel meant it. "Really."

Iggy settled onto Merlynda's head. "I've grown some too, you know."

They sat in silence for a while as they settled into their escape. Merlynda glowered as she stroked Iggy's tail. Their escape had drained her. She knew she hadn't caused any irreparable harm to Oceanus despite the size of her explosion, and part of her wished she had. She pushed those thoughts away. The Oceanids had been in the wrong, but that didn't give her any right to dole out punishment. It would make her no better than them.

Neci also fumed, not only because Lady Phelia had tried to kill her, but also because of how she'd lied to and manipulated each of them. Talking with Arjia *had* helped, but to force a sneaky rehabilitation program on them lacked honor. How could the Oceanids know what any of them needed, having only just met them? Now Neci saw that all those days of sitting quietly had been meant to make her resentful, to drive a wedge between her and Merlynda.

Batu stared at his ocarina, deep in his own thoughts. He'd noticed Xanthe wasn't at the cavern. She'd always struck him as being different from the other Oceanids, separate somehow. Had she only given him the ocarina as a part of his "rehabilitation"? That was difficult to accept.

He couldn't see anything outside the bubble beyond Iggy's light. Being trapped underwater in a bubble wasn't much better than being trapped underwater *outside* of a bubble, in his opinion. There wasn't much separating them from the rest of the ocean.

Batu stole a quick peek at the others, grateful they'd thought to bring him along. After his behavior, he certainly didn't deserve their consideration and hoped he could be worthy of it. "Shall I play something?"

"Yes, please," Neci said. Batu being nice was still weird, but the silence was almost as suffocating as the darkness.

The minstrel picked up the ocarina and blew a warm breath into it, playing up and down a scale. It was high and clear, the musical companion to his voice. He grinned—not at anything in particular, just at being able to play. He took another breath, almost forgetting the darkness, and began an old song he loved playing on his lute.

Halfway through, a wailing moan pierced the water— from *outside*. A shadow deeper than the darkness around them glided past. Iggy's glow flashed across a terrible face with ferocious stained teeth and black eyes.

It slammed into their bubble, and Iggy's light blinked out.

They all tumbled and bumped into one another in the darkness until Neci finally called for them to quit moving. "Are we all still thinking about getting away?"

"Yes," Batu answered. "But I can't tell if we're moving."

"Do you think we could use some light?" Iggy asked.

Everyone chorused their agreement. Iggy made himself glow a little—only a little, at first. When that seemed all right, he glowed a bit more. A shadow moved behind Merlynda, and in a panic Iggy glowed with all his might.

It would have been better if they'd stayed in the dark.

A Word about Mermaids

The mermaids you are likely accustomed to are from ill-informed and fanciful storybooks. Mermaids are often portrayed as beautiful young women lazily sunning themselves on a rock. They might flip their tail playfully to splash friends, or mischievously to splash enemies. If this is what you think mermaids are like, you are wrong.

Mermaids belong to the undead and hunt for magic. They both crave the Aether and fear it. This mermaid knew nothing of traveling bubbles or wyverns or ocarinas, but it knew the scent of magic better than even the scent of the ocean it lived in.

When Iggy glowed, the mermaid moaned from pain but also from pleasure. Light is love, but after such a long time spent in darkness, it can be difficult to embrace what is good. So the mermaid did what mermaids do when driven by a mindless hunger for magic.

It attacked.

The mermaid flung itself at the bubble and tore furiously with its claws. Half of its face was missing from decay, picked away by hungry fish. The travelers yelled and tried to back away, but they could only move so far. Iggy scrambled from Merlynda to Neci, to Batu, and back again.

"It's following Iggy's light!" Merlynda exclaimed.

"Don't let it get me!" Iggy wailed.

Merlynda thrust a finger at Batu. "Play something," she ordered.

"But I don't—"

"Play!" Merlynda roared.

Batu swept up his ocarina and played a single long note. The mermaid stopped.

The minstrel began a slow, haunting tune, capturing the feeling of the endless depths of the oceans, the terror of being trapped, the isolation of being countless fathoms deep beneath the surface and the sun.

The mermaid listened. Then it let out a terrible wail, again and again and again.

"Is it working?" Iggy asked from inside Merlynda's collar.

"No," Neci whispered. "It's calling for more of them."

She was right. Dozens of the creatures darted around them, and more arrived every second. Batu locked eyes with the first mermaid, staring into its horrible blackness and stumbling over his melody.

The mermaid charged.

The others followed, swarming so thickly around the bubble that there was barely any space for the water. They shrieked and clawed to get inside. A small stream of water sprayed into the bubble, followed by a second, and then a third.

"Plug the holes!" Batu shouted, ocarina forgotten. He lunged to suit action to words.

"With what?" Neci cried. She shoved her finger into one, then jerked it back when a mermaid snapped at it.

"Anything!" Batu ripped his tunic into shreds to stuff into the holes. "Merlynda, *do* something!"

"I can't! What if I make our bubble disappear, or magic one of them inside?"

"You can do it, Merlynda," Neci shouted over the mermaids' wailing. The water was ankle-deep.

"You saved us in Oceanus," Batu said. "You can save us here."

"We can do it," Iggy whispered into Merlynda's ear.

Merlynda shut her eyes and focused. Iggy's magic melded with her own, and they stumbled along. She found the place where the magic was, where it sat laughing at her, and she tugged on it. Not on the Water elements, or the Air elements, or any elements alone, but on the magic itself. *Hard.*

There was a brilliant flash of light outside the bubble. Hundreds of the terrifying creatures were silhouetted against the brightness. An explosion like cannon fire radiated through the depths, knocking any mermaids between the light and the bubble miles away. Merlynda held on to the magic long enough to know the mermaids were scattered, that she and her friends were safe.

Then the light disappeared, and she collapsed with a splash.

"Merlynda!" Neci cried. She fell to her knees and pulled Merlynda's head onto her lap, out of the water that had leaked inside. The wizardess was out cold. "Iggy, can you help her?"

Iggy swam over, sluggish. "Look, Merlynda," he mumbled. "I'm a sea serpent." He laid his head on her chest and closed his eyes, faintly glowing.

"Think about getting away again," Batu said. "Think about going up."

Neci did. They were still taking on water. "Is it working?" she whispered.

"I don't know." Batu glanced at Merlynda and Iggy. If they all had to think the same thing at the same time for the bubble to move—

They tore strips of clothing to stuff into the holes. This helped, but the Oceanids had apparently realized that bubbles weren't the most defensible means of transport. Already, the scratches and bite marks were healing on their own.

Neci propped Merlynda up so that she stayed above the water, and gently adjusted Iggy's tail. Merlynda had never fallen like this before. She'd never done *anything* like this before. Between blasting things in Oceanus and then blasting those horrible creatures—not to mention Lady Phelia's brutal training schedule—the wizardess was probably totally spent.

Merlynda had stirred somewhat awake by the time the bubble had healed. Groggy, she recalled the horrible scratching claws and the deadened eyes of the mermaids—

She bolted up, startling Neci and flinging Iggy off her chest and into the pool of water trapped inside the bubble.

"I beg your pardon!" the wyvern yelped.

"Sorry!" Merlynda fished Iggy out and propped him up on her shoulder, then slumped against the side of the bubble and shivered. She was too tired to do anything else, and the water was *cold*. She'd done more magic today than in the rest of her life put together—which was saying something, she reflected. She might have been pleased if she weren't so exhausted. Things still exploded, but at least they'd mostly exploded on *her* terms.

Iggy looked down at himself. He held his breath and glowed, warming up so that the water evaporated in a little puff of fog.

Batu stared at him. "I didn't know you could do that."

"Oh, I'm full of surprises."

Neci sat next to Merlynda so the wizardess could lean

against her. "Are you all right? How did you do that?"

"Just c-c-c-cold." Merlynda's teeth chattered, and Iggy wrapped himself around her shoulders to help warm her. "We did it by making another magical explosion."

The wyvern shifted so he could better warm his wizardess. "I'd say we're getting better. At explosions, that is."

Merlynda looked outside. The mermaids were gone, but dark ocean stretched in all directions, darker even than the portal that took Percy. Her brother's terrified face flashed in front of her again, and the tightness in her chest returned. She pushed it aside. "I know where we need to go."

She reached inside her sleeve and pulled out a waterlogged page. She stared at it, then made it good as new, the way she had with Neci's trading parchment, and handed it to Neci.

Neci unfolded the paper, and Batu leaned over to see. It was the same as Percy's parchment! "How did you—"

"There wasn't time to explain before," Merlynda rushed out. "But I found it! It's called the Omnivia. I had loads of other notes, but they fell out in the cavern." She remembered the Oceanid's deception, and fury rose in her once more. "Lady Phelia knew the whole time but didn't tell us."

Batu and Neci let out cries of outrage, then glanced at each other in surprised solidarity before looking away.

"Also," Merlynda went on, seething at the memory of the cavern, "are you both all right? What Lady Phelia said about you two back there, what she tried to do—she's *wrong*. Who does she think she is, deciding who's worthy of anything?"

"Oh, that," Neci said. "Being strangled by sponge arms wasn't my favorite, but Lady Phelia clearly didn't know what she was talking about."

"Bit controlling, that one," Batu agreed. He'd learned a long time ago that if someone needed to have that much control, it would probably be impossible to earn their respect, so their opinion shouldn't hold much weight.

Neci studied the page Merlynda had handed her. "Did *you* actually rip this out of a *book?*" she asked her.

"I also stole a scrying shell. Don't tell the Curator—he's scary. It's in your satchel."

"Hey," Batu said. "You got a token!"

Merlynda considered this as Neci handed her the shell. "I don't think it counts if it's stolen." She scooped some water up, then stared at the full shell. She tipped it, spilling the contents out to form a water model of the illustration.

Despite everything, Merlynda grinned. The scrying shell had formed the ring of standing stones in every detail. It even showed which pillars had a third stone stacked across them, creating empty doorways to nowhere. "This is the Omnivia. Merlyn made it and then conjured a Concursus to trap Morgan le Fey beyond the In-Between. And then he destroyed it." She leaned her head back and closed her eyes, weariness seeping in. Her whole body felt heavy.

Neci peered at the water stones. "That seems like a waste."

Merlynda opened her eyes. "Merlyn had to. He'd created a place so full of magic, it was a direct doorway to the

In-Between—to the Aether. That's what Morgan le Fey wanted. After he trapped her *beyond* the In-Between, he broke the Concursus and the Omnivia so that she couldn't get out. And then he quit making his own portals and refused to tell anyone else how he did it. He said no one *should* know—it was too dangerous."

The water stones splashed into the bottom of the bubble. "And you think the Hollower wants to use this place's power?" Batu asked.

"I don't know. Probably?" Merlynda thought for a moment. "Stories about the Hollower have been around for *centuries*. That's a long time to be storing up magic. And he has Percy." Who happened to be particularly magical. "There are only stories of the Hollower taking magic, not using it. My guess is that he's planning something big, and if the Hollower needs to open a powerful portal, this is the place to do it." If that were true, then what would be on the other side?

Merlynda scooped more water into the shell, tipped it again, and thought of Percy. She watched eagerly as the water swirled, but it stayed blank the way it had in Oceanus. Disappointed, she allowed the water to fall back into their bubble.

I'm coming Percy, she thought, clinging to the hope of the Omnivia. *We're coming.*

The adventurers all thought very hard about the Omnivia, and eventually the water around the bubble grew lighter and clearer until it rushed up to the surface and popped into the cheerful morning sunlight near the shore.

"Oh, happy day!" Iggy crowed. He set to sunning himself on top of Merlynda's head. It had been hard work to keep glowing this entire time, but he was happy to provide light for his friends. His friends and Batu, that was.

They guided the bubble to the shore, then pushed themselves out, relieved. It rolled itself back over the water, descended, and was gone.

The travelers scanned the wide, empty beach, drenched from the water that had leaked into their bubble. Neci had somehow managed to keep her hair dry, but the other two hadn't fared so well. They jumped and stomped to warm themselves in the sun. "Which way do we go now?" Neci asked.

Before Merlynda could answer, the travelers heard a familiar screech.

"It's the falcon!" Batu shouted. The bird shot across the sky, then dove straight for Merlynda.

"Run!" she shouted.

The children dashed off along the sand. The falcon swooped close, and Neci slashed at it with her dagger. A chill crept through Merlynda—the bird felt cold, or empty.

A silver flash streaked toward the adventurers from above, forcing the falcon to abort its dive. It screeched, then wheeled and turned, trying to get past the newcomer.

The children gaped as they ran, awed. A magnificent silver horse, dappled with black spots along her flank, twirled and darted after the falcon with flashing silver-and-black wings. A single onyx horn spiraled out from her head.

"Look at those wings!" Iggy marveled from where he was hiding in Merlynda's collar. "Have you ever seen anything so wondrous? Do you think mine will be like that, Merlynda?" He flapped his little nubs, but they were barely big enough to wiggle.

Merlynda couldn't answer because of the stitch in her side from running.

The falcon cut to the side, and the horned pegasus—for that is what the new arrival was—overshot it, unable to turn as fast as the smaller creature.

Merlynda didn't think. She grabbed at the Air around her, then smashed it together. Sand burst out in all directions from the sudden force, and the falcon crashed into the Air wall. It tumbled to the beach, then stood and shook its head. A black void blossomed next to it.

Before anyone could grab it, the falcon hopped up, glided inside the portal, and was gone.

The horned pegasus gracefully landed before the children. "Are you all right?"

The children nodded, but Iggy was so starstruck all he could do was blush.

"I am Dame Illondria, knight of the Air, pledged to serve the Aether." She stood to her full majestic height and looked at Merlynda. "Are you the Septimum Genus?"

Now Merlynda blushed. "Um—technically, yes. Were you—are you looking for me?"

The horned pegasus knelt on her forelegs and bowed. "Not directly, but I am glad you are found. I am sensitive to the ebb and flow of the Aether in all its elements and sensed the desperate magic used beneath the waters. Desperate, but powerful—enough to scatter an entire school of mermaids?"

"Those were *mermaids*?" Batu exclaimed.

"I've never met a mermaid I liked," Iggy said.

Merlynda reached up a finger to stroke him. "That's only because all the mermaids you know just tried to kill us." Merlynda introduced everyone, then turned back to Dame Illondria. "Thanks for going after the falcon. This isn't the first time it's attacked us."

The horned pegasus stood tall and studied where the falcon had disappeared. "There's something deeply wrong with that creature."

"Yes." The wrongness of the falcon made Merlynda shiver even though she was warm and dry again. Iggy clambered out from his hiding place to her shoulder, pricking her skin with his claws. "It felt—cold. Dark."

Dame Illondria glowered. "Twisted."

Neci sheathed Faithful. "We think it works for the Hollower."

In overlapping jumbles, they told Dame Illondria about their journey. She pawed at the ground in thought. "The Shadow Sun is in two days' time. The day after tomorrow."

The adventurers looked at one another. "That's impossible," Merlynda said. "We only arrived at Oceanus a few weeks ago. We should have months until then."

The horned pegasus narrowed her eyes and gave a short snort. "I see the Oceanids were not entirely forthcoming about their city. Time operates differently in Oceanus, Septimum Genus. It's always in motion, like the current or tide, but varies its pace just as the rivers and oceans do. If the Oceanids had you in their city, then you may have spent weeks that felt like years, or months that felt like days."

Everything slowed around Merlynda then, became dim and muffled. Dame Illondria's words settled onto her skin and stung her mind like an allover itch. Neci's and Batu's cries of disbelief felt miles away.

Iggy's fury was immediate, ever present, united with Merlynda's own rush of betrayal and *hurt*. She had worked so hard, come so far. She had put everything into finding Percy, and even though she'd always heard her doubts whispering that it wasn't enough, that *she* wasn't enough, she took comfort in knowing time was on her side. With that knowledge came the hope that when the Shadow Sun finally arrived, she'd know enough, be strong enough, *be* enough.

Lady Phelia had tried to take Percy from her by lying about the Omnivia, which Merlynda had thankfully discovered. She'd tried to take Neci by killing her, which Merlynda had miraculously thwarted. But now the Oceanid had snatched away weeks and months of training, of preparation, and Merlynda could never get that back.

Lady Phelia had stolen her hope.

She screamed then, loud and long and wild, dropping

to her knees, overwhelmed by grief. It clawed through her, devastating her with its waves, crushing every last wisp of hope in its wake. Merlynda clutched her head, shaking with failure.

Two days? To find this Omnivia, to defeat the Hollower, to rescue Percy? Any one of those tasks felt impossible, but saving Percy depended on accomplishing the most unlikely feat of all. How could Merlynda learn to control her magic in what amounted to a few hours when she'd been unable to her entire life?

The world sped back up, and Merlynda realized she was still screaming, her throat stripped raw. She looked down at a pressure on her wrist and found Iggy curled up there, offering what comfort he could. She swallowed, tried to breathe, but still the grief crushed her.

"Why didn't they say something?" Neci was roaring. "They knew we needed to find Percy!"

"They don't care," Merlynda croaked out, defeated. "Lady Phelia doesn't care about Percy. Only about stopping the Hollower, whatever it takes." The grief pulled her toward the sand, but Merlynda struggled to her feet. "Remember what she said when she tried to kill you and Batu? 'Even now, we race toward the Shadow Sun.' She was manipulating time so that I'd explode things at the right moment. I bet she had a way to get to the Omnivia already planned too."

Dame Illondria nodded. "The Oceanids believe themselves on the side of good, but their methods do not always match their intentions. You were wise to make your escape."

"I only wish we'd done it sooner," Merlynda said bitterly. "She probably never sent any messages home, either. Merlyn's goat, we've been missing almost seven months! Our parents must be out of their minds with worry."

Merlynda grabbed a fistful of her hair in despair. Iggy clung to her wrist and didn't complain. He knew his wizardess was going through a lot.

The thought of Merlynda's parents returning to find an aggrieved Uncle William and no twins was troublesome enough, but then another dilemma struck her. "And how much more magic has the Hollower been able to steal?"

"Long have there been whisperings of the Hollower's growing power, but do not distress, Septimum Genus." The horned pegasus's eyes were bright. "The Omnivia is not so far from here, less than two days' flight. There is time yet. I will carry you and your knightly companion and help you defeat this evil."

Neci couldn't help beaming. A knight had just called her knightly!

Merlynda bowed her head, unable to speak. Being so close to the Omnivia should have felt like an enormous stroke of luck, but what good would she be when she arrived? She doubted a failed wizardess could stop the Hollower.

"Thank you, Dame Illondria. I'm going to try to get a message to my parents before we leave." Merlynda stepped apart from the group with Iggy. She didn't have any spare parchment since her notes had scattered during the flight from Oceanus, so she pictured a scroll in her mind, and what she wanted it to say. She reached for the Air and felt Iggy's magic intertwining with her own, their power working together as it had never done before. Together they pushed past the Air and into the Aether—

Fwoosh! The sand shot up in front of Merlynda like a geyser. Her Aether shield sprang into place unbidden. Merlynda watched as the sand sputtered out (the others were thankfully upwind), refusing to cry again. She was exhausted, and another hard cry might do her in.

"Well, then," Merlynda said, ignoring the laughing magic as she turned back to the others. "I suppose all that's left to do is head to the Omnivia."

Dame Illondria turned to Batu. "And what will you do, Master Batu?"

Her eyes bored into him with such intensity that Batu was sure she could see his very heart. He'd been wondering the same thing. "I'd planned to travel abroad. . . ." He drew the words out. "Alone. But . . ." Batu's eyes darted at the girls and Iggy, then down at the sand. "But I was wondering if maybe you wouldn't mind your trio becoming a quartet?"

Merlynda blinked in surprise. "You want to come with us?"

Neci hadn't expected this either. "After all that talk about wandering on your own?"

Iggy eyed him suspiciously. "You're willing to share your food?"

"All of it!" Batu burst out. "I've never had anyone to share anything *with* before. Not . . . friends."

There was silence.

"You can talk about it." Batu hurried back a few steps to give them some privacy.

The trio huddled up.

"He's hiding something," Iggy said.

"What?" Merlynda asked.

The wyvern stretched out to sneak a glimpse of Batu. "I don't know. But I think we can trust him anyway. I vote yes."

"That's good enough for me," Merlynda said. "I vote yes too. Something happened to him in Oceanus."

Neci agreed. Something had happened to each of them in Oceanus. Nearly being devoured by mermaids together meant she and Batu had reached a truce of sorts, and he *had* been nicer since their escape. They stepped back toward Batu and faced him as one.

"Dame Illondria." Neci turned to the horned pegasus. "Can you carry three people to the Omnivia?"

The tension in Batu's shoulders vanished. "You mean it?"

Iggy twisted to catch the sun at his favorite angle. "I still haven't decided if you can call me Iggy."

"He'll come around," Merlynda whispered to Batu.

"I heard that. But you're probably not wrong."

The newly minted quartet carefully climbed onto Dame Illondria's back. No one needed to tell them that riding the horned pegasus was a great honor. Even regular pegasuses rarely offer themselves as transport, so you can imagine how much prouder a horned pegasus would be.

"Hold tight," Dame Illondria called back to them. She broke into a trot, sped up to a gallop, and then with a powerful leap they were airborne.

"We're flying!" Iggy shouted. "Merlynda, we're flying!"

Her familiar's pure delight rushed through her. It beat back the despair, if only a bit.

They flew for hours, zipping past meadows and rivers until they were far beyond the edge of a dark forest, denser than even the Howlwyn. When the sun was nearly set, Dame Illondria began to look for a clearing to spend the night in. Strange, dark shapes covered the sky ahead of them, blocking what little sunlight remained.

As they glided down, something small and sleek whistled past Merlynda's ear. At first she thought it was the falcon, but the falcon didn't whistle. Another whistle shot past, tearing a hole in Merlynda's sleeve.

Neci ducked. "We're under attack!"

They were arrows—volley after volley, so many that in the fading light, it looked like a swarm of angry black bugs coming for them.

"Hold tightly!" Dame Illondria neighed, then dove into a tight spiral, dodging this way and that, looking for an opening to escape. She flew her finest, but she'd already had a brief battle that day, and she'd carried three children and a wyvern for most of it, and, magical creature or not, she was weary.

One of the arrows dug into her flank, and she bucked.

"Batu!" Neci reached back for him, but he was gone. "Batu!" she screamed again.

A second arrow found its mark in Dame Illondria, and a third. Arrow after arrow sank in, until she couldn't beat her wings anymore, couldn't keep them going.

The magnificent horned pegasus, servant of the Aether, fell.

*In which Merlynda receives
an unwelcome accessory*

Batu plummeted down, down, down, coal-colored hair flying behind him. There were worse ways to meet death, but he was so terrified, he couldn't think of any. He wondered if his parents would be happy to see him, or sad that they would be reunited so soon.

The trees rushed closer. Maybe he'd get impaled on a branch instead of splattering all over the ground. Splattering might be better—things would be over quicker. He hoped for that.

He gripped his ocarina and faced his death like a noble minstrel.

+ + +

Neci held on only a moment longer than Batu before she was hurled off. She stared up at Dame Illondria as she fell, watching the beautiful silver-black wings flap and strain.

There was nothing to be done. Her dagger had come loose from its sheath in the chaos, but that was all right. Whoever found her body would find Faithful back inside the sheath, strapped around her waist, safe and sound.

At least something would survive. Neci turned to face her death head-on like a knight.

Merlynda and Iggy fell last. The fierce wyvern squeezed his wizardess's wrist, wailing and feeling Dame Illondria's pain as if it were his own.

Merlynda felt it too. She watched as the magnificent horned pegasus fell away beneath her, graceful even as the earthly forces swept her down.

Her friends seemed to fall so slowly. Batu and Neci weren't quite out of sight yet. Dame Illondria's wings continued to flap as she tried to regain control.

Merlynda listened to Iggy as he screamed with Dame Illondria. Merlynda screamed too.

In that scream she pulled at all the magic, every speck and fiber, every sinew and breath. From the Air around her and the Earth below her, from the Fire and Water inside her as every element was supposed to be, every possible strand.

And in that moment of screaming and pulling and connecting with all the elements, she touched the Aether.

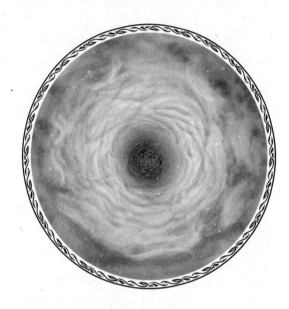

A Word about Aether

The Aether is the origin of everything. It created the In-Between and is present in all of creation. It holds all things together to this day. It is the purest magic.

When Merlynda touched the Aether, fully and with abandon, she shattered the blocks against her magic. The walls and gates and barriers that seemed too difficult for her to overcome burst into a thousand tiny fragments, never to be reassembled.

But she still needed more practice. She still did not fully understand. And she still did not have control.

And, as always, when Merlynda touched the Aether, it laughed.

Merlynda grasped onto the Aether's laughter as hard as she could. She wrestled and twisted and held on tight, held on to the feeling of the Aether. It wasn't a single element—it was all the elements, together at once. Why hadn't anyone ever told her that?

She shot her hands out to her sides, and she stopped falling.

She would not face her death. Not today. And neither would her friends.

Neci and Batu tumbled, so fast, so far. Of Earth and of Water, but not filled with the Aether. Not brimming over, like Merlynda was now.

Dame Illondria plummeted like a boulder. Of Air, but so hurt, so injured.

Merlynda screamed, all anger and frustration and fear for her friends. There was no way out.

No way except for the Aether.

It gripped Neci and Batu in a shield, so that even though they crashed through the branches, even though they rattled and bounced and screamed, when they finally stopped, they were safe.

Merlynda didn't wait to see that Neci and Batu were all right. She knew they were. She reached into the Aether and searched for Dame Illondria, but she was a breath too late.

A huge net spun out from the trees, wrapping itself around the proud majestic beast and sending her spiraling away from Merlynda's protection spell.

And then Merlynda was spent, because while it was nice to finally fully meet the Aether, it was all too much. She closed her eyes.

The fire in her burned out, and the water dried up, and she plummeted through the air toward the earth.

Iggy woke up shivering. He tried to curl more tightly around Merlynda's wrist to warm himself, but her wrist wasn't soft and reassuring, as it usually was. It was rough and scratchy. He peeked open one eye to see what was the matter.

It wasn't Merlynda's wrist at all!

Iggy bolted up and looked around in every direction. It was dark, and cold, and he was surrounded by enormous trees, and instead of being snug and cozy in his spot on Merlynda's wrist, he was hugging a branch.

There was no Merlynda! There wasn't even a Neci or a Batu or a Dame Illondria.

He was all alone. He'd *never* been alone before. In the In-Between there were all the other waiting familiars, and ever since leaving there had always been Merlynda.

Iggy thought back. Dame Illondria had been pierced with arrows, and Batu and Neci had fallen, and then Merlynda had decided that was enough of that, thank you very much, and she'd called upon the Aether—the Aether!—to save everyone. But it had been too much, and Iggy didn't know how to help her, so they'd both been overwhelmed and fallen to their doom.

Except they hadn't fallen to their doom—they'd just fallen. Merlynda was alive somewhere. Iggy could feel it. Familiars weren't any sort of familiar at all if they couldn't tell where their wizardess was.

Only he was on the floor of the forest, and Merlynda was *up*. And what's more, she was somehow *away*.

Despair filled his small body from his head to his tail, and a tear or two threatened to slip out. But he swallowed down the despair (he went ahead and let the tears slip) and took in a deep breath.

If Merlynda was *up*, he'd figure out a way to get to her, just the same as if she were down the trail or a touch to the east or halfway to the moon. And then after he'd found her, he could sort out this *away* nonsense.

He checked to see if his wings had grown in after touching the Aether—the Aether!—but they were still nubs.

Iggy stared up at the mighty tree before him. His wizardess needed him.

"I'm coming, Merlynda," he whispered. And then with his two small feet he began to climb.

Neci landed hard on the forest floor. She was fine, other than being shaken. Not a single bruise or scratch was anywhere to be found.

A thud sounded nearby, and Batu stumbled out of the brush, looking dazed. "Neci?"

"Batu!" They rushed toward each other and almost hugged, then caught themselves. Neither of them was afraid of being alone in the forest, but it felt much better to *not* be alone.

"I think Merlynda saved us," Neci said.

"Yeah. My skin is tingly from the magic."

Neither of them mentioned how wounded Dame Illondria had looked.

Neci collected her satchel from where it had landed nearby and took inventory. Everything was intact, and Faithful was already back in its sheath, strapped around her waist. She had supplies and a weapon, but no idea what had happened to the others.

Clunk, clunk, clunk, clunk.

Neci and Batu both froze. Nearby, twigs crunched and branches broke. They ducked behind a tree to see what was coming.

It was a human man. He wore a long curved sword on his belt, and his boots were strapped to heavy slabs of iron. He called out something, and another man's voice answered in a language Neci didn't know. Batu *did* know it, and he gestured at Neci to stay quiet.

Knight and minstrel shrank deeper into the shadows.

The second man, who was a dwarf, came into view. *Clunk, clunk, clunk, clunk.* His boots were also strapped to iron, but he held a longbow, arrow nocked and ready.

The sight of the arrow made Neci furious. This was who had hurt Dame Illondria! She reached for Faithful, but Batu grabbed her arm. She scowled at him but didn't struggle.

The two men exchanged a few more words, then put their weapons away and clunked off into the forest.

"That's who attacked us!" Neci hissed.

"Yes, and chucking your dagger at them wouldn't have done any good. There are two of them."

"Faithful always comes back."

"It wouldn't have been in time. Those men are Rusvokian raiders, from the east."

"Let's follow them! They might already have the others." She started forward, but Batu blocked her.

"You don't know what you're dealing with."

"We'll learn as we go." She tried to get past him again, but Batu stood his ground.

"They're dangerous!"

Neci lowered her voice but kept all the heat in it. "I thought you wanted to be a part of a quartet. Friends are always there for each other, and right now our friends need us."

Batu seethed. Of course he wanted friends, but he'd prefer the sort who didn't rush off on doomed campaigns. Then again, the regular sort of friends sounded boring.

Neci and Batu crept behind the two raiders. It was easy to track them because they were so noisy.

"How do you know they're raiders?" Neci whispered after a while.

Batu didn't answer immediately. He could probably be honest, but the full truth was difficult for him. So he opted for partial truths, which unfortunately are often still a bit like lies.

"They're Fenrir's archenemies," he answered at last. "Only Fenrir has an honorable side. If the Rusvokian warlord learns the Nordvings helped us, he'll be furious."

"Even though Fenrir kept you prisoner?"

Especially then. "Yes" was all Batu said.

The clunking stopped. They listened for another moment, then crept forward.

The two men weren't far ahead, but now they were arguing. One kept gesturing to a rope ladder that hung between them.

"The one with the sword thinks they should wait for the others," Batu translated.

Neci reached for her dagger to be ready, then paused. "How do you know what they're saying?"

Batu kept watching the Rusvokian men. The one with the longbow won out, and they began climbing the ladder. "I pick up languages easily."

"Where—"

"Hear that?" Batu interrupted.

"No—"

"Exactly. Now's our chance."

Before Neci could ask any more questions, Batu darted toward the ladder. He craned his neck to look up. It swayed as the men climbed. "I can't see where it goes, but once it quits moving, let's climb up after them."

Neci did not like that Batu was keeping something from her, and she especially did not like him telling her what to do. "Why should we follow them up there? Merlynda is probably somewhere in the forest, like we were."

"She's not."

Neci felt her face get hot. "You don't know everything, Batu!"

"You're right," Batu snapped, "but I *do* know how to speak Rusvokian!" He grabbed the ladder and pulled himself onto the first rung. "Are you coming or not?"

"Climb," Neci spat. She'd always suspected Batu was more than a musician. Now she was sure of it.

They climbed the ladder up, up, up through the trees, waiting to see where they'd end up and hoping the raiders hadn't realized that they were being followed. When they at last cleared the forest, the ladder stretched even higher—up to a floating raft.

It appeared to be a raft, anyway. Neci and Batu hugged the ladder, gazing around them. Five enormous dark objects floated above them, blocking out the starlight like massive ships on the ocean. They kept climbing.

When they reached the bottom of their raft, Batu stuck his hand out to feel it. "It's *dirt*."

Neci looked up to investigate. Batu was right. The rafts were enormous flying pieces of earth, and must have been the strange objects darkening the sky just before they'd been attacked. Even as high up on the ladder as they were, they still had at least another fifty feet to go before they reached the top. They continued their climb.

Iggy's lovely scales were scratched and filthy, and his poor little body was stiff and sore, and he was completely tuckered out, but at long last he made it to the top of the tree and looked out over the forest.

He was *up*. But he still hadn't found Merlynda.

What he did find was a roaring fire and the scent of something delicious roasting. Duck, perhaps, with thyme and rosemary and a hint of lemon.

But a fire in the trees didn't make any sense, so Iggy summoned the strength to ignore his stomach and crawled farther out onto the branch to get a better look.

There *was* a fire. It was on top of the forest, in the middle of a kitchen that had no walls and sat upon a wide wooden floor that floated above the trees.

Iggy pushed with his feet and grabbed with his teeth to scramble his way onto the platform, then scurried out of sight. Climbing and walking were tiring work. He missed riding on Merlynda's shoulder. Or her wrist! How he missed her lovely wrist. He'd grown a little, but it was just his size.

He took one last sniff of the delightful roast duck, then moved on. Merlynda had touched the Aether. They'd be able to have roast duck anytime they wished once she got more practice.

He crawled and slithered and wished for wings, but with every inch he got closer and closer and closer to Merlynda.

+ + +

Merlynda felt like she was floating. Not in the pleasant way that the Nordvings' longships had jostled on the water, but like there wasn't any ground to stand on. Like she was surrounded by blackness, alone, in a constant free fall with nothing to catch her.

The Aether. She'd found the Aether on *purpose*. And oh, how it had felt! To finally, fully embrace the Aether. Joy bloomed, a warm memory, and she reached for the Aether again—

But felt nothing.

Her eyes flew open. She was on a hard cot in a small shack made from wood. A lantern flickered in the corner.

Merlynda sat up and clutched a blanket around her, trying to block out the cold. The Aether had been pure and power-ful, and she'd at last felt like the Septimum Genus. But she couldn't control her magic, and she'd blacked out.

"Iggy?" Merlynda whispered.

There was no answer. She couldn't feel him, couldn't sense him at all. Merlynda panicked. What did that mean? If he was hurt, wouldn't she know? Wouldn't she feel it, feel his pain?

She couldn't feel *anything*. Not the wood or the ground or the air that was all around her. None of the tiny Aether fibers that were supposed to be a part of everything.

And she was so cold. Especially her wrist. It was always so warm when Iggy curled around it, but now it felt frozen. She pushed back at feeling ungrounded, at the free fall inside her, and looked down.

Someone had clamped a wide bronze bracer around her forearm, from elbow to wrist, too tight to tug off and too strong to break. Harsh etchings raced around it, all sharp edges and shadows.

This was why she couldn't feel Iggy, or anything. It wasn't an ordinary bracer—it was a shackle cutting her off from her magic, from the Aether. She was a prisoner.

Fury sparked through every part of her, and she pulled and thrashed at the bracer, at the cold it sent along her arm. She pounded it against the wall, and then she screamed.

A human woman rushed through the doorway—as much as she could, anyway, as her boots were strapped to heavy slabs of iron. The curtain that hung across the doorway swirled behind her, and the lantern flickered.

The woman saw Merlynda, then calmed down. "Do not trouble yourself." She spoke with an accent Merlynda didn't recognize. "It will not come off."

Terror turned to fury. "What is it?" Merlynda demanded as the woman walked back out.

The woman glanced back. "To keep us safe. From you."

Merlynda stared at the bracer after the woman left. It was unsettling, to be severed from something she'd known her entire life. Was this how the sick Oceanid felt? This constant free fall inside?

The bracer was clearly made just for Merlynda, but she somehow doubted her captors had crafted it. This meant someone had put them up to attacking her and her friends. Someone who didn't want them interfering.

The Hollower.

He knew they were coming and was trying to stop them. She slammed the bracer against the wall again, more to vent her helplessness than anything. She didn't have time for this! She *had* to get to the Omnivia, to save Percy.

A trumpet blared and Merlynda jumped. The air shimmered in front of her, and a daffodil-skinned fairy appeared in a poof of sparkly dust. It was the same chubby fairy she'd caught in the Howlwyn Forest.

"Presentin' the Right Honorable Lumont of the Oak Tree, Prime Minister of the Woodland Fairies, Duke of the Dancing Acorns, et cetera, et cetera," the fairy droned.

The air burst into a few more sparkly *poof*s, and the sky-blue Lumont and his retinue appeared.

Merlynda opened her mouth, but before she could speak, the prime minister flew forward and produced a scroll (in another *poof*) that he let roll out in front of him. "I have come to collect one favor, as outlined in this contract and signed by Merlynda of Merlyn Manor, Septimum Genus."

"Hello to you, too," Merlynda snapped. "I'm a bit preoccupied at the moment." She held up her bracer.

Some of the fairies gasped, but Lumont barely flicked his eyes at it. "You need only concede a lock of your hair to our possession. No magic, direct or indirect, is necessary to fulfill your contractual obligations."

Merlynda studied the fairy and his many-feathered hat. "Why do you need a lock of my hair?"

Lumont adjusted his monocle and peered at her. "I am not obligated to disclose the purpose. A few strands will suffice."

Merlynda bit back her frustration. Offending the fairies would do her no good. "My friends and I were attacked, Dame Illondria was seriously wounded, and Batu and Neci are somewhere in the forest. I'm being held a prisoner—and you want a *lock of my hair*? Can't you help free me?"

Lumont repositioned a feather that had bobbed in front of his face. "To interfere would violate the parameters of our diplomatic mission."

"What if I owe you another favor?" Merlynda tried to keep the desperation from her voice. "In return for you freeing me."

"Even if I were willing, I am unable," Lumont said. "That bracer has been powerfully enchanted. Your hair, if you please."

"Take it and leave," Merlynda spat.

The daffodil fairy zipped forward, tied a golden ribbon around a few strands of her chestnut hair, snipped it, and then zipped back.

Lumont removed a feather from his hat and offered it to Merlynda. "Sign here. Your contractual obligations are fulfilled."

Merlynda signed and threw the pen at the fairy. It disappeared with Lumont and the others in a sparkly *poof*.

She was alone.

In which our questers cause a
great deal of chaos

Batu reached the top of the ladder and peeked over the edge. The coast was clear. He pulled himself up and moved over for Neci to do the same.

Their flying piece of earth had to be bigger than all of Avonshire. Smaller earth rafts filled the sky around them, large enough to fit dozens of families comfortably. The sky islands were connected to one another with bridges and ropes, and in the middle was the smallest island, connected to all of them. Tiny floating animals dotted the sky, tethered to railings that ran along the edges.

"Are those boars?" Batu whispered. "With wings?"

Neci stared, fascinated. "Yup." She watched the boars swoop and tug on their ropes, then remembered she was mad at Batu and moved away to find a hiding place.

Dozens of haystacks spread out in front of them. She crouched behind one. "Why do they have so much hay?" She snuck along the rows to see how far they went.

"Stay here!" Batu hissed.

"I'm scouting the terrain," Neci snapped.

Batu muttered to himself but followed.

Neci stopped, and Batu almost bumped into her. At the end of the haystacks were rows and rows of cages. Hundreds of cages. Countless cages. And every single cage held an astonishing animal: a winged bear, a six-legged dog, a gryphon, a bright purple snow leopard, half a dozen feathered beetles, and more. So many more.

They wandered among them. Neci had never seen so many fascinating animals all in one place, but she'd read about them. In her adventure books they were proud and full of life and power. Here they were sad and crushed. They couldn't spread their wings or stretch their legs or leap with all their might.

Batu, on the other hand, *had* seen a number of fascinating animals in his lifetime. His eyes darted around. "We shouldn't be here."

He was right, but Neci was rooted to the spot. In front of her was a creature that she'd never read about. It had four legs like a deer, but its body was spotted like a leopard's—except for its swishy tail, which was more like a lion's. Its neck stretched up higher than any animal she knew and was particularly striking (you'll remember that Neci was short for her age). The neck rose up like a furry snake, covered in beautiful brown spots like its body, until it tapered into a narrow head. Its ears stuck straight up, and there were two little nobs in between them.

Never before had Neci seen anything so glorious—not in her adventure books, not in her studies, and not in the most wildly adventurous realms of her imagination.

"Have you ever seen anything so beautiful?" Neci whispered.

Batu looked the animal up and down. It was something to see, that was for sure, but not something he'd call beautiful.

The giraffe (for that's what the creature was) stared down at Neci, then lowered its head and nuzzled her hand.

Neci stroked the creature's head. "She likes me."

"Probably because you smell like her dinner from all the hay," Batu said, exasperated. "We need to keep moving."

He was right, but Neci wasn't going to say so. "I'll come back for you," she promised.

They moved deeper into the maze of cages, twisting and turning along the path. The animals looked pitiful, despondent. Neci and Batu wanted to free them all, but first they had to find Merlynda.

They rounded a corner, and in between a lizard monkey and an animal that had a pocket on its stomach, there was a cage with a shining silver-and-black horned pegasus.

Neci and Batu faltered—how dare anyone put Dame Illondria in a cage?—then darted toward her.

Dame Illondria lay down, wings folded behind her. There wasn't enough room for her to stretch them out to their full glorious span. Bandages wrapped around her flank, covering the wounds from the arrows. The proud beast lifted her head. "Neci the Ardent?"

Neci knelt on the ground next to her. "Yes, it's me!"

"Keep your voice down," Batu pleaded.

Neci examined the cage's lock. "We'll get you out. Then we'll fly away and find Merlynda."

"No, Neci." Dame Illondria sounded weary. "You must find the Septimum Genus on your own."

"Don't be silly." Neci drew her dagger, ready to twist the lock open. "We'd never leave you behind."

"It is not your choice, brave one. Look to my wings."

They did, and something inside broke a little—in Neci, but also, to his surprise, in Batu. The majestic silver-and-black wings had been clipped and mangled at the ends—*on purpose*. Even if Dame Illondria were free, she couldn't fly.

Fury blazed like a fire in Neci. "How *could* they?"

"They will grow," Dame Illondria said gently, "and I will take to the skies once more, but it will not be quickly enough. I suspect the Hollower instructed our hosts on our capture. I overheard their leader say that I am adequate payment."

"For what?" Neci cried.

"I do not know, but you must find the Septimum Genus as soon as possible."

"We'll get you out," Neci promised. She raised her dagger to jam it into the lock.

"Wait." Batu blocked her arm. "They'll know we're here if we do that. We've got to find Merlynda."

"We can't leave Dame Illondria like this!"

"I know! I'm upset too, but we need a plan. Pugachev—"

"Who's Pugachev?" Neci demanded. She'd had enough of Batu's secrets.

Dame Illondria's eyes bored into Batu. "That is the name of the Rusvokian warlord. But I suspect Batu has a great deal more knowledge than I on this matter."

Batu started, but of course Dame Illondria knew. Even if she hadn't known what his secret was, she'd likely always known that he had one.

Neci felt like she'd been body-slammed. Of course Batu had betrayed them, with his fighting know-how and hazy past. He'd tricked them into trusting him!

"You!" she accused. "You told them how to find us! You speak raider talk!"

"It's Rusvokian," Batu snapped. "And of course I didn't!"

"Iggy said you were hiding something," Neci bit out. She was nearly shouting now. "Where's Merlynda?"

"I don't know! Keep your voice down!"

Clunk, clunk, clunk, clunk.

Before Neci could run, a slight Rusvokian guard rounded

a corner of the cage maze and pulled up short. His eyes flicked to Batu, to Neci, to the dagger she held over the lock of Dame Illondria's cage.

Batu called out something in Rusvokian. Neci assumed it was something like "hello," because he grinned and opened his arms wide in a greeting.

The guard was confused, but this boy spoke Rusvokian, so perhaps he was a young relative of another clansman. Besides, he looked familiar. He answered.

Batu responded, and Neci's gaze darted between them. It sounded like Batu was carrying on a regular conversation, but as far as she knew, he was telling the guard everything about her campaign to save Merlynda.

The guard gestured at Neci, and Batu shook his head. Then the guard gestured at Neci's dagger, and Batu hesitated. The guard reached for his sword.

That was all Neci needed. She plunged Faithful into the lock and twisted.

Dame Illondria burst out of the cage. She neighed, high and long and furious, and charged at the guard.

"Go!" Dame Illondria said. "Find the Septimum Genus!"

Neci hurled herself down the row, springing locks and freeing animals left and right. Cages toppled and shattered, and animals screeched and howled and brayed. They kicked and they ran and they flew.

Neci stared in awe at her handiwork.

It was chaos.

Iggy's scales were rubbed raw from slithering across the ground, so he'd gone back to walking. Closer and closer and closer to Merlynda.

At last he saw a small hut and he *knew*. Merlynda was inside.

There were a few problems.

The first problem was that there were two guards posted near the entrance, and the hut was on a corner of the island, so he couldn't sneak in through the back door.

The second problem was that he couldn't breathe fire or do anything more impressive than bare his exceptionally sharp but tiny teeth.

The third problem was that even though he knew Merlynda was there, he also knew she wasn't. She wasn't bright and warm and comforting. She felt like the wisp of smoke that comes after a candle is snuffed out.

Did Merlynda know he was close? Did she miss him?

What a silly thing to worry about! Of course she missed him. But for some reason she didn't know he was near. Or *couldn't* know he was near.

Something was very, very wrong.

Merlynda had accepted that she wasn't well suited for quests. She'd nearly caused her home to be plundered by Nordvings, had almost drowned, had been attacked by a falcon (twice), and now was a prisoner and couldn't access her magic. It wasn't a record that spurred confidence.

But whether or not she was any good with quests, she was smack in the middle of one. So she decided to think like Neci instead of Merlynda.

"Get away!" Merlynda shrieked. "Get away! Help!"

Heavy clunking sounded as the guards outside rushed into Merlynda's little hut. Their iron boots caught on the cot that she'd moved across the doorway, and they tripped, tangled in the curtain that came loose around them.

Merlynda scrambled over the jumble of arms and legs and bolted away into the cool night air.

Something seemed off as she ran. On one side she could see other huts and what appeared to be a village. But on her other side there was nothing.

She looked in front of her and dug her feet into the earth. She slid and stumbled, managing to grab onto the grass and stop.

Merlynda lay there for a moment, then carefully pulled her feet back from where they'd disappeared. She crawled over to the edge of the earth to look.

Below her, dozens and dozens of feet below her, was the top of the forest. Other pieces of earth floated nearby. Fires were lit on some. Crashing and animal cries rang out from another.

Percy would love this. The thought slammed into her unbidden, reigniting the *missing*, and the urgency of the nearing Shadow Sun. But it was true. He'd love the ridiculousness of giant pieces of earth magically floating through the air, and no doubt have some scheme for seeing how far he could push them, or carving silly faces into the bottoms for everyone on the ground to gawk at.

Merlynda focused back on the here and now. How would she get down? Where were the others?

From the sounds of shouting happening back at her hut, she'd need to solve those problems later. She started moving again, afraid to run in case she missed where the earth disappeared.

"Merlynda!"

She froze. "Iggy?"

The wyvern half slithered, half ran toward her. He glowed so that she could find him.

Merlynda dashed to him, all relief and happiness.

Before she could reach down and scoop him up, a big dark shape blocked her. She bounced off of it and fell onto the grass.

The dark shape chuckled, but it wasn't pleasant. It was a big man, with more shoulders than belly. His chin reminded Merlynda a little of Batu's, though this man's skin was a few shades lighter and his black eyebrows were exceptionally bushy. The iron slabs his boots were strapped to shone in the starlight, newly polished.

The large man plucked Iggy from the ground right behind his little head. "Let him go!" Merlynda shouted. The wyvern squirmed, but he couldn't twist around to get a good bite in. If only he could breathe fire!

"So you are the little wizardess," the man said with a booming laugh. It wasn't a kind laugh, and he had the same accent as her other captors. "I am Pugachev."

A Word about Pugachev

Pugachev had not always commanded a horde of flying raiders. He'd started as a circus ringmaster but left Rusvokia with great haste due to questionable practices involving illegal cosmetics and unreasonable circus admission prices. Many of his circus workers fled with him, and for the most part, they lived in peace on a tract of land no one wanted. When Pugachev decided it was time for a career change, he became a warlord. His workers became his raiders and ransacked the occasional village or traveling caravan.

Every night Pugachev would think about the creatures he'd been forced to leave behind: trained hamsters, a multicolored bear cub—there'd even been a blue liger for a time. Every day he'd fantasize about the animals waiting to be thrown in a cage for him to spoil and adore and stare at whenever he wanted.

Pugachev managed to control his love for exotic animals until his nephew died. The boy was all Pugachev had left of his beloved sister. After Dmitri perished, Pugachev again became obsessed with finding new and more interesting creatures to entertain himself.

It started small, like most addictions do. One jewel-eyed rabbit named Carrots led to a two-tailed lizard named Scales, and after Pugachev caught an embermouse, it snowballed until his fantastical menagerie was rivaled by none. Yet still Pugachev wasn't satisfied.

One day he made the mistake of trying to capture a sprite. Wind smashed through the cages of Pugachev's animal collection, and the raiders dove out of the way in fear.

"Human, you desire to hold things of the air?" the sprite boomed.

"Not particularly," Pugachev answered from behind a wagon.

"Take flight! Be one with the air!"

A shower of sparkles rained down over the entire camp. When they'd settled, the sprite was gone and the air was still. The sparkles hadn't hurt at all. They hadn't even tickled. The raiders laughed at their close call, until they realized they were rising in the air and couldn't stop.

Most of them managed to grab on to a tree or a tent pole (one made the mistake of grabbing on to the embermouse). Eventually someone came up with the idea of making iron slabs for their boots, which wasn't such a bad strategy except for the fact that the sprite's curse did not fall only on the Rusvokians. It sank into the earth, burrowing deep into the soil.

Which meant their land became airborne too.

Pugachev considered this a great gift. No other warlord could claim to be a master of the skies. He was a king, a flying king! This way of life was far superior to ground-dwelling.

When Pugachev was asked to keep the Septimum Genus pre-occupied for a few days, he asked what was in it for him.

"She would travel with a winged unicorn" was the answer, and he was welcome to keep this creature if he so desired. There was also a tiny wyvern, a rare specimen of unknown potential. Its magic would need to be taken, but afterward the warlord could keep it.

Pugachev accepted. Besides, that falcon had scared him out of his wits. He never would have tried to keep a beast like that in a cage.

Merlynda gave Pugachev a withering glare. "You'll let him go now if you know what's good for you! What's a Pugachev anyway?"

The man grinned. "I? I am the mighty conqueror of the skies!"

Merlynda scoffed. "You've hardly conquered them," she said. "That bit over there is still free."

Pugachev's grin soured. He'd been on his way to check on his pets, and this was an inconvenient development. He wanted to get back to sitting on his throne and thinking about how clever he was for capturing the Septimum Genus.

Behind her, Merlynda heard the *clunk, clunk, clunk* of the guards.

"You are surrounded, little wizardess." Pugachev drew his curved sword. "It would be best if you returned to your tiny house now."

Merlynda held her ground. "Not until you've released Iggy."

"Is that what she calls you?" Pugachev asked Iggy. "I'll think of something better. You can be Scales Two!"

"I chose my own name!" Iggy shouted. "Unhand me, fiend!"

Pugachev laughed. "He's a feisty one!" The warlord had been disappointed to find Merlynda without the promised wyvern. Capturing it now brightened his mood.

Pugachev stuck out his finger as one might when playing with a small baby. Iggy, already aghast at being handled in such an undignified manner, lashed out and clamped his jaw down hard.

His teeth may have been tiny, but Iggy was not called a very fierce wyvern only because of his dashing appearance. His teeth were sharper than needles, harder than diamonds, more piercing than even the delectable scent of roasted garlic. Pugachev yowled and let go to clutch his finger.

Iggy hit the ground and scrambled to Merlynda, who met him halfway and scooped him up and continued running past what she assumed were curses in Pugachev's native tongue.

"What is *that*?" Iggy demanded when he saw the bronze bracer around her forearm.

"I don't know," Merlynda panted. "But we need to get it off."

"That's why you feel like smoke."

"What?"

Clunk! Clunk! Clunk! Clunk!

Iggy peeked over Merlynda's shoulder at the guards. "We can talk later."

Merlynda dashed down an alley of huts, searching for somewhere to hide. She ducked behind one and waited for the raiders to clang on past.

Clunk, clunk, CLUNK, CLUNK, clunk, clunk . . .

She waited several more seconds, then poked her head around the hut.

Pugachev was waiting. He grinned.

In which our questers
discover a problem

Freeing Dame Illondria was an excellent tactical move, no matter what Batu said. The Rusvokian guard—and his reinforcements—were terrified to go anywhere near the horned pegasus, who was smashing animal cages open left and right. Neci ran in the opposite direction, springing every lock she could.

"Neci!" Batu tried to follow her, but she threw a broken piece of cage at him. "I didn't have anything to do with this! I almost fell to my death too, remember?"

"No!" Neci yelled back. She'd gotten out her sling and used it to chuck another piece of cage at him. "For all I know, you can fly too! *Like this chunk of land that should not be in the sky!*"

Batu ducked. "I don't know why it's in the sky!"

"Why can you speak raider?" Neci shot back.

"It's *Rusvokian.*"

A cage toppled over, and Batu scrambled back before it crashed into him. The path was blocked.

He and Neci stared at each other through the cage's crumpled bars for a long moment.

"Leave us alone," Neci finally said. "We were fine as a trio. All you've done is sink our boat and get us attacked."

She dashed away through the maze of cages. Batu watched her run. He'd only just found friends, perhaps even friends with whom he belonged, and now he was on his own again.

He should have told them the truth, straight from the beginning. It was who he was, after all, no matter how he tried to change it. No matter how out of place he'd felt with the Rusvokian horde.

But, he realized, Neci and Merlynda didn't feel like they fit in their families either, which was probably what made the children feel like they fit with one another.

He wanted back in the quartet.

"Come out, little wizardess!" Pugachev called. His curved sword glinted in the starlight. "You cannot use your magic. You have nowhere to go."

"No, thank you!" Merlynda answered. "I'm on a quest of great importance!"

"I've been instructed to keep you under guard for a few days. You may finish your quest later."

Merlynda forgot herself and stepped around the corner. "Who instructed you?" she demanded.

"I do not betray the confidences of my business partners." Pugachev sheathed his sword. "But I will make a new deal with you. I am a collector."

Merlynda arched an eyebrow, waiting.

"Your tiny wyvern would make an excellent addition to my collection. Trade him to me for your freedom. I will even deceive my business partner so that he doesn't take the wyvern's magic!"

Take the wyvern's magic. Only one person did that.

The anger boiled up so hot and high inside Merlynda that she thought she might tap into the Aether right then and there, bracer and all.

But she didn't. She couldn't. Which made her madder. "Never!" she spat.

Pugachev drew his sword again. "Then, little wizardess, it seems we must return to the original plan. Why not make this easy and surrender?"

"They all wear boots strapped to iron," Merlynda whispered to Iggy. She kept her eyes on Pugachev and his sword. "Are they enchanted? I can't sense anything with this bracer."

"This whole place is enchanted," Iggy answered. "Sprites, by the feel of it. Imprecise magic. They tend to be lazy."

"I've got a plan."

"A good one?"

"A start." Merlynda walked toward Pugachev. "I give up! Put your sword away."

"Not a good plan!" Iggy wailed. "You need to get further with your plans!"

"There's a good girl," Pugachev said. He sheathed his sword.

Merlynda dove at his boots, scrabbling to untie the straps that lashed them onto the slabs of iron. With a yelp Pugachev kicked out, then reached down and grabbed Merlynda by the back of her neck.

"You dare try to trick me?" he bellowed.

"I do!" Merlynda roared back. "I dare!"

Iggy twisted around and sank his teeth into the warlord's hand again. Pugachev yelped and dropped Merlynda.

"You little—"

But whatever Pugachev thought Merlynda was wouldn't be known, for at that moment a tall blur of brown-and-yellow legs crashed into the warlord, bowling him over.

He didn't go far because of his boots, but Merlynda wasted no time. Before Pugachev could right himself, she unsheathed his sword, sliced through the straps, and backed up toward Neci and the strange beast.

"No!" Pugachev yelled as he lifted into the air. He strained for the iron slabs, but his fingers barely brushed them as he rose.

"No!" He cried again. He tried to grab hold of some taller tufts of grass, but they came away in his hands.

"No!" He screamed with such anguish, Merlynda almost felt sorry for him.

She and Neci watched in fascination as Pugachev rose higher and higher in the sky. He clawed at the air, howled in rage, and spat every curse he could think of at Merlynda (they were in Rusvokian, so she wasn't bothered).

"What's he saying?" Neci asked. She rode the giraffe she'd freed like it was a horse.

"Probably something awful about my lineage." Merlynda took a deep breath to calm herself. The Hollower knew they were coming and had been planning to steal Iggy's magic. Her indignation boiled into rage, but she clung to the fact that they were closing in. Otherwise, why would the Hollower have bothered with the bracer?

Knowing they were headed to Percy gave Merlynda a surge of energy. The lost hope-spark flickered back to life. She turned to Neci and got a good look at the creature her friend rode. She'd also never seen a giraffe before, and it was a sight to behold. "Thanks for trampling him."

Neci patted the creature's long neck. "That was all Fang. Isn't she marvelous?"

Iggy took to Fang immediately. He scurried up her neck and sat on her head, right between the two nobs.

Merlynda grinned up at Neci. "You've finally found your noble steed!"

Neci beamed.

+ + +

Batu charged back the way he'd come, dodging creatures and shards of smashed cages. He had no idea if Neci or Merlynda would ever believe him, if he'd ever be able to rejoin them on their quest, but he could still do the right thing and help Dame Illondria. He snagged a heavy shaft of wood as he ran.

He rounded the corner to find Dame Illondria flashing in the starlight, a silver maelstrom lashing and kicking out at any man that dared approach. She was fierce and noble, but without her wings she would eventually be captured again. There were too many raiders.

"Dame Illondria, behind you!" Batu shouted. He charged forward, wildly swinging his makeshift club.

Dame Illondria kicked back with her powerful rear legs, catching a sneaking swordswoman. The raider flew back and crashed into more cages.

Yet still they came, with their nets and their swords and their arrows. There were too many for a flightless horned pegasus and a boy minstrel. But perhaps there weren't too many for a kinsman.

Batu scrambled to stand on top of a cage. "Stop!" he shouted in Rusvokian. "Stop in the name of Pugachev!"

At the mention of their great leader, the raiders stopped. When they saw who was speaking, a few laughed.

"Go home, little boy," one of them called out in Rusvokian. "This is no place for you."

"It is," Batu answered. "Put down your weapons, or you'll have me to answer to."

This was met with more guffaws.

"And who are you, to make such bold demands?" another asked.

"I am Dmitri, nephew of Pugachev."

Sharp intakes of breath were heard throughout the clearing. Everyone stopped, even Dame Illondria.

"Little Mitya?" A faun stepped forward. Batu managed not to flinch at hearing his old nickname. He'd never cared for it, or how his uncle had tried to rename him Dmitri.

"Yes, Nikolai. It's me."

"We thought bears had gotten you!" Nikolai yelled. "Alert Warlord Pugachev. His nephew has returned!"

"No!" Batu said. "I haven't returned. My friends and I were attacked by your archers."

Nikolai hesitated. "The warlord won't be happy if we let you go. You know what he's like when he's unhappy."

Murmurs spread throughout the Rusvokians.

"I'm not staying, Nikolai. I can't."

Nikolai motioned to a few of the raiders, who moved to flank Batu. "I'm sorry, Mitya."

Batu raised up his club and held it high for a moment, waiting. Then he tossed it aside.

He'd never been a fighter, or a circus master, or even a great friend of animals. He was a musician.

He took up his ocarina and played, pouring all of his sadness and frustration, his feelings of not belonging and his longing to belong, into the ocarina. The haunting melody flowed out from the ocarina and through the air and swept all of Batu's feelings into the hearts of the horde.

The raiders were frozen. At first they were merely caught off guard (who chooses to play a flute when they are under attack?), but after several tense seconds Batu realized they *couldn't* move.

He'd somehow tapped into the magic of the ocarina. He didn't stop playing.

"Help!" a voice yelled. "What are you idiots doing standing around? Help me!"

The voice came from above them—but nothing should be above them except for the stars. Batu was so startled, he stopped his song.

The spell broke. Every eye looked up to see what could possibly be in the sky.

It was a huge man, floating away.

"Look who's here!" Nikolai yelled. "Mitya has returned!"

"What?" Pugachev said.

"Your nephew!" Nikolai shouted.

"Mitya? Truly? Then grab him! And get me down!"

The raiders surged into motion, some grabbing for Batu and others scrambling around beneath Pugachev.

"We'll get you, great leader!"

"We'll grab him, mighty Pugachev!"

"Mitya! Come here!"

But Batu wouldn't. He kicked the hands away from him, stomping on any that tried to climb up closer.

A mighty neigh sounded, and a silver streak charged into the men surrounding Batu, bowling them over like they were nothing more than twigs.

"Climb on," Dame Illondria commanded.

"That's my winged unicorn!" Pugachev whined.

"She's a horned pegasus, Uncle," Batu shouted back, "and she belongs to no one!"

Fang galloped as she had never galloped before. The wind was delicious and the running was delightful and stretching her not-insignificant legs was *marvelous*. The little humans on her back were much kinder than the Rusvokian raiders. They didn't prod her with sticks or urge her to go faster than she could. They knew she was trying her best.

The tiny wyvern sat on her head between her bone nobs and whispered into her ear. It had been a while since she'd had a friend. The yeti hadn't been a sociable neighbor, and the gardenfox only ever fretted about the pretty flowers growing from its back.

She wondered what would happen next.

The island was in chaos, with Pugachev's menagerie running rampant. Some animals had found bridges to cross to other sky islands. The Rusvokians raced after them, or away from them (depending on the creature), and a few guards chased Fang.

A silver streak galloped across their path and almost collided with the giraffe.

"Let her go, fiend!" Neci shouted at Batu. She thrust her dagger at him.

"Batu is not at fault, as I'd previously thought," Dame Illondria said. "There is no time to explain. He has an idea for escape." She darted away.

"Go on, Fang," Neci nudged, and the giraffe loped after her. She might not have trusted Batu, but she trusted Dame Illondria. Also, the raiders were starting to get organized.

The fugitives clattered across a narrow bridge at full speed, and Merlynda gasped when she looked down.

They were in between the islands. Far, far below them the forest stretched out in every direction.

"Cut the bridge!" Batu cried when they were across. They were on another island, but this one was dwarfed by the others and had a small palace in the middle. Flying boars soared overhead, tethered to railings that lined the edge of the earth, which revealed they were on the center island of the archipelago. Bridges connected it to each of the other islands, presenting an immediate concern for the escapees.

Neci leapt from Fang and hacked at the bridge ropes with Faithful. Batu slid from Dame Illondria as she ran to attack a second bridge, tearing through the ropes with her teeth, moving on to the next as soon as one was severed.

The Rusvokians who'd followed saw what was happening and ran back to safety as fast as their ironbound boots would allow. The last of the guards leapt from their bridge just in time. The ropes and wooden planks snapped away from the travelers and swung down, down, down, to hang from the other floating earth pieces, and the small island slowly broke away from the archipelago.

The children collapsed. Somehow they'd made it. They were safe.

"Who's the best beast out there?" Neci crooned to Fang once they'd all caught their breath. "Who's the best Questing Beast in the whole world?"

Iggy crawled onto his second favorite spot, on Merlynda's shoulder, seeing as how her wrist was still occupied by the offensive bracer. "What's a Questing Beast?" Merlynda asked Neci.

"We're on a quest, aren't we? And Fang is a marvelous beast. So she is a Questing Beast." Neci beamed, pleased with herself.

"She's a lovely Questing Beast," Batu said. He stood a little ways away, unsure if it was all right for him to come closer.

Fang nuzzled him. He could say more nice things about her if he wanted. She wouldn't mind.

Dame Illondria knelt down. "Batu of the Lake, forgive me. I reached an erroneous conclusion regarding your loyalty. I will not repeat this mistake in the future."

The girls exchanged a look. If Dame Illondria said Batu was innocent, then he was innocent. But that didn't make it any easier to trust him.

Batu didn't feel that he deserved for Dame Illondria to even nod her proud head at him. "It's fine. Please, stand up. I haven't exactly been . . . forthcoming."

He turned to Neci and Merlynda. "I may have given you the wrong impression about me," he began, "but I did not betray us to the Rusvokian horde."

"Explain," Neci commanded.

"Pugachev is my uncle. My mother—Pugachev's sister—left Rusvokia when she met my father. The rest of her family . . . well, they didn't approve of my father, given that he was an outsider and all. So we lived in the village where my father was from, with his people and away from Rusvokia . . . until a plague came."

Batu paused, brushing his mop of hair out of his eyes. He thought about this every day but couldn't remember ever sharing this part of him with someone else.

He pressed on. "My parents got sick and . . . and didn't make it. Most of the village didn't. I don't know how I—why I'm not—" He swallowed. "So I was sent back to Rusvokia, to live with my uncle."

Merlynda's anger faded. Knowing Batu's past made it hard to stay mad, but there still hadn't been any reason for him to lie. "Why did you leave?"

"Because he's awful!" Batu exploded. "He made me change my name to Dmitri and wanted me to lead the horde one day. I don't want that. I'm not a raider—I'm a musician! But he wouldn't accept that. He'd take away my lute and punish me if I skipped combat lessons or if he thought I wasn't acting enough like him."

"And your mother was the one who taught you about

music," Merlynda said, remembering what Batu had told her that day with the Nordvings. "So you'd do whatever it took to keep your music."

"Whatever it took," Batu agreed.

This explained why he knew enough about fighting to always correct Neci. "How do they fly?" she asked. "Can *you* fly?"

"No. I don't know anything about that. When I left, we lived by a river."

"Sprite magic," Iggy said knowingly.

Merlynda scrutinized Batu. "Did Fenrir actually capture you?"

The minstrel shuffled his feet. "Sort of. I wasn't sure I could survive on my own, so I let myself be captured. Uncle hates Nordvings, so it was a sort of revenge. Fenrir never knew who I really was. I thought I'd be able to escape eventually—but then I couldn't. I changed my name back to Batu—that was also my father's name—but I guess I couldn't run forever."

Neci crossed her arms. "You could've told us."

"I didn't think I'd be around you for long. I really did plan to go off on my own. But then we went to Oceanus and almost died, and dealt with those awful mermaids, and everything changed."

Merlynda looked at Iggy. "Does he still have a secret?"

Iggy leveled his gaze at Batu and squinted for a moment. "Everyone has secrets. But this was the one he was hiding."

Batu clasped his hands, wishing he could go back and be

honest from the beginning. "Thanks for saving me when I fell from Dame Illondria, Merlynda. Once we land, I'll go back to being a wandering minstrel."

"Oh, no, you won't!" Neci ticked things off on her fingers. "You grew up in a far-off land, are heir to a horde of raiders, traveled with Nordvings, and you think I'm going to let you leave without telling me all about your adventures?"

Batu blinked, caught off guard. "Really?"

"And you have to teach me how to fight like a raider."

"But no more secrets," Merlynda said.

The minstrel nodded. "No more secrets."

"Excuse me." Iggy cleared his throat. "No one has asked my opinion."

"Make sure you're kind," Merlynda warned.

Batu bowed his head. "I'm at your service, Ignus."

Iggy drew the moment out. "I say—" He paused for dramatic effect until Merlynda nudged him.

"That you may call me Iggy."

Batu grinned.

Iggy stretched lazily. "You did save us from the raiders."

Dame Illondria had been silent, observing, but with Batu's confession resolved, she approached Merlynda. "Septimum Genus. A grave offense has been played against you. Show me."

The full attention and concern of the majestic creature made Merlynda self-conscious. She slid her sleeve aside so that the bracer shone in the moonlight.

Dame Illondria snarled. "What fiend crafted this?"

"The Hollower," Merlynda said. "He knows we're coming. He bribed Pugachev to keep me out of the way."

Batu examined the bracer. "What is it?"

"It's—it's taken away my magic," Merlynda said. "I used the Aether to save you and Neci, but I couldn't control it. I fainted. I must have been out when the raiders found me."

When she'd needed to escape, it had been easy to distract herself, but now the fullness of what she'd lost rushed in on her. She'd never lived a day without feeling her magic. The emptiness echoed inside her, unbearable.

Iggy nuzzled her ear. "Your magic is still there. It's just trapped."

"Ignus is correct," Dame Illondria said. "This bracer has been alchemically forged, and further enchanted with these etchings. It steals your connection with the Aether, but it is only for as long as you wear it."

Merlynda glared at the bracer. "Why *this*? Why not drain my magic, like he did to the others? Pugachev said the Hollower was planning to take Iggy's! I bet that's why that falcon keeps attacking."

Iggy gripped Merlynda's shoulder tighter.

Neci tapped the bracer with Faithful, testing it. There was no keyhole, no lock to pick. "Can we cut it off?"

Dame Illondria inspected the bracer. "This is a powerful wizardry. The magical objects that might be able to remove it are rare, and there is no assurance of their success. Beyond those, only the one who cast the spell can lift it."

"This magic smells old," Iggy said. "It's a bit musty."

"It is an ancient and rare magic," Dame Illondria agreed. "And wicked."

Iggy took a closer look at the bracer. It still offended him that it took up Merlynda's wrist. "It feels familiar. Like that falcon."

Merlynda couldn't feel anything but the cold bronze of the bracer. No Aether, no elements, no power, just the free fall inside her—the emptiness, mingled with despair, dragging her down into the void. How would she save Percy now? The fullness of her failure rushed through the emptiness, drowning her.

Dame Illondria moved closer. "I may not be able to remove the bracer, Merlynda of Merlyn Manor, but I can bestow a gift. Ignus."

Iggy started. "Who, me?"

"Step forward."

Iggy crawled to Merlynda's hand—the one that didn't have the bracer—and she held him up to the horned pegasus.

"Would you like to fly, little Ignus?"

Iggy tried not to squirm from excitement. "Would I!" He looked at his back and wiggled the little nubs.

Dame Illondria gently touched her onyx horn to Iggy's head. Winds howled around them, forming a circle. A flash of light pulsed from the center. The children and Fang shut their eyes and looked away.

The light flashed brighter, then stopped. The winds settled. Eyes opened.

Iggy was gone.

"Merlynda!" A voice cried from above. "Merlynda, have you ever seen anything so wonderful?"

Above them, the tiny but very fierce wyvern darted and wheeled and swooped through the air.

"I'm flying!" Iggy shouted. "I'm flying, I'm really flying!"

He landed on Merlynda's shoulder and twisted this way and that, admiring his wings. They were a beautiful golden red, speckled with shining flecks. It looked like his little body was on fire.

"Aren't they marvelous? Don't I look like an especially fierce wyvern now?"

Merlynda hugged him. "They're magnificent."

"Thank you, Dame Illondria!" Iggy launched himself into the sky once more. Batu and Neci chased after him, laughing.

"It's a wonderful gift, Dame Illondria." Merlynda watched Iggy circle and whirl above them. "A lovely token."

"I only wish I could do more," Dame Illondria said. "If the Hollower knows we are coming, we must proceed with caution."

Merlynda agreed, but the truth was, she didn't know how to proceed. Only hours ago she had finally, *finally* touched the Aether! In that moment she'd felt elated, unstoppable, *whole*.

And now that wholeness had been snatched away, replaced with a never-ending free fall. Without her magic, without her connection to the Aether, she didn't know how to *be*. And if she couldn't even be Merlynda, she had no idea how to be the Septimum Genus.

+ + +

Unfortunately, between the children, the newly aerial wyvern, the horned pegasus, and the Questing Beast, no one knew how to direct the flying boars, so the questers were at the mercy of the floating island.

It was lunchtime on the day after their escape from the Rusvokian horde, but this didn't matter as there was no food on the island. Even the small palace Pugachev had built for himself was empty except for a ridiculous, oversized throne. The merciless sun beat down around a few fluffy clouds that somehow never offered shade. The Shadow Sun was tomorrow. And given their exhaustion and the desperation of their situation, the children were feeling a bit testy with one another.

Merlynda in particular was not having her finest hour. They were all tired, and hungry, and possibly condemned to float forever in the sky, but Merlynda didn't have forever, she only had a day before it would be too late to save Percy. They didn't know if the island had taken them closer to the Omnivia, or away from it, and until Dame Illondria's wings healed, they had no way to leave. Being trapped made all of the worry and fear and hopelessness bubble back up inside her. "Can't we do *anything?*" she asked for the thousandth time.

Neci adjusted her satchel wearily. They'd been having the same pointless conversation for what felt like hours. "I'll go on another reconnaissance mission. Maybe we missed something."

"Something that we didn't see on our six other reconnaissance missions?" Merlynda asked bitterly.

"It's better than doing nothing," Neci snapped. She turned to Batu. "Are you sure you don't know anything that could help us?"

"You think I *like* being trapped up here?" Batu said, indignant. "I told you, I'd never seen these islands until last night."

Dame Illondria looked up from where she'd been resting. "It may be that our only option is to wait. That is no one's fault."

Merlynda knew the horned pegasus was right. But Percy needed her, and she was worse than useless trapped up here. "I'm going to find Iggy," she said, and rushed off before she said anything else she'd regret.

"Do you want to come check the island again with me?" Neci asked Batu.

He shook his head and sat on the ground next to Dame Illondria, then picked up his ocarina. "It's a waste of time."

"Stay here then," Neci snapped, and stormed off.

She kicked at the ground as she walked. She knew they weren't actually this angry with one another, and that really they were upset about the dire turn their of their circumstances. Even so, the frustration felt very real. She needed to regain her focus.

Neci sat down and pulled *The Official Quest Requirements for Knighthood* from her satchel and flipped through the pages. Her Ye Knoble Knights Decoder Ring with Customizable Crest glinted in the sunlight. Neci took it off and shoved it into her satchel.

She hadn't earned a single point. There was nothing in the book about defeating mermaids or saving animals from an obsessive warlord or even about learning new fighting techniques. She'd never be a knight at this rate.

She put her head in her hands. Merlynda had a marvelous destiny. Batu had a glorious past.

Neci had only a middling present.

Frustration and despair blazed through her. She leapt up and raised her arm to hurl the book out into the sky.

Only when she looked up, there was a good deal more sky than she remembered seeing that morning, and the clouds were farther away.

She dropped to her stomach and scooted over to the edge of the island.

The treetops were close. So close, in fact, that the taller ones brushed up against the earth. Clods of dirt and scattered roots fell away beneath her.

She leapt up and sprinted toward the others. Their island was falling!

"We've got to leave!" Neci shouted.

Batu crossed his arms. "Found something, did you?"

"The island is *falling*. We've got to get off it!"

Merlynda and the others (even Fang) rushed to the side of the island and peered over the edge.

Iggy flew down to assess the damage. Even the trees of

usual height were scraping against it now. "The enchantment is wearing off," he reported. "The spell was probably tied to Batu's uncle."

Everyone exchanged worried looks.

Dame Illondria stretched her wings. "I'm afraid I am still beyond flying condition." It was true that she healed remarkably fast, but her wings had not fully recovered.

"And I'm only a tiny flying wyvern," Iggy said. "I can't carry anyone."

"Can't we just brace ourselves for impact?" Batu asked.

Neci rolled her eyes. "What happens when you toss a dirt clod into the air and it hits the ground?"

"It . . . breaks. Oh."

Neci looked around. "What about the boars?"

But the boars, realizing they were under new management, had chewed through their tethers and disappeared.

"Could Batu help?" Merlynda directed the question to Dame Illondria and Iggy. "If this magic was linked to Pugachev—well, Batu is his blood relation. . . ."

Iggy nuzzled her cheek. "You're brilliant."

"Him?" Neci exclaimed, then turned bright red at her outburst.

"I agree with Neci for once," Batu said. "What can I do?"

"When magic is linked to an individual, it will often respond to family members," Merlynda explained. "The spell holding these islands together was probably linked to your uncle, so it will have a link to you, but it will be weaker."

The island shook as it rammed into a large tree.

"Feel the enchantment," Dame Illondria instructed Batu. "Will the island to hold together. Use your ocarina."

The island rumbled as more trees ripped away at the bottom.

"All right!" Batu flung himself on the ground and clung to the tufts of grass. "Please don't crumble like a giant dirt clod!"

"Into the throne room!" Neci shouted, and everyone crammed inside the small palace. Neci got Fang to sit and crouched down beside her. The Questing Beast didn't understand what all the fuss was about. Flying was already an unnatural thing for a giraffe, so crashing only made sense.

Iggy clutched Merlynda's shoulder. "I won't leave you, even though I can fly now."

Merlynda grabbed onto one of the throne's legs. "That's noble of you."

Dame Illondria kicked the door shut as another tremor shook the island. "Brace yourselves! Batu, play!"

Batu didn't know how to both brace himself and play his ocarina, but in a few minutes it wouldn't matter anymore. He climbed up onto Pugachev's throne and played—a song of togetherness, of different people and elements all uniting— and they prepared for impact.

*In which our heroes embark
upon another side quest*

The landmass sank through the sky, every second bringing it closer to the earth. The sprite's magic was fading, losing its battle with the natural forces of the world (namely gravity). Trees scraped away at the island's underbelly, gouging out large sections of dirt and soil. When it cleared the forest and plowed into a meadow, the bottom layers crumbled, the edges shook loose, and the island shrank from every direction.

Every direction except for one. The questers, huddled together, felt the piece of earth shake and bounce and tear as the once-enchanted terra firma ground into the greater earth below, until at last it was over. The island was nothing more than enormous heaps of dirt, tree roots, and grass—and in the center of it all stood the small palace.

The door creaked open, and the questers piled out. They took in the annihilation of the island, then turned as one to gaze at Pugachev's throne room. It wasn't even all that dusty.

"Well done, Batu," Dame Illondria said. "You've saved us all."

"You were amazing," Merlynda agreed. "Also, sorry about . . . you know. Earlier." She looked between Neci and Batu. "Both of you. I'm sorry for acting that way."

"Me too," Batu said.

"And me," Neci chimed in.

"Villainy!" a voice roared, cutting into the moment. "Surrender, ne'er-do-wells!"

Pounding feet sounded from every direction, and the questers looked up, bewildered.

They were surrounded, but the attackers weren't anywhere near as intimidating as the Nordvings, or as wise as the Oceanids, or even as fearsome as the Rusvokian raiders. They were, however, something to look at.

Every person in the crowd, which was made up of people from what seemed like every possible species—gnomes, goblins, humans, ogres, at least one centaur, and countless others—held a bright white candle or a jar of water. Many clutched talismans around their necks (one was wrapped in a string of garlic), and every single one of them was dancing.

They leapt and hopped from foot to foot. The candles had all been snuffed out, the water sloshed around in the jars, and the talismans (and garlic) bounced around.

In short, they weren't particularly threatening.

"Hello," Merlynda said.

"Don't come any closer!" a tall elf warned. His pointy, straw-colored beard and pointy, important-looking hat made it look as though his head were shaped like a diamond. This was only further emphasized by his pointy ears. He brandished a candle as he leapt and flicked water at Merlynda. "I must ask how you came to the fair land of Quaesitum on that abomination."

Neci looked at the loose dirt around them. "Abomination?"

"Land of Quaesitum?" Batu asked. "I've never heard of it."

A hush fell over the delegation—as much as a hush was possible with every member leaping and dancing.

"The noble land of Quaesitum is its own independent state," the tall elf said testily. "We recognize no ruler except our own."

"Who's that?" Merlynda asked. None of her geography books mentioned a place called Quaesitum. Then again, between traveling by bubble and then by air, she wasn't sure which part of the known (or unknown) world they were in.

The tall elf stood up straighter, dancing a jig. "I am."

No one was surprised, and not just because he was the only one with a pointy hat (which was tied beneath his chin so it survived every turn and shuffle).

"I am the Inquirer," the elf went on. "I inquire about things."

Merlynda tried not to bob her head up and down to follow him. "What sort of things?"

"All sorts. I've asked many questions during my tenure as Inquirer. Grand, lofty questions, such as 'Why is the sky blue?' and 'What is the significance of the number forty-two?' and"—he fixed them with a sharp look—"just today I had reason to ask, 'Why is an unidentified flying object landing in our beloved country?'"

Batu shifted to the side to avoid a pirouetting minotaur. "Is it possible for everyone to stop dancing?" He was getting dizzy watching them.

"I have asked this question many times," the Inquirer said, stroking his beard. "Every step we take feels like stepping on burning coals. We are cursed with a dancing plague, you see, so we are rather suspicious of magic." He looked meaningfully at their demolished island.

Neci was about to ask for further explanation when a screech rang out from the skies.

"Not again!" the children cried, ducking as the falcon buzzed over them.

Iggy popped his head out from Merlynda's robes where he'd been hiding (it was much harder with wings) and narrowed his eyes at the falcon. It was time he found out what was so mysterious about it. The tiny wyvern launched himself into the sky, golden wings glittering in the sunlight.

The falcon didn't expect to be met in the air. It didn't expect to be met at all. Iggy plowed into it with his clawed feet.

The shock didn't last for long. The falcon's prey had swooped right into its outstretched talons.

"Iggy!" Merlynda screamed. She strained uselessly against the chilled bracer that blocked her magic, that prevented her from feeling Iggy, that kept him from sensing how strong and brave she thought he was.

The falcon and the wyvern spiraled toward the earth, locked together as they tore at each other. Right before they hit, the falcon ripped itself away, and Iggy smashed into the ground.

"No!" Merlynda shrieked. She sprinted to her familiar, her friend, her very fierce wyvern. The bracer separated her from Iggy's pain, but she knew he was injured, broken, and she couldn't help, couldn't offer him her magic.

The falcon screeched in triumph and circled around, preparing to dive.

Merlynda stood over Iggy and threw her head back and screamed, daring the falcon to try to take Iggy from her. She wouldn't allow it. Magic or not, she *would not allow it*.

A portal opened by her feet, and a robed arm reached through, grasping for Iggy. Merlynda stamped her foot down, hard, grinding the probing hand into the earth before it reached the wyvern.

Neci ran up behind her, whirling her sling. She flung a stone at the falcon, connecting with a satisfying *thwack!* The crooked familiar fell toward the earth.

The arm wriggled away from Merlynda's foot and slipped back into the portal. Another black void opened up to catch the falcon before it hit the grass.

Merlynda threw herself down at her familiar's crumpled form. Iggy's long body was twisted, one beautiful new wing broken, legs still. He turned his head when Merlynda's shadow fell across him. "There is something," he croaked, "very wrong about that bird."

"Oh, Iggy," she whispered, her eyes stinging. "Oh, my funny, fierce Iggy."

She tried to reach into the Aether, to pull it into herself, to move it toward Iggy with all the power the Septimum Genus was prophesied to have—

—but of course, nothing happened.

Merlynda wanted to keep screaming—from rage and pain, yes, but mostly from her absolute helplessness.

She was hauled to her feet, arms tied behind her, and before she realized this was happening, it was too late to struggle. She struggled anyway, toward Iggy, her Iggy!

Neci loaded a new stone into her sling and whirled it around. "What are you doing?"

The Inquirer watched as Merlynda was dragged toward a wooden shaft stuck in the ground. "Witches are servants of evil and purveyors of disaster," he said. "Your friend is sentenced to be burned at the stake. Immediately."

The statement registered slowly in Merlynda's mind. She

was too wrapped up in the falcon, and the portal, and the mysterious robed arm that had tried to grab Iggy. Why was she being taken away from him? It clicked into place when she saw the kindling and straw piled around her.

She tried to pull away. "I'm not a witch!"

"That's wot they all say, i'n't it?" said the man tying her to the stake. This was already a difficult task because he was doing a quickstep, and his strand of garlic bobbed with him, knocking into Merlynda, who kicked the kindling away.

"Now, now, stop strugglin'," the garlic man said. "Quicker you accept it, quicker we move on. It's two-for-one fish fry day down at the inn, an' I don't want to miss it."

"But I didn't even do any magic!"

"Didn't need to, didja? Mysterious portals is openin', an' you've got that flying lizard thing an' those other beasts. Only witches keep unnatural creatures. Besides, your fingernails are dirty."

"So are yours!" Merlynda bit out.

An old woman jigged forward and struck some flint. The sparks danced onto the straw.

"I'm not a witch! I'm a benevolent wizardess in training!"

Flames sprang up around Merlynda. The crowd cheered.

"I'm the Septimum Genus!" she howled.

"She's casting a spell!" the old woman shouted.

Batu and Neci rushed up with two full buckets of water and flung them at the stake, soaking Merlynda and stopping the flames. Neci sliced through the ropes with her dagger, then held Faithful toward the crowd to discourage anyone from rushing them.

"Garlic is for vampires," Merlynda spat at the garlic man, then rushed to Iggy, who was being guarded by Dame Illondria.

She knelt next to him, afraid to move him, but stroked his head.

Merlynda turned desperately to the majestic knight. "Can you heal him?"

The horned pegasus shook her head. "The evil of that twisted falcon is beyond me. Ignus needs healing magic of the greatest caliber." Dame Illondria looked down at Iggy. "Were it not for that bracer, I believe you would have that power."

Hot tears slipped down Merlynda's face. She was broken, yes, but she was more than that. She was *angry*. Furious. She couldn't even feel him through their bond, their magic, couldn't make sure he knew that she was there for him and would find a way to make him better.

Merlynda tore at the bracer, to slip it off, to break it. She snatched Neci's dagger and sliced it toward her arm just above the metal—

"Merlynda!" Neci knocked Merlynda's hand aside before the dagger could cut her arm, then wrestled it away. Merlynda tried to struggle, but the knight in training won out.

Neci was breathing hard, but it wasn't from the tussle. She looked incredulously from Merlynda, to the bracer, to her dagger. "What were you thinking?"

Merlynda stared at the bracer. Faithful wasn't strong enough to remove her bracer. She knew that. But her arm?

"Whatever it takes," Merlynda promised.

"We'll find a way," Neci reassured her. She sheathed Faithful but kept an eye on Merlynda.

Batu studied his ocarina. On the sky island with the raiders, he'd played what he felt—alone and frustrated, how he couldn't be himself. In the throne room when their island was falling, he'd played a song of unity and togetherness. He'd played *honestly*. What was honest now?

He wanted Iggy to get better, to feel at peace, to not worry, to rest, and that's exactly what came out—a lullaby for Iggy.

As they watched, Iggy's breathing slowed back to normal, and instead of twitching he relaxed into Merlynda's arms.

"Thank you," Merlynda whispered.

Neci studied Batu. "What did you do?"

"I—" Batu looked at his token, unsure of how to explain. He told them how the raiders hadn't been able to move.

"Can you do anything you want?" Neci asked warily.

"I don't think so." Batu thought it through. "I think whatever I play has to be what I really want. No, that's not right. It has to be honest. In my heart."

Dame Illondria inclined her head. "Ignus still needs medical attention. His wing must be seen to immediately."

The denizens of the land of Quaesitum had kept a cautious distance. Merlynda shot a withering glare at the hovering Inquirer. "We need a doctor."

"Ah, Mistress Merlynda." The Inquirer's legs kicked out in a dance variation, which made him look more distressed. "While we have great respect for your—*abilities*—it is difficult . . . one might say 'awkward' . . ."

"Do spit it out," Merlynda snarled. Besides being upset about Iggy, she hadn't forgiven them for mistaking her for a witch. Her robes were singed.

"Magic is outlawed in the land of Quaesitum," the Inquirer finished. "Ever since we were deceived and ill-treated by a witch—"

"*I'm not a witch!*" Merlynda shouted. "My familiar is hurt, and my magic is useless!" She thrust the bracer into his face, and the Inquirer recoiled. "I'm on a quest to find my brother and defeat an evil wizard, so the sooner you help us, the sooner we'll go!"

The garlic man danced over and splashed his jar of water onto Merlynda. It was a good thing Merlynda didn't have her magic, because she would have blasted him on the spot.

"She ain't meltin'," the garlic man said.

"Let's leave them for Zahilda!" the old woman called. "Maybe that'll give us a break from her!"

"You are not to speak of the banished," the Inquirer barked.

"Who's Zahilda?" Merlynda demanded.

The Inquirer cringed. "She is the witch who cursed this community. She lives up in the mountains and torments us whenever the fancy strikes her."

"You probably deserved it," Merlynda snapped. "Can she help?"

The Inquirer sniffed piously while pirouetting. "Perhaps. I doubt she'll be inclined to aid your lizard."

"He's a very fierce wyvern," Merlynda said in a dangerous tone.

Neci stroked Fang's neck, considering. "This sounds like another side quest."

Batu cocked his head to the side. "A what?"

"I'll explain later."

"Septimum Genus." Dame Illondria bowed her head. "With every moment the Hollower grows stronger, and time grows ever shorter."

"Zahilda cursed all these people," Merlynda said. "Even if she can't or won't heal Iggy, what if she has a snow cactus, or a sandrose—something that can break this bracer? You already said that I could heal Iggy without it. And I don't think I can stop the Hollower without my magic."

Dame Illondria ruffled her wing feathers. "Time is of the essence. A side mission may delay our ultimate goal."

Merlynda held Dame Illondria's gaze. She loved and respected the horned pegasus, and of course she knew time was running out, but she couldn't go on without Iggy.

The Aether's servant dipped her horn. "But I, too, see the wisdom in seeking to remove that cursed bracer. I will agree with whatever the Septimum Genus decides."

Merlynda's voice was firm. "Let's find the witch."

The Inquirer sniffed. "Don't expect her to help you. And *do not* incite her wrath any further against this community."

Neci was finding it more and more difficult to treat the Inquirer with courtesy. "We'll be exceptionally diplomatic. Where is she?"

The elf offered a cold smile. "Follow the crows."

The witch was rumored to live partway up a nearby mountain in a dank, dark cave, where she had full view of the land of Quaesitum and could lash out with her hexes and curses to her evil heart's content. The children left Dame Illondria and Fang behind to watch over Iggy.

It didn't take long to understand what the Inquirer had meant by "follow the crows." They were everywhere, flitting up and down the mountain. The farther the questers went, the more crows there were. They cawed and cackled and made the children huddle closer together.

The questers climbed up and over a particularly treacherous bit of mountain and stopped. They were on mostly level ground now, and ahead of them was the witch's cave. Countless crows pushed and shoved to roost over the entrance. Those that were tired of jostling settled on nearby branches and rocks.

Neci fiddled with her dagger. "She'll see us coming."

"It's the only way." Merlynda took a step forward. "And I suppose I'd prefer a witch who is expecting us to one who isn't. They can be unpredictable when surprised."

The trio approached the cave, on the alert. There was no

birdsong, no chirping bugs, no sound at all except for the occasional rustling feathers and scuffling talons.

"What are they looking at?" Batu whispered.

"The crows are looking at me," a lovely voice called from the cave. "I'm not prepared for company, but you may as well come in."

The trio glanced at one another, then moved forward.

The cave was not dank and dark, as the Inquirer had led them to believe. Cheerful floral wallpaper lined the walls, lit by bright torches. The scent of rose water wafted toward them and mingled with the cherry pie cooling by the entrance. Tea was set on top of a daisy-patterned tablecloth with a bouquet of freshly picked wildflowers in the center.

The single occupant wore a fluffy bathrobe. Her brown hair was tied back in a loose bun, and she gazed intently into a tall full-length mirror.

Merlynda studied the woman before her. This person didn't look particularly witchy. "Are you Zahilda?"

"Yes." Zahilda scooped out some sparkly orange sludge from a clay pot and began smearing it on her face. As she did, the orange swirled into other colors, always complementing her copper skin.

Merlynda took a timid step forward. "We were hoping you could help us. Our friend is injured."

The witch bent closer to the mirror and dabbed some more goop on her nose. "Then find a doctor."

"He isn't a person. He's a . . . wyvern."

Zahilda paused mid-dab and peered at them in the mirror. "A wyvern."

"Yes."

The witch straightened and turned to face them. "Who are you? Don't lie to me now. A witch always knows."

Merlynda stared Zahilda straight in the eyes. Witch or not, fluffy bathrobes and sparkly sludge masks weren't especially intimidating. "Merlynda of Merlyn Manor, Septimum Genus. My familiar needs help."

"Hmm, so the prophecy did decide on a twin." Zahilda narrowed her eyes. "Not much of a Septimum Genus if you can't heal your own wyvern, are you?"

The words stung. Merlynda bit back a retort and pulled her sleeve up.

Zahilda cast a careless eye down at the bracer and nodded. "That makes sense." She went back to the mirror and scooped up more orange goop.

"That's it?" Neci said. "'That makes sense.' Nothing else?"

"I'm busy. Wart masks have to be applied within twenty minutes of mixing or they spoil."

"To remove warts?" Batu hazarded.

"Of course not." Zahilda scowled at her reflection. "That would be a wart-*removal* mask."

She moved to a bowl of rose water and vigorously washed away the sludge. The witch patted her face dry and peered into the mirror.

"Typical," she muttered. Her skin was clear and smooth.

She gave up and faced the children. "I won't help you."

"Why?" Merlynda asked.

"Because witches are evil."

"No offense," Batu said, "but you don't exactly look like an evil witch."

Merlynda examined Zahilda's immaculate hands. "Your fingernails aren't even dirty."

Zahilda shot Merlynda an icy glare. "That is a nasty stereotype, and I will thank you not to perpetuate it. Have you ever met a witch before?"

"No," Merlynda said, surprised. "But I've read all about them."

The witch huffed. "And I'm sure all of those books were written by wizards, or unicorns, or other ilk who tend to find witches distasteful."

Merlynda felt her cheeks redden. "Actually, um, yes. They were."

"Then perhaps you ought to pay more attention to *who* is saying such things and why they might want you to assume all witches have dirty fingernails." Zahilda sniffed haughtily.

Then she let out a heavy sigh and poured herself some tea.

"You're right, though. I don't look much like an evil witch. But I'm trying. I'm not offering you tea because evil witches aren't hospitable. Natt the Nefarious—that's my role model—never offered guests tea."

Neci watched the tea splash into the bright pink cup. It was purple and had globs of something nasty-looking in it.

"Are you trying to be evil, or trying to be a witch?"

Zahilda didn't look eager to drink her tea. "I'm trying to be a good evil witch. You understand."

They most certainly did not.

Zahilda's face brightened. "I know! I'll chop you up for my stew. That's what Natt the Nefarious would do."

The children edged back, but the witch stood and clapped. The ground shook, and an ornate gilded armoire leapt across the cave and blocked the entrance. Two flowery dresses zipped out of it and floated in front of them menacingly.

"I'd prefer to be a vegetarian," Zahilda said as she formed a fireball in her hand. "But eating children is a perfectly evil thing to do."

She selected a butcher's knife from her stove with her free hand and beamed. "Who would like to go first?"

A WORD ABOUT WITCHES
(or at least about Zahilda)

*W*hile it is true that witches are generally evil, it is not at all accurate to say that every witch is evil. You can't assume every individual of an entire group embodies a single characteristic. How would you feel if I said that all children are frightful, or that they love being gifted socks? On your next birthday you'd probably end up with an unfortunate number of argyle stockings.

Zahilda was, at the moment, somewhat evil, but she hadn't always been that way. It was true that she'd cursed the land of Quaesitum with the dancing plague, and it was true that she terrorized them when the fancy struck her, but she only did those things because they expected her to.

Zahilda's sisters were proper evil witches and had bullied Zahilda relentlessly for her cheery floral dresses and perfect pies. So Zahilda, recognizing that she wasn't wanted as herself, picked up her white-and-orange tabby cat from where he was hunting twigs (because of course she didn't have a proper black witch's cat) and left the coven. She and Prince Whiskerkins settled in the land of Quaesitum and got along quite well knitting doilies and making daisy chains with the others in the village.

Until the crows came.

Crows are a common enough bird, but when they gather in large numbers for no apparent reason, it is usually a sign of witches. And when the crows all alighted on Zahilda's cottage roof, the game was up.

Would her new community still embrace her now that they knew her? Would they still invite her to birthdays for their children and cousins and great-aunts?

The answer, I am sad to report, was no. They came to Zahilda in a mob, torches and all, to rid themselves of the evil witch for good.

Zahilda felt a fury like none other, even greater than when her sisters hexed all her pies. This wasn't just anger. This was betrayal.

It was a defining moment for Zahilda. There and then she decided to emulate the evilest witch who'd ever lived: Natt the Nefarious. She already had wavy hair like Natt, so she'd just *need to grow an iconic wart or two, and maybe cook up a spell that would make her taller, but she was determined to see it through. Cursing her former neighbors and friends would be an excellent start.*

Every single torch flame leapt up to circle in a roiling fireball above the mob, then a thousand tiny flame darts struck the feet of each and every citizen of the land of Quaesitum.

Zahilda picked up Prince Whiskerkins and swept away into the night. If an evil witch was what they wanted, then that's what she'd give them.

Zahilda launched her first fireball, and the children scrambled.

"Stay still now," the witch scolded. "I don't want to singe my curtains."

Another fireball hurtled toward Merlynda, and she ducked behind the armoire, kicking at one of the floating dresses. "You don't have to eat us! You said yourself that you like vegetables better than children!"

Zahilda sighed as she prepared another fireball. "Yes, but you don't know what it's like. Every time I try to be who I want, I'm run out of town. So I thought, why not really give being evil a go?" She flicked a reluctant finger at the stove, which began to boil a pot of water. "Everyone already expects it."

Merlynda peeked her head around the armoire. "It doesn't sound like they knew you at all."

"Well, I'm evil now. Just like Natt. I'm doing my best, anyway."

"You don't have to be evil," Batu pressed. He'd hidden beside the stove, which upon reflection wasn't the best choice.

"Please," Zahilda snorted. "Have you ever heard of a good witch?"

"Why can't you be the first?" Merlynda dodged a swipe from the dress. "I'm the heir to Merlyn's legacy and can't use magic."

Neci poked her head out from under the daisy tablecloth. "I'm a root vegetable farmer determined to be a knight."

"I'm a raider who ran away to be a wandering minstrel," Batu added.

Zahilda's fireball shrank a little. "And did others think it was all nonsense?"

"Absolutely." Batu smiled at Merlynda and Neci. "But not everyone."

Zahilda set the butcher's knife on the table and sat down once more by her tea. "I don't think the villagers will ever forgive me." She snapped her fingers, and the water stopped boiling. "There's only one way to find out, I suppose."

*In which Merlynda makes
a difficult choice*

ahilda wanted to make a fresh pot of tea and be hospitable, but Merlynda described Iggy's injury and begged her to come right away. The children explained their quest while Zahilda magicked herself into a cheery floral dress and shook her hair out of its bun, then everyone piled onto her broomstick.

It was a tight fit, and Prince Whiskerkins kept crawling all over them trying to play, but it got the job done. Merlynda was glad she was no longer allergic to cats.

Zahilda let out a low whistle at the sight of Dame Illondria and Fang. "I never thought I'd see a horned pegasus in my life-time. And what on Earth is *that* creature?"

"That's Fang." Neci beamed.

Merlynda was off the broom and at Iggy's side before everyone else had come to a full stop. "How is he?"

"The same," Dame Illondria answered. "Batu's song is long-lasting."

"This is Iggy," Merlynda said to Zahilda. "Can you help him?"

"What," a sharp voice asked, "is *she* doing here?"

"Hello, Wallace," Zahilda said coolly. Prince Whiskerkins arched his back and hissed.

"Zahilda." The Inquirer's voice was curt (as much as it was possible to sound curt while twirling). He whirled toward Merlynda. "When I suggested the witch might be able to assist your friend, I was not granting you permission to bring her here."

"Oh, blow down a house with all your hot air," Zahilda said. "I've come to apologize."

The Inquirer stumbled, then continued with his dance. "You've what?"

"She isn't welcome here!" a turtle person called from a long dancing line.

"As I am well aware," Zahilda shot back. "But even if *you* are all ghastly and awful, it doesn't mean that I should be."

Zahilda raised her arms.

"Look out!" the old woman screeched.

"Shut up, Agatha." Zahilda clapped her hands together.

There was a deafening crack at the moment her fingers touched, and thousands of tiny flames sprang up from the feet of the dancers. The flame tongues gathered above their heads in a roiling fireball, whipping up clothes and hair and dust.

Then Zahilda snapped her fingers, and the fireball shrank in on itself. A small gem dropped from the flames into the surprised Zahilda's hand, and that was that.

No one danced.

"We're cured!" old Agatha cried, and collapsed from exhaustion. Everyone else followed her example.

Batu stepped over a villager, narrowly avoiding Prince Whiskerkins, who batted at the fallen villagers playfully. "What's wrong with them now?"

"They'll be all right," Zahilda said, distracted by the gem. "Hydration and rest are all they need."

"Zahilda." Merlynda tried to keep the pleading out of her voice, but she couldn't help it. "Can you save Iggy? Please. A wicked sort of familiar did this to him."

"Ah." Zahilda bent closer to examine Iggy, careful not to touch him. "That explains the wizard magic. Can't you feel it? Oh, that's right." Her eyes flicked to Merlynda's bracer.

Neci stroked Fang's fur. "You can heal him, right?"

Zahilda straightened. "No. My particular brand of magic has never played well with that wizard nonsense."

Merlynda crumpled to the ground. Her whole world was collapsing and breaking inside her. They'd failed. *She'd* failed. Zahilda had been right. What sort of Septimum Genus was she?

A sob rolled through her, taking with it any lingering fragments of hope. She balled up her fists. The Shadow Sun was tomorrow. They'd come so close, and none of it would matter.

"Hush, child. There is a new possibility, but it will not be an easy choice."

Merlynda wiped her face and took a shaky breath. "Anything."

Zahilda held up the gem that had fallen from the flames. It was hard and black, but a reddish light glowed from within.

"This is pure fire," the witch explained. "Highly compressed flames, forced into a solid form. I've been hoping to summon one my entire life."

Merlynda stared. It was an Elemental Stone! The very thing she and Percy had been trying to find the day that Iggy arrived and then Percy vanished through the portal. The day she got the parchment. "It can save Iggy?"

"Yes." Zahilda hesitated. "These firestones are rare, child."

"I know," Merlynda said eagerly. Hope blossomed again, and she dared to let it.

"I never expected one to come from any of my spells," Zahilda continued in earnest, "though I've tried my whole life. They form once every few generations."

"But we've got one," Batu said. "That's all we need, isn't it?"

"Perhaps. And after today I am more than willing to give it to you. But it can only perform one spell, so you must choose how it will best serve its purpose." Zahilda gave the bracer a meaningful look.

"Oh," Merlynda said in a small voice. She tugged her sleeve up so that her bracer was fully displayed. "You mean that stone can remove this?" she whispered.

Zahilda nodded. "I can't heal Iggy, but you might be able to."

Merlynda didn't understand. "Even without the bracer, I don't know anything about healing magic."

"You may not need to. The bond between wizardess and familiar is an extraordinary one," the witch answered. "Perhaps with your magic restored, you can heal him."

Perhaps she could, Merlynda agreed—but perhaps wasn't good enough. It had *never* been good enough. *She'd* never been good enough. She'd lost Percy because she couldn't control her magic, and if she made the wrong choice, she'd lose Iggy, too.

Zahilda held out the firestone, and Merlynda took it gingerly. It was heavier than it looked and warmed her hand from the bracer's chill. She hesitated.

Dame Illondria nuzzled Merlynda's shoulder. "You know what you must do, Septimum Genus," she said. Her voice was warm and sad and comforting. "Use the stone to remove the bracer, and then heal Ignus with your magic. It is no choice at all."

Merlynda inhaled shakily. "You're right. It's no choice at all."

She dropped to her knees and thrust the gem at Iggy.

It slipped into Iggy's scales as easily as a rock dropped in a lake. Light rippled up and down the wyvern's body and shot out in all directions.

His tail and wings straightened. His two feet scratched at the ground as he stretched.

Then his eyes burst open, and a stream of flame shot out of his mouth.

Iggy looked around, embarrassed. "Excuse me."

Merlynda scooped him up and hugged him.

"Hello, Merlynda! What did I miss?" He craned his neck around Merlynda's head. Everyone was staring at him. "Do I have something stuck in my teeth?" he whispered to her.

Batu blinked the spots out of his vision. "You just shot fire out of your mouth."

"I did?" Iggy paused, then blew gently. Another jet of flames came out.

"Did you see that, Merlynda?" He darted into the air, showing off his new skill. "I'm a proper wyvern now!"

"You were always perfect." Merlynda wiped at her tears, then flinched as the chill from the bracer touched her face.

Iggy landed on her shoulder. "What's wrong?"

"The Septimum Genus had a difficult decision." Dame Illondria's voice was as noble and steady as ever, hiding the disappointment Merlynda was sure she felt. "She's only just chosen."

Merlynda felt the heat rise in her throat. "I did choose! And I'd choose the same again."

"I'm sure you were brilliant," Iggy said. "What did you choose?"

Merlynda tried to hold on to the anger, tried to keep her brave face. But it was too much, and all at once the heat collapsed. "You!" She choked down a sob. "I didn't believe that I could heal you with my magic, so I used the firestone to save you instead of getting rid of this cursed bracer."

Iggy wiped her face dry with his tail. Merlynda hugged him again.

"How will I defeat the Hollower now?" she whispered. "How will I save Percy? But I thought—instead of losing both of you, if I could save one—"

Iggy nuzzled her cheek. "You're lucky to have saved me because now you've got a very fierce *fire-breathing* wyvern for a familiar. And I'm not as tiny as I used to be."

"I'm scared," Merlynda confessed.

"There's nothing wrong with fear." Zahilda eyed the Inquirer, who was still lying on the ground. "What matters is how you handle it."

"And you've got us," Neci told her. Batu and Fang nodded.

"I will stay by your side as well," Dame Illondria said. "Saving your friend was a noble decision."

"I didn't do it to be noble," Merlynda sniffed, wiping at her face. "I did it because I was selfish."

"Loving others is quite the opposite of selfishness."

Merlynda stroked Iggy's tail. That sounded true, but what

if she'd made the wrong choice? "Neci, do you have my scrying shell? I want to check in on the Omnivia."

Neci rummaged around in her satchel and pulled it out. Merlynda dunked it into a bucket of water, then paused. She couldn't actually do anything with it this time.

"Let me." Iggy hovered over the shell, cocked his head at it, then slapped the water with his tail. It leapt out of the shell and swirled into a half-moon shape, with the flat side on the bottom.

Iggy landed on Merlynda's shoulder and ducked his head beneath a wing. He'd flubbed using the scrying shell—how embarrassing!

Merlynda walked around the half-moon. "Where's the Omnivia?"

"Give it here," Zahilda said. The water splashed to the ground, so she dunked the shell again, muttered a few words, then tossed the water into the air.

Iggy peeked his head out to watch. The droplets fell down into a perfect half-moon like before.

Zahilda peered at it. "You were right. Your Hollower is definitely there."

Iggy flew around the water. It didn't look anything like the Omnivia they'd scried before. He poked it with his tail, but that didn't tell him anything either. "How do you know?"

"He doesn't want us to see what he's up to." Zahilda prodded the Inquirer with her foot. "I assume my cottage is as I left it, Wallace?"

"Yes." The Inquirer lifted his head from where he lay on the ground. "No one wanted to risk being cursed again."

"Typical," Zahilda huffed. "How I lived among such narrow-mindedness, I'll never know." She picked up Prince Whiskerkins (who had given up trying to play with the villagers and was now stalking leaves) and started off.

"Where are you going?" Merlynda asked.

"With you," Zahilda called over her shoulder. "But if we're going off on this fool's errand, we're going to need pie."

Merlynda's heart swelled, and she felt the hope trying to spark, to win its way back. It was a dangerous thing, hope, but Merlynda was beginning to think it was necessary. Hope that they would save Percy had brought them this far, and she was determined to see things through to the end.

The people of the land of Quaesitum were more than happy to help the questers be on their way, as they still wished to have nothing to do with magic. Merlynda wanted to head out immediately—the Shadow Sun was *tomorrow*—but she saw the reason in getting a good rest and showing up fresh, for all the good it would do without her magic. Besides, it was no use arguing with Zahilda.

Bags were packed with food and water, directions were given, and Zahilda even managed to heal Dame Illondria's wings the rest of the way while her pies cooled.

"It's nothing to thank me for." Zahilda smoothed out her dress. "She'd already done most of the work herself, but it's not every day one meets a horned pegasus."

"I like her," Iggy whispered to Merlynda. "She smells like flowers. Do you think she can make funnel cake?"

A harness was made for Fang, who kept trotting in circles. She didn't know why they needed to strap her into a silly thing attached to that pie-maker's broom, but Neci kept stroking her neck just the way she liked, so the Questing Beast decided to see things through.

Merlynda wasn't sure if the Hollower knew they were still coming, or if he was just being cautious. She asked Zahilda to do a little more magic for her, just to be safe.

"And what good will it do, sending these messages to—who was it? Lord Fenrir of the Nordvings and Lady Phelia of Oceanus?"

"Possibly more good than if we sent nothing," Merlynda snapped, matching the witch's tone. Zahilda might not be evil, but she was certainly cranky. "At the very least, the Nordvings and Oceanids deserve to know!"

"And the Rusvokians?" Batu asked, adding another small scroll to the stack in front of the witch.

"*And* my parents," Merlynda added. "They must be back from the Forfle realm by now. I've tried sending them messages but don't think any have made it." She didn't mention how worried they must be, or how much she missed them. "And Mother can help us."

"Fine!" Zahilda muttered a quick spell, and the scrolls zipped up into the air like shooting stars before streaking off toward their destinations.

Preparations made, the children and Iggy—the bonded quartet—shared a pie that evening. It was delicious, and not just because Zahilda was an excellent baker. It was the final eve of their quest. Tomorrow would decide whether they succeeded or failed, whether they rescued Percy and defeated the Hollower or if more dreadful things would befall them. Sharing a meal on such an evening nourished their bodies, yes, but also their spirits.

There were also things that needed to be said before they headed off into what was sure to be a grueling battle.

"Batu," Neci said, feeling uncomfortable. But knights acknowledged when they'd done wrong. "My deepest apologies for being so rude to you on the flying island. I beg your forgiveness." Thank goodness again for the wording in *The Compendium of Knights and Their Noble Deeds*! She wasn't just repeating the words, though. She meant them, which is the only way an apology is any good. "Also, thanks for saving us from crashing to our untimely doom."

Batu swallowed his bite of pie. "Oh, sure. I mean, I didn't want to crash either." Batu hesitated, then went on. Hadn't he promised no more secrets? "I'm sorry too. My uncle used to like it if I was a jerk to people. If he was happy, things were easier."

Neci was appalled. Her parents might keep trying to make her be someone she had no interest in being, but they would *never* want her to treat others unkindly.

"So I got in the habit of being . . . well, someone who isn't very nice," Batu continued. "But I don't like treating people that way. I really am sorry."

Iggy lifted his head from his pie and bared his teeth. "Your uncle is the one who needs to be sorry if I ever see him again!"

Neci seethed in agreement. "Family is hard when you're not what they wanted or hoped for." She looked from Merlynda to Iggy to Batu. "But I'm glad that here, we can be just who we are."

Everyone chorused their agreement, then returned to the business of finishing their pie and thinking about tomorrow.

"Are you sure about this?" Neci asked Merlynda. "It's bound to be dangerous, and we still don't know how to get that bracer off."

Merlynda didn't look at her forearm. She was acutely aware of the bracer. Every. Single. Moment. "Do knights back down when they know they have to head into danger?"

"Nope."

"Then neither do wizardesses."

"Or minstrels."

"Or exceptionally talented wyverns."

They finished their pie, then turned in early, each wondering what the next day would bring. Merlynda settled onto her sleeping mat and removed the familiar parchment from her robes. It was already crumpled and worn. Oceanus felt like it had been ages ago, but it had hardly been days.

How had Percy spent these past months? Was he all right?

Iggy nuzzled her. "We'll know tomorrow," he mumbled sleepily. The bracer might disrupt their ability to sense each other, but they were still bonded. Like any good friend, he knew his wizardess was worried about what the morning would bring.

Merlynda slipped the parchment back into her robes. He was right, but she couldn't sleep just yet.

"Iggy," Merlynda whispered. "What if . . . What if we can't save him?"

Iggy turned in a circle a few times before settling down next to his wizardess. "We'll get there in time."

"Not that." Merlynda licked her lips, afraid to say what she *really* feared, but also needing to. "What if we get to Percy in time, but the Hollower still wins? What if . . . What if I'm not good enough to stop him?"

Merlynda fought to keep her voice down as her fears rose to the surface.

"I'm the one who bungled my magic so badly, he vanished into a portal. I'm the one who is supposed to be the great Septimum Genus, but I can't even use magic! It's my fault! If we can't save him—if I can't—"

Merlynda buried her head in her arms so the others wouldn't wake from her crying. A small warm body pressed against hers. She lifted her head to see Iggy curled against her.

"We are going to get there in time," he told her. "And the Septimum Genus and her very fierce, flying, *fire-breathing* wyvern are going to make the Hollower wish he'd never Hollowed anyone."

They were both afraid. Even so, Merlynda felt a tiny bit

of reassurance that if anyone could defeat the Hollower, it was them.

But that would be tomorrow. For now, all she could do was rest.

Merlynda was up before dawn and roused the others. The Shadow Sun would appear this afternoon, and if they hadn't found Percy by then—

She savagely tightened a supply pack, refusing to take that thought any further. They *would* find Percy. The ache of missing her twin and the hope of soon finding him filled her so much, she thought she might burst like the flames of the dancing plague.

The Inquirer came to make sure they were truly leaving. "Have everything you need? Heading out soon? I'm sure you must be on your way—you've magic to bother, or whatever you said."

"Stop tattering, Wallace," Zahilda snapped.

The questers flew fast toward the Omnivia, the sun rising higher with each passing minute. Dame Illondria's wings were still infused with the remnants of healing magic, beating steadily, determined and strong. Zahilda, for all her reluctance to appear witchy, was proud of her broom. It was barely slowed at all by Fang. The Questing Beast had thrashed and panicked in her harness during takeoff, so Zahilda cast a sleeping curse.

"She'll be fine," the witch promised an indignant Neci.

"Give her a gentle stroke once we land—she'll come around."

"There might still be a bit of evil in her," Neci grumbled to Merlynda.

The wizardess, for her part, was trying very hard to think of ways she might defeat the Hollower without her magic. She hoped Mother had gotten her message, which would help a great deal in that area. "Are you sure you sent the messages correctly?" she asked Zahilda.

"Of course I did," the witch snapped, and that was the end of that.

An hour before midday, a brilliant bluish purple light appeared on the horizon. As they flew closer, they saw that the light came from an enormous dome. Dame Illondria and Zahilda circled it so they could take a good look.

Merlynda squinted. They were so close! "Where's the Omnivia?"

"Hidden beneath this strange light. Proceed with caution, Septimum Genus," the horned pegasus warned. "Our enemy has great power."

"Pfah," Zahilda said, unimpressed. "If he's trying to tamper with the In-Between, he's not *that* clever."

They landed. Neci woke Fang right away, who had no intention of ever traveling by air or sleeping curse again, and the group turned to examine the dome.

It was made of pure magic, and shimmered as they approached. Dame Illondria snorted at the offensive barrier. Neci poked it tentatively with her dagger. A slight ripple moved along the surface, then stilled. She reached out to touch it. "I can see the grass on the other side, but I can't push through."

"Perhaps he's cleverer than I thought." Zahilda peered at the dome so closely, her nose touched it. Prince Whiskerkins did the same, batting at it. "It's an Impedimentum, and one of this size is nothing to sneeze at."

Merlynda inhaled sharply. "It's a barrier against magic," she explained to Neci and Batu. "Against the Aether. Magic can't pass through it."

Neci wrinkled her nose. "But I haven't got magic."

"Me neither." Batu rapped his knuckles on the Impedimentum.

"Everyone's got magic," Zahilda said. "It's just that some people have a good deal less than others."

Merlynda tugged her sleeve away from her bracer—the bracer that *separated* her from the Aether.

"Iggy," she said in a hushed voice. "You'll have to stay here."

The fierce wyvern looked from the bracer to Merlynda. It didn't block *his* magic. "You're right," he answered softly. "But I want you to know I don't like it."

"I know. But you must be brave. I'll be back."

"I'll try to be as brave as you." He nuzzled her cheek one last time, then fluttered his fiery golden wings and perched on Fang.

"Good luck," Zahilda said. "I'm glad I didn't turn you into stew."

Dame Illondria bowed. "Go with courage."

"We'll find another way to break through the barrier," Batu promised.

Neci threw herself at Merlynda in a huge hug. "You are the best friend a knight could ever hope for," she whispered. She pulled away and pressed Faithful into Merlynda's hands.

Merlynda tried to push it back. "No way. I can't."

Neci crossed her arms, refusing to take it. "You have to. You have no idea what you're up against."

Merlynda knew it was pointless to argue, so she accepted the dagger and turned toward the Impedimentum, gazing up at the sun. How much time did she have? An hour? Two? She wished Mother would arrive soon, but she couldn't wait any longer.

"Well." She took a deep breath. "Here I go." She reached a hand toward the barrier. It passed through as easily as air.

Magic or not, it was time to be the Septimum Genus. She stepped forward.

The inside of the Impedimentum was ghostly quiet, as if cut away from the rest of the world. Merlynda looked up at the top of the dome, high above, then glanced behind her. She could just make out the outlines of her friends, now shadowy figures beyond the barrier. But they couldn't help her, so she clutched Faithful and moved on.

Ahead of her stood several enormous stone pillars, roughly arranged in two circles, one inside the other—the Omnivia. Several stones were lying on the ground, knocked over from eons of existence. A few of the standing stones had a third gigantic pillar stacked across them, forming a doorway to nowhere, just like the parchment Percy had sent her. And through one of the doorways stepped—

"Percy!"

*In which Merlynda meets
the Hollower*

The tension Merlynda had carried ever since Percy had disappeared through the portal vanished. The lightness blooming through her was the most wonderful thing. She could *breathe* again.

She sprinted for her brother, not caring if the Hollower was nearby, not caring if she'd given herself away, because Percy was there and he was all right—

Percy whirled around, caught off guard. No one was supposed to be here! The figure barreling toward him, purple robes billowing around her, was—*Merlynda*.

Percy sliced his arm through the air, and the earth between

him and Merlynda shot up in a geyser of dirt, rock, and pebbles. When the dust had settled, a narrow but deep trench ran between them.

Merlynda skidded to a stop before the trench, puzzled, not quite to the outside ring of enormous stone doorways. Percy had traded his usual robes for a darker, more formfitting outfit, but this was definitely her twin in front of her. She'd know those blue eyes and that chestnut hair anywhere, and not just because they were the same as her own. But there was something new *behind* those eyes. Something shadowy and dark. "Percy?"

"What are you doing here?" he demanded.

Merlynda took a tentative step forward. "I'm rescuing you. You sent for me."

"I didn't."

Merlynda could not believe that after all she'd been through to get here, after finally finding the Omnivia and Percy, that this was the welcome she got! She huffed and jumped across the narrow ditch, still holding Neci's dagger as she strode toward him. The stones towered above her, gray and rough and covered in moss and lichen, far wider and thicker than her entire arm span spread fingertip to fingertip. Shorter blue-tinged stones, as tall as Merlynda, were also scattered between the rings of doorways. "You did! Iggy arrived—that's my familiar—and then somehow we created that second portal and you vanished, but then a third portal opened and you sent me this message!" She thrust the parchment with the Omnivia clue at him.

Percy snatched it and glared. His eyes widened when he noticed Merlynda's bracer. "Why are you still wearing that?" he growled. "You were supposed to use the firestone!"

"Iggy was hurt and—" Merlynda stopped. "How do you know about the firestone?"

"I know everything, Merlynda," he sneered. "At least, I *did*, except you kept meddling."

"Meddling?" Merlynda's temper flared. Weeks and months of trying to find Percy, of worrying and imagining the worst possible scenarios, and this was how he thanked her? "You get sucked through a terrifying portal to Merlyn knows where, pop up again looking terrified, and send me this clue about the Hollower"—here she jabbed her finger at the parchment Percy still grasped—"and say that by trying to rescue you from losing your magic, I'm *meddling*?"

Merlynda paused to catch her breath, and a screech sounded from above. She instinctively whipped up the dagger as the twisted falcon swooped down toward them.

"Watch out, Percy! That falcon's attacked us more than once. . . ."

Merlynda trailed off as the falcon alighted on Percy's shoulder. He reached up to stroke it, smiling.

Understanding froze Merlynda like a wave of ice, but she shied away from it.

She had to be wrong. *This* was wrong. Not her partner in crime, who always had a mostly harmless scheme up his sleeve. Not her talented twin, who was always there to clean up her magical messes. Not her brother, who had promised that they would figure out her magic *together*.

But then she glimpsed the shadowy *something* that was now behind Percy's eyes as he went back to magically digging his trench, and she couldn't deny it. She tried to breathe, but her lungs felt like the wind had been knocked out from them.

Percy was the Hollower. *Percy* had stolen the magic from the Oceanid, and countless others across the centuries. *Percy* had ordered the falcon to hurt Iggy, and Pugachev to—

"*You* did this to me?!" she shrieked, thrusting the bracer in Percy's face and startling his falcon away into flight. Her voice shook from the anger and from the tears she fought back. "*This* is how you keep your promise to help me with my magic? By taking it away? By being the Hollower?"

Percy paused from his work to smirk and offer a mocking bow. "Do you think Merlyn knew his seventh descendants would be the Septimum Genus and the Hollower?" he asked, straightening. "Two of the most powerful people of all time." He glanced at her bracer with disdain. "Well, at least one of us is."

Merlynda had never given much thought to what a broken heart might feel like, but it had to be exactly what she felt now. Empty. *Emptier* than empty. As if she'd already been Hollowed, but instead of her magic being taken, it was everything she was. Everything she trusted. Everything she'd believed.

Percy sliced his arm through the air again, extending the ditch farther around the Omnivia. "I've got a schedule to keep, Merlynda."

Merlynda wrenched her focus away from her broken heart and back to her brother. To his betrayal. "But *why*?" Her confusion spiked her anger, and she clenched her fists. "Do you know what I've been through to find you?"

"I do, yes." Percy didn't look up from the trench he continued to carve just outside the stone doorways of the Omnivia. He blasted air at the exploding earth to keep it away from himself. He did not extend the same courtesy to Merlynda, who ducked behind one of the stones. "I inherited Grandfather Merlyn's foresight, remember. But as Merlyn always said, foresight can't be trusted entirely."

Merlynda lifted her arm to protect her face from the blowing dirt, stepping over and around the huge fallen stones while she followed Percy around the circle. "You saw me using the firestone on my bracer," she accused. "If I'd done that, I wouldn't have been able to enter the Impedimentum."

Percy blasted one final section of earth. He brushed specks of dirt from his robe, pleased with how the ditch had turned out. "The bracer was only supposed to be temporary. It's not my fault you kept it on."

"It's your fault I'm wearing it at all!" Merlynda shouted. "But if I *had* removed it, you'd be free to—to do whatever it is you're doing." She looked at the trench, which formed a deep circle around the outside of the entire Omnivia.

"The bracer was supposed to keep you from interfering. With you out of the way, stealing your familiar's magic was supposed to be easy. My falcon almost got the little worm that last time." He studied the parchment she'd handed him, puzzled. "I could've gone back to when it first arrived and drained its magic then, but the potential would've been significantly less prior to your bonding with it."

This was another layer of information for Merlynda to process. "You travel through *time?*" But of course it made sense. If Percy was the Hollower, he'd have to time travel to steal magic from all those centuries.

"Just like Merlyn," he said, distracted, then finally looked up from the parchment. "Almost, anyway. I can only go backward. I can't travel beyond our present like Merlyn could, to see if my foresight is right."

The shadows in Percy's eyes deepened.

"I went back and listened to his prophecy about us," he almost snarled. "All this time, we've been looking at him as some sort of great wise wizard, but he was a bumbling twit! And so *selfish*. He had access to all this power"—he gestured at the Omnivia—"but kept it to himself!"

This darkness and anger were not Merlynda's brother. "What happened, Percy?" Merlynda whispered. "What made you like this?"

"I made myself," he said coldly. "I was furious your familiar came first. How could it be possible that you were the Septimum Genus and not me?"

His voice was so icy, Merlynda felt like he'd slapped her.

"And then I was terrified, getting sucked into that portal. The In-Between is an empty place. Time doesn't make any sense there. I was trapped alone for ages, with only my fear and anger and confusion echoing back at me. It was awful."

Percy was haunted by the memory for a moment, then shook himself loose. "But then I found this." He reached up to a silk cord tied around his neck, and from beneath his robes he lifted a flat silver disk. Beautiful, intricate etchings surrounded a glowing amethyst in the center.

It was the amulet of Morgan le Fey.

He moved toward Merlynda, who took an involuntary step back. "I summoned my own familiar, and Vis arrived. And when we went back and listened to the prophecy, I realized something."

Percy's gaze was frenzied. Merlynda kept backing away until her foot slipped into the ditch. "And what's that?" she asked, because she knew she was supposed to.

"We make our own destiny. And I'm going to be the greatest wizard of all time."

"Yes, well, you're already one of the world's greatest terrors, well done," Merlynda spat. "Are you going to travel back and magic Merlyn away?"

Percy grinned, but it was maniacal. "Even better. I'm going to make a Concursus."

Merlynda was stunned for a moment, sure she'd misheard. But no, of course she hadn't. "You're delirious!" she shouted. "Percy, this isn't you! Merlyn broke his Concursus for a reason—he didn't leave instructions on purpose—"

"Because he didn't want anyone else to be better than

him!" Percy bellowed back. "I'm going to open up the In-Between and be more powerful than he ever was!"

He calmed down, breathing hard. The amulet flared, and his eyes hardened. "I tried to protect you, you know. The amulet's whispers wanted your magic, but I planned to give it your familiar's instead. I gave you that bracer to keep you out of the way. To keep you safe."

This was by far the most twisted reasoning Merlynda had ever heard. She started to say so while Percy gazed at the amulet, but then he looked at Merlynda with such intensity, she froze.

"But now I don't have a choice. If I can't have that little worm's magic, I'll have to take yours."

Iggy, Neci, Batu, Dame Illondria, Zahilda, and Fang stared at the spot where Merlynda had vanished.

Iggy sniffed at the Impedimentum. "It smells like the In-Between."

"We've got to help her." Neci looked at Zahilda. "Don't you know *anything* that will get us inside?"

"Oh, sure," Zahilda said. "Expect the witch to solve everything. Haven't a clue, dear."

A familiar *poof* sounded from behind them, and Neci groaned. As one, they turned to find a group of fairies.

Zahilda raised an eyebrow. "Who are you, bug-brains?"

The chubby, daffodil-skinned fairy with the goatee darted forward. "Presentin' the Right Honorable Lumont of the Oak Tree, Prime Minister of the Woodland Fairies—"

"That's quite enough, Horace." Lumont flew forward, squinting through his monocle down his sky-blue nose. Horace backed into the group.

Neci glowered. "You're a ways outside of fairy territory." She hadn't appreciated the fairies much to begin with, but she'd never forget how they refused to help Merlynda with the Rusvokians.

Lumont cleared his throat. "We have been tasked with the protection of the Impedimentum."

"You are on the wrong side of this conflict, Master Lumont." Dame Illondria's eyes narrowed. "I suggest you leave."

"I'm afraid we can't do that," the prime minister answered. "Our instructions are to stop you, by force if necessary."

"You and what army?" Neci challenged.

Clouds of sparkly dust *poofed* all around them, and the air filled with fairies winking into existence. There were scores and scores of them, all growling and wielding tiny weapons.

"Great," Zahilda muttered. "Looks like those messages we sent were invitations to a party."

"But the fairies weren't invited." Neci turned to Lumont. "What's happening in that Impedimentum?" she demanded.

Lumont lifted his feathered hat from his head and brushed it off. It sparkled, then morphed into a battle helmet. "It is no concern of yours."

"Here's a concern for you, fairy scum!" a deep voice boomed.

"Aye, you tell that twinkletoes!"

"More concerning than Freiydin's wrath!"

"Hail, Fenrir!"

A host of Nordvings marched in from the west. Neci spotted Brynhild and waved, and even Batu was excited. Iggy bobbed a greeting to a still-hovering Vilhelmina, who pawed a lazy hello and then eyed Fang.

"This conflict isn't yours, Lord Fenrir," Lumont said testily. "You'll want to return home."

Fenrir swung his battle-axe around as if it weighed nothing. "I was thinking the same of you, Master Lumont. I'm glad we were already pillaging in the area when we received Merlynda's message." He looked at Vilhelmina. "These the fairies that imprisoned you, my precious?"

The aerial liger bared her teeth, and the fairies flinched.

Lumont tried to compose himself, but the feathers on his helmet shook. "There will be no mercy offered to the beast this time."

Pop! "None indeed," a voice cackled from the east.

Prince Whiskerkins hissed, and Zahilda whirled around, furious. "You were most certainly *not invited*."

Pop! Pop! A mass of black-robed figures appeared, each accompanied by a *pop* and a black cat. The lead witch removed her hood, revealing a face that looked very much like Zahilda's. "We received an invitation from the good Master Lumont," the witch crooned. "How disappointed we were to hear that our own dear sister was having a soiree without us! Wizards have kept the In-Between's power from us for far too long."

"And you'll be kept away a bit longer!" a voice called from above.

"Nikolai!" Batu waved.

The three mini armies and the travelers looked up to find a horde of raiders swooping and gliding on the backs of the flying boars. "Hello, Mitya!" Nikolai called down. "We received your message!"

"Oh, ho!" Fenrir cried. "I've been waiting for another chance to give Pugachev's ilk a taste of my axe!" He raised his weapon, but Batu stepped forward.

"No, Lord Fenrir! We're allies now. And . . . I'm sort of their leader? Since my, er, uncle has disappeared."

Fenrir looked at Batu, astonished. Then he belly-laughed. "Very clever, Batu of the Lake! If I'd known who you really were, things might have gone differently for you. But if you say we're allies, then allies we are!"

A piece of cloth fluttered down from Nikolai. Batu tied it around his wrist, to show his true colors. "I guess I'm a raider after all," he told Neci.

Neci could have hugged him for bringing reinforcements. Instead, she turned to Lumont and the witches, to Fenrir and the Rusvokians.

She drew her sling and loaded it with a rock.

It was going to be a glorious battle.

In the past when in danger, Merlynda unconsciously summoned a mysterious Aether shield to defend herself. With the bracer, she knew this was impossible, so instead she took the only other recourse she knew.

She tackled Percy.

Light flared up from the amulet and zapped into the top of the Impedimentum high above them, missing Merlynda by a breath. She'd caught Percy by surprise and pinned him, scrabbling with Neci's dagger, trying to cut the amulet's cord from his neck. One thing had become clear to her—whether or not Percy realized it, he was under the sway of Morgan le Fey's favorite evil item.

An invisible force slammed Merlynda back, sending her tumbling across the grass. She frantically stabbed Faithful into the ground to stop herself before she crashed into one of the Omnivia stones. Even the shorter bluestones were a great deal thicker than her and would pack a wallop.

Percy stood, panting. "Don't make this harder than it has to be. It's your turn to help me, like all those times I helped you."

Merlynda scrambled behind one of the towering gray pillars on the outer ring. "I'm not going to help you steal magic!" she shouted, edging around the stone and away from Percy's voice. She wished she had a shield instead of Neci's dagger!

She was about to make a run for it when Percy's hand shot out from behind the stone, holding the amulet. Merlynda was slammed back again, this time landing hard on the grass inside the Omnivia's inner ring. She blinked, dazed, holding on to Faithful like a lifeline. Now she could see that there weren't two rings of broken stone doorways, like she'd thought. The inner circle was actually arranged like a horseshoe. Time had broken the stones so that instead of five clear doorways, only three stood on their own, the remnants of the others strewn about the ground.

Percy chuckled as Merlynda struggled back to her feet, idly swinging the amulet. "Morgan lost to Merlyn because she was arrogant," he said. "I don't plan to make that same mistake."

"Could've fooled me!" Merlynda shot back. She tensed, trying to remember any of the battle tactics Neci had babbled on and on about, but they all escaped her. "Mother will be here soon," she threatened, then winced at how pathetic that sounded.

"Oh, because your witch friend sent her a message?" Percy pulled a scroll from his sleeve. "This message?"

Dread snaked into Merlynda's stomach, wispy tendrils that twisted and squeezed. "How did you know about that?"

The scroll burst into blue flames in Percy's hand. He let the ash blow away. "I wasn't taking any risks. I made sure all magical correspondences to Mother were routed to me. Thankfully"—he gave her another infuriating smirk—"none of *your* attempts to contact her were anywhere near successful."

Merlynda ignored her crumbling hope, stumbling over a fallen bluestone as she tried to put more distance between her and Percy. Mother wasn't coming, but hopefully the other messages Zahilda sent had been successful. Percy had no reason to monitor Fenrir or the others.

"You know, I think Merlyn was afraid Morgan would

come back," Percy mused. "He put a charm on this amulet so that only his blood relations could touch it. Funny, isn't it? Only descendants of Merlyn can wield the amulet of Morgan le Fey."

He jumped toward her, amulet outstretched, and again Merlynda was blasted back. She bashed into one of the pillars, gasping.

"Then why can't *I* get near it?" Merlynda growled, trying to get her footing for the third time. He was *playing* with her.

Percy's cocky smile grew. "Because I'm smarter than Morgan *and* Merlyn." He reached into his robes and pulled out a lock of hair, bound with a shiny gold ribbon. "The fairies were more than willing to help once they learned what I could do."

The coils in Merlynda's stomach tightened. Percy really had thought of everything. He'd sent the fairies to take a lock of her hair and then used it to put a restriction spell on the amulet. As long as the hair was bound, she couldn't touch the amulet, couldn't get near it, couldn't stop Percy from making a Concursus for whatever malevolence the amulet had planned.

The hopelessness of what was happening crashed into Merlynda, and Percy beamed as he saw it spread across her face. The dread dug deeper.

"Percy." Merlynda tried to keep the desperation out of her voice. "This is wrong! You know Morgan only wanted to destroy things, rule everyone—this amulet was supposed to help her do that!"

Percy either didn't realize the amulet had its own designs,

or didn't care. He slipped the cord over his neck once more, the shadows flickering behind his eyes. "It's my amulet now. I'm sorry, Merlynda."

The amulet flared. A beam of amethyst light shot from it, catching Merlynda full in the chest. She was lifted up, up, up into the air, higher than even the tallest of the towering stones, surrounded in swirling purple light. Merlynda shouted and struggled, twisting and turning, trying to escape. Why didn't the bracer block *this* feeling?

She felt her magic being ripped out of her, fiber by fiber, every last tendril and wisp, absorbed into the gem in the amulet. It didn't laugh anymore, didn't say anything as it seared her from the inside out.

When she'd been scraped clean of every last breath of Aether, Merlynda collapsed to the ground. She lay there, enveloped in her new reality, in this new heavy emptiness that left her foggy and cold.

She'd been Hollowed. Her magic—*her magic*—was gone.

In which a dastardly plan comes to light

The four armies stood their ground (or flew on their boars), eyeing one another. The questers were tensed, ready, backs to the Impedimentum as they faced their unexpected foes.

Then a fairy let out a warbling war cry (which is a terrifying thing, you'll remember), and everyone charged.

A Rusvokian woman tossed a curved sword down to Batu, who caught it and began batting fairies out of his way left and right. Vilhelmina growled and took a swipe at a flying boar.

"They're our friends now!" Batu scolded her. "Go after the fairies."

She flicked her tail at him but pounced on Horace.

Dame Illondria and Zahilda set to work deflecting hexes and curses and sending them back at the witches.

"You've baked your last pie, sister!" the head witch crooned.

"Hardly!" Zahilda shot back. "I've got something in the oven right now!" She blasted the coven with a hex of her own, scattering them. They stumbled to their feet and hissed. Prince Whiskerkins launched himself at the throng of black cats, yowling.

Iggy darted up and down the battlefield, nipping at fairies and blasting plumes of fire and thoroughly enjoying himself.

Fang didn't understand what all the fuss was about, but Neci didn't like the little chubby flying things, and she definitely didn't like the robed figures who knew Zahilda, so the Questing Beast kicked out at anything that Neci attacked (or that tried to attack Neci). It was much more exciting than being Pugachev's pet had ever been.

Neci found herself back-to-back with Brynhild, who tossed her a spare sword. They stabbed and parried at the fairies, and Neci even got into a brief grappling match with a witch (she knocked the witch out cold before the hex was finished).

Flashes of light shot back and forth, arrows darted past, and flying boars dropped down to crash into enemies and give their archers closer targets. It was, indeed, a glorious battle. Everything a knight could wish for!

Everything, that is, except for her best friend. This battle was just a distraction to keep them from helping Merlynda.

"Iggy!" she yelled as the wyvern darted by, chasing a witch with his fire. He soared back around and perched on her shoulder as she ran. It wasn't as nice as Merlynda's shoulder, but it would do.

"We have to get inside the Impedimentum." Neci swung her sword up to block a hex, then stopped outside the magical barrier. The bluish purple dome was turning more purple. She raised her sword and stabbed it with all her might. It clanked off, rattling her arms so badly, she dropped it.

Iggy belched out a stream of fire at a fairy who was trying to sneak up on them. He poked the Impedimentum with his tail. "We need magic."

"You said it smelled like the In-Between."

"Yes."

"And when we were in the Howlwyn Forest, you said that in the In-Between, the elements are all jumbled."

"Yes."

"Well . . ." Magic was not Neci's area of expertise. "What if we gather all the elements together?"

Iggy thought for a second. "That might work. Or it also might not."

A hex blasted into the dome right over Neci's head. She sprinted away to find Batu. "Have you got a better idea?"

"Nope!" Iggy launched himself into the air toward Zahilda and Dame Illondria.

A few moments later the questers gathered once more outside the barrier. Dame Illondria pawed the ground. "Your plan has been explained, Neci the Ardent. I will stand vigil over your scheme."

"Hurry," Iggy urged. His tail whipped back and forth nervously. "Something bad is happening."

Zahilda considered the Impedimentum. It was much more purple than blue now. "I don't think this will work."

"If you have a better idea, now's the time," Neci snapped.

Zahilda flicked a finger at an enchanted shrub barreling down on them, and it disappeared into a cloud of smoke. But she didn't say anything.

Neci held out her Nordving sword to the witch. "Do it."

"Fine," Zahilda said. "But only because the lizard is right. Something *is* happening."

Zahilda held her hand over the blade of the sword and muttered something cranky-sounding. Ice crystals formed along the blade—solid Water.

While she muttered, Batu played a melody. It was of Air and lightheartedness and flight, wrapping around the ice and the blade and binding them together.

Iggy perched on Neci's shoulder. They had to get to Merlynda *right now*.

"Ready?" Neci asked Iggy.

"Ready!" he answered.

Neci took a deep breath and raised the sword. Each of the elements—Earth in the blade, Water from the ice, Air from

Batu's ocarina, and Fire from Iggy—was present. All together, they made up the Aether.

And all together, they plunged as one into the Impedimentum.

Iggy blasted his fire to combine with the other elements, and the sword sank into the barrier. Neci pushed and twisted, struggling to keep it in place. Ripples cascaded across the surface of the dome. The purple dimmed, then the rich color shot back across the surface and into Neci's sword.

The blade shattered and Neci flew back, crashing to the ground. Batu rushed to her and played a song of healing.

"Merlynda!" Iggy shouted. He threw himself at the barrier, bashing it with his tail and blazing fire. "Merlynda!" Merlynda had felt like smoke ever since that awful bracer was snapped on her, but now Iggy could feel her being scraped, being seared, being *emptied*.

"Hush, little one." Dame Illondria kicked a fairy. "We will find a way."

"It's too late," Iggy sobbed. "It's too late! Can't you feel it? It's gone!" He fell to the ground and curled up, shaking. "He took it. Her magic is gone."

Merlynda lay on the soft grass, floating in this new emptiness. She felt the earth beneath her, and Neci's dagger, which she'd continued to clench lest it disappear on her. She saw the stones of the Omnivia towering above. She smelled the freshly dug dirt and tasted her sweat and the blood from where she'd bitten her lip by mistake.

But she couldn't feel how these things were connected, how they were alive and full of the Aether.

The hated bracer clung to her arm, though she no longer felt its chill. She felt only a void, a blackness, a bottomless nothing. She wanted to rest in that nothing forever, but Percy was still trying to start his Concursus, and she was still the only one who could stop him.

Merlynda pushed herself up, testing this new heavy emptiness.

Percy stood over her. He wiped the sweat from his face with a piece of cloth, then wiped roughly at Merlynda's forehead. "Don't strain yourself."

She watched as he turned away, facing the broken horseshoe of stone doorways. The ground trembled and shook, and Merlynda watched in awe as the stones dug themselves out of the earth, like a giant's fingers floating through the air. She flinched, fearing for a single, heartrending moment that Percy was going to crush her with one. Instead, the pillars righted themselves, burrowing upright into the ground and stacking on top of one another.

Percy's trench made a ring around the entire Omnivia, and just inside it there was now an endless ring of enormous stone doorways. A few feet in toward the center, the shorter, narrower bluestones were arranged in their own wide circle, and

farther in still was the horseshoe: five gargantuan stone doorways, separate from one another, curved toward the center as
if waiting to see what Percy would do next.

The Omnivia was restored.

Percy jabbed his hand once, twice, and two new chan-
nels burst through the earth, cutting from the outer trench
and through the center as if Percy had drawn an X across the
Omnivia.

Merlynda struggled to her feet as Percy whispered an
incantation into the sweat-covered cloth, then flung it into the
cross section of the trenches. It levitated in the exact middle of
the X, as if this was what the Omnivia stones were waiting for.

Percy held the amulet close and whispered a few fluid
words. The magic from the amulet melded with the cloth as
he circled it, and water began to drip from it into the trenches.

Merlynda struggled to her feet. The drip grew into a
stream, and before long it would flow from the X and fill the
circular ditch with water from—somewhere. The In-Between
maybe? She couldn't sense it, couldn't feel the Aether.

"Percy," Merlynda croaked. She tried again. He seemed so
far away. "Percy!"

He ignored her. This was a complicated spell, one he needed
to focus on. Not just any wizard could make a Concursus.

Merlynda stumbled closer, reached toward him, but was
slammed back once more by that invisible force. She fell to the
ground again, dazed.

Percy didn't look away from the flowing water. "The

restriction spell, Merlynda." He pointed his finger and jerked it toward the cloth. A pile of kindling assembled above it like an altar, safe from the stream. Flames sprang to life. He swept his arm around in a wide circle, like he had that day in the orchard so long ago, only this time he guided each of the elements at the same time. Four shimmering rings of light appeared in the center of the Omnivia, stacked on top of one another like pancakes.

Merlynda was tired of being knocked into grass. Then again, she was just tired. Percy had his Water and his Fire. Earth was obvious, and Air was all around. And of course, there was the amulet that had stolen so much magic, from every sort of creature, over centuries. He had everything he needed to open the Concursus, to do the one thing Merlyn warned to never, ever do.

Merlynda stared at Neci's dagger, an idea forming in her soupy thoughts—there was no restriction spell on Faithful. Percy was too focused on his shimmering rings to pay her any attention.

Merlynda took aim and threw.

It was a decent throw, but Merlynda wasn't a knight. She was a wizardess, and not necessarily a good one. The dagger flew past Percy and landed with a splash in the trench.

Percy darted his gaze to her, shook his head, and went back to his spell. He lifted the amulet from around his neck, and it floated to the center of the glowing elemental rings. Light poured from the amulet, binding the elements together with the stolen magic—*her* magic—until their power flared and twisted together. The elements roiled in a dark sphere above them, fed from Earth, Water, Air, and Fire, boring a hole into the In-Between and to the Aether. The void was only the size of a pebble, but it would grow.

The Concursus had begun.

You'll recall that Neci's dagger was no ordinary blade. It was fashioned from the purest refined Earth, carefully culled to highlight this single element's properties. It was as loyal as any blade could possibly be. So while Neci sat holding her head on the battlefield after being blasted back by the Impedimentum, Faithful reappeared in her sheath.

She jumped up, ignoring the pounding in her head, and wiped the blade dry. Batu's playing had helped her feel better, but there wasn't any more time. She grabbed a broken spear shaft. "Fang! Iggy! To me!"

They hurried over, and Neci rushed to her noble steed. "Give me a boost," she ordered Batu. He clasped his hands together, and she stepped on them to climb up on Fang.

Neci spat on the dagger. "I hope that's enough," she told Iggy.

Fang craned her long neck around and added her own glob of saliva, which mostly landed on the dagger and not on Neci, so that was a success. This was an odd game, but she was happy to help.

Neci held out the dagger to Batu. "Play."

He stared at it. "But didn't you just—"

"Play!"

Batu obliged, whistling out a variation of the tune he'd played earlier.

Neci ripped a strip of cloth from the bottom of her tunic and lashed the dagger to the spear shaft to make a passable jousting lance. She turned Fang to face the Impedimentum.

While Batu played, his eyes darted to her, to the magical barrier, and then back again. He finished his song. "Are you sure?"

"Yep. At least, I'm pretty sure this will work." Faithful vibrated at the end of the shaft. Because of magic, Neci hoped. "Ready?" she asked Iggy.

Iggy hovered nearby, golden wings flapping and glinting in the fading light. He bared his teeth in acknowledgment.

Neci adjusted her grip on her lance. "Ready, girl?" she whispered to Fang. The Questing Beast nodded and tried to bare her teeth fiercely like her flying friend.

"Wait!" Batu called up. "Let me see your lance."

Neci lowered it toward him. He untied his raider scarf and wrapped it around the dagger's handle. He looked Neci straight in the eyes. "Joust like a girl."

"How else would I joust?" Neci smirked and faced her opponent.

She nudged Fang into a trot, then a full-blown gallop. Iggy sped along beside them. Right before they hit, Iggy shot out a jet of fire.

They smashed into the Impedimentum.

+ + +

The Concursus roiled above Merlynda, the elements flickering and blending and melding until it was impossible to tell where one ended and the next began. She stared at it from the grass. It was very like that morning so long ago in the orchard, though a different sort of terror seized her now.

Percy stared in awe at his creation—his *power*. The Shadow Sun was almost upon them. "Did you think it would be so stunning, Vis?" he whispered to his twisted familiar, who was once again perched on his shoulder.

The Impedimentum flickered above the twins as if straining to hold, then shattered. The magic-dome pieces were whipped up into the roiling void, and the sounds of battle rushed into the empty space.

The amulet was busy feeding the Concursus, but Percy was still a wizard to be reckoned with. He whirled around, furious—

—which was exactly when a gangly giraffe bowled him over. A reddish-gold streak flashed alongside it, sending the falcon screeching off into the sky.

Fang skidded to a stop next to Merlynda, and Iggy swooped back around to land on her shoulder. "I'm sorry," he whispered. Tiny tears trickled down his cheeks, and she scooped him into her arms. "I'm sorry we're too late."

Merlynda hugged him tight. "You're just in time." Affection welled within the great emptiness inside her. At least Iggy and Neci were okay.

Neci slid down from Fang. Merlynda was all in one piece, but she didn't *look* whole. "Iggy said—your magic—what happened?" she shouted over the storm of the Concursus, and the sounds of battle spilling toward the Omnivia.

"Percy is the Hollower," Merlynda managed to shout back. Her head throbbed.

Iggy growled. Neci helped Merlynda to her feet. "*Percy? How?*"

Merlynda pointed to the center of the storm, where the purple light pulsed and fueled the widening portal. "The amulet of Morgan le Fey. It's done something to him—twisted him somehow."

"Merlyn's goat," Neci breathed.

The crumpled bundle that was Percy started twitching. "Fang!" Neci shouted. "Don't let him move!"

The Questing Beast dutifully trotted over and sat on the wizard. The falcon tore out of the sky, grasping for Fang's eyes. The giraffe bellowed and ducked. Iggy launched himself from Merlynda's shoulder, spouting fire at the twisted familiar's feathers as they raced across the battlefield.

Neci and Merlynda darted toward Percy. A portal opened beneath him, swallowing him. Fang followed—but only half of Fang. The portal sealed, leaving the Questing Beast half buried in the earth. She panicked and kicked and bellowed, but she couldn't free herself.

"Fang!" Neci darted toward her noble steed, but another portal opened in front of her, and Percy leapt from it, blocking her. He shoved his hand out, and Neci flew back, narrowly missing a bluestone as she tumbled across the ground.

Percy breathed fast, eyes wild. "You sent that filthy beast to attack *me*?" He stepped closer. "You think you can stop the Hollower?"

"Percy, listen to yourself!" Merlynda cried. "That amulet has gotten inside your head!"

"Leave, Merlynda." Percy's eyes were cold. "Leave, and you might have a chance to stay safe." He opened another portal and stepped through, reappearing atop one of the great stone doorways in the middle of the Omnivia. He settled onto it in a comfortable position, unconcerned with the battle. From here, he had a prime view of the doorway in the center of the horseshoe. The In-Between was nearly open, and he wanted a front-row seat to watch his completed Concursus.

Merlynda rushed to Neci, who had pulled herself up and was trying to calm Fang. Overall, the battle wasn't going well. At least half of the Nordvings and raiders were hexed, several more were injured, and still the magic spells flew. Batu ran around playing healing melodies, but he couldn't help everyone at once. Dame Illondria and Zahilda were forces to reckon with, but more than a dozen witches and fairies had surrounded them, and Zahilda's sisters were one-hundred-percent evil.

The earth rumbled, and then with the force of a tidal wave, a wall of water rose from the trenches, and a bubble shot out onto the battlefield. An *Oceanid* bubble, Merlynda realized, and a tiny hope-spark flared in her empty chest.

Neci hefted her lance. "Why are they here?"

"I invited them," Merlynda said. "After a *lot* of wondering whether I should. They're wrong about a lot of things, but they want to stop the Hollower. We're on the same side."

Bubble after bubble shot from the wave. Oceanids leapt out and into the fray as soon as they landed. Fairies popped some of the bubbles in midair, but the Oceanids tucked and rolled and sprang up again, unharmed. The display of Oceasha was dazzling, and the arrival of more magic-wielders helped even the odds.

Lady Phelia gracefully dropped from a bubble and landed before Merlynda, carrying a lethal-looking mace. She bowed. "Septimum Genus."

Neci leveled her lance at the willowy woman, making sure she stayed between the Oceanid and Merlynda.

Lady Phelia bowed to her as well. "Your caution is warranted, Neci the Ardent, but rest assured, we have the same goal."

"You tried to kill me," Neci spat.

"And I would again, if I thought it would benefit the greater good." Lady Phelia stared at Fang, then with a wave of her hand the earth around the giraffe crumbled and separated, allowing the Questing Beast to stumble out and hide (unsuccessfully) behind Neci.

Neci gritted her teeth. "Thank you," she said.

"The amulet—" Merlynda ducked a fairy charm that Lady Phelia blasted back with her mace. "My brother—he's the Hollower—"

"Then let us end this!" Lady Phelia snarled.

"*No.*" Merlynda put as much command into her voice as she could muster. "You will *not* hurt him. The amulet has twisted him, or made something in him worse, I don't know. It's the center of the Concursus." She gestured to where the amulet channeled all the magics into one another.

Lady Phelia hefted her mace. "Then we remove the amulet, and stop the Concursus."

"About that." Merlynda outlined how it had been enchanted so that only Merlyn's relatives could use it—but that Percy had used a restriction spell so that *she* couldn't.

Lady Phelia hissed in a most unnerving manner, but before anyone could move, the battlefield dimmed.

The fighting stalled. Overhead, a dark circle blanketed the sun until all that could be seen was a thin ring of bright yellow around the edges of a blackened disk.

"The Shadow Sun," Merlynda breathed.

The amulet flared a brilliant violet, and a blinding beam shot from it toward the center of the horseshoe, filling the middle stone doorway with dazzling purple light. The sun was already brightening again as the dark blanket crept on.

Seconds later the Shadow Sun passed, and the amulet ceased its flaring and dropped to the grass. The soft amethyst light trapped between the stone pillars pulsed, filling the doorway—the completed Concursus.

Merlynda hadn't even begun to process what that meant when a laugh filled the clearing. Not the laughter of the

Aether—this was softer, but not friendly. It sent chills through every creature on the battlefield. Merlynda felt it cut through her, though her magic had been taken and she still wore the bracer. It even sent ice through Percy, though he'd heard it before.

A pale hand stretched out from the amethyst Concursus, and then a woman followed it, plain but regal. She wore a simple tunic that had seen better days. Her thick, curly blond hair was tied back with a leather cord.

She pressed her hand against the nearest pillar, feeling its weight, its strength. She allowed the soft grass to tickle her feet. She turned slowly, once, twice, looking at herself, looking around her, relishing in all the scents of the world. It had been so long since she'd *breathed*.

She drank the air for several moments, then looked up. "Hello, dears. Don't stop on my account. Percival, darling. Come here." She beckoned him forward.

Percy, still perched on the gray stone, didn't move. He'd heard the laugh before, from the amulet, but he didn't recognize this woman. "Who are you?"

She laughed again, a delightful tinkling laugh, undercut with darkness. Merlynda shifted. Even without sensing the Aether, this woman made her uneasy.

"I'm surprised you don't recognize me." The woman took a graceful step toward the amulet, stumbled, and put her arms out to balance herself. "Been ages since I've walked." She winked at the crowd. "But I'm sure I'll get the hang of it."

The woman's gaze stopped when she saw Merlynda. "Ah, yes, the Septimum Genus. Seventh descendant of the great *Merlyn.*" She said "Merlyn" as if she'd stepped in something unpleasant.

Neci, back on her feet after Percy's attack, moved her lance to point at the newcomer. Lady Phelia adopted a fighting stance next to her, mace at the ready. "Don't take another step," Neci warned.

"Little Neci," the woman crooned. "Foolish, brash Neci. Put that down, love. You might hurt yourself."

"Last warning," Percy said. "Who are you?"

The woman was at the amulet now. She smiled. "I am the voice that has been whispering to you all this time, Percival. The ear that listened to your confusion and hurt at the Aether choosing *her* over you. The spirit that made your magic soar, that told you where and when and how to accomplish your thefts and powerful acts of magic. All to bring me home."

Her smile turned wicked.

"I am Morgan le Fey."

In which an old family
foe returns

Merlynda heard the woman's words—everyone had, though she hadn't raised her voice—but they didn't fit. This couldn't be Morgan le Fey. Merlyn had banished the sorceress beyond the In-Between.

Merlynda looked once more at the amulet, which was undoubtedly Morgan le Fey's. She glanced at the Omnivia around them, a place created by Merlyn and then destroyed by him, to prevent anyone else from using it.

No, she realized as the pieces clicked into place. She pushed away the emptiness inside her to focus. Merlyn hadn't destroyed the Omnivia to stop others. He'd destroyed it to stop *Morgan*, to prevent her from escaping.

"Merlyn's goat," Merlynda whispered. "It's her."

Lady Phelia exhaled sharply next to her but didn't move.

Morgan appraised the wizardess, as if she could sense Merlynda's recognition. "Yes. It's me. And now I can finish what I started."

Merlynda struck what she hoped was a brave pose. "Not if I can help it!"

Morgan narrowed her eyes but kept smiling. "As a matter of fact, you *can* help, dear. I want revenge against Merlyn. He's long dead, of course, so I'm going to murder his descendants instead. Won't be a moment."

She reached for the amulet, but it leapt away across the grass. Morgan frowned, then tried again.

The amulet jumped, like a purple-and-silver frog.

"Ah, yes." She stood, resuming her regal air. "Percival," she sniffed, "I require your assistance until we can remove Merlyn's pesky blood charm."

Percy stepped through another portal, this time appearing next to his twin. With both Merlynda and Morgan here, and the amulet on the ground instead of next to his heart, the angry fog clouding his mind thinned, and the amulet's whispers grew fainter. In their place was a sense of dread and remorse about what he'd done as the Hollower. How he'd let Morgan trick him, use him. "I don't think so."

The corner of Morgan's mouth crooked up. "After all I've done for you, you would deny me this?"

"You just said you were going to kill me, so, yes? You're denied."

Morgan waved her hands airily. "Pishposh! I can't kill you if I need you. Not until you've undone this irritating blood-magic binding of your great-grandfather's."

Percy's falcon swooped down to land on his shoulder, and they stood at the ready.

The sorceress let out an irritated huff. "Have it your way, then."

Faster than anyone would have expected of a woman who'd been trapped for seven generations, Morgan blasted Percy—*Zap! Zap! Zap!*—with purple lightning. Percy blocked the first bolts, but even after centuries of banishment, Morgan's power was too much. He cried out and collapsed, clothes smoking. The falcon took to the air.

Percy stumbled to his feet and sent his own volley back, slipping past the Air and into the Aether, gripping at the powerful magic to barrage the sorceress. He pulled on his fear, his betrayal, his growing horror at what he'd done, raining down blast after blast on Morgan.

When he'd finished, he collapsed to his knees, exhausted. There was silence. The armies stared at the dust cloud obscuring Morgan, waiting.

"Oh, Percival." The dust lifted away with an airy wave of the sorceress's hand. "I could show you so much more."

Percy stood, stunned. He'd given everything he had, and Morgan hadn't even been scratched. An angry howl started in his throat but was cut short as an invisible cord lurched him to the center of the Omnivia and slammed him into the ground at Morgan's feet.

"You're mine, Percival. You've welcomed my amulet's whispers into your heart." She tousled his hair as if he were a favorite nephew, then snapped her fingers. Unseen strings lifted his legs like a marionette's, jerking him toward the amulet. His hand shot out and grasped the disk, then dropped it clumsily around his neck.

"For the Septimum Genus!" Fenrir roared.

The battle unfroze, and the armies converged on one another once more. Merlynda ignored the chaos, rushing through the battle toward her brother. He twitched this way and that, violet light prancing from the amulet and turning anyone it struck into stone, into grubs, or inflicting grievous wounds. Percy screamed terrified warnings when he could, helpless to stop Morgan. He hadn't foreseen this, not in any way. He wished he'd never found the amulet.

"Fight it, Percy!" Merlynda shouted. "You can fight it!"

Percy wrenched in the air to face her. "Run, Merlynda," he pleaded. "Please. I can't—"

"You can!" Merlynda clenched her fists.

A stray burst from the amulet shot out, and Merlynda dove to the side. She scrambled behind a gigantic gray pillar. "Merlyn's goat, Percy, *fight!*"

Morgan laughed her delicate laugh. "How sweet! Percival stole your magic, yet you're still trying to save him."

Merlynda whirled on the sorceress. "You did this to him!" She ducked back behind her pillar as another blast came at her.

"Nonsense. His disappointment and envy led him to the amulet all on his own."

"Liar!" Merlynda furiously dodged another blast. "You sent it to him after the portal Iggy and I made trapped him!"

"Oh no, Merlynda." Morgan's voice was sweet. "*I* created that portal, but it wasn't for Percy. It was for *you*."

Merlynda popped her head back out. "*You* made that portal? Not me?"

The sorceress laughed again, though this time it was mocking. "Of course that portal was mine. If half the stories your dear brother has told me about your magical disasters are true, I'm impressed you're alive at all."

Despite the circumstances, Merlynda felt a rush of relief. She hadn't made Percy vanish! It had been Morgan all along, trying to . . . do what?

"Why was the portal for me?"

Morgan flicked her finger idly, and Percy began to rotate in the air. The amulet fired at random. "Even beyond the In-Between, I'd heard Merlyn's prophecy. He'd banished me far too well to kill *him*—but I could watch and wait for his precious Septimum Genus to come. Do you know how *boring* it is to wait for seven generations with nothing to do but plot your revenge? And *then*, just when that insufferable prophecy comes to fruition—twins!"

The amulet gave a vicious blast to punctuate Morgan's

anger (it thankfully missed Dame Illondria and instead hit the witch she'd been battling). Merlynda dashed away, trying to put more stones between her and Morgan. A Hollowed wizardess was hardly a threat to the evilest sorceress to ever live.

"I followed the trace of the Aether's portal and snatched up the first thing that blew in." Morgan sliced her hand through the air, and the earth in front of Merlynda burst up into a wall. She slammed into it and fell to the ground, dirt raining down all around her.

Morgan stalked closer. "How was *I* supposed to know that only one twin had gotten their familiar?"

Merlynda scrambled backward and pulled herself to her feet. "You're not the first person to be thrown off by that, if it makes you feel better."

"It doesn't," Morgan snarled. "But killing you will."

The sorceress had herded Merlynda back toward the center of the Omnivia, the shimmering purple doorway of the Concursus at Merlynda's back. Morgan glided across the grass, a stricken Percy floating behind her. "I'd relish drawing your death out, but theatrics are what got me into trouble last time. Percival, darling."

Morgan pulled the invisible thread that jerked Percy forward. He met Merlynda's eyes.

Morgan's face twisted into a wicked smile. "Finish her. For me."

Merlynda held Percy's gaze. He wouldn't do it. He wouldn't blast her.

The amulet glowed, ready to fire. Merlynda stood her ground.

"Do it, Percival," Morgan said through gritted teeth.

Percy fought and struggled, willing the amulet to stay silent. The sorceress's power clashed with his own.

"Do as I say!" Morgan snapped.

Percy kept fighting. This wasn't the way things were supposed to go, wasn't what he'd meant to happen! He wrestled against the pull of the amulet—he'd let it burrow so deeply into his heart, into his hopes and dreams, and now he wrenched himself back. It hurt, like hot needles were searing every inch of his body, but still he pulled. He felt the amulet begin to flare, begin to channel its magic at his sister—Merlynda, who was still trying to save him, despite everything he'd done.

And in that moment, he knew what to do.

He waited for the amulet to charge, then reached for it with his own magic and *twisted*. A small portal appeared right in front of him, a window to another time. He glimpsed the orchard back at Merlyn Manor and Merlynda-of-the-Past's startled, tear-streaked face, then shoved the crumpled parchment he'd taken from *this* Merlynda through—the parchment Merlynda insisted he'd sent to her, summoning her here to save him.

The portal winked out. He grinned, then gave Morgan a triumphant, defiant look. "I'm not yours anymore."

"If that's the way of things," Morgan said coldly, "I will break you so that I can rebuild you."

She spun toward Merlynda and sent a bolt of violet lightning sizzling across the space.

"No!" Percy screamed.

The lightning slammed into Merlynda, lifting her from the ground and blasting her back. Fire raced through every inch of her body as she flew across the Omnivia, whirling away from her battling friends.

Morgan turned back to Percy while Merlynda was airborne, unconcerned. She closed her hand into a fist, then swung her arm down and opened it like she was hurling something at the ground. Percy's body dropped with the sorceress's hand, plummeting toward the earth.

Before her brother shattered on the ground, Merlynda passed through the Concursus.

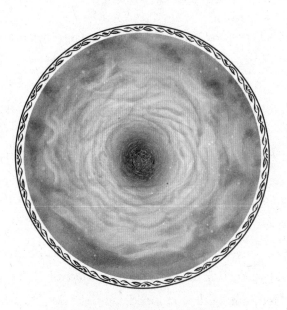

A(NOTHER) WORD
ABOUT AETHER

A s has been mentioned, the Aether is not the sum of all magic, but the origin. It isn't a single element. It is all of them.

Merlyn knew this, but the wizards that came after him forgot. They studied the Aether, and the more knowledge-able they became, the less they knew. They congratulated themselves on their experiments and accomplishments, highlighting individual elements of the Aether instead of the Aether itself.

They forgot the whole.

The Aether lived in the In-Between, connected to the world

and all worlds, observing. It allowed the foolishness of wizards and other magical types to continue, because it knew this day was coming.

The great Merlyn had been different from the others. He used the In-Between to travel through time and space, and he was able to do such powerful things because he understood that individual elements were only a tiny piece of the whole.

Merlynda, in spite of her vast book knowledge and allegedly great power, didn't have a clue.

Merlynda was enveloped in darkness as soon as she crossed through the Concursus. The sounds of battle and violet light vanished. Her momentum stopped, and she settled to the ground, unharmed.

The image of Percy about to splatter rocketed across her vision. She tried to stand, the last crackles of the purple lightning fizzling out of her body. Had Morgan sent Merlynda to the very place the wicked sorceress had been banished for all those centuries? She had no sense of up or down, no sense of anything at all in the great blackness. Is this where Percy had found the amulet?

The chill from the bracer returned, sweeping through her arm and into her bones. What did that mean, since Percy had taken her magic? "Hello?" Merlynda called.

Something stirred through the empty space. A voice spoke, rich and full, warm and terrible. "You are separated from us, child. From the Aether."

"Please, I need—"

"Did you choose to be apart?"

"No," Merlynda said immediately, but it was the sort of answer you give without thinking. The darkness, and the return of the chill, and the certainty with which the rich voice spoke made her focus on the question.

She thought back to how she could have used the firestone to remove the bracer and connect herself with the Aether once more. She'd chosen to save Iggy instead, but that had been about saving her friend. She hated being separated from her magic, but making sure Iggy survived was more important.

"No," she repeated, sure of herself. "I don't want to be separated anymore, especially after knowing what it's like. I used the Aether to save my friends once before. I think I might control it better now."

The voice laughed, but it wasn't mocking. It sounded amused, the way a parent might laugh at their child's silly antics. "You do not control the Aether, Merlynda. No more than you control the wind or the earth."

"But—the elements—"

"Are not what you think. Tell us, have you discovered an affinity for any one element?"

Merlynda's face flushed. She felt remarkably small, here in the void. "All I do is bungle things."

"This is because you are trying to dilute the Quintessence—the Everything. You are looking at only a portion of what is available to you."

"I don't understand."

"Think back to the Rusvokian raiders' attack. Did you use a single element to save your friends?"

Merlynda remembered what it had felt like, to finally touch the Aether. The power, the immensity, the fullness. "Was that you?" she whispered.

"Yes. Do you wish to be free of that which binds you, Merlynda?"

"Of course I do!"

"Then be free."

Warmth spread through her arm. The bracer clicked open and fell away, and the darkness vanished.

She was next to a lake, calm and still. The vibrancy of the grass and reeds seeped through her skin and into her bones, washing away all weariness. Merlynda took a deep breath, drinking in the Aether fibers. *Feeling* again. Feeling *alive* again.

Not a stone's throw away, farther along the shore, a vicious crack scarred the ground, and beyond it—emptiness. Merlynda could see where it had ripped trees and plants and broken the earth. Already it was healing, somehow, but the wound was fresh.

She felt other presences nearby—other familiars, perhaps, waiting to be sent into the world. Or maybe they were more servants of the Aether, like Dame Illondria. They flickered and shifted, constantly on the move.

Except one, standing next to her.

"Grandfather Merlyn?" Merlynda hazarded.

He was a properly wizened man, but not ancient. He

smiled and shook his head. "No. We are the Aether, but you may call us Quint. We've taken Merlyn's form to make you more comfortable."

Merlynda didn't think there was anything comfortable about speaking directly with the source of all life and magic. "Am I—am I in the In-Between?"

"You are."

Merlynda looked back at the crack. It was already much narrower, leaving nary a trace. The emptiness she could feel must have been from *beyond* the In-Between. It was the scar from Morgan tearing her way through with the Concursus.

"Is that—" she whispered. It was hard to imagine. "Percy was trapped *there*, wasn't he? Not here?"

Quint nodded, pained. "Morgan herself couldn't leave, but she is evil and cunning. She pulled Percy in to twist him and released him once the amulet had taken over."

Merlynda shivered. No wonder he'd been drawn to the amulet, stuck in a place like that. She rubbed her bare wrist. "Do I have my magic back now?"

Quint laughed. He was—they were?—so joyful. "Yes, Merlynda. The amulet stole much of your power, but we never left you. Not truly."

"Never left?" Merlynda cried, incredulous. "I don't think you were even there in the first place! You weren't there when the mermaids attacked us, or when Dame Illondria got hurt. You weren't there when the raiders put this bracer on me, or when that twisted falcon almost killed Iggy!"

"We were there," Quint said. "We were the herald who gave Neci her dagger, to show her the level of her potential. We were the Oceanid who gifted Batu his ocarina, to heal him from his pride and his past. It was through our servant Dame Illondria that Ignus received his wings. And it was because of our power that you received the firestone from the witch Zahilda and were given the choice of how to use it. We could not decide your path, but we could equip you for your trials."

"Did you equip me with *that?*" Merlynda snarled at the bracer.

Such sadness filled the Aether that Merlynda felt it through her anger, her hurt. She felt Quint's heartache. "Just as you were equipped and allowed to choose, so are others. Not all choose as well as you have."

This didn't make Merlynda feel better. "But why even let it be made?"

"As we said, others must make their own choices. We cannot choose for them. Unfortunately, the choices of others always have the potential to harm. But look where that bracer brought you, Merlynda. If you'd never worn it, would you have come to the In-Between? Would you have found us?"

Merlynda sulked at the bracer. "No. I would have missed out." She looked up at Quint.

"Those other times, when I found you without realizing—why did you laugh? Why did you always laugh at me?"

Quint laughed now, but it wasn't unkind. "We were

delighted that you'd found us, child. Before, when you were so focused on one element, you were like an enormous river trying to push through a small bend. There was too much power, and you spilled over the riverbank."

Understanding rushed through Merlynda. "That's why things always exploded."

"You don't need an element to find us, Merlynda. You can go straight to the source."

"Is that why you chose me to be the Septimum Genus? Because Percy only has affinity for Air?"

Quint rubbed their forehead, and for a brief moment Merlynda thought she saw the weariness of all their many lifetimes. "As we said, we can equip you for your journey, but we don't make your choices. Percy might have joined you, but instead he chose to follow the power of Morgan's amulet."

Quint bent down and picked up the bracer. They held it out to her.

"Alternately, *you* chose to be the heir of Merlyn's prophecy."

Merlynda stared at the bracer but didn't reach for it. She'd only just gotten rid of it and wasn't eager to take it back.

"You're doing a fine job, if we do say so ourselves." Quint winked.

Merlynda was inclined to disagree, but who was she to argue with the Aether? She reached for the bracer, and instead of being icy, the bronze was warm.

A portal swirled opened behind her. She glanced back to Quint, but they were gone.

Gone, but not gone—Merlynda knew this somehow. She glanced once more at the broken earth, which was all but healed, then strode through the portal.

Merlynda launched through the portal to find everything exactly as she'd left it. Morgan's hand still sliced through the air, and Percy plummeted, half a moment from splattering on the ground.

She didn't have time to think, to savor this fresh awareness, this life, to drink in every magical fiber. She slipped into the Aether—why had it ever been hard before?—and tugged. The magic didn't laugh at her this time. It laughed *with* her.

Merlynda spun, gripping the fabric of the magic, and flung it toward her brother. Instead of smashing into the earth, he stopped inches from the grass. He looked at Merlynda, terror turning to disbelief.

The Septimum Genus grinned at him.

Merlynda flung up a magic shield and swirled away from the amulet's flare, one with the Aether. She blocked the blast easily, but it was a good reminder that she still didn't have a lot of practice.

"You." Morgan zapped more purple lightning, and Merlynda hastily created Aether shields to match them. "What *is* it with your family? Merlyn *always* showed up when he was least wanted, and I could—never—get—rid—of—

him!" She punctuated each word with a bolt of lightning.

A red-gold streak flashed across the sky, and a plume of fire set Morgan's tunic alight. The sorceress cursed and set to beating out the flames. Merlynda took the opportunity to duck behind a stone pillar.

Iggy shot across the field to Merlynda, who caught him and held him tight. "You were gone!" the wyvern exclaimed. "You didn't feel like smoke anymore, you felt like *nothing*! And I was so worried, but then a second later you came back, and you were Merlynda again!" He nuzzled her wrist, which he was now far too large to wrap around but was fond of just the same.

Merlynda pulled the bracer from her robes, and Iggy cocked his head. "It feels different."

"It *is* different." The bracer, alchemically forged to block and absorb Aether, had been overwhelmed by being in the In-Between, in the full presence of the Aether. It was whole, overflowing, no longer drinking in and stealing the Aether around it.

Merlynda felt for the magic laced through the metal, then reached out to each element at once, and to none at all, directly into the Aether—the Quintessence.

Her magic melded with Iggy's, and together they grasped at the fibers of the bracer, tracing the magic of its curves and contours. They smoothed out the etchings and pulled and stretched until they'd reshaped it into something new.

Merlynda stared at their creation. "I'd say we've figured out our magic."

Iggy examined his reflection. "I always said we had potential."

Merlynda hefted the bronze shield they'd created, thin and light and perfect for warding off magical lightning. She looked at her very fierce wyvern. "Let's go defeat a sorceress."

Merlynda leapt out from behind the stone, brandishing her new shield. Iggy darted into the air and hovered above her. He let out a little burst of fire to be extra intimidating.

Morgan sent another blast of lightning, but Merlynda blocked it with her shield. The lightning danced across the surface, then dissipated.

"You've got a new toy, I see. Clever." Morgan swung her arm around, and Percy flew in front of her, dangling as if his arms were tied above him. The amulet he still wore flared, and purple light shot out, but Merlynda caught this blast on her shield as easily as she'd caught Morgan's lightning. Percy smiled in relief.

A corner of Morgan's mouth twitched. Merlynda readied herself.

The ancient sorceress let fly an enormous burst of lightning, but she missed Merlynda entirely—and blasted the pillar behind her, one of the massive gray stones holding up the Concursus. The sorceress twisted her hands in a complicated ritual, sending another flare from the amulet into the same spot her lightning had cracked, then pulled back on an imaginary rope.

The pillar splintered at the top, crackling. It fell, breaking away from the shimmering purple light. The Concursus folded in on itself and vanished, no longer anchored in the world.

They couldn't send Morgan back, Merlynda realized. Not the same way she'd come, at least. Just as this thought flickered through Merlynda's mind, the entire crushing weight of the stone toppled toward her.

Iggy dove toward his wizardess, to his newly whole Merlynda, but the amulet flared violet once more. He dodged, but a chunk of falling debris bashed into him, knocking him off course. He spiraled up and away, dizzy, then looped back around in time to see Merlynda buried beneath the enormous crumbling stone.

"Merlynda!" he howled. "Merlynda! Merlynda!" He could feel her but couldn't get to her. The rocks were too massive, too heavy! He could fly and breathe fire, but he was still a somewhat small wyvern.

He dove at Morgan, swirling this way and that to avoid her lightning. He shot fire and scratched at her head and looped around to go again.

"Begone, rodent!" the sorceress screamed.

Before Iggy could tell her that he would *not* be gone, not while he could fly and breathe fire and scratch her, the pile of rocks that covered Merlynda glowed, then exploded in every direction. The pieces stopped, hovering above the battlefield. Beneath them, in the center, stood Merlynda.

Not just Merlynda.

The Septimum Genus.

The stones glowed, and Merlynda launched them, one after another, at Morgan. Some transformed into flocks of hummingbirds, others into fireballs, yet more into sharp fragments or biting bugs or sweets. Others burst into magical chains that tried to bind the sorceress. Merlynda forced Morgan to retreat, to protect herself against each new assault, to be too distracted to force Percy to use the amulet. The armies cleared away from the Omnivia, dodging fallen stones and fragments as they continued their own battles.

"What is this?" Morgan shrieked. "You attack me with tiny creatures and hard candy?"

"I'll attack you with whatever I want!" Merlynda slammed another bluestone toward the sorceress, morphing it into a Nordving battleship. Morgan whirled out of the way before it could ram her, but bashed into a life-sized statue of Merlyn that had dropped in her path. The sorceress screeched before incinerating it.

Merlynda flung spell after spell, sometimes using rocks, sometimes magicking snow or thorny flowers or hungry mice. "I've spent *months* thinking I sent Percy straight into the Hollower's clutches, but *you* kidnapped him! Let—my—brother—go!"

Morgan twisted to avoid being splattered by a pair of cheese-filled stockings. "Percival is mine," she hissed.

Merlynda grinned. "Guess again."

The sorceress whirled around. Her puppet still floated in the air, but a strange beast with a small girl riding it charged at him. Morgan twisted her fist, and Percy spun around.

A blinding purple light hit Fang square in her chest, stopping the Questing Beast cold. Neci flew forward from their momentum, slamming into Percy and skidding across the ground. The would-be knight struggled to stand. "No!" She reached toward Fang, but Morgan slashed her arm to the side, and a chunk of rock crashed onto Neci's legs, pinning her. Neci screamed.

Her noble steed, her faithful beloved Questing Beast, watched from where she'd been hit by the amulet's light. Fang's body and legs were already stone, and her neck was fast hardening.

"No!" Neci screamed again, unable to move from where she was pinned. She reached out a hand, straining. "Fang!"

Fang barked for Neci to come, to help her, to explain why she couldn't move. But before Neci could do any such thing, the stone took over, and she was frozen.

Neci let out a string of the most unknightly things she'd ever said about anyone (or their crops). Purple lightning flared over her body, and she fell on her back, writhing.

"Such ignoble behavior." Morgan swept her hands, and the stones Merlynda held flew away. "Percival? My amulet, darling."

Percy jerked through the air toward her, head hanging.

Morgan straightened. "Let's wrap things up, shall we? We must break this pesky enchantment, and to do that, I'm going to need some of your blood."

Percy raised his head, smug. "You'll also need the amulet."

She glanced down. His neck was empty. Neci had grabbed it and ripped it free when she'd slammed into him.

Morgan slammed Percy into the ground. He laughed through the pain. "The mighty Morgan le Fey, bested by a ridiculous beast and her knight."

Morgan clenched her fist, and Percy felt his whole body tighten. "Quiet, fool." Her voice was dangerous. "You still belong to me."

"No, he doesn't!" Merlynda pulled at the Aether and wrenched Percy from Morgan's power. In a brilliant purple and blue light storm, the last threads of the amulet's bond were broken. Percy had already done most of the work himself, but then he'd always been a powerful wizard.

Morgan growled and turned to face Merlynda. The amulet lay in the grass between them. They circled it, ready, even though neither of them could touch it.

"Do you know why your grandfather banished me?" Morgan asked.

Merlynda held her shield at the ready. "Because you wanted to enslave all of humanity."

"Enslave, liberate—everyone would have been so much happier with me telling them what to do. No more wars, no more famine. Sure, I'd be giving the orders, but I would have brought peace. Doesn't that sound nice?"

"No, it sounds like tyranny. People should get to choose." Merlynda risked a glance at Percy. "Even if they sometimes choose wrong."

Morgan sneered. "You sound like your grandfather. You have his nose, by the way."

"So I've heard." Merlynda focused on Morgan and the amulet they circled. Each wary step brought them a little closer.

"He and I were friends once, you know," Morgan continued, as if they were on a picnic and not in the middle of a raging magical battle that might decide the fate of the world. "Quite close friends. We had a falling-out because Merlyn thought our talents should be used to serve mere mortals, and I thought we should rule them. All that power, and what did he do with it? Pop in and out of time! Parlor tricks! Bicker with his imperious owl!"

"He defeated you," Merlynda pointed out.

They were an arm's length apart now, the amulet at their feet. "We could have changed the world," Morgan said. "Now *you* have that opportunity. You can do what Merlyn didn't."

The sorceress darted her hand out and grabbed Merlynda's arm, scratching viciously. Merlynda howled, struggling to pull away.

"Not yet, darling." Morgan fought to hold Merlynda where she was, scratching deeper. "I need a few drops of your blood to fall onto the amulet. Percy's restriction spell won't interfere with *that*. Merlyn's blood enchantment will unlock, and I'll be on my way."

"Merlynda!"

"Kinda busy, Perce!" The wizardess flashed her eyes to

Percy. His falcon swooped down and picked up something from his fist, then flew up toward Iggy.

It was her lock of hair.

Morgan saw it too and hissed. She jerked Merlynda's arm closer to the amulet but was too eager. The amulet's protection spells triggered, and it leapt away. Morgan dragged Merlynda after it, gouging her nails deeper. Merlynda's skin broke, and blood welled up while she gasped and struggled.

The falcon dropped the lock of hair before Iggy.

The wyvern blew a stream of flame, incinerating the lock of hair, the golden thread that bound it, and the restriction spell that prevented Merlynda from grasping the amulet.

With a cry of triumph, Merlynda twisted around and reached toward the amulet with her free hand, but Morgan yanked her back with an outraged growl. Merlynda swung her shield, bashing Morgan with a satisfying *thud*. The sorceress stumbled back and let go.

Merlynda scrambled to the amulet, then hesitated. It had woven itself into Percy's heart. Would she be strong enough to resist? If she'd found the amulet instead of Percy, she could have easily given in to the temptation to be skilled with her magic, to do what no one thought she could.

"Grab it, Merlynda!" Percy struggled to his feet. He knew her fear, so made sure he locked eyes with her so she could see he meant what he was about to say. "You're going to be *amazing*."

Morgan screamed and sent a desperate burst of lightning

at Merlynda, which she blocked almost nonchalantly. Then she smashed the bottom of her shield into the amulet.

Purple light flashed and sparked, and Merlynda shut her eyes so she wouldn't be blinded. She could feel the Aether fibers in the shield and the amulet, the magic binding and holding them together. She unwound the threads and wove them together again, urging the two to fuse, to forge something new.

The dark tendrils of the amulet binding it to Morgan were severed. The overwhelming presence of Aether in the shield poured into the amulet, filling it, until it was no longer possible to tell where one ended and the next began. They morphed and shifted, bronze intertwining with silver, becoming whole, together.

Merlynda stood. Instead of her shield, she held an elegant staff, crested at the top with the amulet's amethyst. Engravings flitted across the shimmering metal, shifting and changing.

It felt good in her hands. It felt right.

She faced Morgan. For the first time the sorceress looked uncertain.

Merlynda took a step forward and slammed her staff into the ground. "I am Merlynda of Merlyn Manor. I am the Septimum Genus, a title offered by the Aether, and a destiny I have chosen to accept."

She took another step, and Morgan shrank back.

"I have been to the In-Between and back. I have spoken with the source of all life and magic." Merlynda swept her staff around so that it pointed at the sorceress. "I will defeat you, Morgan le Fey, just as my grandfather did."

Morgan let out a terrible cry and launched herself at Merlynda. The sorceress magically pulled her own staff from the air and slashed it down.

Merlynda caught the blow and returned it, blasting Morgan, blocking more attacks. She danced and twirled with the Aether, sensing the magical assaults before they arrived and rapidly snapping back her own.

Iggy swooped in and set Morgan's blond curls on fire. The sorceress tried to zap the wyvern with her lightning, but Merlynda magicked a chain around Morgan's foot and yanked, knocking her off-balance. Merlynda felt she could go on like this forever, moving with the Aether—but Morgan needed to be stopped. Her friends on the battlefield needed her. Percy needed her.

Morgan jammed her staff into the ground, and a shock wave rippled across the earth. Merlynda flew back, caught off guard. Her new staff flew from her hands.

Morgan pointed her own staff at Merlynda, pinning her. "You may be powerful, little wizardess, but you are inexperienced. I'll have my revenge at last by destroying Merlyn's namesake."

The end of Morgan's staff glowed. Merlynda flung up her arms, but before she could summon a barrier, a rush of wind billowed up and knocked Morgan back.

Percy stumbled closer, laughing hoarsely. He was covered in

bruises, and blood trickled down his cheek. He gripped his side and winced. "You've destroyed enough," he spat. He flicked his finger, and Merlynda's staff flew back into her hands.

She stood and looked at Percy. "Together?"

He nodded. "Together."

They faced Morgan as one. Percy concentrated, focusing past the pain of whatever bones were broken and honing in on how Morgan had tricked him, how he'd done awful things, and how he needed to make them right. He pulled at the Air around him and beyond it into the Aether until a small void began to open behind the sorceress.

Morgan lashed out at Percy, but Merlynda was there to defend him. She parried the spells with her staff and tossed up shields, and Iggy and the falcon swooped from above to distract the sorceress. The void grew, and clouds raced around the edges. Pinpricks of light flashed then vanished as the portal spiraled deeper, wider, opening *beyond* the In-Between.

"Morgan le Fey," Merlynda shouted over the wind. "You are hereby banished beyond the In-Between. Your link with the amulet has been broken, and with it your last ties to this world."

"I'm not going back!" Morgan shrieked. Her attacks became wild, desperate, but Merlynda and Percy pressed on.

Merlynda twirled her staff, then slammed it deep into the ground. A blinding light shot from the amethyst and into the portal. Merlynda felt it tear through the In-Between, clearing a way to the emptiness beyond.

"No!" Morgan screamed. She leapt for the twins, but as one, they pushed their arms out and caught Morgan in the air with their magic. Together they launched her through the void and beyond the In-Between. Merlynda twirled her staff, sealing the rift they'd created, once again locking Morgan in the emptiness.

The light from Merlynda's staff faded, and the portal winked out.

In which our loose ends are
(mostly) tied off

Percy collapsed, coughing. Merlynda knelt beside him, frantically checking him over. There were a number of scrapes and bruises, and blood trickled down his face. Every breath he took seemed a struggle, which probably meant there were injuries she couldn't see.

"I'm sorry," he wheezed. "I'm so sorry."

"Stop moving," Merlynda scolded, but she squeezed his hand to comfort him. "Where does it hurt?"

"Everywhere." Percy looked at the battle around them. He'd never forgive himself. "But I deserve it."

"Stop moving and shut up," Merlynda commanded.

The battlefield was littered with shrubs and stone figures and small animals scurrying this way and that. Many
of the towering pillars and bluestones from the Omnivia
were gouged or fallen over, and several were missing
entirely, which at least helped ensure no one would try to
summon a certain evil sorceress again anytime soon. Much
farther out, beyond even the trench Percy had dug, a deep
rift scored the ground in a wide circle around the Omnivia,
a scar from the shattered Impedimentum. Leftover hexes
settled onto the ground, traps for anyone who might
stumble on them. And everywhere were the wounded,
the weary—Neci was still trapped beneath the stone and
badly injured, Dame Illondria thrashed under a heavy net,
Zahilda's cackling sisters bounced her up and down, and
Batu was cornered with some of his raiders.

Merlynda glared at Percy once more so he wouldn't move,
then stood and jammed her staff hard into the ground. Purple
light blasted out from her, rippling across the Omnivia.
"Morgan le Fey has been defeated!" she announced, amplify-
ing her voice through the light.

Cheers went up from the Nordvings and raiders, but the
fairies and witches redoubled their efforts.

Merlynda growled. She was exhausted, but this needed to
end. Percy wasn't the only one who was wounded. She freed
Dame Illondria, who set about herding fairies. A blow from
her staff scattered the witches surrounding Zahilda. They vanished along with their cats in clouds of ash and smoke.

"Show-offs," Zahilda muttered, brushing soot from her flowery dress.

"Should we be worried about them?" Merlynda asked.

"Probably. But no more than usual."

Zahilda cast a particularly witchy binding spell to keep the fairies from using their magic. Lumont adjusted his monocle in a superior manner, and the others responded with as many obscene words and gestures as they could. Vilhelmina strolled over to guard them. She lazily *snnkt*ed her claws out, licking her lips and baring her teeth at the fairies. They quieted down after that.

Dame Illondria, Batu, and Merlynda set about healing the rest of the wounded while Zahilda uncursed the hexed. The stone pinning Neci to the earth was slid aside, and Dame Illondria touched her horn to the would-be knight's legs.

"It will take time to fully recover," the horned pegasus said, "but the worst of the damage is healed."

Neci stood gingerly, testing her weight. "Thank you, Dame Illondria." She waved away the crutch that was offered and hobbled over to Fang, which was no easy task when she was accustomed to darting and dashing as she pleased. She hugged the stone beast, eyes stinging in the corners. "You were the best noble steed a knight could wish for," she whispered.

Merlynda stepped up behind her, appraising the stone. She hefted her staff. It thrummed with power she was only beginning to understand. Or perhaps it was her own magic that thrummed. "Stand back."

Hardly daring to hope, Neci hopped a few steps away. Merlynda spun her staff and focused on the life trapped within the stone. The glimmering amethyst pulsed with magic. The Aether felt like an old friend now. Merlynda didn't understand it completely—how did you understand something so huge?—but she felt she knew it better.

She whispered a word, then gently touched the amethyst to Fang's stony chest, right where the hex had caught her midgallop. The stone splintered. The curse pushed back at the staff, straining against this new power, but Merlynda held firm.

The stone popped and crackled. Cracks webbed and spiraled across the Questing Beast, racing up the long neck and down each gangly leg. Neci hugged herself so hard in anticipation that her arms went numb.

With a deafening *crack* the stone fragmented into a thousand tiny pieces, and beneath them all was Fang, whole and alive. The Questing Beast kicked wildly, but Merlynda blocked the hooves with an Aether shield and scurried away.

"Fang! Hey, girl!" Neci shouted. "It's okay! You're okay!"

Fang stopped kicking long enough to look around her. No one was fighting anymore! She barked joyfully and trotted toward her human (for at this point, she considered Neci hers). Between a sleeping curse, being trapped in the earth, and then turning to stone, Fang thought that magic was probably something she didn't need to bother with anymore.

The reunion of knight and noble steed made Merlynda grin. She gazed across the Omnivia to see how the others were faring, then flushed with anger. Lady Phelia stood over Percy with two of her Oceanids, mace ready to strike. Batu stood between them, shouting, and Zahilda looked like she was about to cast a curse. Undeterred, Lady Phelia's mace swept through the air with deadly force.

Merlynda dashed toward them, whispering to her staff and flinging a ray of violet light from the amethyst. It shot out, creating a purple barrier between the Oceanids and the others. Lady Phelia's mace bounced off of it. She whirled to see where the shield had come from.

"Septimum Genus." Lady Phelia narrowed her eyes but lowered her mace. "You interfere with justice."

"It isn't for you to decide what justice is," Merlynda said. "I thought *rehabilitation* was more your style, not murder."

"There is no rehabilitation for one such as he. And while you may be the Septimum Genus, you have no authority over our actions."

"True," Merlynda agreed. "Everyone makes their own choices, and Percy will face consequences. But if you try to hurt him, or anyone else here, you'll have to answer to me."

"And me." Batu hefted his sword.

"And me," Zahilda spat. She almost *wanted* the Oceanids to give her a reason to hex them.

Merlynda adjusted her grip on her staff. "I don't agree with you on everything, Lady Phelia, but we're on the same side—the side of the Aether. If you can't see that, you should leave. Thank you for your help."

Lady Phelia stepped back. "Perhaps it is for the best." She swept her arms across herself and toward the water that filled the trench, moving through graceful Oceasha forms. The water rose to form a sphere, and the Oceanids across the battlefield filtered over to it, diving in one by one.

When they were all gone, Merlynda flicked her fingers, and the swirling water fell back to the earth.

She knelt by Percy. He looked terrible, but at least it was the same amount of terrible from before Lady Phelia tried to attack him. "Are you okay?"

Percy tried to flash her a weak grin. "Your friends got here in time."

Merlynda looked gratefully up at Batu and Zahilda. "Thanks for that."

"Sure," Batu said, relieved that the Oceanids were gone. "I mean, I don't think I could have done much, but he's your family."

"Batu played him a song to help with the pain," Zahilda said. "I was just putting those Oceanids in their place. Anyone that self-righteous could do with a curse."

The falcon swooped down and nipped Percy's ear affectionately.

"Time for you to go, Vis." Percy didn't want to say goodbye, but he also knew now that this was right. Vis wasn't whole. Not yet. "Maybe I'll see you again one day, when the Aether sends you. When we're both ready."

With an effort, he formed a small portal. Vis nipped

Percy's finger one last time, then glided back to the In-Between.

Percy stared at where the portal had been for several seconds. He'd never been the Septimum Genus, and now he was no longer the Hollower. Hopefully Vis would come back when Percy was ready to be whoever he was supposed to be.

Merlynda studied her brother. His eyes no longer had shadows lurking behind them, but now they were almost empty, as if Percy himself had been Hollowed. His magic was there, but Merlynda suspected parts of her twin were changed, or maybe even gone, forever.

"Hey," she said to him. "We'll get through this together. Like always."

Percy's eyes welled up, and he nodded.

Merlynda stood. "I'll ask Dame Illondria to heal you," she told Percy. "My staff can reverse magical ailments, but not this."

"No." Percy grasped the edge of her robe. "I stole your magic. I hurt people. I *should* be in pain."

Merlynda suspected he would be for a long time. Taking care of Percy's physical wounds would be a start, but Merlynda had a feeling that true healing—for both of them—would take a good deal longer.

As soon as Dame Illondria had seen to Percy, Merlynda applied the first part of his penance. In addition to having foresight and raw talent, Percy was also gifted when it came to kitchen tasks. Merlynda made him responsible for making sure their armies and prisoners were well fed. Everyone needed a good rest after the battle before heading out.

Percy moved through his chores like a ghost. He cooked and scrubbed dishes and did whatever was asked of him. If he didn't keep busy, he heard echoes of the amulet's whisper, saw flashes of his time as the Hollower. He'd have to face what he'd done, but for now the work was a welcome distraction. There was hope that Merlynda would be able to restore the Aether to those he'd stolen it from, but that still wouldn't erase his actions.

Things would never be like before—not really. The amulet's grip was gone, but it had forever scarred his heart, and the knowledge of his choices was unbearable. Morgan may have been behind the whispers, but Percy couldn't deny that he'd allowed it. He'd believed Morgan's lies because he wanted to believe them. He wanted to be the greatest wizard who ever lived, and when he realized he wasn't the Septimum Genus, he'd chosen to be the Hollower instead.

Percy went out of his way to make something special for Iggy, given how particularly awful he'd been to the wyvern. He took up his dish and found Iggy lounging across Merlynda's shoulders.

"I'm sorry I called you a worm and that I sent Vis after you when you left the Nordvings," Percy said.

Iggy sniffed and turned away. "And?"

"And on the beach, after you left the Oceanids."

"And?"

"And in the land of Quaesitum. I'm really, really sorry for all of it."

Iggy twisted his head away. "I'll consider accepting your apology."

Percy uncovered the dish he'd been carrying. "I, um, I made you this."

Iggy didn't turn his head, but he could smell it. "Is that . . . ?"

"It is."

"With a sprinkling of sugar?"

"Just a hint."

Iggy whipped back around to Percy and stared at the dish. Finally—finally! *Funnel cake.*

He snapped up a bite and gobbled down three more before he remembered his manners. He straightened, sugar smeared on his face. "Apology accepted. But you have to call me Ignus."

The camp settled and dinner was served. Those who remained on the side of the Aether dug in gratefully, while the fairies continued to sulk (Prince Whiskerkins had decided to "help" Vilhelmina guard them, which the liger graciously permitted). Percy served up funnel cake to anyone who wanted it for dessert (which, of course, everyone did).

Merlynda found some parchment and dashed off a quick note to her parents to say they'd all be home soon. She kept the details sparse so that Mother wouldn't know where to send a reply. She missed them terribly, and even missed Uncle William, but wasn't sure where to begin.

She wondered if the battle at the Omnivia was what

Merlyn had seen with his foresight, and if his prophecy that the Septimum Genus would do great things had been fulfilled. She was definitely the Septimum Genus, and most people would consider defeating Morgan le Fey a spectacular and miraculous thing. But, Merlynda would argue, saving Percy was just as wondrous. Perhaps even more so.

Maybe Merlyn's prophecy didn't matter. Foresight was fickle, after all. Maybe all that mattered was that Merlynda believed she'd fulfilled the prophecy.

Neci fiddled with her dagger as she flipped through *The Official Quest Requirements for Knighthood*, reading by the light of a campfire. She'd had marvelous adventures, visited interesting places, and helped save her friends and probably the entire known and unknown world from an evil sorceress. She'd fought against witches and alongside Nordvings and was likely the only person with a Questing Beast.

Batu nudged her with his shoulder. "What's wrong, lady knight?"

"That!" Neci exploded. "None of the things we've done are in this stupid book! Listen to this: 'Help an elderly crone cross the street, then defend against her hexes when she betrays you—ten points. Discover the enchanted legumes of the air— three points.' There isn't anything about putting a witch in a headlock, or visiting underwater cities, *or* surviving the total destruction of a magical flying island!"

She slammed the book closed. Merlynda picked it up. The once-fine leather cover was battered from their adventures. She flipped it open and scanned the pages, then paused. "Where did you say you got this?"

"I sent away for it."

Merlynda opened to the last page and held the book up. "From your Ye Knoble Knights Defend the Civilized World trading parchment game?"

Neci grabbed the book from Merlynda. "An *expansion* pack? It's for the game? You mean I never could have earned my knighthood anyway?"

Batu studied the page. "Merlynda, how many points do you think are awarded for valiantly rescuing a horned pegasus?"

Merlynda caught on. "Oh, that's tough. Fifty? Sixty, at least."

Batu cocked his head, considering. "And what about seeking out an allegedly evil witch to right a wrong?"

"A hundred, easy."

"And I don't suppose you can count how many points you earn by being a real friend."

Iggy lifted his head from his third helping of funnel cake. "Also, always providing snacks to a wyvern in need."

Neci's frustration melted. She settled in next to her friends. "You're right. A true knight's worth can't be measured." She stared at the book for another second, then tossed it on the ground.

The evening wore on in a pleasant sort of way. Batu was called on to play his ocarina, which he did with gusto. The Nordvings and raiders were friendly with one another and even swapped stories and taught one another campfire songs.

The stars above the Omnivia were bright. So bright, in fact, that it didn't take long to realize that some of the stars were moving.

And getting bigger.

And closer.

Everyone scrambled to grab the nearest weapon, in case the magical events of the day hadn't yet reached their conclusion (they hadn't). The fairies were particularly distraught.

"Let us out!" they hollered, flinging themselves against Zahilda's binding hex. Even the threat of Vilhelmina didn't stop them.

The twinkling lights winked out, then flared in the center of the camp so brilliantly, it seemed like the sun had risen in the middle of the Omnivia. The light faded to reveal a battalion of fairies.

"Reinforcements!" Neci warned, whirling her sling.

"Reinforcements? Nonsense." The fairy who spoke wore a fluffy teal dress that was stunning against her deep-purple skin. She carried a scepter made from intricate vines and leaves— hardly proper battle attire. She hovered ahead of the others.

Merlynda lowered her staff and curtsied. This wasn't a general with an army. It was a queen with her court. "Your Majesty."

This pleased the Fairy Queen to no end, but she waved her hand and curtsied herself. "It's an honor, Septimum Genus. I apologize that we meet under such embarrassing circumstances. I am here for the traitors." She made a few swift motions to her court, and a couple of fairies split away toward Lumont's group.

Vilhelmina snarled and prepared to leap, but Iggy flew over and sat on her head. The liger relaxed.

"Your Majesty!" Lumont squeaked. His war helmet *poof*ed back into the ridiculous feathery hat. "How gracious of you to come! I—"

"Do shut up, Lumont," the Fairy Queen snapped. "Conspiring with Morgan le Fey! I couldn't believe the news. You are a disgrace to all fairykind."

"If I may explain, Your Eminence, *all* fairykind were to be protected. . . ."

Lumont trailed off as the Fairy Queen's face flushed a deeper purple. It was difficult for someone so small to hold in such large emotions. *"Protected?* By evil sorcery? Magic that isn't even half the age of our own? You are a disgrace, Lumont! A disgrace! You shame us all!" She bowed to Merlynda. "Please accept my deepest apologies for the actions of my *former* prime minister."

"Of course, Your Majesty." Merlynda bowed again. She didn't question how the Fairy Queen had received word, or that she knew where the Omnivia was. The queen wouldn't have told her, anyway. Fairies were like that.

"You've done well, Merlynda of Merlyn Manor. Your great-great-many-times-great-grandfather would be proud. If we can ever do something to show our gratitude, please let us know."

Merlynda looked at Neci, who had lowered her sling (but not quite put it away). "Actually, Your Majesty, there *is* something you can do."

She explained her request, and the Fairy Queen beamed. "It would be my honor, Septimum Genus."

They cobbled together the ceremony in a rush, but that only added to the excitement. The fairy court fanned out in a semicircle behind their queen. The entire camp stood before them, waiting. Merlynda and Batu had positions of honor in the front.

The crowd parted to let Neci through, whispering encouragement. A fine piece of cloth was draped across her shoulders like a cloak, and Faithful was buckled to her waist. Her Ye Knoble Knights Decoder Ring with Customizable Crest was back in its rightful place on her finger, proudly displaying the gryphon crest. She stood tall, trying to move with grace on her not-quite-healed leg, to look strong and knightly. Her palms were sweaty.

When she reached the Fairy Queen, she knelt, then drew Faithful and offered up her blade.

"Neci the Ardent," the Fairy Queen said, "you have shown exceptional bravery on your journey with the Septimum Genus. You've proven yourself an eager learner, a clever warrior, and a loyal friend. You have acquired a valiant and singular steed, and you have grown and flourished."

Neci stared at the ground. She didn't trust herself to speak, so she only nodded. The queen took the dagger.

"To recognize your achievements and your noble heart, I bestow on you this honor." The queen tapped each of Neci's shoulders with Faithful. "I dub thee Dame Neci of the realm of Faelor, protector of all the known and unknown world, fairy friend, and Knight of the Most Honorable Order of the Faithful Dagger."

Neci rose and accepted her dagger back. The armies erupted into cheers as she turned to look at them.

It may not have been very knightly, but she couldn't stop grinning.

The next morning everyone packed up to return to their respective defending, journeying, or pillaging duties. It was the beginning of the end. Sometimes this point is clearly defined, and other times it passes by without you ever noticing. This was one of the noticeable times.

Merlynda offered to unhex Vilhelmina so that she could run on the ground again, but the liger flicked her tail politely to decline. She already considered herself one of a kind, but to be an aerial liger was truly to be a liger above all others.

Fenrir volunteered to escort the questers home, but they assured him they'd be fine. "You'll be able to go back to pillaging right away," Merlynda said. "But please be gentle about it."

Fenrir boomed out a laugh. "If any other Nordvings ever try to give you trouble, you tell them you're friends of Fenrir the Mighty." He slapped everyone on the shoulder in a friendly way (nearly bowling them over), then he and his Nordvings began the hike back to their ships. Their songs rang through the air far after they'd disappeared from sight.

Merlynda, Iggy, and Neci stared at the path the Nordvings had worn into the ground. It felt a bit like when they'd set out on this quest with just the three of them, only now Merlynda really was the Septimum Genus, Iggy was a full-grown and truly fierce wyvern, and Neci was a royally dubbed knight.

Or maybe they'd always been those things, but now they felt like them.

Batu and his horde had decided that while they disagreed with most of Pugachev's methods, traveling by Air wasn't so bad. The Nordvings had helped them lash and hammer together wood to make ships, and the Fairy Queen enchanted them to fly (Batu had been reassured that fairy magic was far more reliable than sprite magic). The boars even had their own roomy pens to rest in.

The wood of the airships was much sturdier than crumbling earth, which Neci and Merlynda found comforting as they floated across the wild and lesser-traveled countryside toward Faelor, toward home. Fang didn't like it any better—there were gaps! In the wood! *Where she could see the ground.* But she had Neci and Iggy and the lovely silver-horned pegasus and even that witch lady who flew on a broom to make her feel better.

Iggy liked sneaking up on the Rusvokians to startle them. He had mostly forgiven them for what they did to Merlynda and Dame Illondria, but not quite.

Percy spent the journey by himself. Merlynda would find him staring across the land, eyes vacant, seeming much older than eleven. Centuries older. In those moments, she sat next to him.

"It really was all my fault," Percy said one evening. Ever since the amulet's hold had been broken, he'd felt a deep and infinite ache about what he'd allowed to happen. About what he'd done.

Merlynda waited for him to continue when he was ready.

"I couldn't believe that you were the Septimum Genus," he said. "I thought the Aether must have made a mistake, or that it was holding out on me. I didn't know it was Morgan talking to me through the amulet, but the things she said . . . I wanted them to be true. The amulet said I could be an even greater wizard than Merlyn. I wanted that more than anything." He swallowed. "And really, that's what Morgan wanted too. To be the greatest. The most powerful. I was willing to do whatever it took."

Merlynda said nothing, feeling this was something Percy needed to get out. He finally met her eyes.

"I hurt you," he whispered. "And I hurt others." He hesitated, but decided to give words and shape to what troubled him even more than the ache. The thing that gnawed and gnashed outside of the emptiness and curled the edges of the ache into terror. "That wickedness, Merlynda, it's inside me. What if it comes out again? What if . . . What if I'm just like her?"

"It won't," Merlynda said firmly. "And you're not. You made mistakes, and you're going to have to do a lot more than cook and clean to make up for them, a *lot* more. I imagine you're in for a lot of trouble once we tell Mother and Father. But if that wickedness tries to come up, you're strong enough to fight it. And you're not alone."

She took his hand.

"You have me, Percy. You'll always have me."

She sat with him awhile longer. Percy would never be the same again. But, Merlynda was sure, the rest of them wouldn't be the same either.

Before too long, and also perhaps too soon, the enchanted airships arrived on the horizon of Avonshire and Merlyn Manor. Merlynda fiddled with her staff, uncertain about the homecoming she'd receive.

"I'm sure they'll understand once you've explained everything." Neci tried to reassure her. "You're the Septimum Genus!"

"Yes, and Percy is—was—the Hollower. That's a lot to take in."

"Bet they'll have an easier time with it than my parents." Neci fiddled with her Ye Knoble Knights Decoder Ring with Customizable Crest. "I ran away with a wizardess to pursue forbidden dreams of adventure and glory. Not exactly the life respectable root vegetable merchants envision for their only daughter."

"But now you're *Dame* Neci the Ardent. That's something to be proud of." Merlynda smiled at her, and Neci nodded. She stopped fiddling with her ring, leaving it on her finger for all to see. Together they looked toward what would come.

A crowd gathered from the town, whispering and pointing and following the strange flying contraptions until at long last they floated just over Merlyn Manor. The crowd kept a healthy distance.

Dame Illondria allowed Merlynda and Neci the honor of riding on her once more. Iggy swooped alongside them, followed by Zahilda and Prince Whiskerkins on her broom with Fang in tow. Batu rode down on a boar with Percy.

"Are you sure you don't want to stick with the quartet?" Neci asked Batu once they'd all landed.

He smirked. "Friends are too much trouble. You're always bickering, and chasing after them to make sure they don't get killed." He pulled a small square of parchment out of his tunic and handed it to Neci.

It was a poorly painted Ye Knoble Knights Defend the Civilized World playing parchment. The figure had splotchy, short dark hair and a dagger. Beneath the portrait were the words "Dame Neci the Ardent."

"I'm not very good at painting—"

Neci smothered Batu in a hug.

Iggy landed on Merlynda's shoulder. "You can visit me anytime you want," he told Batu.

"Same to you, Iggy." The corners of his mouth quirked, and he bowed to Merlynda and Neci. "Dame Neci, Septimum Genus."

Neci clutched her parchment. She'd keep it safe, right next to Dame Joi. "Whip that horde into shape."

Merlynda gave Batu a quick hug. "I think she means we'll miss you."

"That's what I said."

Dame Illondria stepped forward. "It has been an honor to serve with you, Merlynda of Merlyn Manor and Dame Neci the Ardent." She bowed deeply. "I hope we meet again under joyful circumstances."

Merlynda bowed back. "Us too."

Percy couldn't bring himself to look at the majestic servant of the Aether. "I am so sorry," he whispered.

"You are forgiven, young one. Very few could resist the amulet's pull, particularly given your circumstances. You will carry these scars through your life and will have consequences to face—sooner rather than later, I suspect—but you must move forward."

"Take care of yourself, Dame Illondria." Zahilda poked a finger at Batu. "And you, minstrel boy, you watch after that ocarina."

Batu climbed back onto his boar and took flight, Dame Illondria leapt up in a flash of silver, and they were gone.

Merlynda, Iggy, Percy, and Neci stood for a few moments longer, watching Batu and Dame Illondria disappear, holding on to the moment. Zahilda finally gave an irritable "ahem," and they turned to look at the crowd that had formed.

When you've experienced something wonderful or awful (or something that's a mix of both), it can be difficult to return to your life as it was. This is because life *isn't* as it was. Not anymore. Not for you. You've been on a journey, and changed, but parents and friends and other regular-life things haven't.

Five figures (and a hedgehog) edged out from the crowd, gaping at the questers. They stared for a handful of heartbeats, recognizing the familiarity of who stood before them, but also the strangeness. Then the parents (and uncle) rushed forward, and the children sprinted toward them, and everyone was caught up in a jumble of worry and assurance and relief and shock.

"Only *one note*," Father managed. "Only a single message in all these months you've been gone!"

"I *tried*," Merlynda managed to squeeze out from her mother's crushing embrace.

"When the mirrors didn't work, we weren't worried at first," Mother said, clutching her children. "But then when no other messages came, we didn't—we thought—we came back early, and you were both *gone*."

Uncle William seemed unable to find any words but kept patting both of the twins on their heads as if to make sure they were really there.

The children gave an abbreviated account of their adventures, unable to keep up with all the questions and scolding and hugs. Mother and Father admired Merlynda's new staff, and Uncle William declared it was a prize to be heralded through literary epics. They admired Iggy, who struck a regal pose on Merlynda's shoulder.

While they didn't yet know all the details, they could

tell Percy needed to be held more gently. Not because of his injuries, which through the wonders of magic had healed, but because of the wounds they couldn't see. The darkness he'd carried and given into and then beat back, but that continued to lurk in the corners.

Lady and Lord Ardent tried to usher their daughter away from these magic users, but Neci held her ground, arms akimbo, ring dazzling for all to see. "I'm Dame Neci now," she told them. "I'm a knight. I don't want to carry on the family business—I want to have glorious adventures and help those in need. And Merlynda is my best friend and always will be." She set her jaw to show them she meant it, but still her lip quavered. Would they accept this? Would they accept *her*?

Lady Ardent started to say something, but her husband touched her arm to quiet her. He didn't understand any of it, but he could see this was important to Neci. He wrapped his arms around his little girl, and she melted into him. Lady Ardent was sure she didn't approve of any of this, but Neci had come back safe and whole. In that moment, nothing else mattered.

After the children had been squeezed for so long they weren't sure they'd be able to breathe again, Mother finally loosened her hold (though she didn't let go entirely). "So the Hollower is real? How? Who is he?"

Merlynda hesitated and glanced at Percy. It wasn't her story to tell.

Percy looked squarely at each of his parents. "It was me.

I'm the Hollower." He glanced at his sister. "But Merlynda saved me." The ache inside Percy threatened to swallow him, but he acknowledged it. He knew he'd carry the awful things he'd done with him forever, but he'd face that ache head-on and do what he could to make things right.

The adults were stunned for a moment. On the one hand, Merlynda had fulfilled Merlyn's prophecy and done miraculous, wonderful things. She'd mastered her magic, created a marvelous staff, and spoken with the Aether face-to-face (hadn't Mother said that Merlynda would dazzle the world?).

On the other hand, while their son had succeeded in opening a highly advanced (though dangerous) magical portal to the In-Between, he was also one of the most dreaded villains in history. They'd have to sort out how to punish him, and also how to help him grapple with the consequences.

"I *specifically* told you not to use your foresight while we were gone," Mother scolded Percy. He had no plans to use it again anytime soon. It was too easy to be misled, and too unstable. He suspected he hadn't been able to see if he and Merlynda would be successful in summoning an Elemental Stone all those months back because at that point the future had too many possible paths. He'd rather experience life the normal way, without knowing the future, from now on.

Father looked at Mother with a serious expression. "The Round Table is sure to want something more than grounding him. You don't suppose . . ."

Mother's face twisted like she'd eaten something unpleasant.

"I expect so. But we'll deal with that when it comes."

"Round Table?" Merlynda asked. "What's that?"

"Not what," Mother answered, her face clouding. "Who. The Round Table is a group of magical beings who occasionally meet. They'll probably want to chat with you and Percy, that's all."

The twins could tell Mother was trying very hard to make the Round Table sound like a harmless weekly book club. This only convinced them that it was, in fact, something much more serious. Some sort of magic council? Would they punish Percy for being the Hollower? How?

But Mother beamed and said they'd worry about it later, and the twins were so happy to be home with their parents (and Uncle William) that they let it go.

Neci's parents didn't know what to feel. Their little girl, who was supposed to carry on the noble family business of root vegetable farming, had run away from home, fallen in with all sorts of magical creatures, owned a weapon, and was knighted by a fairy. They didn't know what to make of it all, which is a thing that sometimes happens with parents. They usually try their best, but in the end they're still just people trying to sort out their own ideas about the world.

Zahilda had kept a respectful distance for this initial reunion but now cleared her throat.

Lady Ardent eyed Zahilda's broom and flowery dress. An orange tabby cat wound itself around her feet. "Who are you?"

"This is Zahilda," Neci said. "She helped us save Iggy."

"I'm a witch," Zahilda offered. Neci cringed.

Lady Ardent tightened her grip ever so slightly on Neci's arm. "Are you staying in Avonshire long?" she asked in a voice that was an octave too high.

Zahilda surveyed the town. "That depends. How do you people feel about good witch's pie?"

Neci's parents paled, but her father saw how fond his daughter was of this witch. If she'd helped save that flying lizard thing on the wizard girl's shoulder, she probably wasn't all bad. "Pie is good. We like pie."

"And we have lots of vegetarian root vegetable soup," Neci added.

Zahilda grinned.

"Neci, dear." Lady Ardent pointed. "What is that?"

"That's Fang!" The Questing Beast perked up at her name and trotted over. Neci rubbed her neck. She knew this was difficult for her parents. They didn't understand her. Maybe they *couldn't* understand her.

"Every knight needs a noble steed," Merlynda explained.

"Come over to the manor," Merlynda's mother said to Neci's parents. "We'll have tea and hear every detail about their quest. Nordvings, you said? And mermaids? I've always wanted to meet a mermaid."

"No, Mother." Merlynda shook her head. "You really don't."

"And where did you find that gorgeous winged unicorn?"

"Horned pegasus," Percy corrected his father.

Hortensia raised one of her hedgehog eyebrows at Iggy. The wyvern faked a yawn, which he casually turned into an impressive burst of flame. Merlynda's parents and the hedgehog nodded in approval.

Neci thought her parents would refuse the invitation to Merlyn Manor and insist on going home that instant and grounding her forever. Instead, Neci's mother reached out a tentative hand to stroke Fang, and Neci knew she was trying. Which was all she could hope for, in the end. That her parents would try.

A pony with a scorpion's tail galloped across the road.

"Oh!" Lady Ardent stumbled back, voice strangled. "What is *that*?"

Father sighed. "It's only Harriet. She's been incorrigible since Percy disappeared." He looked at his son. "See what happens when you neglect responsibilities to pursue evil magical goals? William refuses to go anywhere near the creature." But he tousled his son's hair and pulled him close, like he might never let him go.

Percy kicked at the ground. His father didn't even *have* magic and had no idea what the amulet's whispers had been like. But Percy didn't pull away from him.

"We'll need to calm Harriet and get her back into her pen," Mother said. "Merlynda, dear, would you do the honors?"

Merlynda turned to Percy. "Together?"

He smiled weakly, then stood straighter. Despite everything, they were still a team, and each of them knew that.

They'd face the future, and whatever this Round Table business was, hand in hand.

The twins both reached toward Harriet with their magic, grasping directly at the Aether. They felt its warmth and its pull, its power and its strength.

They heard its laugh, and they laughed back. Together.

ACKNOWLEDGMENTS

Writing a book is a mostly solitary endeavor, but it still takes a village. *Hollower* is the result of many years of work, and the support of many people, to whom I am eternally grateful:

Kelly Dyksterhouse, my amazing agent and friend. My stories are infinitely better for her feedback and wisdom.

My brilliant editor, Jessica Smith, and the entire team at Aladdin/Simon & Schuster (most especially Heather Palisi, Chel Morgan, Rebecca Vitkus, Olivia Ritchie, Sara Berko, Alissa Nigro, and Tara Shanahan). Also the wonderful illustrator Kristy de Guzman, who brought these characters I've lived with for so long to such incredible, vivid life.

Adam Rex, Jennifer J. Stewart, and Janni Lee Simner welcomed me into their circle when I was but a youngling and desperate for writing friends. Their wisdom, advice, feedback, and encouragement over the years have meant everything.

I am fortunate to have many friends who have championed me throughout my writing journey: Matthew Karolak, my childhood friend and partner in crime; Diana Ro, who gave me a tough-love talking-to exactly when I needed it; Natalie Maikoski, for giggling at my silly spontaneous "fairytales"; Adriana J. Boyd, for celebrating every milestone; and Lindy Koenig, for being my fiercest cheerleader.

So many people gave their time to read *Hollower* and give me feedback to help it become what it is: Adam Rex,

Jennifer J. Stewart, Kathy Quimby, Kathi Appelt, Joi Lakes, and Kyla Kupferstein.

I would not be who I am without my VCFA community. This is especially true of my Magic Ifs, who were my first writing family, and Kathi Appelt, who was the first person who told me I have what it takes to do this.

And of course to my family, everyone else who believed in me and cheered me on, and to every reader who joined Merlynda on her quest to save Percy from the Hollower: from the bottom of my heart, thank you. May your quests always be full of funnel cake.

A WORD ABOUT THE AUTHOR

CALLIE C. MILLER writes for animated television shows, a video game company, and (most importantly) herself. When she's not writing, Callie is most likely reading comics or playing video games or dreaming about hot chocolate. (Hot chocolate is very important nourishment for writers.) She received her MFA in Writing for Children & Young Adults from the Vermont College of Fine Arts. *The Hunt for the Hollower* is Callie's debut novel. Visit her at CallieCMiller.com.